SWEET INSANITY

Graham Thompson

MINERVA PRESS

LONDON

MIAMI RIO DE JANEIRO DELHI

SWEET INSANITY
Copyright © Graham Thompson 2001

ISBN 0 75411 511 9

First published 2001 by
MINERVA PRESS
315–317 Regent Street
London W1R 7YB

Printed in Great Britain for Minerva Press

SWEET INSANITY

To Lesley, my lobster, my life

Acknowledgements

I would like to acknowledge the following for their assistance, inspiration and encouragement:

Helen Bogan:	my invaluable secretary/typist
Jason Dickson:	a police officer and my mate
John Douglas:	FBI agent and author
Graham Farrow:	a playwright and friend
Sergeant William Ottaway:	a police officer and gentleman
Debra Robinson:	a hairdresser and friend

I would also like to thank Robert L Bell for his permission to reprint material from 'Desiderata'.

Chapter One

The serious-looking man stood in the cold winter drizzle at the bus stop with four miserable members of the public.

It was 6.20 and he was becoming impatient. Depressing, really, he mused, the thought that all the buses in town may have collectively stopped running because they know I'm waiting! He certainly hadn't seen one in either direction in the twenty minutes that he had been there.

'Goddamn useless car,' he muttered under his breath.

The elderly woman standing next to him glanced at him, swapped her seven shopping carriers between wet hands and again looked forlornly at the damp pavement.

Damn radiator! Another £60 down the pan and God knows when I'll get it back! Garages these days just charge what the hell they like and the long-suffering, soft-bellied masses simply shrug their shoulders, complain to their neighbours and pay every penny. Fools! All because nobody wants to stand at the damn bus stop in the cold and the rain, waiting for dirty, unfriendly buses that are invariably late! Still, he would have to be patient, because tonight was another special night.

The other people standing alongside the man in the queue were never going to notice the ordinary fellow for any special reason; after all, he was surely the personification of the word 'inoffensive'. They had, of course, like all people stuck in a queue, sharing a ride in a lift or sitting together in a tube train, given their fellow sufferers the once-over.

The old gentleman with the military bearing had thought of the man as a 'smart chap, nicely turned out, decent haircut'.

The lady with the bags was very tired after a long, long day shopping and was wishing that she had for once broken her rules about never wasting money on a taxi from town. She desperately wanted to sit down, get her shoes off, put the kettle on and get rid of the bags that were making her arms ache and her hands sore.

She didn't want to put the bags down on the wet ground but any minute now she was going to have to. Although her head was bowed down, she had earlier registered that amongst her immediate company was a shortish man who was not unattractive, a bit weaselly, definitely too much aftershave, but there was something appealing about him.

The young girl going to her friend's for tea before hitting the local night spots was more concerned with the fact that wearing her 'party frock' – as her mother so annoyingly called her best clubbing miniskirt – had indeed been a mistake. She really should have listened and taken the skirt to change into at Jennifer's. Her legs were freezing and wet, raindrops running down the back of her bare, falsely tanned legs. And that will probably run, she thought with irritation. What a start to the night! Worse still, the odd gust of cold wind was lifting her skirt, what there was of it, exposing too much thigh for this weather and this time of night. To cap it all she was pretty certain that the funny-looking little man a couple of places down the queue was looking at her in a sideways sort of way; somehow he appeared to be enjoying not only her legs but also the discomfort that she was suffering... pervert!

Think of somebody nice, she told herself. Now if Mr Brad Pitt was to look at her wet streaky legs, well, she would probably do a headstand!

The fourth bus stop associate of the man was a twenty-six-year-old graphic designer who was still coming to terms with having been made redundant a month earlier, not long before Christmas. How the company had lost that contract, after servicing it so well for six years, he would never understand. No amount of talk of downsizing, competitive tendering or recession-driven consolidation would clarify it for him.

'Too many eggs in one basket' was the most understandable explanation he'd heard. That and management complacency. Whatever the cause, it was difficult not to feel bitter.

Christmas with his young wife had been completely overshadowed by the horrible news. The redundancy package was negligible; after three years what could you expect? And the prospects of an immediate return to another local firm of designers were not good. Baby plans were suddenly on hold. The most immediate economy to be made was the huge sacrifice of the car, although he knew that they would have to get a little runabout sometime... sooner rather than later, if he wasn't to crack up one day whilst standing at the bus stop. He wanted to scream out, 'I've been made redundant. I've done nothing wrong, except taken out too big a mortgage. I love my wife and I'm scared. Don't you understand?'

He wanted to, but of course he didn't. He just bottled up his seething frustrations and looked bleakly and enviously at the people around him, making instant snap judgements. Old woman. Loads of shopping, loads of money, cosy house, couple of cats, comfortable, comfortable, comfortable.

Bloke about thirty-five years old. Probably a clerk, can't do too well, would have a car. Steady as a rock, job for life.

Retired soldier. General, big army pension, neat home and garden, regimented but nice life.

Kid on the razzle. No worries really, everything ahead of her, fun, blokes, mates, school or college – just a breeze. Big bad world yet to hit home. Poor bitch, got it all to come!

And *me*, scrap heap at twenty-six. Money worries, family worries and all these people. Like everybody and anybody else, not a care in the world. It's so bloody unfair, so unfair!

He pursed his lips tight together to stifle a sob that had arisen from the huge ball of bitterness and bile that was lodged in his guts. His assessments were incorrect.

The old man thought of the wet, rain sodden battlefields of World War II where he had lost so many comrades and friends. Never a day went by without him thinking of those brave men, and it was a constant battle now to convince himself that the guilt he felt gnawing away at him, day after day, was indeed, as a psychiatrist had told him so many times, misplaced.

The lady thought of walking through her front door and the warmth of the welcome from Frankie, her dachshund, but darker thoughts crept in as the prospect that she had been pushing away all day rushed back. How on earth was she going to tell her eighty-seven-year-old mother that she, at a sprightly sixty-eight, had been diagnosed as having cancer?

The young girl dreamed of Mr Pitt but as he faded away she reminded herself of the promise that she had made to herself earlier, that she must, absolutely *must*, stop 'borrowing' money from her mother's handbag.

They had all looked at the man, allowed thoughts of him to cross their minds. They would never have suspected in a hundred – no, a thousand years – any of the worries that were flitting around inside his head. For a start he was a little concerned that this incessant rain would thoroughly soak his neat brown macintosh, that the sodden coat would then possibly reveal the outline of the three unusual items to be found clipped tidily inside it. They were a screwdriver, a small claw hammer and a Stanley knife. Secondly, he was concerned that although God had undoubtedly had a hand in the damn radiator blow-out, maybe the non-provision of a bus was also a message from above; that tonight wasn't just a tester involving transport obstacles, but that he had got it wrong and tonight wasn't supposed to happen.

The distant green outline of a vehicle dispelled his fears and he allowed himself a tiny smile. Seeing the girl's uneasiness earlier as he had watched her little skirt flutter in the breeze had given him pleasure and now he was convinced he had been right to interpret this as a positive sign that he was correct in his analysis of the night.

The serious looking man would get to use his tools tonight. First to kill his stranger, then to mutilate the stranger's body.

For tonight was killing night, *again…*

Chapter Two

God, he was getting really sick of this! That was the fifth person, at least, who had said that he was putting on weight. The comments had ranged from the relatively innocent like Auntie Doris's, 'Just a hint of a little love handle there, Jeffrey dear,' to the downright bleeding outrageous '…Turning into a right fat get', from that plonker, Harry Dean, a man with the observational qualities of Blind Pew and the diplomatic skills of Saddam Hussein. His ever-expanding jumper sizes tended to cover the ever-spreading spare tyres, so the conclusion had to be that these people's comments were made from the sight of his ballooning face and copious chins: depressing. He could joke that it wasn't his weight that was the problem; that was fine. It was just that he was too short. Oh to be a six footer, and what's an inch or two between friends?

Diet and exercise, that was all that was needed. Both just took will-power and he had some of that, didn't he? A bit of will-power, well, okay, a lot of will-power. Surely he could manage that, of course he could! Right, he had decided, he was determined, he was confident. He would start tomorrow, set targets for measured weight loss and how many people he wanted to hear say, 'Strewth, you look good, Jeff, lost some weight?'

He promised himself again, tomorrow was going to be the first day of a new era. No excuses for non-compliance. It had to be tomorrow, of course, because tonight he was going out with the lads. Five or six pints of good, strong lager, a bit of a bop at a local nightclub, a good ogle at the semi-naked talent and a good nosh on the way home at either a kebab takeaway or an Indian sit-down. Marvellous! He'd felt a pang of guilt, given his intention two minutes earlier, but pushed it to the back of his mind and consoled himself with the thought (excuse!) that he couldn't have gone jogging now anyway because it was piddling down; not that rain would stop him once he was in the swing of a disciplined exercise regime, no way. It would just be a bit much on the first night.

He glanced at his watch: quarter past six, bit tight anyway, he had to get ready. Maybe he should do fifteen minutes on the exercycle that was rusting in the garage, just to show willing: the famous bike that was going to shed the pounds last time. The bike on which he had clocked up a whole sixty-two miles on the mileometer so far. Probably needed a drop of oil to loosen it up a bit, bit of maintenance generally; no point rushing at it and having a flipping accident.

He dismissed the idea of the bike tonight and considered instead the old, very old, Bullworker, or perhaps the few weights that he had kept since his teen years when he had taken fitness very seriously. Might strain something if I just dive in, he told himself. I'll have to get into it first, draw up the agenda tomorrow using all the available bits and pieces around the house and in the garage. Chuck in regular jogging, the odd game of squash with Toddy and Jonno, and it wouldn't take too long at all. Don't forget the baths he thought, enthused by his plan. God, in a few weeks he would be as fit as a lop, whatever a lop was. Reinvigorated by his positive outlook and decisions, he turned his attention away from his flabby appearance to the forthcoming attractions of a night out with the 'happy crew'. That was his pet name for what the others called 'the old mob', 'the survivors', or simply 'the lads'.

This was a gang of five men who had quite a history behind them, ranging from primary school through to current status as wage earners. Five or six years ago the gang would have numbered nine, but the recent years had taken their toll, what with three marriages and Gerry just upping sticks and disappearing off into the sunset seeking his fame and fortune. They had not heard from him and often speculated on what the hell he could be up to.

It wasn't as if marriage formally barred you from the happy crew, it was just that the gang knew that the marital band of gold seemed to move the goalposts some distance from the happy crew's playing field. As if by some telepathic acceptance of the situation, the married lads slowly parted company from the happy crew and their outings.

So now there were five, which in itself was quite a feat given that they were all in their late twenties. Mind you, they didn't get together that often, blaming work, girlfriends, other social commitments and occasionally lack of funds. This, 8 January, was the first night out together since over Christmas, and they all feared that after two nights in a couple of weeks the next time could be weeks away. That was why they all anticipated this occasion with relish. It was a guaranteed sure-fire good laugh, mickey-take, drink and knees-up and, with a little bit of luck, maybe a kiss or two off some willing piece of skirt. Nothing more serious than a kiss or two and maybe a bit of a fondle; because this was, first and foremost, a night out with the happy crew, and no girl, unless truly stunning, should get in the way of that. You could go on a fanny hunt in ones or twos, but the full complement of five was too difficult to organise to chuck away.

Mike would probably fancy a curry rather than a kebab, but what the hell, drinking the water out of the vase of flowers on the curry house dining table, which was one of Mike's specialities, was always a giggle, even if they had seen it many times before. Of course there's a few more calories in a curry, but hey, you're only twenty-eight once!

Jeff hummed and half-whistled along to the latest Elton John top twenty hit. He chuckled at the term 'hit'. In his teenage years you had to sell hundreds of thousands of records to get near to number one in the charts. Now, if you could sell about one hundred and thirty you would probably top the charts for weeks.

Pathetic! He smiled at this nostalgic look back at 1986 when he was sixteen. Twenty-eight and he was harking back to the good old days. Not that these days were so bad and today was better than most because of the night to come.

He was not a big drinker by any stretch of the imagination, far from it. Indeed, if he even got close to keeping pace with the rest of the lads then he would certainly be ill at a later juncture. Probably sooner rather than later, like on the way home. It wasn't that he was a wimp, or didn't like alcohol, it was just that it somehow never quite agreed with him once it got beyond the five or six pint mark. When his mates got to the realms of seven, eight or nine he would quietly slow down, either nursing a pint for hours or conspicuously going on to soft drinks.

He once used to envy those of his peers who could so easily down a gallon of ale, then knock back a couple of shorts, wolf down a beef Madras then get up next morning only complaining of a 'thick head'! With Jeff it always went to his stomach and once past his limit the vomit was inevitable. He did not like being sick, never had done. Somehow it always made him feel so flipping ill. Others might claim that a good puke was cleansing, but not him. So tonight there was just that little note of caution. Amidst all the general revelry and mayhem that would be going on, he would have to keep sight of the running tally of what was being consumed. This was not always the easiest task as the night wore on, as rounds had been known to get confused, as well as his requests for halves or shandies being derided or ignored. He had to admit that his mates were pretty damn good about his lack of capacity. He supposed that their acceptance of his 'inadequacy' was due to two reasons. One, he had a more than adequate sense of fun, humour, mischief – call it what you will – without the need to be paralytic. Secondly, in their increasing maturity, perhaps they had just come to accept that that was the way he was and he was not going to change now.

If the lads had a night when the mickey-taking got a bit heavy, there was no harm in adopting his simple but effective old trick of discreetly depositing half-full pint glasses around the nightclub. He decided that maybe tonight he should do a little depositing; after all, he was on a diet.

Elton John had finished as Jeff looked in the mirror. He was satisfied, if not exactly overjoyed, at the image facing him. The large collar and tie hid those damn jowls quite well, along with the childhood scar under his chin that he would always be conscious of. The stick would be severe, but he would take it in good spirits. Anyway, he would give as good, and better, than he got, and that was the greatest attraction of this night out – the banter, the crack. It was a fact that all five members of the happy crew were of above average intelligence; but when they were all together, indulging in collective piss-taking, then the wit and repartee moved on to a different level. It was so sharp that at times they would actually take a moment out from it all and marvel at a previous exchange. It was not particularly self-congratulatory, more an appreciation of the English language and the world-famous English sense of humour.

They had to have something to talk about, of course, and like most men, age being irrelevant here, they tended to concentrate on football and women. If someone suggested at the outset of a six-hour meeting that five bright young men could only talk about football and women during that time, it would have been deemed a hard target. Yet stretch that meeting over a couple of pubs, a nightclub and an Indian restaurant, and six hours just wasn't enough.

Yes, the night held the promise of beer, laughs, banter and curry. Cracking!

It was seven o'clock and Jeff was ready to go downstairs and wait for the taxi that was due at seven fifteen. If Jeff had had the tiniest inkling of what lay ahead that night he would have turned around, disrobed and gone to bed. He did not realise that just a few miles away, in the town centre, a bus was pulling up at the town hall. A couple of young men, a courting couple and a man in a brown macintosh disembarked.

A man in a brown mac who was going to make Jeffrey Sanders' world very extraordinary. A man who was going to make Jeff wish that he had never left the house that cold and miserable night. In time, this man would make Jeffrey Sanders wish that he'd never been born.

Chapter Three

He got off the bus in the town centre and stood for a second or two in the rain, which was a little harder now. It had taken him forty minutes to get to this town from his home town and most of that had been spent on the move. A few people had stood at the bus stops that lay scattered through the countryside linking the two towns. During the journey had had recounted in his head his favourite lines from 'Desiderata':

> You are a child of the universe no less than the trees and stars;
> you have a right to be here. And whether or not it is clear to you,
> no doubt the universe is unfolding as it should.[1]

Max Ehrmann was right, he did have a right to be, and his plan with God was unfolding as it should.

He looked up and down the High Street as if unsure of himself. In fact all he was doing was counting the third pub from Woolworth's corner. It was that random a selection process, decided upon in the forty-minute bus ride; a selection policy which for somebody that night was literally a matter of life and death.

That last time had been in Manchester on 31 October, some fourteen months before. The policy that night, chosen in the car on the way over there, had been the nearest pub to WH Smith's. He didn't know Manchester at all, but knew that there would be a City Centre, Smith's and a pub not far away. He was right and was pleased with the pub itself; it was big and rambling. Selecting a girl in there was easy, as he'd had no difficulty whatsoever in mingling with the crowds.

The randomness of selection was part of his strategy, as the complete lack of pattern was vital in maintaining his anonymity.

No pattern to timing, location, victims; absolutely nothing to link them.

God had seen to the timing. Last time there had been that stupid junior at work spouting on, 'No man could really be called a good lover, they didn't know what they were doing; no man could be called a gentleman, they didn't know what manners meant!' And she was only seventeen! The final straw on that occasion had been when she said, 'Most of them are mummy's boys at heart, I know it's true.'

He had realised that this was God speaking to him, saying quite clearly, 'Go, son, and extract a price!'

And so it was today when that old spinster, Marjorie Radley, had started explaining at the next station just why she had remained a spinster.

'I just don't trust men, I'm afraid, simple as that. They are dirty, untrustworthy liars and cheats. Basically, their problem is that they are not women. We are obviously a different species and we are superior. Why lower your standards by getting involved with them? That's what I think, anyway.'

He had to admit, God had novel ways of communicating, but communication this surely was. So here he was, in downtown Stockton, ready for retribution.

He had supposed that there was a good chance after tonight there would be connections made with his girls in Darlington and Sunderland. The police would surely bust a gut trying to firm up the links between the murders in the North-East of young women carried out over the course of nine years. Maybe not; he didn't know and he wasn't really bothered. He reasoned that there was a good chance that the deaths of girls in London in 1978 and Manchester in 1997 would not be linked. Why should they be? The only connection was the gender of those murdered... and the viciousness of the attacks, of course.

He felt that as nobody would ever know the motive behind his work, that there was nothing to stop him carrying out his duties for many, many years to come. He sometimes fantasised about going to the police in his dotage and announcing proudly, 'Officer, I wish to advise you that I have sacrificed one hundred women over the last thirty years. My work is done, thank you and goodbye!' In his dream the police officers around him broke into applause and slapped him on the back in congratulatory fashion.

He shook himself from his idle thoughts and gave himself a mild rebuke. Naughty boy! he chided. That appears to be complacency creeping in. Don't get sloppy. God would not like that and He might just punish you for it. He focussed again on the task at hand and walked slowly to his chosen pub.

As he strolled down the street busy with people scurrying to pubs and restaurants, he allowed himself one final thought about previous nights like this. He had thought a minute ago that nobody would ever know his motives. That was not completely true, of course, because to date he had explained his motives, indeed his story, to three people. It was just unfortunate that those three people had each had about five minutes to live when they heard his story. From his point of view he had found it strangely satisfying that they were fully aware of *why*, if not *why them*. The first had been spontaneous; no story explained with that one.

He walked up to the pub and looked through a steamy window. Pretty packed, he thought, as he knew it would be. They're busy on a Friday night in this bustling town. The busier the better as far as he was concerned. He knew that it was so easy for him to disappear into the crowds and he could studiously observe all that he wanted.

He strolled casually into the pub and made his way to the nearest bar. It was busy, but not impossibly so, as it would be later when it would be four or five deep at every serving point. He got a pint of beer quite quickly and moved over to a corner where he propped himself against a wall. A nearby window ledge was used as a place to put his beer. He carefully loosened his mac, undoing the belt and buttons. He did not want it to swing open, giving a possible glimpse of its peculiar contents. He looked around at the full tables and at the pockets of people standing around in their close groups. He was not too bothered about picking any definites this early in the evening, but was curious to establish the nature of the clientele, as it could have a bearing on his choice later on.

What he wanted, of course, was the ideal stranger. Plenty of strangers round here, but they had to meet his rigorous criteria.

For example, it was no good selecting a real looker; too many people kept their eye on them.

He picked up his pint from the window ledge and held it tight to his chest. People squeezed past him but nobody gave him a second glance. By contrast he gave everybody a second glance, and sometimes a third and a fourth. In particular all the females, his apparently casual appraisal taking in all the details that he needed to know.

He knew that it would very quickly fill up and then he could do some more serious observational work. He had a few moments, he felt, to consider the bigger picture. So, whilst still conscious of his surroundings and the people around him, he thought about the long-term strategy that he and God had devised.

As long as he did not make a fundamental mistake, enjoyed a little luck and continued to believe in the unavoidable rationale behind it all, he saw no reason why he shouldn't go on and on and on forever into immortality. He should become one of the true greats, as famous as the Yorkshire Ripper or his predecessor, Jack the Ripper. Funny that, two of his earlier role models both being given epithet 'Ripper'! He speculated whether he would be known for generations to come. Generations… That was a hell of a thought. He didn't want to be known as a 'Ripper', that suggested too much of a sexual deviant, and he did not want any such association. He wondered if the media would give him a nickname or tag that would stick. He would have to admit, if pushed, that he was a little disappointed that there had been no positive linking of his murders, in particular the ones in Darlington and Sunderland. There had been a little speculation, naturally, and even mention of a possible new Ripper, but it had not stuck. He guessed that the police were involved in blocking the establishment of a name as it might have created both panic in the streets and a media frenzy. His thoughts drifted back to the other Rippers. By all accounts both of these men were driven by the need to rid the world of prostitutes, although both had made mistakes and killed non-prostitutes. Or had they? What if they were driven by the same God and demons that he was? Maybe all they chose to do was take out women of the night because they were easily accessible. Maybe they were motivated just as he was; nobody would ever know.

He noticed that the pub was filling up quicker than he had anticipated, so he focussed on his locale.

The noisy throng made the bar like a frenzied chicken coop in which he was the fox. A few couples, a handful of people on their own, but mainly gangs of young men and groups of younger girls, all eyeing each other up, the girls giggling and flirty, the boys macho, raucous and leering. Eye contact was often made but rarely followed up; after all, this was a pub, and pubs were for drinking. The chatting up was for later at the nightclubs, even though it would have made a lot of sense to do the chatting up at the pub, as it was several decibels quieter than the clubs and it was where a conversation could take place comfortably at distances of two feet, rather than uncomfortably at two inches. Still, it was the ritual, and rituals must be followed.

The clever trick for him now was to find a stranger who was going to stay in the pub all night without getting attached to a party of males or females. Preferably they would spill into the street along with other die-hards who had seen last orders, and then they would take tipsy steps into the roads leading off the High Street. He had had plenty of disappointments before but tonight it felt right, he felt confident.

With the university so close to the town centre, there were plenty of students who would fit the bill, particularly as they could not afford the nightclub prices – neither admission nor refreshment. The massive local general hospital had the same effect, bringing hordes of thirsty nursing staff to the town's hostelries.

At nine thirty he moved from his spot just to ensure that he would not be noticed as a man on his own who'd stood at the same point all night. He calmly and slowly moved through the crowded bars towards the back of the pub. The last thing he needed was to annoy some half-drunk thug who would ask, 'Who're you pushin'?' or 'Who're you looking at?' So he moved firmly past people, always apologising quietly when he had to bump somebody to get past. He picked a spot, again against a wall, that he thought was sufficiently anonymous without him losing the ability to watch all around him.

He was wearing a short-sleeved T-shirt under his mac as he knew that it would get very warm in the pub around this time. He was now grateful that he had made this decision as he was not feeling too comfortable. He had also decided this afternoon to change his shoes, as he knew that he had worn his first choice of footwear on Halloween two years ago. He wore brown patent leather shoes, and as they were new he wondered if they would start to pinch if he had to walk very far later that night.

Something in his head clicked and he started the serious business of picking a girl. It was nearly ten o'clock and several of the larger groups left the pub, obviously heading for one of the many excellent nearby clubs. Stag nights, hen nights and birthday parties were all in evidence, but although their leaving thinned the crowds, all the tables were still occupied and there were plenty of people standing. This suited him fine: still sufficient cover but easier vision. He preferred to stand because it excused him from having to share a table with anybody and possibly having to exchange conversation or avoid the dreaded eye contact. He wanted neither.

As ten o'clock had passed he was confident that what he saw around him were people who were not going on to other pubs. It was only a question of whether they would be going clubbing. The numbers swelled a little as a group of seven girls, apparently drunk, burst in and rowdily ordered drinks.

He had made a provisional choice of girl when he had first settled at his new spot. He checked on her again. Plumpish, gauche, a touch awkward, sitting with the others some distance from himself. They had pretty much kept themselves to themselves, leaning together occasionally to discuss in a secretive manner the physical attributes of the nearest bunch of lads. Their eyes usually gave away the results of their conspiratorial whispering. They looked settled and he guessed that they had done the circuit of the latest four or five pubs being deemed to be 'in' and 'cool'. It always struck him as silly to want to traipse all over town, battling through the crowded bars at each different pub, just so you could claim to have visited the right places. As a drinker in his early twenties, his remembered youth, getting a seat at a table, staying out of the wet and cold was deemed sensible. It did not mean that you did not have a good time and it was certainly more comfortable.

Kids, he thought, meaning anybody under the age of twenty-five. They don't know what a good time is. Now, he was different. He knew a good time when it came along. Like tonight. God yes, tonight was a very good time. All day, and so far tonight, he had felt detached, very cool and unemotional. Now, as if someone had flicked a switch, he was conscious of the blood pumping around his body. It surged through his head and he felt good. He felt so alive, so sharp in his senses that it was almost frightening, almost not fair. He felt physically and mentally strong, he felt superior. Shit! he thought, I am superior.

God had given him these powers, these abilities as compensation for those unforgotten horrors. It crossed his mind again that it was unfair that he was quite so powerful. But if God so decreed, then who was he to argue? Anyway, didn't he really deserve it after... all that...?

He thought that the girls' clothes suggested they were students; bright and cheerful tops, baggy jeans and chunky boots. He didn't look out of place himself with his youthful looks, his trim figure (no middle-aged spread allowed here), short back and sides (which he noticed some of the younger lads had taken to) and his natty brown mac. His advantages were that he was not what you would call particularly handsome or striking, and had no distinguishing features. He was just an ordinary Joe. Well, it just proved how appearances could be deceptive, didn't it? A smile passed his lips as he thought how he was anything but average, and he turned back to his girl.

He lifted his glass to his lips, but only as cover, as the beer in the glass was very warm and almost undrinkable. He saw that the attractive girl on the right was picking up her handbag from the floor. She stood up and rearranged her hair in a fluffing motion as if making a statement that no matter what the time, no matter what state of inebriation the remaining clientele were in, she was still prepared to strut her stuff. She moved towards him and brushed past him as she headed in the direction of the toilets. His privileged sensory abilities kicked in and he took a second to analyse the sweet smell inhaled as his target's friend passed by. He was able to distinguish the perfume from the smoke that hung around him and told himself, Cheapish perfume – Charlie, I think. Not at all unpleasant, either the perfume or the girl. He half turned towards the target.

Certainly not ugly, he thought. If she lost a few pounds, well, maybe half a stone, she could be okay. Pity she won't get the chance… He felt no pangs of guilt, shame or embarrassment. This was business, and was ordained by God Himself.

The friend returned and the three girls gathered up their belongings and put their jackets on. They made their way to the exit. He let the first two girls go through the door before he quickly followed. He left the pub and knew from his observations before entering earlier that evening that there was no close alley or passageway that they could disappear down. Despite this he was keen to see them again. Cool, cool, cool, he told himself as the cold night air hit him. He welcomed the shock to his overheated system. Invigorating and stimulating, just right to hone his buzzing senses.

He looked left down the High Street and failed to spot the three girls. Plenty of others, but not his chosen ones. He looked right and for a second felt a shock ripple through him as he again could not immediately see them. Surely God wasn't just teasing him? He released a sharp misty breath as he glimpsed the Charlie girl behind a larger group of revellers. He was aware that there were a whole host of reasons why his simple plan of 'pick a girl, follow her, kill her' was seriously flawed. The victim could get in a taxi, get a bus, walk with her friend to her own front door, all giving him no chance of contact. But he deeply believed that God only allowed the selection of the right type; the rest of the business to be transacted by him.

He shifted slightly to his left, pulling the collar up on his mac both for protection from the rain and from sight. He started off after them, pleased that he could see 'Plump' some twenty or thirty yards ahead of him. The only niggle that he felt was that he knew enough of this town to be aware that the obvious way back to the student digs was the other way down the High Street. Still, his voice was telling him to remain convinced that the girls were not going on to a party or other function and that his spirits should stay high. He splodged along through the puddles, comparing himself to a lion stalking, at a distance, a zebra. He meandered down the street, trying not to let his adrenaline carry him too close to the girls. Although the rain was probably keeping the numbers down a little on the street, those people who were about were either running to their destination or walking with their heads bowed. Either way it meant a lot less chance of casual attention being given to a man sensibly dressed in a mac.

He was conscious that he was becoming more tense, but was equally aware that he was entering the mode of self-control that was always going to be essential for the tasks to be performed on these special nights. He loved this sensation, the knowledge that his body wanted to run, to panic at the slightest difficulty, but that his mental strength would not allow that to happen. The control was total now: control over his own movements and emotions; control over the girl. She was his payback time.

And then a moment to test this control, this resolve. The girls turned into Ward Street, something which was not supposed to happen, as it could only mean one thing: The Strand nightclub. He looked beyond the girls and saw the tiny neon sign shining brightly in the gloom of the distance. People were gathered, he could see, around the entrance.

Damn it, damn! They're just not Strand people, he thought. Far too expensive a place to go. What the hell are they doing? Anyway, Target and Charlie have jeans on, they'll never get in… unless they know someone. Shit! What if they've got complimentary tickets, or – worse still – know one of the heavies on the door?'

He slowed a little, thinking it through. It had to be The Strand, as Ward Street was effectively a cul-de-sac, leading only to a few industrial units.

He was thinking furiously. Could go into the club and do it later. Could get someone else… Neither was appealing. Going to the club meant a potentially very late night and then that meant transport problems. To pick somebody else would firstly be difficult and secondly not really what the plan was about. Too risky, the club… Although his anonymity was relatively assured to date, why chance one of the three girls just scraping a recollection of him from the pub and pasting it to his appearance in the club? To choose another girl at this late stage would smack of hasty decision and he was not about to make that sort of basic, sloppy error.

So if I'm thwarted tonight, so be it, he thought, without bitterness. If God wants to test me out, so be it. He isn't going to catch me out with something so simple.

He was disappointed, sure, but he felt good that it was this clinical, rational thought pattern that, amongst other things, set him apart from the crowd; that and the fact that he butchered women. For a fleeting second his thought was, the fact that he murdered *innocent people*, but the notion was strangled at birth.

Go home now, then? Or go a little closer for a last look at the lucky, lucky girl. Must be fate, God's decision. He decided to go close. You should buy a lottery ticket tomorrow with luck like this. A 'tomorrow' that five minutes ago you were not going to see. Are you really just teasing, Lord? Just a little spanner in the works to see how I will react? Hah, no problem! It doesn't bother me, same again soon.

And then, a few yards away, a sight to behold, to rejoice at. One of the girls, the skinny one, was being given what looked like a bear hug by a large young man. At about 6'3" and probably at least fifteen stones the lad, who was twentyish, dwarfed the girl. Indeed, he picked her off her feet without the slightest hint of exertion. A boyfriend! A goddamn boyfriend, of course. So that's what they were doing at The Strand. Two pairs of jeans and a pair of trousers, jeans no; trousers yes.

Sure enough, the threesome said their giggling goodbyes, and Skinny and the Incredible Hulk disappeared into the muddle of a queue that led into the throbbing gloom that was The Strand.

He was moving very slowly towards the end of the queue himself, giving the impression of either looking for somebody or being unsure about going to the club. He looked down at his shoes as Plump and Charlie girl strolled past him, arm in arm, and laughing. He just caught Plump saying to her friend '…Told you he was big! Suzie reckons he's massive all over…' More giggling ensued.

He quickened his step to the intimidating bouncer on the door. He was aware that a few people at the head of the queue, waiting impatiently and getting wet, were watching him. Any hint of him jumping the queue and he knew that they would be down his throat very quickly and they might remember that. So he deliberately looked at the front two couples and said, 'No worries, I'm not going in.' They immediately relaxed and turned their attention back to each other. The big coloured gentleman glared at him silently.

'What time you open till?' he asked, knowing the answer full well, as his workmates divulged this sort of information every week.

The bouncer growled back in a voice that started and finished in his boots, 'Doors shut one thirty, kicking out is three thirty.'

Aye, with the emphasis on the kicking, he thought wryly.

'Cheers!' he said, not sounding at all cheery.

He turned on his heel and started off back down the street. The girls were not too far ahead. They were soon back on the High Street, where they turned left. There were still plenty of people about; lots of cover. The girls seemed to pick up pace a little, perhaps the rain in their faces influencing their stride pattern. All good news, he thought. Heading for student land, and no taxi.

They went a few more yards, past a few shops then turned left into Bullen Road. He was a little puzzled. They could go this way for digs, but the more obvious way was back further down the High Street. Bullen led to other pubs and another club so there were still people milling around. He glanced at his watch and saw it was just after 11.20. Couldn't be going for another drink, surely? He got a surprise when the two girls stopped abruptly outside The Medal Man and embraced. Now what…? He smiled; God really was giving him the run-around tonight. Not like the others, who had been very straightforward. Charlie girl was approached by another girl and they exchanged greetings. Then they waved to Plump as they moved away, presumably to a party of some description.

So Plump was alone, and now he knew he would find out whether tonight was going to happen or not. She returned to the

High Street and turned left, not right, to the taxis. She moved quickly and soon came to Langdale Street, which she turned into. He knew now that he was in business. He knew that Langdale headed into suburbia quite quickly, without knowing intimate details of the geography.

He was right, for Wendy Fell was not a student in digs. She had just rented a small flat in the suburbs.

Without consciously arriving at a decision, he found himself crossing to the other side of Langdale. He knew that it was going to be much, much quieter down here; in fact a scan of the street showed only one couple some way off on the girl's side of the street.

The rain splashed in the gutter puddles, the drops getting bigger and more frequent. If she hasn't gone for a taxi in this weather she can't have far to go, was his first thought, followed by the question, Do I catch up now, or wait?

Both sides of the street quickly rid themselves of offices and shops and suburbia sprang into being. There was a short rough area of old, battered properties, but only a couple of hundred yards later it was as if somebody had drawn a demarcation line and stated, 'That side, don't touch, leave to rot. This side, start again, nice dwellings, nice places, nice feeling.'

This was not so far off the truth, because 'nice suburbia' was a result of local governmental inner city regeneration policies. That is to say, an idea to build houses near the town centre in order to keep the High Street alive in its deadly battle with the out-of-town malls.

He had dropped back as far as he dare without still leaving him a distance that he could not cover quickly. He might have to act fast... but he needn't have worried; the girl was only thinking of her warm, snug Winnie the Pooh pyjamas, her cosy bed and a cuddle off Mr Flopsy.

Have to get closer, she can't have far to go, he was thinking, as the girl stopped abruptly at a bus stop.

What the hell now? Can't be for a bus, for Christ's sake, all the stops she had passed. The last bus had probably gone anyway. Then he realised that she was just stopping to check for any taxis that might be passing, fortuitously. In her case, he thought, it would be *very* fortuitous. There were none, he was relieved to see, but was worried by the paradox of her having gone this far and now looking. He couldn't have known that Wendy was really regretting that seventh and last Bacardi and coke. She was not far from her flat but the bile was rising to her lips. She spat a couple of times, but figured that if she could get home then a pint of water might settle her. A pound on a taxi, daft as it was for such a short distance, would be worth it. If she had to, she could vomit in the street but she preferred option one. She guessed that she might make it on foot anyway; it certainly didn't feel critical.

He had made a snap decision, forced upon him by her stopping and looking. He could not find an instant hiding place; to stop would look very suspicious and to walk on would look as if he was possibly following her. So, as she looked for her taxi in his general direction, he immediately dug his hands deep into his mac pockets and broke into a gentle trot. His intention was to give the impression that he was jogging home, and because he was already moving at a slow trot when she first spied him that was exactly the impression that she got. In fact she never gave him a second thought, not even at this hour, on this deserted street, in this gloomy, brooding weather.

He did not look up but was aware that the girl had seen him. The street was empty apart from the two of them. Then a car splashed by, coming from the direction of the High Street.

He was conscious of the neat, semi-detached houses that he was passing. Neatly painted and maintained houses, fronted by neat gardens: suburbia, a safe haven – usually.

His mind was working fast, covering the options. Had to make a decision now. *Now.*

He felt as if he then physically obeyed subconscious decisions, as if on some divinely guided autopilot. He was rapidly making up the ground between himself and the girl as he mixed a few paces of jogging with a few quick steps. He knew she was his and the thought sent a charge of electricity coursing through his veins. He felt a giddy rush of excitement to his head and he wanted to shout, 'Yes, yes, yes! Thank you, God, thank you!'

The only action that came was that his right hand unbuttoned the top two buttons on the front of his mac. Then he undid the belt with both hands. His right hand slipped into the left inside lining of the mac and his fingers ran across the three weapons that were held there. His fingers selected the screwdriver, with its viciously sharpened point. He carefully pulled the Velcro tab away from it, gently handling it between two fingers as it became free. He drew it from his coat and clasped it in the palm of his right hand.

He was nearly level with her now. As he drew opposite her he was aware that she had glanced at him through the pouring rain. He moved on a few yards, then took a diagonal route across the road. He slowed as he crossed, taking exaggerated deep breaths as if exhausted from a long run.

He never gave any indication that he was even aware that she was there. He slowed and tried to give the impression that he was trudging home after a depressing night out, that he was cold, wet and miserable, and was now fatigued from an overtaxing run. He had judged his angles perfectly. He had arrived on her side of the street far enough ahead of her not to arouse suspicion or worry, but close enough so that the pace at which she was moving soon brought her splodging up behind him. As she neared him, his sharp senses told him that she had inevitably and noticeably quickened her pace, so she was not oblivious to potential danger.

'Got the time, luv?' he asked as she went past.

'No, sorry,' she said without pausing her stride or looking at him.

Lying bitch, he thought, having noticed in the pub her garish red watch.

He looked ahead and saw on their side of the street a dark area that was obviously not built on. She was only a few yards ahead of him as they reached what he could now see was some sort of wasteland. Even better; he'd have been happy to deal with her in a garden, but this was truly heaven-sent.

In a second he was upon her. His left arm went around the girl's throat, snapping her head back. She grunted a strangled scream. His right palm produced the screwdriver and he jabbed it into her back. He knew that the severe sharpness of this cruel weapon would penetrate her jacket and then her top and then her flesh. Her squeal confirmed this. He did not want to kill her here, not yet, but she was kicking and wriggling too much for his comfort, so he jabbed the screwdriver again. This time it had the desired effect of paralysing her, either by pain or fear or both. He did not care. He tightened his grip around her throat and her cries were stifled.

His shins hurt where she had kicked back at him, but he managed to push the girl towards a path that led to the dark area. The entrance to the area was illuminated by a light atop of a ten-foot pole, the light emitted being apparently about forty watts' worth.

He suddenly stiffened as the headlights of a car swept into the street from a side road some hundred yards ahead of him. He instantly spun the girl around as if in a grotesque ballroom dancing manoeuvre. She found herself facing him; indeed their faces were only an inch apart.

'Don't move!' he hissed at her.

She tasted his breath and the intimacy terrified her. He held her right arm in his left hand and his right arm held her pressed against him in a vice-like grip. As the car drew near he pressed his lips to hers in a passionately obscene embrace. She wriggled in his grip and his lips could feel the vibrations as she tried vainly to scream. His very effective hug stifled both noise and movements as the car went by. Still kissing her, conscious now of a stickiness on her back where blood seeped through her clothes, he thought he heard a shout from the car.

'Go on, mate, give her one for me!' boomed out, followed by raucous, drunken laughter. The car careered away and his mind drifted for a second to a day long ago when careless driving took a terrible toll. He snapped from his thoughts as the girl tried to bite him. His little cry of 'Ow!' sounded loud in the night whose silence was only broken by the splashing rain.

He thought of the comment from the car. He was going to give her one all right, and he was going to violate her, but not in any way that the shouter could have imagined.

He pulled back from the girl and whipped his right hand from behind her back to slap her hard on the left cheek. He looked at her stunned, terrified, bewildered features and felt nothing. He spun her back to the original position and marched her down the path on the wasteland. He bent close to her and growled into her ear, 'No noise.' She whimpered, so he barked, 'No noise!'

She offered little resistance, other than being a dead weight as he dragged her into the darkness.

He looked along the path that was only dimly lit every thirty yards or so. It was quite a big area, and probably the usual haunt of druggies, perverts, queers and flashers, but not tonight, not in this rain. He had pushed her some two hundred or so yards from the main road and had just passed under the fifth, fairly useless little lamp post. He swung her right and moved off the tarmac path. The ground was uneven and slippy and she was more difficult to push here as she stumbled along. He only went a few yards before stopping to catch his breath. It was very quiet and eerily dark, with a strange pale light emanating from the nearby lamp.

'Let's talk,' he said into the girl's left ear.

'Please… my back…! Don't hurt me again.'

Such was his grip that the words could barely be heard by the man, and he grinned wickedly at his total control. Although he was only carrying out a function designed by his Lord, he could not stop himself enjoying the final moments of another successful task.

The girl started to shake and choke and he immediately loosened his grip a fraction. He did not want her passing out, not at this, the most interesting, part. No, she had to listen now, and understand, even if only a little, about *why*. She continued to cough, quite gently, almost apologetically, but he could see that she was over the worst. Then she unexpectedly vomited. Fortunately for him she was turned a little away from him and the mess splattered into grass rather than down his mac. She threw up a second time, and sick dribbled down her chin.

'Lie down!' he ordered, pointing to a grassy patch of ground at their feet. The girl did not react, probably couldn't, so he dragged her roughly to the ground. She hit the wet ground with a squelching thump and her knees were immediately raised off the ground in a defensive movement.

'Don't worry, this isn't rape,' he said, in an almost conversational tone. She registered no consolation. He tapped her knees as if gently chiding a youngster, saying, 'Down please, put them down.'

The girl lay on the grass, shaking with terror and although she saw his lips move, she was no longer able to hear his words. If she had been capable of rational thought at that precise moment, the girl might have wondered why this madman was gently but firmly placing his left hand over her mouth. The gentleness of the movement, given what had gone before, and the casualness of it, should possibly have alerted her. It didn't, so the shock was even greater when he produced a screwdriver and rammed it into her left knee. Her back arched off the ground and her mouth opened wide. Her eyes bulged and her legs flailed for a second before she slumped flat on the grass. He immediately sat astride her, across her stomach.

He had pinned her left arm to her front and it was trapped under his right leg. Her right arm was held by his left hand. He leaned forward and said, 'Now then, I asked you nicely and you ignored me, do we understand each other now?'

She was crying quietly and she mumbled over and over, 'Please, please let me go, please, please let me go!' The words came between sobs.

'I'll take that as a yes, then.'

She couldn't comprehend these words, this man, this situation.

'No noise now, please,' he said. 'You have to listen.' He waited, as if expecting a cogent response. If he was, he was disappointed because none was forthcoming. A whiff of her perfume touched his nose and he stopped to enjoy it. He did like the smell of a woman's perfume, even cheap stuff like this.

The blood from her knee soaked into the lower part of his trouser leg; her back bled into the dirty ground.

'I'll try not to bore you,' he started. His voice was low but clear and he leaned forward as he spoke.

'Don't know whether you could say the problems were always there, grew as I grew, or even if they really were my fault. I don't think that "my fault" is a genuine option, but hey, who will ever know for certain? Anyway, I do believe, totally, without any shred of doubt that that life, those conditions, that hell on earth, was more than anybody, absolutely, literally *anybody*, could be reasonably expected to take. To tolerate. Not without some compensation. Really, you understand, don't you?'

He was unaware that the girl was still repeating, 'Please, please, let me go!' His questions were now rhetorical; it was a speech that he was making, not a discussion that he was holding.

He went on in monotonous tones, knowing that it was somehow important that the girl realised the justification of this deed.

'I know it is an old cliché, but it happens to be true, and many clichés are, by the way; but you would not treat an animal like that, you really wouldn't, for fear of getting hammered by the RSPCA, and getting loads of bad publicity.'

The girl made an almost involuntary movement, which even she couldn't have said was a pathetic attempt at escape or just a spasm trying to gain some comfort from the pains hitting her body from all angles. Without being aware of any decision or thought about it, he reacted by pressing down harder. She gasped as firstly the air was forced out of her lungs, and then two ribs cracked. She shouted out in pain and he immediately slapped her into silence. He stared at her with a look of disgust and spat out angrily, 'Firstly I tell you no noise, then I tell you to listen. You do neither, as if to deliberately annoy me!' Tears coursed down her cheeks. 'You believe in God, don't you? I never used to, not at all. God, no. Not for a long time. Just wasn't possible, suffering as I did. But then you see I found Him and He found me, and really I think even He got a shock at what I'd been through. He'd overlooked me, you see. A complete genuine oversight, nothing deliberate, too much big stuff to worry about. But when He found out He said, "Whoa, this needs to be redressed!" So we talked, and we hatched a plan.'

He leaned further forward and his left hand released her arm. The arm remained limp on the grass, his voice dropped to a whisper.

'It was a good plan. Simple but good. Seeing that we both agreed that it was mothers who were the problem, we then agreed that we should remove a few. In lieu, if you like; as compensation. You see, God cannot stop people being born – free will and all that – and anyway he accepts that he made sex too attractive. So, given that women are going to be born, the next best thing was to kill a few. Those of child-bearing age, just for the irony of the timing.'

Of all his talking the first thing that registered with the girl was the word 'kill'. Although not hearing the context, she knew that the use of that word meant a great deal.

She wriggled, this time in a conscious effort to try and get away. She lifted her left arm, but it felt so heavy and tired that it just flopped onto his shoulder rather than delivering a stunning blow as intended. He picked up her right wrist and threw her arm to the ground as if throwing a piece of meat to a dog. She desperately tried to unscramble her thoughts. 'Talk to him, talk to him!' something shouted inside her. She was trying to think of something, anything, to say as he continued. Neither of them heard the door of a motor vehicle slam shut nearby.

'He is fair, you know, and powerful. And don't tell me you haven't, like everybody else, said a prayer when in need. Like exams... and boyfriends.' He grinned at what he saw as humour. She missed the joke. 'So very fair. You know, He said to me, "You've had the shitty end of the stick, no kidding, so now it's payback time. How does half a dozen sound? That's about even, isn't it?" Anyway I negotiated and got that number up to eight. You see, in negotiating, I reminded the Almighty about the cupboard, which you've got to agree is worth two in anybody's language.' He chuckled at the memory of the uplift to eight. 'Anyway, you are five, because I don't count my mother, of course – my dear departed mother. Ha!' He spat out a triumphal exclamation.

The girl listened but didn't understand a word. She knew the pains that racked her body, strangely the one that she was most conscious of was not in the back, the knee or the ribs, but the cheek, where he had punched and slapped her. She felt dizzy and sick again, as he continued.

'That's why He made me strong and cunning. Just to give me the tools to make a go of it. A fair chance. I mean, there wouldn't really have been much point giving me the green light to even up if I was thick enough to get caught first go, now would there?' He paused and then said wistfully, 'Of course, there was that big gap between one and two, one not being mother, you understand?

Eleven years, three months. Then two years, four months, five years, four months, now one year and two months. Not regular, I must admit, but hey, I'm new to this!' He laughed a low, guttural laugh. 'So you see, He's been scrupulously fair, as you'd expect, and I hope you realise that you are totally random. Nothing personal. Quid pro quo and all that. So that's how we ended up here.'

He looked into the distance, staring blankly ahead, and the girl took the chance to speak.

'I know you have reasons, good… good reasons… anybody can see that. Just… just let me go now. You go, I'll stay here!' she stifled a sob. 'I won't tell anybody.'

His head turned down to her. 'Sorry, pet! As I said, this is not rape, where you talk to me and I change my mind and like, feel sorry for you; this is different. It's a joint mission with God that He has authorised, I thought I had explained.'

He got angry at his own words, bent down and hissed loudly into her ear, with the spittle splashing her ear and neck, 'Which fucking bit didn't you understand, bitch? I don't think you have tried to understand, and that *annoys* me!'

His conversational tone had evaporated and she detected the hate in his voice. She started a scream but he immediately reacted, so quick he might have anticipated it. The punch was short and sharp, full into her face, and she saw stars other than those in the heavens above her.

'"An eye for an eye", as the Bible says. It's the only way. I had no life in those years. Worse, in fact, because I was alive and had to live through it. Death would have been greeted with open arms. As you should do now.'

The girl recognised that the moment was upon her. If she had had any hope through the brutal last ten minutes then it vanished now. She closed her eyes and thought of her family. She didn't see him draw the Stanley knife from his coat. He still sat astride her so he raised himself a little. He placed the tip of the blade under the right side of her chin. He drew the blade firmly and in one motion under her chin and across the top of her throat. He watched, expressionless, as the blood poured down on to her neck, shoulders and beyond. He had deliberately avoided the jugular vein; he didn't want blood showering everywhere. The stroke of the blade was meant to be sacrificial; it felt sacrificial. A sacrifice to the good Lord's great godly companions in the firmament: justice and revenge.

He sighed as if the moment was an anticlimax, but the truth of the sigh was that it was an exhalation of satisfaction. He knew that any independent observer of the proceedings would be screaming, 'Get away, run!' But he was calm, he was sated. He started to draw back when the girl suddenly coughed, loudly, splattering blood over his chest. His involuntary reaction was to lunge forward and he slammed the girl into the ground. Her head lolled lifelessly to one side and he saw her staring eyes in the light cast by the lamp. Something about the stare made him look in the direction that they pointed. He thought he heard the girl mocking him as he saw, to his complete amazement, not more than forty feet away, a young man staring at him.

Chapter Four

It had been a good night, no question, but the amazing and wonderful thing was that it was because of a girl, rather than just the usual belly laughs (several), dancing with some top totty (a couple) or dancing with seriously ugly dogs (a few).

The banter in the taxi was all about Jonno's latest sexual conquest, a twenty-three-year-old barmaid from a club in Middlesborough that they had been to two weeks earlier over Christmas. Jonno – John Nugent – was not what you'd call handsome, obviously handsome that is, but women and girls saw something in his open, smiling features and his easy, confident but not cocky manner. The barmaid was a typical Jonno girl, in that he had only spoken a few words to her that night, acquired an address and met her a week later on her first available night off. They all roared with laughter, envious but not jealous, as he described graphically how she had allowed him to do whatever he wanted on their second date.

In the pub which they settled on as first choice they managed to find a table that they could all sit around. From the pub Toddy rang Mike on his mobile and told him where they were. Mike Horsham was a Project Leader at the local division of an international chemical giant. He was working on a rush job at the moment and couldn't finish work until seven o'clock. His intention was to drive down to town, enjoy the night on soft drinks and then take a couple of the crew home.

As the chat concentrated on women and football, with the odd diversion into television, film, work and cars, it was decided that they should go for an early dance at a local pub where there was a small, atmospheric area that was basically a dance floor and four rooms. They hadn't been there for a while; they guessed that the place would be busy with people still spending Granny's Christmas money.

Baz and Toddy were going to a thirtieth birthday bash tomorrow, and anticipated a major night. The birthday boy was a prop forward who believed that if he could drink twelve pints, then everybody should be able to drink a gallon and a half of strong beer (or lager, he wasn't going to complain about that, even if lager was a girly drink).

They had considered calling off tonight, but didn't want to risk going several weeks without a happy crew night, so here they were; and at just after eight, the crew was complete with the arrival of Mike.

For an hour and a quarter they discussed and digested the recent results of the local football teams, the performances of the overpaid stars and prospects of good cup runs. At 9.15 they left the pub and walked briskly to the venue of the dance floor, which was only a few hundred yards away. They knew that there would be a small queue, but anticipated comfortable access before ten o'clock, after which there was a cover charge of £4 per head. Their timing was spot on, the queue being only six or seven long, probably because of the wet, miserable weather.

They entered the front door and then turned left into a corridor which led to the room with the dance floor. Just outside the dance area was a bar with a long recess in which you could stand and rest your drink on a series of shelves. It was noisy in this area, with the thump, thump of the bass line from the music next door. They got served pretty quickly, not for the lack of customers, but because of the large number of staff behind the counter, another plus point for this particular venue.

Jeff nipped off to the toilet, again, and that was another nuisance which only he seemed to suffer. Beer and lager just seemed to go straight through him, when others around him only went once or twice a night on gallons. Life is so unfair, he thought to himself mockingly.

In the toilet he peed into the urinal proudly bearing the name, as so many do, Armitage Shanks. Why, he wondered, since the age of about eleven, have I always wanted to write *Does he?* after the name?

He couldn't answer his question, so he shook the droplets from his penis, washed his hands and rejoined the crew.

When he picked up his glass he was aware that they were giving Mike some stick.

'What's he done?' he asked Baz.

'He just let an absolute monster go, could have cut it with a knife, and Jonno said it was about time Mike strapped an air freshener to his leg – permanently – his arse is so stinky!'

Jeff laughed and joined in the baiting of Mike. 'You'll never be an astronaut will you, Mike? Christ, one of your specials in your spacesuit – what a horrible way to die!'

Everybody laughed, even Mike, who would have to admit that he was both frequently flatulent and often smelly with it.

They moved en masse to the arch that led to the dance floor and stepped just inside to take stock of those dancing. Busy, but not silly, was the popular verdict, and they indulged themselves in a happy round of 'Spot the dog'. Baz won when he spotted a short, plump girl with owl-like spectacles and a very peculiar haircut.

'Strike one for Baz!' cried Jonno. 'Now get over there and give her one!'

Baz knew the rules,: win the point, lose the dance. He boldly announced, 'It is a far, far better thing I do, Macduff...' and strode off.

The four non-participants watched intently as Baz walked up to the girl, smiled at her dancing partner, put a hand on his target's shoulder and leaned conspiratorially to her ear. They noticed that she appeared to look twice at Baz but then, even at that distance and in that light, they could see the size of her smile. Baz, at 6'2", towered over the girl, who was probably about one foot shorter.

'Christ!' exclaimed Jeff, 'if she had a flat head Baz could rest his pint on it whilst she gave him a gobble!' He laughed loudly at his comment, and the others joined his laughter.

Baz was courteous enough to have a second dance with the girl, then said a polite, 'Thanks, luv,' before rejoining the crew.

The beer and laughs flowed and Jeff started to feel that perhaps he had been drinking a bit too quick. He did not fancy the thought of calling for Hughie down the big white telephone later, so decided to slow up. Maybe the food to follow, whatever it might happen to be, would settle that slight queasy feeling.

Pairs of girls swayed and jiggled to the music, hoping that some good-looking blokes, preferably two together, would pick them out of the masses and start a beautiful romance. Several lads stumbled around, too tanked up already to dance smoothly, bumping the girls whom they asked to dance, grinning stupid leering grins, hoping only to avoid instant rejection and praying for a dance that would lead to a later smoochy fondle.

The happy crew were on schedule for their anticipated night when Jeff noticed two girls on the far fringe of the dance floor. Toddy and Baz were crucifying Mike over an incident a few minutes earlier when a flying elbow had half emptied Mike's pint glass. He had turned angrily with a 'What the bloody hell—?' and found himself staring into the chest of an enormous black man, built like a fit Arnold Schwarzenegger.

The tight white T-shirt only served to enhance the hugely intimidating presence of this modern Goliath.

Baz had whispered to Mike, 'Steady, tiger, be gentle with him,' and Mike had literally raised his head and uttered a whimpish 'Sorry.'

'No problem, sonny!' boomed a resonant voice and Mike slunk back to the group.

'Did you see the colour he went?' Jeff asked, pointing at the man-mountain. 'You scared the shit out of him, Mike, you vicious bastard!'

Toddy and Baz were still ribbing Mike as Jeff said, 'Toddy, hey, Toddy! Take a look!'

Toddy came to Jeff's shoulder and Jeff pointed out the two girls who had caught his eye.

'You mean the skinny bird with a mate who looks like a bulldog chewing a wasp?' asked Toddy mischievously.

'No, prat, the two behind them,' retorted Jeff, knowing Toddy knew exactly whom he was pointing at.

'Why not?' said Toddy rhetorically.

Jeff made sure that he got to the girls slightly ahead of Toddy, so as to ensure getting the particular girl he had noticed.

Mike, Jonno and Baz discussed the possibility of not going for a major nosh as a grand finale. Mike declared himself knackered from work, Jonno was running short of cash and Baz was conscious of the tough night that lay ahead on Saturday. They were all aware that for possibly the first ever time an integral part of the night was in jeopardy. Mike made a half-hearted attempt to turn the opinion around, but his comment, 'I could murder a vindaloo,' was squashed by Jonno's, 'Think of your arse in the morning!' and, 'No need to stock the bog rolls in the fridge!'

They decided that to grab a burger from a chuck wagon would be a satisfactory middle ground.

Toddy was a confident young man who would normally get to the pretty girl first, but Jeff had felt that it was important to be ahead this time. Mind you, Toddy's choice and taste in girls was highly debatable, so the other lads never challenged his race to get there first. Jeff grinned at Toddy's slightly surprised expression; it wasn't what he normally experienced.

Jeff was not particularly sure of himself with girls until he really got to know them, and given his current state of podginess he was feeling pretty insecure.

'Hi, okay, if we join you?' was his sparkling opening line. He was very encouraged by the lovely smile that greeted his words. He glanced at Toddy, who was already jiving like a demented frog, hopping from foot to foot, but the girl he was performing to was laughing in a happy rather than mocking fashion.

Jeff did not mind dancing at all; he felt that he had a certain rhythm, even if the crew sometimes described him as dancing like a crab on heat. In fact he was not too self-conscious about moving about, at least to music that he was familiar with. What he did struggle with, always, was the communication thing. It wasn't that he was medically deaf, just that for some reason he could never hear clearly what a girl would be saying to him amid the hullaballoo of a dance floor. He was staring at the girl thinking, God, there's something about this girl that is wonderful, exciting, special! Then he realised that her mouth was moving and he felt panicky. Shit, she's saying something and I can't hear a word! Cher blasted out her smash hit and for a second he felt like screaming at the top of his voice, 'Shut the sodding music off, the magic girl's talking to me!'

He shouted 'Sorry?' and leaned forward towards her. He concentrated hard. She also moved forward a little and their heads were very close.

Jeff thought that she smelt gorgeous. He thought that she said something like, 'Oove... oo... ud... ite?'

'Sorry?' he said again, apologetically, now desperately straining his ears and concentration. How the frig did people conduct full-blown and easy conversations on these floors. Shut the fuck up, Cher!

'Have you had a good night?' she shouted into his ear.

When he looked into her face he wanted to say, 'Since I saw you, you wonderful, sexy thing,' but thought better of it. He answered, 'Yeah, great thanks, just out with a few mates. How about you?'

The 'you' was hardly out of his mouth before he had moved even tighter to the girl and turned his ear to where the girl's words were coming from. He didn't catch all of her answer but got enough to make sense of it, something like, 'Yeah, it's been good, me and Helen.'

They both looked to Helen and Toddy, who was now gyrating like a man possessed. Jeff jabbed a thumb in Toddy's direction and shouted to his dancing partner, 'Bit subdued tonight!'

His girl nodded and laughed.

She was not what your average punter would call stunning, or beautiful, or sex on legs; but to Jeff she had a certain indefinable 'something' that was attractive, appealing, sexy – and more. Just 'something'.

'What's your name, then?' he asked.

'Jayne, what's yours?'

'Jeff,' was all he said, and then a great big smile burst through on to his face. A smile beamed back and something jumped inside his chest. A shot of electricity ran through him. The music faded and he took the opportunity in the brief interlude to ask, 'Can I get you a drink?'

'Yes, please,' she replied and smiled, so he placed a gentle, unobtrusive hand behind her and, barely touching the small of her back, guided her across the floor to the arch that led to the bar.

As they walked, the thought crossed his mind that he was not supposed to be doing this, this was not part of a happy crew night. However, the rules were allowed to be waived for a special woman. Now, yes, that was meant to be reserved for totty who had male eyes on stalks, with legs, arse and tits on display, and all quality. However, special was special, and every instinct in Jeff's body was shouting, 'Hey, whoa there, fireworks zipping, heartstrings twanging!'

He barely glanced at Mike, Jonno and Baz as he passed nearby. He heard a distant, 'Get up there, Henry! Hubba, hubba!' from Jonno, but took no notice. They just did not realise, just did not see or feel what he was seeing or feeling.

The bar was busy but Jeff was delighted that he would at least be able to talk and listen clearly. The talking that ensued was simple chit-chat really, establishing basic facts such as addresses, modes of transport that evening (Jeff taxi, Jayne bus), and where they worked.

Jeff did not feel the need to impress, to fire off sharp dialogue and clever witticisms, and for this he was extremely grateful. It all felt so comfortable, so right, as if they had been friends (lovers!) for a long, long time. He knew that this was different, because with a girl for a first time Jeff always faced the 'job' dilemma. Although he had no personal worries about admitting that he worked at an accountant's, and he knew that the truth was that it was often an exciting and invigorating working environment, the theory was – and sometimes reality confirmed – that others felt that such an admission was tantamount to admitting to no life, no personality and a 'sense-of-humour-ectomy'. Tonight the information was imparted without compunction. So this was different, and better, than any girl Jeff could remember – going back all the way to Beth, if not further.

Time was short because Jayne and Helen were set to leave at eleven thirty and it was almost that now. After the few minutes that they had been together Jeff was now faced with three options. One: do nothing, say goodbye and wallow later in the satisfaction of a few precious moments with an angel. Two: go for it, grab her, in a nice way, and snog, she must be up for it. Three: do something unusual, be polite, be courteous, ask for a telephone number and arrange to see her again. There was no real option, and he said words that did not sound like his own.

'It's been great, Jayne… can we swap numbers and maybe get together in the next few days?'

Before he could wonder at his politeness – or even allow the unthinkable thought to cross his mind, like What if she says, 'No thanks'? – Jayne was bringing a pen and diary out of her handbag. She tore a page out of the back of the *Marie Clare* diary and wrote *Jayne Gilmour*, with her address and telephone number. She wrote a little *X* at the bottom of the page and it made Jeff's racing pulse squeeze another beat or two through his veins.

He was still looking at the piece of paper, beaming, when Jayne moved closer, kissed his cheek and, pressing her lips to his ear, said, 'Call me, bye.'

He hadn't even noticed Helen return to Jayne's side, and as he said, 'I will,' they moved off down the long corridor to the front door of the pub. He lifted himself on to his tiptoes and shouted, 'Bye, Jayne!' to the back of a distant head.

He lowered himself down with a jolt and, as if that small motion brought him back from a distant dream world, he was suddenly aware of the noise, smells and movement around him. He could also sense four pairs of eyes burning into him from the right side of the arch. He turned slowly, to emphasise the moment, acutely aware of what he would see. He was not disappointed: Toddy, Mike, Jonno and Baz were grinning like four happy Cheshire cats. Each held a bottle raised in their right hands and each held their left hands on their groins.

Mike bawled, 'Let's hear it for Jeff-er-rey Sanders, lurrve machine!' and the four of them broke into American-style whooping and hollering, as if drawn from an excited US quiz show audience.

He moved back to them, traded insults and listened to Toddy detailing the firmness of Helen's buttocks and the flexibility and suppleness of her tongue. Jeff took it in his stride and heard some of the banter, and even responded to some of it on autopilot. His thoughts were elsewhere. That kiss on the cheek. Wow! Wonderful, subtle, sophisticated, sexy, wonderful, attractive, smiley, smart, working as a nursery teacher meant she was nice as well. Wonderful…

He was getting quizzed again about the piece of paper that Jonno had seen being exchanged and he answered, 'We exchanged a message of lurve, she knew I was Mr Right,' he declared.

'Right then, who's for a kebab?' Mike asked. 'I certainly am, I could eat an Alsatian!'

Jonno responded, 'You're in luck mate, it probably is frigging Alsatian!'

They watched a little more dancing, cruelly identifying a pair of girls that they deemed 'most unattractive' on the dance floor.

'The one on the left's definitely been hit with the ugly stick,' declared Jonno, 'and her mate looks like a clumsy bee-keeper – spotty or what?'

The two girls abruptly stopped dancing, picked up their handbags and strode towards them.

'Oh my God!' declared Toddy, 'they're coming to get us!'

They marched straight past where the young men were standing and after they had passed Jonno commented, 'Yours looks like she's been chopping sticks on her face!'

They laughed callously and decided to make their way out of the club.

They went outside and were disappointed to see the steady rain. A quick debate took place and, surprisingly, they decided to call it a night and avoid getting soaked. Mike was to take Jonno and Baz; Jeff and Toddy were to get a taxi that was to take them in the opposite direction.

It was not a long taxi journey, and on the way Jeff told Toddy that he would get out at the 'brickie' and take a short cut. Toddy said that Jeff should stay with the taxi, but Jeff insisted that the rain was easing and it would save a few bob.

They were soon parked at the 'brickie' – a piece of derelict wasteland or a patch of natural wilderness in deepest suburbia, depending on your viewpoint.

Jeff had two main reasons for getting out here and neither had to do with gaining a few pounds or a few minutes. He wanted to have a little time to think about Jayne, and the rain would help, he hoped, to clear his beery head. Toddy only lived half a mile farther up the road that they were parked on, but said the taxi could take him to his door.

Jeff got out from the taxi and at that instant thought he heard a noise somewhere into the brickie. He was going to say something but Toddy was saying his goodbyes and taking the mickey one last time about Jayne.

Jeff slammed the taxi door, a little loudly, he thought, Shit, maybe I am a bit drunk... On previous occasions when he had taken a little air before getting home it had only worked on about fifty per cent of the time. He often suspected that if he had that one drop too much, no walking in fresh air, no amount of food, water or coffee would make any difference. At least not to the ultimate outcome, although it may buy a little time. That ultimate outcome meant noisy, painful choking and vomiting. On the way to that horrible finale was the almost equally unpleasant room-spin. He would gently lower his head to his pillow, picking out the point on the ceiling to focus on. He would concentrate desperately on that point, straining to keep it steady as it tried to wobble away from view. Then he would close his eyes slowly, as if speed of eyelid movement was a factor and hope. He obviously never hoped enough because everything started spinning immediately – sickening, dizzying spinning that lurched and dipped, no matter what he concentrated on. Once the mental motion had started, opening his eyes was another bad move. Lampshades would jump and sway, and the portable television would shudder as if on a rickety washing machine that was wobbling around a kitchen.

He glanced ahead into the gloomy area known as the brickie. It was many years since the old brick works had been cleared away from the site, but the name had stuck. The planners had worked around it when building the new developments which formed the backbone of the urban regeneration schemes. They had done, it was universally agreed, a good job of the housing areas, with nice properties and facilities, but the brickie was controversial. The idea was to leave a green belt, and it was a large area, that could accommodate play areas, trees, walks, a beck and picnic areas. Supporters said that it still served this function, just needing a little tidying. Detractors said that the whole area was dirty and dangerous, a haven for illicit sex and the provider of cover for flashers and perverts. It was true that there had been early problems after the housing areas were first occupied. Young girls walking home were often accosted by men high on drink or drugs. The outcry was finally listened to when a girl was raped by two older men who had been drinking all day on a summer Bank Holiday. That was a catalyst for the authorities, police and Council to act, and the human filth was swept away over the course of a couple of months. The Council built a path through the area, running from the main road out of town to the heart of the suburbs. It was lit, but done on the cheap and the lamps were weak and spaced well apart. However, the message seemed to have been received, because no further incidents had been reported. The path was known as the 'M1' because it was such a well-worn path, well trodden by dog walkers, revellers on their way home and joggers of both sexes.

So on this cold, wet, unfriendly night, Jeff stepped onto the M1 and thought nothing of the brisk ten-minute walk that lay ahead of him. At the back of his mind a tiny, squeaky voice whispered, 'You heard something, you know, something that didn't sound right, didn't sound nice.' But he wasn't listening to that, he was already thinking very happy thoughts about Jayne, that kiss and how soon he could see her again.

He moved quickly because although the rain had eased considerably from what must have been a cloudburst at the pub, he didn't want to dawdle and get soaked. He was not conscious of how scary the brickie could look to a stranger not familiar with it. The swaying trees, dim lights, scudding clouds and moving shadows would not have been attractive to many people, but Jeff was simply a local who remembered the brickie as a place for football and cricket matches on sunny afternoons. On a different night he might have been more aware of his surroundings but tonight Jayne filled his head (and heart?).

He had only gone a minute into the brickie when he heard the slightest of noises ahead. It wasn't the wind, it wasn't trees or bushes, nor a babbling brook. It was slight, but it was scary; the noise dragged his thoughts from Jayne. She wasn't Miss World... she wasn't Meg Ryan, Sharon Stone or Michelle Pfeiffer... she wasn't... Bollocks to that, she was Jayne, she was lovely and she wanted to see him again. God, life was good! And then that little noise wiped the smile from his lips and made him slow his stride.

He looked slightly ahead and to the right, into some bushes that moved a little in the damp breeze. Was that something in the bushes? No, just the changing light and shadow as the rain clouds blanketed the moon again. Jeff felt very sober. He approached the point where he imagined the noise had come from. He felt a chill run down his back and he didn't think it was caused by rain droplets. Thoughts of sunny sports pitches had long evaporated. Maybe it was a bird or animal, but he knew that the kids who played there all day had ensured that there was no significant wildlife in the brickie.

Thoughts of Jayne were pushed aside, and then he heard an unexpected sound: the sound of somebody talking, quietly. He moved a few paces forward and then stopped. The voice was only a few yards from the M1 and he leaned forward to peer behind some small shrubs. His first thought was that a couple were having sex, as he could see a man astride a girl. He was on the verge of smiling when the muscles in her face froze solid. Spot-the-dog, man-mountain, Jayne, the earlier than expected finish to the night... If Jeff had been asked to recall the evening he could not, at that moment, recollect a single detail. He was paralysed with fear, as his wide eyes stared at a man placing a weapon to the girl's throat. A second later he moved the weapon across the girl's neck, and in the half-light that the distant lamp created, Jeff was aware of a darkening patch below the girl's neck, and it wasn't shadow.

The man astride the girl did not seem to be in any rush and that in itself was terrifying. The calmness of the man, his apparent detachment, having just done what he had done. No sensible thoughts entered or left Jeff's head. Not even *Run*. He simply watched the scene a few yards away, in horror and stunned disbelief.

And then, to compound the horror, the girl gurgled and coughed, before her killer slammed her down into the wet earth. The motion turned the girl's face in Jeff's direction. He was literally staring death in the face, but his awareness of the pun did not raise a smile.

Jeff's heart felt as if an icy hand was gripping it – too tightly – and he subconsciously realised that he had been barely breathing for the last forty-five seconds. Now, as he swallowed hard, an exhalation of air escaped his lips before he drew in air with a gasp. Jeff's eyes had been firmly fixed on the girl, firstly her throat, and then her face and that diabolical expression. Now, Jeff tore his eyes from those of the girl and looked into the eyes of a killer. Like a doll being worked from below, the killer's head had turned slowly to look at Jeff, and again, like his nonchalance, the slowness of the motion was terrifying. Jeff's stomach lurched, his bowels seemed to twitch and threatened to open then and there. At last, the chemicals necessary for the job of escape flooded through his torso into his legs and he turned and ran. He stumbled, he flailed his arms, he made a strange mewling noise as he moved. He tripped and lunged forward but managed to stay on his feet. He only stumbled and tripped out of fear, out of his desire to get away from that scene. Those faces, one dead, one alive. Which was the more terrifying?

For a moment he thought he was running into thick, cloying mud because his legs did not seem to be taking him anywhere, but he realised that he was running quickly, even though his body felt as if it belonged to somebody else. He was not conscious of his environment but the image flashed into his head of trees grabbing Snow White as she ran from the Evil Queen. 'Jesus, Jesus, oh Jesus!' he gasped as he ran.

He burst out of the brickie and off the M1 at speed, over-shooting the pavement and hitting the road at quite a lick. If the driver of the white Transit had been less alert he might well have ploughed Jeff into the tarmac. As it was he swerved into the kerb as Jeff hurtled past the bonnet of the van. Jeff didn't think of stopping; home, sanctuary was too near now. He couldn't stop or slow down until he was inside his front door. He needed to be inside the hallway with the door shut.

He ignored the shouts of the van driver, not looking back. He didn't dare look back in case that face was right behind him, tracking him, holding that weapon aloft, ready to strike.

He twisted and turned through the streets, thoughts tumbling around his head. He saw his house and pounded a little quicker to the drive. For the first time since he had broken into his run, he slowed. He was breathing in rapid short gasps, his chest was tight and he could taste the phlegm in his throat that suggested blood. For the first time he turned his head, but gained no pleasure or relief from seeing empty streets.

He started to fumble for his keys but found that he was shaking and unable to locate them.

He banged on the front door with his fist, and it sounded very loud in the quiet neighbourhood.

Lights flicked on sleepily above, then from the hall he heard shuffling footsteps approach the door. He looked anxiously over his shoulder again, as if the monster would take him now, at this moment of salvation.

He turned as the door bolts were snapped back. Jeff's dad shouted through the unlocked door, 'Who is it, please?' and Jeff spat, between heaving breaths, 'Me, Dad.'

The door opened and Mr Sanders stood aside to let Jeff in. 'Left your keys, did you…?' he started to say, but got no further as he saw the pain etched on his son's face.

'Dad, call the police, there's been a murder!' Jeff gasped, before throwing up over his father's best slippers.

Chapter Five

The young mother stared at the tiny baby in the cot. Stared in disbelief. How did this happen, how the hell did this happen? she asked herself. She should never, ever have listened to her mother. She had always known, from the first shocking moment of confirmation of the awful truth, that abortion was the only possibility to consider. It had to be, because how could she hope to look after a kid when she had no job, no boyfriend, no money... and no hope. But her mother, God, her mother! The pressure that she had exerted from that first day, the cajoling, the shouting, the abuse and the persuasion. All these techniques she mixed together into a potent cocktail, and added to the classic, 'I'm your mother, I know what's best in life and I know what's best for you.'

At sixteen she was mature, but not so strong willed that she could resist her powerful domineering mother. The teenager's reasoned arguments about money and space and caring somehow withered away under the onslaught of her parent's persuasions.

So she had gone into hospital three days ago, had as straightforward a birth as she could have hoped for, and now, a few days later, was here, at home, looking down at her baby son.

She was puzzled why she did not feel more for him. She wanted to feel a deep and satisfying love that her mother had talked about, wanted to sense that binding love that was supposed to envelop her at the first sight of her infant. Well, it hadn't happened yet, and something told her it never would.

She wouldn't deny that she was fascinated by the little bundle before her, in a distant, abstract sort of way. Curiosity and interest though, she knew were not love. Maybe, just maybe, those feelings would come. For now, she was content in the knowledge that her mother was fussing like a broody hen around both her and baby Sam. To be given such attention was so pleasant an exception to the norm that she was going to enjoy it while it lasted.

It was not that her mother didn't love her with every single fibre in her body; it was just that as a single working mother who ran a household there were never enough hours to devote much time to quality one-to-one time with her daughter.

Her mother had taken her annual holidays to cover the first two weeks of the baby's homecoming. She was a strong woman; she had had to be, bringing up a daughter alone through the late Forties and early Fifties. Her husband had died just a few weeks after Ruth was born in 1943, their daughter having been conceived during a passionate week of leave in 1942. Cancer, not a foreigner's bullet, claimed him over three short months.

Edie's money, which she had saved with her husband before and during the war, with plans for a new home, had soon evaporated. She knew that she would have to juggle motherhood with a part-time job. She became a packer at a local food factory and Ruth was looked after in working hours by a neighbour who minded three other children.

It was a tough life; times were genuinely hard, both nationally and in the Eastman household. But Edie Eastman had already made the decision that she was going to devote the rest of her days to making the best of their situation and giving Ruth every possible chance to enjoy her life.

And then came the bombshell news in early 1959 that Ruth was pregnant, at barely fifteen. The father was a twenty-three-year-old local lad from a disreputable family and there was never a moment's discussion regarding his or his family's involvement in the future of the baby.

Ruth had fought to be allowed to terminate the pregnancy – a risky business in those days – but her mother was determined that this would not happen. Just as she saw Ruth as the future representative of her beloved husband, she also saw her grandson as the extension of that love.

And so to now. With a new baby in the house, there were even tougher times in prospect, but Edie Eastman was going to see this through, no matter what.

Ruth tried to blank out the thoughts of what was going to happen when this initial honeymoon period came to an end. She knew that her mother would continue to give her every possible support and that inevitably a lot more responsibility would fall on her shoulders. Was it even remotely possible that her mother could continue to look after all three of them? No, not really; but she mustn't dwell on this. For now she had a baby to stare at, to wonder at and, this afternoon, to show off to Mandy and Gemma.

At that moment Sam awoke with a shout which immediately turned into crying, that awful mewling which is meant, biologically, to alert the mother to her baby's needs for food, comfort or love, but which to this mother simply generated panic. She did not move, did not pick him up, but stood there with tears in her own eyes shouting, 'Mam, Mam, Sam's crying!'

The lack of response increased the swelling panic. Ruth started shrieking, 'Mam, Mam, help, please!' She still hadn't touched Sam, who was himself bawling. 'Shut up, shut up!' she pleaded, but then, as if a button had been pushed, the pleading tone turned to one of threat and hate. She lowered her voice and through sobs and gritted teeth she said, 'Shut up, you little bastard, or else I'll make you shut up!'

When Sam made no obvious attempt to heed the warning, his mother leant over the cot and smacked the side of his head, hard and cruelly. The baby screamed louder than ever, and Ruth glared again at the noisy, red-faced object. She had stopped shouting for her mother, as hate had taken over the emotions that she was feeling.

Sam did not realise that he was about to be struck again but was saved by the intervention of his grandmother. She had been hanging out the washing and thought she had heard a distant shouting. She stopped what she was doing and listened, but heard no more. She hung out a few more items but stopped again; something bothered her. A little voice said to her, 'That was Ruth you heard, and now it's gone very quiet, almost too quiet.'

She picked up her basket and peg bag and started moving back to the house. As she entered the kitchen through the back door she heard Sam screaming and she recognised the scream as one of extreme distress. She dropped the basket and bag and rushed upstairs. She burst into Sam's room and raced to his cot, brushing Ruth aside. She picked the baby up and held him with tightly to her chest. She soothed him with sweet nothings in his ear, quiet words of comfort. Whatever she whispered, it worked, for he quietened almost immediately.

Sam's grandmother turned to Ruth and asked in a calm voice, 'What's the problem, Ruthie?' Edie was tempted to shout and bawl but she knew that Ruth was struggling to come to terms with the baby. There was something that was gnawing at her. Ruth had never been one to forge emotional ties with anybody. Friends had come and gone over the years, and no one individual had ever become a best friend or special friend. There was a cold, aloof quality about Ruth that Edie had at first tolerated, then tried to change and finally worried about. Now, at this moment when something as tumultuous and life-changing as a baby was in evidence, that coldness had grown more blatant, more obvious.

In that room now, Edie saw it again. Ruth appeared emotionally oblivious to the child's plight. In answer to the question, Ruth said in a flat, emotionless voice, 'Nothing really. He cried, so I came up.' Then she turned and left the room.

A darkness enveloped Edie's heart when she looked into Ruth's eyes as her daughter walked past her. Those eyes, a little red around the rims, were blank: not scared, angry, sorrowful or pleased, just blank.

Edie saw to Sam's needs, providing some food, a drink and a clean nappy. Then she noticed a red weal on the side of his head. She wondered if it was a heat rash caused by the way he had been lying in the cot, but she sensed that it wasn't this, as it had more of the appearance of a mark left by a slap. She decided that it was something that could not be explained, and attempted to wash it from her pool of thoughts. It wouldn't quite go away and she realised that she was thinking, My Ruthie hits her baby.

Downstairs, Ruth was sitting in the big old armchair that had been her father's favourite seat. She had switched on the wireless and was listening to Dean Martin. Although giving the outward appearance of an average teenager listening to the popular music of the day, the reality was that she was thinking very un-average thoughts – like whether to run away from home, whether to kill herself or whether to kill her entire family.

The days, weeks and months passed and somehow Edie managed to keep all the strands of her life together: her family, her home, her job and her sanity. It was difficult every single day, never getting a break; asking for – and receiving – no help, other than the childminding neighbour who looked after Sam during Edie's working hours. Ruth's feelings in those first few days of Sam's life had been accurate, eerily so. She had not grown to love Sam and indeed resented even more the time and space that he occupied in her life and her mother's. She didn't care that the baby sensed that he had two mothers, and that he far preferred the older one.

The days, weeks and months passed, and the girl grew slightly more tolerant of Sam. He was a lovely looking boy, bright-eyed with blond hair and a cherubic face. The baby's grandmother, after only a week back at work after her annual holidays, had taken a week off sick with bad knees. The truth was that she enjoyed the baby's company, but a deeper motivation behind all this time spent at home was that she sensed something in her daughter's manner that troubled her. It was almost tangible, obvious, like the lack of natural maternal instinct that was conspicuous by its absence. But more worrying was that certain unidentifiable something, that faraway look, and occasionally that dark scowl that crossed Ruth's face.

In the time that she was at home the grandmother effectively looked after Sam on her own, but over the coming weeks the girl started to take more of an interest. She didn't enjoy the baby per se, and certainly not the nappies, feeding and entertaining, and least of all the crying; but the detestation had become irritation, which was something. What forced her hand into helping was seeing the effort and sacrifice made by her mother. She would never say 'thank you' to Edie; it was not that sort of relationship, never had been, never would be. But she had a deep love and respect for her mother that she managed to suppress effortlessly.

The baby benefited from the assistance provided by his mother, and his early days were pleasant enough.

The baby's first birthday came and went, celebrated with his mother, grandmother and a few neighbouring families. His grandmother shared every spare second of her life with her daughter and grandson, and although she knew that her daughter was doing more physically with her son, the lack of depth in the emotional field still niggled away; and so it went on, with daily routines carried out by the two of them and the child well looked after.

The love of the mother grew stronger and stronger, not for the baby, but for the child's grandmother. The elderly woman recognised some of this and tried to channel it back towards the child, but never managed it.

A few days after the baby's second birthday, with Ruth herself just gone eighteen, a bright day dawned that would utterly devastate this family, now and forever.

It was a normal Wednesday morning and on the crackly radio that nice Max Bygraves sang his latest hit. Edie Eastman hummed a little as she busied herself getting ready for work. She was a proud woman who had lost her husband to cancer after only five years of marriage. She had time before his death to assess her future as a single mother. The presence of the girl was a mixture of great joy and terrible sadness and it left Edie a little confused. The cliché, however, proved relevant, as time turned out to be a great healer, and Edie poured all her love into her daughter. She knew over the following years that Ruth wasn't getting the best of everything, not by a long way, but she also knew that she could go to her grave any one of those days and an appropriate epitaph would be, 'She did her best.' And now, in late 1961, there was a new decade under way, a new era, and she was still working around the clock – employee by day, mother and grandmother by night.

In the usual ordinary and chaotic attempt at an orderly Wednesday breakfast, Edie Eastman half heard snatches from the radio. An explanation how the recently formed Campaign for Nuclear Disarmament was promising to change the world, an interview with the popular singer, Mr Pat Boone.

There was a minor baby tantrum over the 'funny' taste of the milk on his cereal. Grandmother was trying to sort out baby and daughter, who took some motivating in the morning, and she was conscious that the deadline for leaving for her bus was rapidly approaching. It somehow all fell into place, and Edie actually left the house with a minute or two to spare. She walked the few hundred yards to the bus stop briskly, enjoying the fresh air, and without consciously admitting it to herself, enjoying the peace of her walk. It was almost the only few moments of the day when she wasn't doing something for somebody else. She smiled and nodded a polite 'Morning' to the four other people queuing at the bus stop. She was not particularly interested in early morning conversation; she preferred the beauty of inner peace and quiet, just for those few precious moments.

The bus duly arrived, on time, and Edie found a seat at the back, downstairs, next to a rotund lady who had a significant moustache and a smell emanating from her that made Edie wrinkle her nose. In twenty minutes Edie alighted, only a few yards from the main entrance to the crisp factory where she worked on the production line. She had worked there many years and was well liked by the management and her colleagues. She always worked hard, caused no trouble and was competent at her job.

Today was no different from the hundreds that had gone before: work, tea, work, lunch (no crisps), work, coffee, work, clock off at five thirty. The factory was operating unusual hours because of a downturn in production, caused primarily by the success of rival brands with high-profile advertising campaigns, and morale was generally low amongst the predominantly female staff. This led to less than usual chatter, the initial gossip and rumour period having passed some weeks ago. Edie did not mind this sombre mood at all, as it again provided her with some time to think, to compose her thoughts.

Five thirty came and the site klaxon blared its happy news. Edie had told her daughter at breakfast time that she would pop into town at teatime to do a baby shop, picking up as much as she could carry of baby items, food, nappies and cosmetics. The bus for town went from a different side of the factory from where Edie worked, so it took her a couple of minutes to get there, by which time the queue was fourteen long. As she joined the queue she was hit by a wave of the horribly greasy smell that often wafted from the factory. Despite the years she never got used to the smell, and she turned her head to one side as if that would make a difference. It didn't, and it crossed her mind, as it had many, many times before, that if the general public got to inhale that odour on a regular basis no advertising campaign on earth would convince people to buy crisps.

It was a bright evening and it wasn't at all unpleasant standing in the evening sunshine. After only a couple of minutes a bus appeared but as it pulled up it became obvious that it was already fairly full. Only eight people scrambled aboard, leaving seven standing at the stop. Edie turned to the woman who had joined behind her and said with a smile, 'Nice night to miss the first one.'

They struck up a conversation about the vagaries of the British weather, and touched very briefly on the afternoon's rumour of a return to shift work in a couple of weeks. Edie was too experienced to get excited about possibilities, and didn't dwell on it with the woman who she knew from the factory was nicknamed 'Boop'. She guessed that she might be called Betty but couldn't be sure.

Edie turned to face the direction where the bus would approach from, looking forward now to getting the shopping done and getting home. Missing that first bus was not a huge disappointment but another fifteen minutes seemed to somehow suggest a long night. See Sam soon, she thought. God, how I love him! She decided to pass the few minutes' wait by remembering as many of the records that had been played over the crackling factory tannoy system during the day. She quickly thought of her current favourites: 'My Old Man's a Dustman' by Lonnie Donnegan, and 'Fings Ain't What They Used To Be' by Max Bygraves. She knew the two or three that the young girls were always chattering about: 'Someone Else's Baby' by dishy Adam Faith, 'Stuck on You' by Elvis the Pelvis and 'Stairway to Heaven' by Neil Sedaka. She had another tune going around her head which was getting mixed up with 'Cathy's Clown' by those lovely Everleys.

'What is that other song?' she muttered under her breath, and she started to hum it to herself.

The two young lads in the battered old Ford Prefect weaved down the middle of Burnside Lane, a side road on the edge of the industrial estate. Although only sixteen, they had both been drinking strong cider all afternoon. The car was owned by the older brother of Ted, the blond-haired thug who was driving. Ted had found the keys in his brother's bedroom, Jim having gone on a bus trip to the coast with a couple of mates. Jim would be home late, pissed and violent, so Ted reckoned a fair price for the anticipated abuse to come – verbal definitely, physical probably – was to borrow the car for an hour or two, go for a spin with daft Dave, burn a little rubber, impress a few peers then get it home to cool off before Jim returned. It was daft Dave who had brought along a dozen large cans of strong cider, stolen from the cache in the larder, the cache that was itself stolen by his father from a local grocery store. After three cans each they were giggly and tipsy; after five each they were drunk. The sixth made Dave feel sick, Ted as high as kite.

They had headed for the industrial estate because it was a good spot to practise handbrake turns and reversing at speed. They had got a little lost in the warren of streets lined with industrial units but could not help but giggle, snort and chortle each time Ted turned into another street and said again, 'Nope, not this one – bollocks!'

They were parked at the kerbside when Dave shouted, 'There, there, on the light, right, flipping heck, right, 'long there,' he burped loudly and Ted guffawed.

'What, what's up there, on the light?'

'Reckon that goes to Warbenby Street.'

'Warrenby Street,' Ted corrected. 'Yeah, could be.'

He revved up the engine, took a long swig from can number six and grinned at Dave. 'Ready to go, Dave?'

'Go for it, my mate,' said Dave, and raised a can in mock salute.

The car lurched forward, noisily and not altogether securely, and both young men shouted out in glee.

'Go for it, go for it!' screamed daft Dave, but quietened for a second as he tasted a little vomit at the back of his throat. Ted did go for it and swerved into Warrenby Street at speed, in third gear. He rammed the stick into fourth and whooped repeatedly. Dave felt distinctly queasy but didn't want to show it, so he forced himself to say, 'Stop pishing about, why don't you hit it like a real man?'

Ted's eyes burned bright as he accepted the challenge with a muttered, 'No trouble!' He literally jabbed his foot to the floor and the car picked up speed, the engine whirring and screeching painfully. Tawny Road approached rapidly on the left and Ted swung the car into it. The car crossed the white lines and clipped the kerb but he managed to drag it back on to the correct side of the road before steadying it. Tawny Road was long and straight and led them out of the older part of the estate, towards an area which was more populated. Dave slumped a little in the seat, but Ted didn't notice. He loved the thrill of speed that buzzed through him as he felt the adrenaline travel through his body. He did not notice the distant junction, took no account of the movement in the distance of people and vehicles.

As he leant forward over the steering wheel Ted was thinking, Fuck you, Jim, fuck you and your screaming fists. Look what I'm doing in your shitty car, I'm hammering it and you can't stop me! He screamed aloud, 'Fuck you!' and turned to Dave for agreement. He was surprised to see that Dave's eyes were closed, so he punched his arm and said 'Dave, Dave, eighty and rising!'

He looked up at the road but was drawn back to Dave as he heard a strange gurgling noise. Dave's vomit first hit the dashboard; then, as his head lolled right, he puked on Ted. 'Hey!' wailed Ted as he shied away from the stinking mess.

The car was now doing seventy and the junction was upon them. Ted squealed, and so did the tyres, as he leant into the car door and pulled on the wheel. He had no chance, none whatsoever, especially as there was traffic on the road which they were joining. They hit a black van a glancing blow which redirected them back across the road.

'Christ, Christ!' screamed Ted; Dave had opened his eyes and just said 'Whoa!'

Their speed barely reduced, despite Ted jamming down on the brake. It swung left and right and Ted wrestled with the wheel. The swinging, lurching motion proved too much for Ted and the aerodynamics of the car. They clipped a parked car and flipped over, somersaulting once and then rolling over twice. It came to rest with a shuddering, sickening thump on its roof. For a second or two there was only the noise of the spinning wheels, and hissing steam from the engine. Then the screams started. Firstly from Dave, who had a broken back, broken legs and multiple injuries. Seat belts really were a good idea… Clunk-click, every trip, especially when drunk. Ted made no noise, probably because his skull was shattered in two places and his brains had spilled out over the car floor against which he was wedged.

And then the really terrible, horrible wailing started. Around the car, and under the car, from those seven people who seconds earlier had been waiting patiently for a bus to town. The pleasant mellow evening had lost its charm now that three innocent bystanders lay dead and mangled and four more were horribly injured. They had had no chance to react to the impending onslaught. The mass of metal and terror that had ploughed into them had hit them as if dropped from the sky by a malevolent God.

Edie had just remembered Cliff Richard and 'Fall in Love with You', when she had heard a squeal of tyres. She turned to see a bright red car career across the road. As it hit the parked car on the opposite side of the street the simple thought entered her head, Dear God, that's going to crash. The next few seconds unfolded before her as if in slow motion. The car swung crazily across the road and then, as if picked up by an invisible power, lifted into the air in spectacular fashion. Nobody in the queue moved; they were all transfixed by this amazing sight. After it bounced and rolled, the car seemed to unfreeze the statutes at the bus stop. But just as they moved, time defeated them. Two or three steps does not move you from the path of hurtling metal travelling at fifty miles an hour.

Edie was typical. Her head said 'Run!' but her legs argued, 'No need, this is not really happening.' As an act of retribution for such stupidity it was surely harsh, but as it passed Edie, the car severed her legs at the thighs, the jagged edge of the driver's door which was hanging at an angle created a huge slicing weapon that alone was responsible for the instant death of 'Boop', and the removal of Edie's lower limbs.

Edie was conscious for a few seconds and in that time looked down and knew what had happened. As her torso crumpled to the pavement she thought of her daughter and Sam. There was an astonishing clarity of thought in those final few moments. She knew death was imminent but the chill around her heart was born not from her own predicament, or shock, or pain, but from some terrible knowledge that without her around her grandson's life would be changed irrevocably, that his future with his undoubtedly unstable mother would be bleak. It could be terrifying. It could be dangerous. Edie died, and that was just the start of the horror.

When the police officer said for a second time, 'Are you okay, luv?' the girl turned her head slowly to the uniformed person before her. 'What?' she asked.

The police sergeant patiently repeated his question. 'Are you okay? Shall we go inside and sit down?'

'Mmm,' was the only response.

Officer Smethurst gently took the girl's arm and stepped inside the house. He pushed open the first door that he came to and saw that it was the living room; a neat room that looked clean. His instinct told him that it was maintained – had been maintained – by the person now lying in the mortuary.

The news that her mother had been killed in a 'road accident', with no further details at this stage, had most definitely not sunk in. She mumbled, 'But she's at the shops... nappies and stuff. Home soon.'

The pitiful, plaintive voice, allied to the look of hopelessness on the girl's face, tugged at the sergeant's tough heartstrings.

'I'm sorry, luv. She was waiting to go to the shops, and then the accident happened.'

She grinned a sickly grin. 'No, there's been a mistake, that's it, you've got mixed up. She's all right after all, I've just realised, that's it.'

He held her hand and looked into her eyes but go no recipro-cal focus. His voice lowered. 'No mistake, luv, she was still holding her handbag and we got her name and address from that.'

She said nothing, but a stunned, blank expression appeared on her face. They sat together for a minute or two like that. The policeman had delivered awful news before, many times, but somehow this time it was a little different. He had experienced people going into shock, people breaking down hysterically, and everything in the emotional range between the two ends of the spectrum. He felt that there was a subtle difference in this girl's reaction; it was difficult to put words to, just something.

He was a good police officer, very experienced, with over twenty-two years of sterling service. In that time he had developed a good copper's gut instinct. He had often been found to be accurate in his assessment of a person's mental state, and degree of guilt or innocence, when others around him had leapt to incorrect snap judgements. His instincts had not let him down here, but even he would have been very surprised if he had known the precise details of 'the difference', as he saw it, in the reaction to bad news of the young girl in front of him.

In the space of only a few seconds she had accepted that her mother was dead, wondered how she could possibly cope alone with Sam, and then felt a surging pain rise in her stomach. She asked if it was all right to go to see her baby, and the police officer stood up and followed her to the room which was effectively a playroom, once having been a formal Sunday best dining room. Sam was playing happily with some colourful building bricks, oblivious to the terrible news and terrible events unfolding around him.

'Lovely lad,' commented the policeman, genuinely compli-mentary about a healthy, happy, blond-haired angel before him.

Seeing Sam there, being physically near him, confirmed what the girl had felt and believed next door, in the living room.

A medical assessment at that juncture might have speculated that the girl's inner turmoil was the physical reaction of shock, nausea and guilt combining unpleasantly.

The girl knew that it was not these things. She said, 'He's a good boy.' Inside she knew that the last five minutes had resurrected the long suppressed feeling, the monstrous feeling that she had fought against but always dreaded would one day come back to destroy her.

She hated Sam, always had done, for what he had done to her life, but more for what he had done to her mother's life. That loathing had been hidden from her mother, whom she did not suspect had any inkling of it. But now, God, now! This present from the devil was directly responsible for the death of her beloved, beleaguered mother. The blond burden that had been visited upon her as punishment for the evil perpetrated in the back seat of boyfriends' cars was not, it seemed, satisfied. He had now exacted this ultimate price. But he had made a big mistake. A really big mistake, because he had massively underestimated her resolve to fight back.

She felt sick all right, but not from simple shock at the news of the demise of her mother. No, she was shocked at the clarity of the realisation that her single goal in life as from this moment was to punish the person responsible for not only the physical end of her mother's life but also the end of her own mental health. She strangely recognised that she was deranged, and welcomed it.

Chapter Six

Jayne had really enjoyed the night; it was always fun with Jessie and Helen. They were good friends who had been through school together and could honestly say that in all those years they had never had a major argument. They simply gelled from the start. They were very different characters, but maybe it was true that opposites attract. Jayne was quiet, polite, a good daughter and loyal friend. Many impartial observers had been led to comment, 'Too good to be true.' That would have been their first impression. Second and third impressions would have strengthened this reaction. Jealous commentators would say that Jayne was a little spooky, a bit freakish. Nobody, just nobody, could be that flipping perfect. Adored by family and friends, she cared for the elderly (part-time), loved animals, worked hard, pretty and intelligent, and, without a malicious or envious bone in her body, she was also generous of spirit... for starters!

The point was, as family and closest friends would tell you, that you had to really know her to understand all this. Her virtues, strengths and qualities were not false, not an act or exaggerated. They were not worn like a badge of perfection; she did not even seem to realise herself what an amazing package of goodness she was. Even this was potentially annoying, but it was no pretence or false modesty. To know Jayne was to realise that she was truly 'nice', in all senses of the word: nice to talk to, to work with, to be around. She had a very special quality which meant that after enjoying her company some of her niceness seemed to rub off and you would feel better for the experience.

Even her imperfections had an endearing quality about them. Having had one drink too many, and she did like a drink, she would get very giggly and find everything everybody said funny. When she had two drinks too many her inhibitions would be totally dissolved and she would sing or dance in the most extrovert fashion.

When she cursed, something she was no stranger to, she did it in a way that reminded onlookers of a six-year-old curly-haired cherub stamping her foot, scowling and shouting, 'Bother!' It just always seemed funny, and the worse the language, the funnier it became. Once, when Jayne and her two closest friends were on a major shopping expedition and trying on clothes in shop after shop, Jayne had decided to try on the skimpiest, most revealing little black dress that she had ever contemplated wearing. She squeezed into it and it had the immediate desired effect of making her feel very sexy. She was showing it off to the girls when Helen bumped into a rail of blouses. A couple fell off and Jayne instinctively bent down to retrieve them but juddered to a halt when there was a noisy parting of the seam at the back of her dress. There was a moment's silence as all three girls stood there open-mouthed.

'Oh, fuck!' wailed Jayne, and Helen and Jessie collapsed in total hysterics. As she surveyed the damage in the mirror, a distressed Jayne said again, 'Oh, fuck!'

This finished Helen off, and she was soon down on her hands and knees on the shop floor. Jessie was bent double, holding her aching stomach and making squeaky noises that meant she had gone beyond laughing and was now at that painful level where your body won't react to the brain's instruction to 'stop it, get a grip and think of something boring!'

Jayne was still shocked at the severity of the damage and turned to her hysterical friends. Though the language could in certain circumstances be deemed offensive, even the approaching shop assistance smiled as a dismayed Jayne said to her friends in shocked tones, 'It's fucked. Totally!'

If her friends ever ribbed her about being 'good', or asked her directly, 'Don't you ever get tired of being so good all the time?' she would answer light-heartedly, 'What's the problem? I'm happy, nobody gets hurt, it's just the way I was brought up. It's the way I am, and anyway I'm no goody two shoes.'

Her friends didn't query the niceness of Jayne very often, and when they did, it was only out of mischievousness.

Jayne was tall, with a lovely figure and fair, bobbed hair. She was not pretty in an obvious drop-dead gorgeous way, but when you studied her face you would see a lovely openness and you could really appreciate those green eyes. Her wonderful complexion was the envy of her friends. She had never suffered adolescent acne, indeed she'd never had a spot worthy of the name. It was if any potential zit had thought about it and decided, Nope, I'm not going to be the one. She had high cheekbones, attractive breasts and shapely legs, all the things that women envied and men desired. Her light was often hidden under a very large bushel, because although she wore nice, often expensive, clothes, they were not what would be called particularly exciting, sexy or flattering outfits. The incident with the black dress only served to convince her that such outfits were not for her. No, she'd leave them for Helen and Jessie, particularly Helen. Quality cardigans do not suggest a vamp, and this primary packaging often generated no second viewing of a girl dismissed as a 'plain Jayne'. She rarely made any particular effort to display her legs, which were beautifully sculptured. It wasn't that she was prudish, simply that she preferred the comfort offered by baggy tops and long skirts.

She had been similarly attired that night, in a dark skirt to the ankles with a moderate split, and a white blouse buttoned up. Her taste in jewellery reflected the same modesty: a bangle at her wrist and one dress ring. It was all very nice, smart and unexciting. She did not care, she knew that she could dress sexy if she wanted to impress somebody who liked that sort of thing, and occasionally, when she had boyfriends she had done so, but she always felt a little uncomfortable doing it. Not because the exposure of leg, thigh or boob attracted such admiring looks, but because the act itself was not her.

When her friends chided her that she had the best figure of all of them and she should share her bountiful assets with all and sundry – after all, she might attract Mr Right – she usually said, 'Each to their own, I'll leave the flashing and flaunting to Helen and Jessie.'

It was true that Helen and Jessie did make up for what Jayne lacked in the extrovert fashion stakes. As Jayne often remarked, 'What they can do with two hankies and a bit of stitching is quite amazing.'

Helen particularly loved the attention that revealing outfits brought. She turned this to her advantage as she was able to wear loose-fitting tops that revealed exciting glimpses of flesh whenever she moved.

Jessie was more fully endowed and often wore tight tops which suggested that two melons were attempting to escape their undersized packaging. She was also the noisy one of the group, loud and excitable. She sometimes overstepped the mark and was a little too exuberant. Life was never dull with Jessie around – she was always good for a laugh.

So the three of them had had a good night, in their own terms. Jessie had brazenly flaunted herself and teased the young men all night long in a seemingly endless production line of willing dance partners. The boy's faces gave away their oh-so-obvious delight at having a few minutes in the company of this wiggling, thrusting, fun girl. And wow! Those tits – pushing their way up towards her chin, threatening throughout to pop out and take them to higher levels of pleasure! The boys didn't even appear to mind getting a fairly rapid brush off, seemingly satisfied with their opportunity to rush back to their groups and describe to envious mates how 'her knockers were right in my face' and 'Christ, I had a cracking stiffy!'

The spin-off of Jessie's shining 'Come on, boys' neon sign was that Helen and Jayne received plenty of attention. Because they did not have Jessie's stamina or desire to dance solidly for hours, they effectively took it in turn to sit out the occasional dance, returning to the side of the dance floor to take a breather. This meant that they were approached on a number of occasions by lads, sensing an easy conquest but a firm 'No thanks' usually sufficed to deter them.

The girls had gone to the club very early because they were going to get away early at the end of the night due to Helen's commitment to a shopping trip to York with her mother early the next morning.

They danced, laughed and enjoyed each other's company. Jessie ran true to form and, as ever, Helen and Jayne marvelled at not only the bees-to-honey effect Jessie had on the male population, but mainly at how the boys were so obviously just pleased for that one dance. They never seemed crushed at her swift rejection, never gave the impression of thinking, The bitch is taking the piss…

As the night drew to its early close, Jayne had found herself dancing with Helen. Jessie had told them an hour earlier that she had her eye on a particularly swarthy hunk who was based at a table not too far away. Despite her several lingering looks in his direction, he'd seemed unwilling to approach her, so Jessie – being Jessie – had gone straight to him. Helen and Jayne could no longer see her, but they were not concerned because Jessie would always, in circumstances like these, find them before the end of the night and advise them of the transport position.

Helen and Jayne were comparing notes on their fellow dancers, and being particularly critical of one man who, while being more man than boy in age, was, to be fair, dancing like a demented octopus, arms and legs flailing in every direction. They were happy to see out the last few dances alone, as they had long passed the days when there was an urgent, desperate need to have a messy snog before going home. However, they were not disappointed when two lads walked up and politely asked them if they could join them. They looked at each other and smiled before turning their attention back to their prospective beaus.

Jayne liked the look of her guy. He was not what you would call stunningly handsome, not chiselled, particularly athletic or whatever passed for 'handsome' these days, but equally he did not appear cocky and full of himself, as so many did. He struck Jayne as 'nice'. He was smiling at her, not talking, which she did not mind, and she sensed that he was genuinely pleased to be with her, that he was not there a) because there was nobody else or b) for a quick snog.

She glanced across at her friend and laughed aloud when she saw Helen and her partner in a tight clinch and smooching.

She turned to her partner and leaned forward, saying, 'Didn't take them long did it?'

The young man nodded and smiled. She thought it funny how he was so quiet. She leaned forward again. 'My name's Jayne,' she offered.

The implication of an expected response was obvious but nothing was forthcoming. Then he leaned towards her, took a step closer and, putting his mouth close to her ear, shouted 'Sorry?'

She tried again, saying loudly, 'Have you had a good night?'

She was starting to wonder if she had been set up when he again said, 'Sorry?' So she leaned to his ear and screamed the question again. She was surprised and a little relieved to get a sensible response.

They had exchanged pleasantries and shared a drink when Jayne had realised it was time to go. She was very willing to give this guy her number; there was an honest look about him that she found attractive. As Helen joined her they saw Jessie with her hunk, waving at them that she'd make her own way home.

In the taxi Jayne and Helen exchanged notes.

'What a kisser!' enthused Helen. 'Awesome tongue... Imagine that all over you!'

They laughed and Jayne said, 'No doubt you will when you get home, you dirty tramp!'

'You're not kidding – can't wait to get to bed,' Helen said with a huge grin. She fell silent for a second or two as she thought of not only Toddy's tongue down her throat but also how she had felt that hard bulge in his trousers as she had pressed against him. That big, very hard bulge. 'Urrmm, lovely,' she murmured.

'What is?' asked Jayne.

'Sorry, miles away,' Helen said, and felt herself redden a little.

'You're on heat, aren't you?' said Jayne accusingly, and laughed at Helen's confirmation that she was certainly pretty damn warm. Helen told herself to try changing the subject. She was too turned on to discuss Toddy; she would have to wait until she got home, when she could pleasure herself. That really had been some kiss.

'So how about you, then? Didn't do so bad, did you?' she asked. 'Come on, J, did you get tongue?'

Jayne was used to the provocative questioning of Helen and Jessie and usually found it easy to dismiss, because nothing was worthy of reporting, usually.

'Well,' she started, 'I must admit...' She hesitated and Helen seized upon the opportunity, Toddy momentarily forgotten.

'I don't believe it! You've had your tonsils tickled, haven't you? And did you feel his affection pressed against you? God, did he squeeze your arse, or did he feel you up or what? Tell me!'

She was excited at the prospect of Jayne divulging details of intimate contact but was immediately disappointed when Jayne said, 'No, nothing like that.' Jayne then teased her with, 'Anyway, you should have been paying attention, shouldn't you, you don't know what you missed.'

Helen laughed at the gentle taunt and said, 'There is something, isn't there? Tell me, J! Come on, we'll be home soon…'

'Nothing to tell, really, not what you want to hear anyway. He just seemed nice, you know, genuine.'

'Screw *nice*!, did he slip you tongue?'

'Christ, you're obsessed with flipping tongue!'

'Just big, wet ones like Toddy's.'

'Oh, so it's Toddy, is it – just good friends, eh?'

'I'd like to be friends with his tongue,' *and his cock* was left unsaid, but Helen was thinking it and shuffled a little in the seat. She dragged her concentration back to Jayne.

'Well?'

'If you must know, I gave him a peck on the cheek and we swapped numbers.'

'A peck on the cheek, is that it?'

'Look, horny girl, not everybody is like you and Jess, gagging for it every minute, every day. Some of us have aspirations to greater things.'

'"Aspirations" – Christ, that's a big word for this time of night! So you're going to see him again.'

'Well, if I do, seeing as they are best mates, there must be a good chance that you'll see Toddy, isn't there?'

'Good point, J. Go out with… What's his name, anyway?'

'Jeff.'

'Wow, Jaynie's got a boyfriend called Jeff! Lucky Jeff, lucky Jayne. Jaynie's got a boyfriend, Jaynie's got a boyfriend!' Helen sang.

'A bit like early days, wouldn't you say, just a little?'

'No, no, I can see that you're into him.'

'No more than you and the tongue monster,' retorted Jayne, but she did not believe this statement. She had to admit to herself that there had been a connection with Jeff – a spark, chemistry, whatever you might call it. She smiled as she thought of him smiling at her and a little tremor fluttered through her.

Helen hadn't noticed Jayne's shiver; no doubt she was dreaming of Toddy and his various working parts.

As if thinking aloud, Jayne volunteered, 'It might not come to anything.'

This was seized upon by Helen, snapping her from her dreams. 'So, you admit it, you hope it will come to something?'

'Brilliant, Sherlock, that's not what I said.' But she made no further defence.

The remaining few minutes of the journey were spent speculating where Jessie was and what she was up to, and there was always the concern that one day, or night, she would get herself into a situation that she couldn't get out of.

Helen was first to leave the taxi, and as she gave Jayne a good-night kiss and hug she made one final comment on the night. 'Remember this as the night that changed your life.'

Neither girl understood the prophetic truth of those words.

Jayne had a couple of minutes alone in the taxi to reflect on the night. A dance, a peck on the cheek; his *cheek*, no real contact. How then did she feel so flipping giddy, like a schoolgirl with a crush on her first ever boyfriend?

Girl, you should get out more, she joked to herself. It was true that she had not had a boyfriend for a long time, not since Gary; but surely that couldn't explain this reaction?

And then there were Helen's words, 'Remember this night,' and the feeling buried deep within her that it was a significant night.

Silly sod! she told herself. You'll probably forget all about him tomorrow. 'It wasn't as if he was that special,' a voice said. But what if he was special? What if?

Jayne was happy, very happy. She paid the taxi driver, gave him a generous tip and walked up the path to her ground floor apartment. She entered the hallway, walked to the lounge and peeked under the sheet that covered her budgie's cage. Dilbert was fast asleep. She dropped her coat and bag on the sofa and went to the kitchen. Lily-Billy was asleep in her basket; she was a scruffy old cat that Jayne claimed was her real best friend.

She took a can of Diet Coke from the fridge and took it to bed. The apartment was very warm because she had left the heating on high and it hadn't been that cold a night. She switched the heating off and snuggled her legs under the duvet. She drank the Coke whilst sitting up, thinking of Helen, Jessie and Jeff. Particularly Jeff.

What a wonderful night! Could it have been any better?

Only a few miles away, as the crow flew, Jeff had been thinking the same, almost telepathic, happy thoughts. 'Had been', because at this precise moment, as Jayne drifted to a content sleep thinking of being with Jeff, Jeff was staring at death, and all thoughts of lovely Jayne were banished from his terrified mind.

Chapter Seven

Gerald Sanders took his son's hand in his own, for the first time in a very long time, and pulled him into the house. Spittle and vomit were splattered down Jeff's chin, jacket and shoes. Gerald was half asleep and struggling to take this in; Jeff never got so drunk that he was sick on arrival home, and it wasn't even the small hours of the morning.

Jeff blurted out, 'Dad, Dad! Call the police, ambulance, everything, I think he was killing her, far side of the brickie!'

He knelt down and retched again. His father was finding it hard to believe stories of murder but the urgency of Jeff's words suggested that something was afoot. He started to talk to Jeff very gently.

'Look, son, it's been a long night. Maybe you've just...'

'Dad, for Christ's sake, just do it! Oh never mind, I'll see to it!'

He started to move towards the telephone, but his father felt a pang of guilt and moved quickly to the phone stand ahead of him.

Mrs Sanders appeared at the top of the stairs in her dressing gown and peered down to her family below.

'What is it, Gerald? What's going on?' Her voice betrayed her anxiety.

'It's okay, Dorothy. It's Jeff, he's had a shock or something. Go back to bed,' he called, but his wife was already on her way down.

'Good grief, Jeffrey! What has happened?' she asked in shocked tones at the sight of Jeff, pale and sickly, still hunched down.

'Nightmare, Mum. I've just seen a bloke hurting a girl, probably...' he swallowed hard '...killing her. Out on the brickie, near the road at the town side.'

Mrs Sanders raised a hand to her mouth in horror and moved to Jeff to put her arm around his shoulder.

'Let's get you cleaned up,' she instructed, 'and then we can get you a drink or something.'

Mr Sanders was struggling to provide any details to the female operator who had answered his 999 call.

'All I know is that my son has just arrived home in a very distressed state and he says that he has witnessed an incident at a local area known as the brickie. A man appeared to be hurting a lady.'

He listened attentively while he was quizzed about the location, time and further details of the incident, but became frustrated as his protestations that he knew no more seemed to fall on deaf ears.

'Just a moment, please,' he asked. 'I'll see if my son can help.' He placed the receiver on the table and went to the downstairs cloakroom where his wife was wiping Jeff's face with a cloth, as if cleaning a baby's face. Jeff was leaning on the basin with both forearms placed on the edges.

'Jeff, could you speak to them, please? I can't give enough detail?'

'Yeah, okay, Dad,' said his son weakly. He filled his hands from the running taps before messily splashing his face. He shook his head to clear the water and his thoughts.

Jeff went to the phone, took a deep breath and said, 'Hello.' He related his story to the operator, giving as precise a location as he could. Although he gave no more details than his father, his version seemed to satisfy the lady at the other end of the line. He provided his own details and he was promised that a squad car would be there soon.

He put the phone down and wandered into the living room. His father sat next to him and asked just what he had seen, suddenly fearful that Jeff had witnessed and completely misinterpreted a courting couple. Jeff was repeating his story patiently when his mother appeared with a tray. On it were three mugs of tea and a plate of chocolate Bourbons.

'I know that mugs will have us up all night, Gerald,' she said firmly, 'but I think we are in for a long night anyway.' Gerald did not argue.

The emergency call and all relevant details were relayed to all the squad cars and vans patrolling within three miles of the town centre. After making the call, the girl on duty at the central control station put her hand over her microphone and whispered to the girl at the next desk, 'Sammy, it sounds like a big one, watch this space.'

Police Constable John Daniels was walking the beat which meandered through the industrial units near to town up to the new suburban estates, and he was just inside the boundary of the suburbs when he heard the call to the cars regarding the brickie. He answered the call and advised that he was on the site and would investigate. This was acknowledged but the call to the vehicles remained in force.

PC Daniels was soon at the path leading across the brickie. As a local man he knew the area well and had a fair idea where the spot being described in the message was. He did not hesitate at the entrance to the brickie; he was professional and brave and a girl's life could be at risk, if the story was to be believed. His personal guess was that the lad had seen something in the murk and rain, and, probably drunk, got mixed up and panicked. Still, you never know.

He walked along the path, mentally calculating how far a 'few hundred yards' were. They'd said something about beyond the first couple of lights, then not far off the path, to the right, and a few bushes. He decided to have a look where he was now and stepped off the path on to wet grass and mud. He shone his torch around the area where he stood but saw nothing. He started to walk along the muddy patch, staying parallel to the main path. He scanned the area ahead of him, swinging the torchlight like a spotlight from left to right and back again. Nothing. He stopped and listened, but could hear nothing but the steady rain splashing around him in puddles and on the surrounding foliage.

He made his way back to the proper path and looked around as if to get his bearings. From what he had been told this felt about right – but it could all be a wild goose chase, couldn't it? He walked a few yards more and looked over his shoulder as he heard a siren approaching. He slowed down as he reached a place where a little mound rose from the path on the right. Just beyond were a few bushes, so he walked the couple of paces up the mound, slipping a little.

He waved his torch towards the bushes and saw nothing, so he took a step to the right to allow the beam to go behind the bushes. His light flashed on something white, like a balloon. He concentrated the beam on the object and started to move towards it. Probably a shopping bag, he thought, but his pulse had noticeably quickened. He soon realised what he was looking at. The girl's face was a ghostly white, and the reason why her head appeared detached from the rest of her was that the necklace of blood around her throat formed a dividing line between her head and her dark, soaked clothes.

'Oh God, no!' PC Daniels said aloud, and repeated it when he bent down to the girl's side. He knew she was gone, but went through the motions anyway of looking for a pulse. When he had confirmed that she was dead he radioed the news to Headquarters. He stood up, and looked down at the girl. This was nasty he thought, this is no lover's tiff or barroom brawl. This had the smell of a vicious, random murder, probably sexually motivated. Nasty. He retreated to the path, lifting his feet gingerly from the ground in an exaggerated fashion, trying not to scrub out any potential evidence.

As PC Daniels reached the path he heard his colleagues further along the way. He moved a little towards them before shouting at the top of his voice, 'Over here, lads, keep going!'

He flashed his torch in their general direction. They were soon there, two officers from a car, and he explained his finding. When he had finished he simply said, 'Routine time, lads. Let's crack on.'

At the police station in Stockton-on-Tees, the supervisor for the night shift took over proceedings. He was Duty Sergeant Bill Newsome and he was a very organised and methodical man. He called the police surgeon at his home and advised him of the details, as he knew them, saying that a woman with her throat cut had been found locally.

He got the paperwork ready to form a detailed log for all the comings and goings that would inevitably occur at the scene and despatched it with an officer immediately, with stern instructions to maintain the log very carefully.

He made a call to the on-duty Scene of Crime officer and volunteered no thoughts on the incident, just the known facts, which the recipient of the call appreciated.

Finally in this first wave of activity he called the senior officer who would lead this enquiry, a Detective Inspector Len Mansell. DI Mansell was watching a late night horror film, quite a good one, and he jumped a little when the telephone rang just behind him.

'Mansell,' was his curt response.

'Len, it's Bill, got a murder for you. Young woman, throat cut down in the brickie. Got three officers there now, SOCOs on their way, so's the quack. Jonno's got the ambulance going and Denny Clark is running the log. One other thing, there's a witness, young lad, lives locally, got some PCs going there.'

'Okay, Bill, thanks. Give Will a ring, please. Say I'll meet him down there. Which side of the brickie, town or houses?'

He ran upstairs to his wife who had just retired to bed, having found the risen dead just too scary in the film on TV.

'Sorry, luv, got a murder, young girl. Got to go, see you when I see you.'

He kissed her on the lips and then on the forehead before rushing downstairs. He grabbed his coat and keys from the front door table and stepped out into the cold air. He shut the door quietly behind him. His car was parked on the drive and he was soon on his way to the brickie. His mind was racing. It wasn't simply a matter of murder. What if it was 'him' again? He would soon know.

Sergeant Newsome had called Detective Sergeant Tom Rogers, known to his colleagues as Will, from the fairly obscure connection with Will Rogers, old-time screen cowboy. He too was soon on his way, having been told that 'Nige' was waiting for him. 'Nige' or 'Nigel' were the more obvious nicknames for DI Mansell, and if Nige was waiting for you, you didn't keep him waiting long.

As he approached the brickie some twenty minutes later, having broken speed limits all the way, DS Rogers marvelled at the fact that firstly there was Nige's car, as if it had been there all night; and secondly the speed at which SOCOs worked. There was already evidence of tape barriers going up and he had no doubt that very shortly the big tents would spring up to cover the scene. They sure worked – and worked well – these guys.

He parked near to Mansell's car and set off for the scene. Denny Clark duly asked him his name as he crossed the line. The arc lights being set up were powerful and it was like daylight as he approached the hub of the scene. He spotted Mansell and went over to him.

Mansell greeted him with no pleasantries, just a gruff, 'Over there, Will... Kid, early twenties, late teens maybe, nasty. Throat's been cut side to side... no obvious sexual interference. The rain means it's messy, but there's got to be footprints if we don't muck it up with our size nines. Member of the public saw some of it, so how about you going over there and shadowing the PC on site?'

Rogers knew that this was an instruction rather than a request so said, 'Yeah, no problem. Just one question, sir.'

'Fire away,' Mansell replied, guessing what was coming.

'Any connection with A, B and C?'

'Don't honestly know, Tom, but we soon will and I'll keep you posted.'

He had guessed correctly that Tom Rogers would be as curious as himself if there was to be any connection with murders over a period of years in Darlington, Sunderland and Manchester, known to a few as A, B and C. Was this D? Forensics would soon tell, as they already knew quite a lot about the man who linked the previous violent deaths of three women.

Rogers headed back to his car and Mansell turned his attention back to the immediate vicinity.

Back at the station, Sergeant Newsome was looking at a map of the town. He had his finger on the brickie and was considering its position for transport implications. He was next to two constables who listened closely as the sergeant expanded on his thoughts.

'Assume he had a car... Well, he'll be well away now, two minutes to the A19 and A66, could be miles away in any direction.' He paused. 'But what if he's not in a car, just walking, what are his options?' He was asking the question of himself, and the young officers recognised this and said nothing. 'If he's local, from

Norfolk Estate, then he's got problems, because that's the way the witness went and our man is hardly going to follow him. So he's got to go the other side. At the road he's got two choices: left into more suburbia; no real outlet there; or go right, back to town. What does he do in town – taxi, bus, what?'

At this point George Stott asked, 'What about the railway station, Sarge, that's not far either.' To emphasise the point he placed his finger on the map.

'Quite right, he's got all sorts of choices in town. Mind you, the chances that he's not in a car are remote. But to cover the bases, how about you two get down to town and check out taxi ranks, bus stops and maybe the station, George, if you fancy it?'

The officers set off in a hurry, keen to impress the sergeant, whom they liked and respected.

At the brickie, Mansell had surveyed the location, the immediate scene and the body. He was keen to minimise the damage to the locale so ordered that only personnel absolutely essential to scene of crime work be allowed to enter the immediate vicinity.

After he had been there half an hour, he made a call to Chief Superintendent Burns, who would oversee the investigation, albeit from afar, whilst Mansell and his team did the real police work. He outlined the position to date and answered 'Yes' to every procedural matter that Burns raised. As Senior Investigating Office, the SIO was responsible for making policy decisions, but had to trust all officers below them to carry out a thorough job. Burns did not trust anybody, which meant he was either a methodical, efficient stickler, or a distrusting, annoying bastard. Mansell favoured the second opinion.

As Burns went back to sleep, satisfied that the routines were being followed, Mansell called up the police helicopter. It was based at Teesside Airport, only a couple of minutes away, and he had an idea that if it flew around the surrounding suburbs for a while, whilst annoying a few folks with its noise, it might just flush out anybody lurking in back gardens or the like. The chopper had a 'night sun', the powerful beam of light that tended to freeze criminals in their tracks, such was its mesmeric strength. The police airplane was fitted with the heat-seeking equipment and it was a source of annoyance that the chopper was waiting for a budget facility for this; still, the night sun would do tonight.

Once this was organised, Mansell found the police surgeon, a guy named Joseph Barrow, who was always genial, no matter what he was working on, no matter what time of day or night.

'What have you got, Joe?'

'Girl, about twenty, dead about a couple of hours at the most; maybe as little as one hour forty-five minutes.'

'That's right, our witness says the murder was happening at about midnight which is…' he glanced at his watch '…one hour forty-nine minutes ago.'

'Witnesses are always useful, Len,' said the surgeon, smiling. 'Death caused by the severing of throat, windpipe and trachea; nasty. Death by asphyxia.'

'Blood?' asked Mansell.

'Fair bit, but the jugular's been missed, deliberately or otherwise, so not necessarily a spurter. Fair bit, mind, but sloshing into ground around the back of her neck rather than outwardly on to murderer. There is something else, or rather, other things.'

'Such as?' asked Mansell, and he suddenly felt a surge of excitement and anticipation.

'Well, early days obviously, but first brief inspection suggests various other injuries.'

'Such as, Joe, such as?' snapped Mansell impatiently.

'Well, wounds in the back, looks like a sharp instrument, and bruising around the face. Possible rib damage… nasty, very nasty.'

'How sharp an instrument, Joe?'

'Yeah, possibly a screwdriver.'

Mansell's mind was alive at the prospect that this was D. Wounds in the back was a common denominator with A, B and C, so surely this was D?

'It will be at least tomorrow, Joe, when we release her. Loads of potential forensics around here, but I'd appreciate it if you and your team can push it through path lab as quick as possible. I think this is a biggie.'

Joe nodded and went back to the corpse.

Mansell battled with various emotions as he stood there in the steady rain. He wanted to go crashing through the crime scene, demanding analysis and answers and quickly getting on to the trail of someone he was sure was a serial killer. However, he knew that he was correctly bound by procedures and routines which themselves in time would give him the raw data and clues to strengthen his hand in the pursuit of this madman. There was nothing more that he could constructively offer at the scene, so he gave a few final instructions regarding careful treatment of the vicinity and set off for home. He reckoned that a good rest, if not sleep, would be useful, as tomorrow was going to be the start of a difficult and tiring case, he was sure of that.

When Rogers arrived outside the Sanders' home he noticed that there were two squad cars parked at the kerb. In one of them, two officers sat quietly. He parked behind it and went to the driver's door. The constable jumped when Rogers knocked on the window and immediately scrambled out of the car, the other PC doing the same from the passenger seat.

'Yes, sir?' said the driver.

'Just what exactly are you doing?' asked Rogers with an edge to his voice that made it clear that he was not expecting a particularly good answer.

'Er… just waiting, sir.'

'For what, exactly – frigging Christmas? There's been a murder a couple of miles away, and you're "waiting"! Get your arses in gear now and get to the station for orders.'

The young officers jumped back into the car and sped off, the passenger complaining to the driver, 'Shit, Mike, I told you "proceed" to the address of the witness didn't mean stay outside all night. We'll have fucking Will on our case now, and God help us if he tells Nige. Shit!'

Rogers knocked firmly at the door and did not wait long before an elderly man opened it. Rogers introduced himself and was led to a pleasant living room where a man in his late twenties sat with an older woman, presumably his mother, and two uniformed constables.

Rogers took command straight away, exchanging pleasantries and offering sympathy for the difficult position they found themselves in. Then down to business. He turned to PC Willow, a young lady whom he thought had real potential to make a good career in the Force. Her colleague, PC Greenhaugh, he wasn't so sure about. Cocky little sod, Rogers always thought. PC Willow recounted from her notebook everything that Jeff had told her. She had obviously followed the standing instruction regarding taking statements, which was to get the interviewee to blurt out everything he or she could remember and worry about the detail later. The scattergun method often worked, and was preferred to a precise statement, focussing on what was deemed important but missing out the odd point that was often crucial.

When PC Willow finished the detailed notes, Rogers turned to Jeff and asked, 'Is that how you remember it? Anything different, anything missing?'

Jeff considered what he had heard before answering, 'Yeah, that's about it, I couldn't see lots of detail – too much rain and mist. Mr Rogers, you haven't said anything about the girl.'

The change of tack caught Rogers slightly unaware, but he quickly recovered his composure.

'Bad news I'm afraid, Jeff. You were watching a murder. She died at the scene.'

Rogers was conscious that Mrs Sanders gasped at the news and he spoke gently when he turned to her and said, 'Yes, I'm afraid so, Mrs Sanders. A bad business all round, but with Jeff's help maybe we can catch him quickly.'

Rogers looked at Jeff, trying to weigh up what he was dealing with. He surmised that Jeff, although obviously shaken by his experience, was a bright, sensible lad who wasn't going to miss anything fundamental. He knew that he had to check, though, because the statement due to be taken later that day could not be changed afterwards. Bits could be added, but nothing retracted; so they had one bite of the cherry.

'Let's just go through the description of the man again. I know it's a drag but the tiniest detail could be significant.'

'I know, I'll do my best,' said Jeff, and concentrated hard on the events of only a couple of hours ago. His first image was of the girl and that coughing noise. He strained his thoughts on to the man and closed his eyes as he fought to identify any details.

'He was obviously very wet, soaked. He had dark hair, wet and short, kind of stuck to his head. He was wearing a coat, a mac I think, definitely not an overcoat. That was dark too, but probably just wet. I couldn't see his feet.'

'What about his face, anything at all?' Rogers was starting to think that maybe the witness who'd sounded so promising was going to give them very little.

'Difficult to say. Nothing special really, not fat, not very thin. His nose seemed normal, his mouth was shut. Didn't seem to have sticky-out ears or anything.'

Rogers had picked up on something so he probed quietly, 'Any other detail, no matter how trivial?' But Jeff shook his head.

'How about his eyes?' Rogers watched Jeff closely and saw him definitely react to the question. Something passed across Jeff's features.

'I – I don't know,' stammered Jeff.

Rogers was tempted to leave it but knew that Jeff was hiding something.

'You won't know the colour, but maybe there was something about them?'

'He did look at me, straight at me.'

Jeff fell silent and his father interrupted. 'Detective Rogers, I think that Jeff has had enough for now, if you don't mind.'

'It's okay, Dad, it's just that – just that – his eyes were kind of scary.'

'Can you explain that a bit more, Jeff? You are doing really well,' said Rogers, encouragingly.

'Well, I think he got a shock when the girl made that choking noise and he got another shock when he saw me. His eyes were quite wide and they certainly seemed dark from that distance, but what I remember is that first of all he stared at me and seemed to look through me, and then – well – then his eyes seemed to smile at me! It was horrible.' He shuddered at the memory of those mocking eyes.

Chapter Eight

After the initial shock at the sight of the man staring at him, Westmain had quickly regained his composure. Even in those circumstances it crossed his mind that this was God's final test of the night. After taking away his car, dumping rain on him, making it tricky picking his girl, now this: a man staring at him! How much had he seen? Presumably not a lot, nobody had enough will-power to stand and watch a murder. He accepted the challenge.

The man spun and ran away, stumbling a little as he made off. Westmain almost welcomed the further surge of excitement as he recognised that he had to be cold and careful in his next moves because God had thrown him a real tricky one this time.

He pulled himself away from the girl, not giving her a second glance. He went to the path and headed back to the road. He walked briskly down the path, but forced himself not to run. By the time he reached the main road he had already made the decision to go to town. The option of heading into the suburbs was not really on, because although quieter, where was he going to find transport?

So he pulled his collar up and moved swiftly towards town. Over the course of the next few minutes he saw a couple of cars, one van and a taxi. As he passed through the industrial buildings near town he saw a policeman walking through the units, fortunately moving away from him.

He reached the busier fringes of town and heard behind him the wail of a police siren. The brighter town lights allowed him to have a better look at his appearance: a bit muddy with some blood down his right sleeve. He stopped by a large puddle at the kerbside and scooped some water up. He splashed it on to his trousers and sleeves and the cloth and waterproof material immediately darkened. He was confident that it would not draw attention from the casual observer.

He was soon back on the High Street, which was alive with late-night revellers staggering homeward, some queuing, some singing, a few puking. He kept moving, slowly, in order to avoid stopping and looking suspicious. He noted that it was twelve fifteen and knew that the trains ran until one o'clock. He could walk to the station but didn't think that he had the time. Assuming that his observer had reached a phone pretty quickly and that the police had found the body soon after then, he had to assume that the police could be about to flood the town. He went to a taxi rank and joined a small queue. He was feeling okay, quite calm and collected, but the slowness of the taxis to pick up was causing him to became agitated. There was suddenly a rush of taxis and he was soon sitting in one.

'Just the station, thanks.'

'The station?' asked the cabbie, as if to suggest a fare this small was not acceptable.

'Yeah, just trying to avoid getting any wetter. I'll give you a tip.' He immediately berated himself. Fool, fool, he'll remember you now, goddamn idiot.

The journey took only a couple of minutes and he duly provided a good tip. He walked slowly on to the platform, just in case the police were already there, but the station was quiet. Two lads stood some distance away, and a courting couple sat in a shelter kissing and cuddling.

He kept his distance and sidled over to the departures board. He tried to look casual but his heart was pounding. He knew that he needed some luck now: a train, soon, and preferably going in the right direction. He would get on any train that came at random, but one home would be great. He scanned the board and found good and bad news. The good news was that a train was due in just five minutes; the bad news was that it was not going to his home in Bishop Auckland. It was going to Newcastle, with stops at Darlington, Durham and Sunderland. There was a train to Bishop but it was twenty-five minutes away and that was too long.

Get on it, worry about the details later. When the train duly arrived, on time, he picked the quietest of the four carriages. He chose a corner seat and tried to turn away from the light, but it didn't feel comfortable so he took his mac off and bundled it up, being careful to ensure that the three weapons stayed in their places! He placed it on his knees to cover some of the stains on his trousers.

The conductor was soon there and he asked for a ticket to Durham rather than Darlington; Darlo was a bit too close, the police might be covering that. For a second Westmain thought that the conductor was looking at him in a funny way, but as the official moved off down the train he dismissed it as paranoia.

He peered out at Darlington Station, but saw no particular activity, and he was soon at Durham. As the train ground noisily to a halt he opened the door and stepped on to the platform. Nobody else was alighting and there was nobody in sight at the station. Paranoia crept in again as he thought, What if the police are hiding behind a corner or a wall? Then he chuckled at the absurdity of the notion; the police were simply not that bright or efficient. He strolled nonchalantly down the platform, having pulled up his mac collar. He was conscious that there would be CCTV about and did not want to make identification easy, not that the images of these systems were ever good enough to make much of a difference.

He knew that the station was high above the city, but it was only a few minutes' walk down the hill and he had decided to walk rather than involve another taxi. As it was there were no waiting taxis at the rank so he did not have the choice to make. He approached the city a few minutes later and passed the first bed and breakfast guest houses without looking at them. He reckoned that should the trail lead the police to this city, they would possibly check the first couple of B&Bs within walking distance of the station.

For good measure he walked a mile and a half, passing half a dozen suitable places. He finally chose The Blue Marlin, a wholly inappropriate named guest house boasting AA and RAC recommendations. It was still open and the weary old man on reception confirmed the availability of a single room. Westmain thought £29.95 a little steep for B&B in a place with no stars, but it offered what he needed: anonymity, refuge and no questions. The receptionist had not even noticed his lack of luggage.

His room was all right, typical of such establishments. A bit stale, in need of some fresh decoration, but big enough and to be honest, comfortable enough. He noticed that the wildlife picture was well and truly fixed to the wall and idly wondered if the management really believed there was any threat of it being stolen. He thought it was hideous, lacking style or grace; a couple of buffalo standing in a plain.

He removed all his clothes and stood naked in the middle of the room. He placed his underpants and socks, vest and shirt in one pile, then his trousers and macintosh in another. All items were neatly folded and placed with care in their separate positions. He then went to the bathroom and stepped inside the bath. He turned the knob on the shower unit and freezing water hit him hard. He barely flinched, for this was something that he practised at home as a test of discipline. He slowly adjusted the temperature until it was hot and then stood motionless as the water cascaded over his head and body. After a minute or two he opened his eyes and, blinking the water away, looked to the nearby basin. There was a bar of soap there, which struck him as very unhygienic but he took it and started to wash himself.

For the first time since he had arrived he started to think about the night. Different, he thought, certainly different. He did not think of the girl, that was just business; but the man who saw him, well that was different all right, and needed to be thought about carefully – but not now.

After he had finished his shower he towelled himself vigorously and felt better for the exercise. He went to the bedroom and brought back the underwear and shirt. He filled the washbasin with hot water and placed the items in it. He then filled the bath with steaming water and brought through the trousers and coat. He dropped them into the bath and noticed the instant discoloration of the water with mud and blood.

He returned to the bedroom and switched on the television. He kept it very quiet; no point generating a complaint from the neighbours, if there were any. For an hour he watched some crass American game show that had a strange fascination in its awfulness. He chuckled when the plump lady who had battled through four excruciating rounds failed that last hurdle to win a dream holiday to Europe.

When the show had finished he switched off the TV and went to the bathroom. He used the soap on the contents of the basin then wrung them out, before taking them to a radiator near the bedroom door. He then scrubbed the items soaking in the bath, concentrating on the knees and lower legs of the trousers and the sleeves of the mac. The water was filthy when he had finished, and after releasing the contents of the bath he rinsed the clothes in hot water. He held both items up to the light for inspection and was satisfied with what he saw. He took the mac and the trousers, again having squeezed water from them, and hung them on the hot radiator under the window. The room was very warm, so he lay on top of the sheets. It was time for sleep and as he drifted to unconsciousness he smiled at a good night's work.

As he felt the approach of sleep he reached out and switched off the side light. On the little unit by the bed were the items that he had placed there neatly when he undressed: the typical things, like his watch, loose change and keys; and some untypical things, like a screwdriver and a Stanley knife.

His last thoughts before he fell asleep made him smile. How proud Grandma would be if she could see me now, was the first; the second was a word for God.

'No problem! One to me, I think. You really will have to try harder next time...'

Chapter Nine

It was seven o'clock on the Saturday morning and Detective Inspector Mansell was discussing the murder of Wendy Fell with Detective Sergeant Rogers.

Mansell was the more imposing character in all ways. At six foot tall and fourteen and a half stones he was a big man. He added to the image by having a crew cut and a hint of five o'clock shadow. His bushy eyebrows seemed to add to the air of menace that exuded from him. His manner was usually aggressive and he often dominated people and situations, sometimes even his superiors. It was rumoured that his apparent lack of ability to tone it down a bit or take the diplomatic route was holding back his career. There had to be something, as everybody knew that he was an excellent policeman who delivered good results. If colleagues had to sum up Len Mansell in a word, the word would probably be 'scary' – definitely a guy who you wanted on your side.

At the age of forty, he had now served twenty years in the Force and he loved his job. He had no ambitions to move upstairs, as he put it, he enjoyed the involvement with cases at hands-on level and was not interested in having a fancy title if all that meant was that you got to discuss budgets, cash flows and the financial implications of catching criminals.

Tom Rogers was like Len Mansell in one regard only, he too was a good thorough policeman. At 5'9" he was dwarfed by his boss, and at twelve stone two seemed only half as bulky as the DI. He was a placid character with a laid-back manner that often belied his inner strength and resolve. At thirty-three his youthful looks emphasised the difference between the two of them, but whatever the disparities, physical or otherwise, nobody would deny that they made a good team. In Rogers' twelve years of service he had worked with several superior officers. In his opinion, nobody came close to Len Mansell, and he had the greatest respect for the man whom he saw as his mentor.

They sat at the back of the main squad room at Stockton Police Station.

'Going to be chaos soon, bloody cameras and pappers everywhere.' 'Pappers' was the derogatory term that the police used to cover all journalists, including those who did not deserve the title 'paparazzi'. The relationship between police and media had soured eighteen months earlier when the visiting Prime Minister had been knocked to the ground in a media-led frenzy at a nearby factory. Certain police officers responsible for security that afternoon had received severe reprimands internally from senior officers, but worse was the coverage in the national press. Despite protestations that security was fine and that it was the media boys who had broken the rules, the named officers were hammered in the eyes of the public. The final straw for the local police was when they received a visit from Home Office security advisers ('Frigging civil servants, can you believe it?') to tell them that they would not be considered for future visits because of their incompetence and attitude.

'What do you mean, "soon"?' Mansell retorted. 'They are already there.'

It was true, the brickie was surrounded by journalists, both regional and national. Television vans and crews were parked a long way down the streets between brickie and town and a police officer wearing the standard yellow jacket was struggling to organise them.

'Plan of action, boss?' enquired Rogers.

'Right, I reckon the following. Tell me if I'm wrong.'

Rogers nodded, knowing that it would be a very rare event indeed if a) DI Mansell was wrong or b) somebody told him if he was.

Mansell laid out his ideas, 'First you go and see Sanders, get his formal statement. I'll go to the brickie and go over the scene. After Sanders, you meet me at the brickie. We'll get Bill Newsome to organise all door to doors and road checks. After the brickie we can send someone to get all High Street CCTV tapes, and we'd better check whether any on the individual units out of town will cover the area between town and brickie. You make a note to chase up taxi and bus data, and the station, I suppose. Bill sent somebody to do this last night – I need those reports now.

I'll get hold of forensics and Joe will have more to say about these other wounds, no doubt. I don't need to remind you to trace the girl's movement through the night, do I?'

Rogers shook his head.

'I'm going to meet the Super and tell him to talk to Darlington, Sunderland and Manchester. I think this is D. So we better revisit A, B and C. He can do that.'

Rogers thought it was typical of Mansell that he intended to 'tell' the Super rather than 'respectfully request of' the Super. He asked, 'What about the media?'

'I was coming to that. Jenny can handle all that; I'll brief her now.'

Jenny Spears was the Police Liaison Officer and was much appreciated by the senior officers at the station. She took a lot of pressure off them by doing all she could to release their time at moments like this when there was a huge workload to get through and the media were screaming for details.

'Let's go, Will. See you later.'

As Mansell rose to leave, Rogers asked a final question. 'What time will the squad meeting be, boss?'

'It should be this morning, but I'm going to call it for three this afternoon, so that I'll have something to report on whether this is D.'

'Okay, see you at the brickie,' said Rogers, and was gone.

Mansell found Jenny Spears in the cubby hole that was designated her office. 'Just a quickie, Jenny,' he said as he entered the room briskly. His size seemed to fill the already cramped space.

'Do me a favour, go to the press and buy us some time on this. Tell them the truth, all we know. Wendy Fell, twenty-two, murdered at the brickie around about midnight. Violent death, no evidence of sexual motive at this stage. Anybody see anything, et cetera. Nothing at this stage to link this to any others.'

Jenny opened her eyes a little wider.

'And are we expecting links to be made?'

'I might be, but you don't know that.'

'Understood, sir,' Jenny replied respectfully.

'Are you clearing this with the Super?'

'I wasn't going to, but if you insist I suppose I'll have to.'

Jenny said nothing, knowing that Mansell knew very well that the Liaison Officer could not possibly talk to the press before the Superintendent had authorised it, anyway, she reckoned that there was a good chance that the Super might well want to be the first to approach the press in these particular circumstances.

'I'll run it by him, then leave it to him and you,' said Mansell. He turned on his heel and left the room. After marching down the corridor and up a flight of stairs, he went through a door on the left and then he was outside the door of the well-appointed room of Chief Superintendent Burns. He knocked firmly and walked in without waiting for an answer. He knew Burns was in because he had seen his car in the car park when he had arrived at seven o'clock. Mansell did not really like Simon Burns, for various reasons. Mansell was suspicious of the motives of a man who had apparently gone flat out from day one in the Force to become a Superintendent. Mansell was not anti-ambition, but felt that Burns was not interested in genuine, nitty-gritty police work, preferring the kudos and the pips on his uniform.

'Morning, sir,' he said, as Burns turned back to him from the window he had been staring out of.

'Morning, Len. What have you got?'

'Getting organised mainly, covering the routine stuff. I really wanted to mention a couple of specifics.'

'Sure, fire away. What's your problem?'

Mansell bristled at 'problem'.

'No problems, sir, just thought it might be an idea if you talked to the Supers at Durham and Northumbria, and Greater Manchester.'

Burns raised an eyebrow. 'You're linking them, eh?'

'Not officially, and I may be off beam here, but I'll know for certain soon – and my water tells me it's going to be D.'

'Okay, I'll set that in motion. Anything else?'

'Yes, I've talked to Jenny Spears, and asked her to buy some time. Press are baying. She can give a statement which they can chew on but which tells them nothing. I don't know whether you want to see her or get more involved.'

'Yes, I think that's a good idea. I'll go and see her and maybe we'll do something together.'

'Yeah,' thought Mansell. Poncing about in front of the camera rather than actually doing police work... 'One last thing, sir,' he continued. 'I've called the squad meeting for three o'clock so that we can take in details from the other forces. Hope that's okay?'

Burns was not going to argue over a matter of procedural detail, even if the meeting should have taken place this morning.

'Okay Len, that's fine. I'll do these things and I'll see you at three.'

'Thanks,' was Mansell's only comment as he left. He quickly made his way to the front desk where he found Bill Newsome.

'Bill, I know you're on back to back and you must be knackered, but can you organise the door-to-doors and road checks?'

'No problem, sir. I've taken the liberty of setting it up – I thought you might want help on this score.'

'Cheers, I'll see you later, I'm going to the brickie.'

When Mansell arrived at the brickie, even he was a little surprised at the scene that greeted him. Although dawn had broken, the area was lit by many floodlights, with some police and some media. There were two uniformed officers at the entrance to the area but Mansell was more concerned about the stretch of ground that ran parallel to the main road. Although there was a fence running the length of the green belt, it was hardly daunting for a member of the press should he or she decide to nip over and get a little closer to the action. And what about the other side? he wondered. Who was covering that?

He squeezed his car into a gap that wasn't really there, between an ITV truck and an unmarked blue van. He marched to the two constables and asked who was covering the perimeter of the brickie. He was pleased to hear that PC Dawson was doing the rounds, going from one side to the other.

Mansell took a moment to assess the situation now that it was easier to see the whole area. It was as he knew it, nothing struck him as unexpected. He moved down the path to where he saw the large white tents set up by the forensic team. As he approached the spot where the girl had died, he saw the many white-suited forensic guys who were working the area literally on their hands and knees. It always struck Mansell that a murder scene was like a series of ever-decreasing circles. There was the large outer circle, in this case the brickie perimeter. The next circle was that area inside the perimeter but not at the hub of the activities that took place. This is where Mansell now stood, on the approach to the main area. Circle three was the area that encircled the central focal point, and this vital circle could be anything from a few yards to dozens of yards in diameter. Then finally there was the inner sanctum, the tight circle around the spot, the actual precise location of the crime. These circles were often just in Mansell's mind, but today there was physical evidence of some of them, being a combination of red and white tape, orange sheeting and white tenting.

Before encroaching any further on the inner circle Mansell watched the paper-suited team go about their business. He was always impressed by these guys; they never seemed to miss anything. It was ball-aching work, the tiniest details being their raison d'être, and they never seemed to get depressed or frustrated at the slow progress of their physical labours and, later, the scientific study of their findings.

He knew that this locale was bad news for the forensics lads, just about their worst scenario. Open spaces, trees, becks, mud and muck. Give them the confines of a house or room any time. They would be here for days and he fervently hoped that they would be able to release the body soon. He hated the thought of the girl's family having to live with her body just lying there.

He moved to the white tent and flashed his card at the officer at the entrance. He was surprised but encouraged to see an ambulance man inside the tent, which suggested that maybe the corpse was about to be released to the local hospital. Milling around the tent were several suited men, one writing notes, one taking a careful slow video of the scene, two talking and one on his hands and knees near the bushes in front of the girl, who was covered with a heavy red blanket.

Mansell looked around the faces and recognised two or three only. He was not surprised, as the SOCOs often included some civilians and these could change from crime to crime. He walked past the scribe and noticed that he wasn't talking or making notes;

he was actually sketching the scene, with a few notes added at the bottom of the page.

One of the men he had recognised was Philip Gonzalez, a native Mexican who had travelled a most peculiar route through life, ending up in the North-East of England.

'Phil! Hi, how's it going?'

'Morning, Len. Okay thanks, everything's in hand.' He spoke with a lilting Mexican accent which seemed so incongruous against his surroundings.

'Any news?'

'Footprints in the mud are pretty solid, we'll get good prints off them; not a lot on the girl, no obvious debris under nails, not much sign of a struggle to be honest. Mind you, Joe was saying last night that she had been battered, so maybe that quietened her down.'

'Is Joe expected?'

'Yes, about five minutes. And you know, Joe, he'll be here.'

'I'll leave you to it, Phil. You know where I am if you get anything. Any idea when the girl can go? I saw the ambulance guy.'

'Sorry, don't know, Len. I think he was only here to change the blanket; the other one got pretty wet during the night.'

'Thought it was too good to be true,' muttered Mansell as he thanked Philip and moved away. He stopped at the exit from the tent and considered for a moment. If the girl had been beaten prior to death, where had that taken place? Here or elsewhere? Why hadn't she screamed or put up a fight?' From what he had seen last night she was not a small girl, or particularly fragile.

At that moment Joe Barrow walked in, carrying a medical case.

'Hi Joe. Okay?'

'Fine, Len. How's yourself?'

'Apart from standing ten feet from a murdered girl, smashing thanks.'

'I suppose you want a chat?' asked Joe rhetorically.

'I could say that. Where should we start?'

'Okay, this is what I've got. Death occurred at just after midnight, that's pinpointed by your witness. Cause of death is the cut throat, causing asphyxia. Pretty quick, seconds probably. Blood we talked about: preliminary examination last night suggested wounds in the back caused by sharp pointed item such as a screwdriver. I also suspect that the lass had taken a severe blow to her left abdomen, could be rib damage judging by the bruise, and she also appears to have had a slap or punch to the face.'

'Sounds like she was beaten up.'

'Possibly. There's one other thing – I'll tell better, now – but it is possible that there was minor discoloration under her chin, which may not have come about because of the cut throat.'

'Meaning?'

'Meaning, a possible arm around the throat to go with the back wound.'

'So the bastard came up behind her, grabbed her, stabbed her and finished her off?'

'Not impossible,' concurred Joe.

'What's your next move, Joe?'

'I'm going to check all these things out, then chase forensics to see if they will release her. I don't want her hanging about her any longer than necessary.'

'Good man! Talk to you later.' Mansell went back to his car and decided to make a few notes whilst waiting for Rogers.

Joe went to work on the girl. He knew that he was known to be genial Joe who was always amenable, but last night had not been one of his best. He and his wife had had an argument at supper time over how much money to spend on her sister's ruby wedding anniversary. She wanted to splash out, make a fuss; he didn't. It ended in a shouting match and slammed doors. Joe had gone to bed and as usual went to sleep quickly. He was having a very pleasant dream about examining the intimate parts of Cindy Crawford who, incidentally, was very much alive in his dream, when the phone had rung at the bedside and it had been Bill Newsome. Not only was Joe miffed at having to leave Cindy, not only was it a miserable night to be called out from your snug bed, but the coldness of the night air reminded him of the reality of the earlier bust-up with his wife.

It was too early to volunteer for apology duty, so he mumbled a message about the phone call and left. He would have to admit now that he had possibly been less than professional in carrying out his duties during the night. Somehow the twin images of his ranting wife and the lovely Cindy spreadeagled on an operating table kept crowding in, and when he got home in the early hours he felt a little guilty that maybe he had not been one hundred per cent thorough. So now he was going to go over some of the same routines again and hope that nobody noticed.

Tom Rogers was sitting in the Sanders' living room holding a cup of tea. Alongside him sat PC Drake and opposite them in a big armchair sat Jeff Sanders.

Rogers spoke. 'I've prepared this statement from what you told us last night, Jeff. Please take your time and read it very carefully. Any detail in it, no matter how small, that you don't agree with, or anything that may be missing, please change it now. Once you've agreed the content, then obviously it will need signing and dating.'

The room fell silent, apart from the loud ticking of the carriage clock that stood on the mantelpiece. Jeff's eyes scanned the lines back and forth and he was soon through it.

'That seems fine, thanks.'

'You're absolutely sure, nothing you want to change?'

'No, that's an accurate description of what happened.'

'Okay, sign the back page please, Jeff.'

Duly signed, the statement was handed to the constable.

Rogers had studied Jeff again this morning and decided that he was bearing up very well. Obviously lacking sleep, he looked okay and had certainly spoken in a calm and thoughtful way.

'Do you think I could take you to the scene, just in case it reminds you of anything?'

Jeff only paused for a second. 'Yeah, that'll be fine, I'll just get my coat.'

Rogers knew that Mansell had not mentioned this, but as the Sanders boy was apparently showing no ill effects, why not?

Jeff told his parents where he was going, and despite the reservation on the face of Mrs Sanders, they were soon in Rogers' car. They passed comments about the weather, 'Lot colder today, might snow later,' 'Could be worse,' and so on, but made no reference to where they were heading.

After the ten-minute drive around the estate, they were on the main road leading to town. They soon saw the build-up of traffic that led to the brickie. Rogers saw Mansell's Volvo and as they passed it he waved acknowledgement to his DI. They parked some way down the road and walked briskly back to Mansell, who was waiting beside his car.

'Morning! Mr Sanders, I presume?' said Mansell by way of greeting. 'Sorry to drag you out, but as Tom here will have explained it's just a matter of seeing whether anything comes back to you that you've possibly not remembered.'

'I understand,' said Jeff, and together they set off into the brickie. Mansell asked PC Drake to check out some pappers that Mansell had been watching in his car mirrors, and he dutifully set off. As Jeff moved ahead, Mansell took an opportunity to whisper to Rogers.

'Good idea to bring him, Will.'

'Okay, boss.'

They caught up with Jeff and asked him to describe the events of the previous night as he had walked down this path. He did so, describing the rain and the poor lighting. They neared the spot where Jeff had first heard something and he explained that to them. A few yards further and Jeff showed them how he stopped, listened, took a step onto the mound and saw behind the bushes the man and the girl.

He stopped talking and a faraway look came into his eye.

'Okay, Jeff?' asked Rogers.

'Yeah, yeah, I was just thinking of that girl. Christ, it was scary enough for me, never mind for her! What must she have gone through?'

'That's why we've got to catch him quickly. Can you see him in your mind's eye, any details at all?' asked Mansell.

Jeff looked back to the spot, peering through the entrance of the tent to see the bushes and imagined it dark and wet.

'Sorry, just the same: wet, normal, nothing special.'

'Right, we'll get the artist over to you later and we can do a composite that should be interesting.'

They both thanked Jeff and led him back to Rogers' car. Mansell said his goodbyes to Jeff and said that he would see Rogers back at the station.

Rogers dropped Jeff at home, and now that he had PC Drake back in the car, he decided to use him for some donkey work.

'Right then, here are the names and addresses of the lads who Sanders was out with last night. Get around to all of them, get their stories for the night.'

Jenny Spears was getting a bit pissed off with Chief Superintendent Simon Burns. He had called her to his room and asked if she could organise a mini press conference just to release a statement confirming the murder and give a couple of details. 'Fine,' she'd said, she could do that. Then he had suggested that he be in attendance at the conference, for support. 'Okay,' she'd said. Now he was saying that he should read the statement and she could back him up. Great, in the limelight again, that's all this asshole ever wanted! Who the hell was supposed to be the sodding Press Officer? She bit her tongue and said, 'Whatever you want, sir, I'll put together a statement for you to look at.'

'Thank you, Jenny,' he said, smiling, and her skin crawled.

Creepy, patronising bastard, was all she could think of as she stomped back to her room. She was pretty sure, though couldn't prove it, that Burns was responsible for this crap room that she had been oh so generously allotted. Nobody would confirm it, but she knew he had overseen the room reorganisation last year when she and Sarah Cook the senior admin girl had had their nice spacious office taken away from them and been allocated two cupboards. Sexist bastard, she thought, God how I would love to issue a press release about him!

Despite her annoyance, she donned her professional mantle and put together a statement in the usual format. She did as Mansell wanted and gave them everything that they knew to date, but actually told them nothing. She included Wendy Fell's name, because the family had been informed. She sent the draft to Burns via a junior clerk and sent it on its way with a wish that he choked on it. She called the various, usual media offices and arranged a news conference at twelve o'clock.

Rogers saw that it was lunchtime and decided to head back to the station to grab a cup of tea before preparing for the three o'clock meeting.

When he arrived at the police station car park he noticed Mansell's car a few bays away and decided to sound him out on the forensic news. He looked in Mansell's room and the neighbouring squad room but had to ask the lads where he was. When he heard that Nige had been summonsed by Burns, he presumed that it must be the feedback regarding A, B and C. Mansell had thought that also when Burns rang and said, 'Pop up, please, Len.' But it wasn't about that.

Mansell had knocked and entered and taken the seat that Burns offered.

'I've contacted Durham, Northumbria and Manchester and they're all digging the files out before we talk specifics.'

So it's not that, thought Mansell.

'I've spoken to Jenny, and we're moving on the conference at midday.'

Nor that,' mused Mansell. So what the hell am I here for?

'I need to talk money, Len. You know the implications of a big murder.'

Mansell's blood started to boil immediately. The linking of budgets to murders always had that effect on him.

When he got no response whatsoever from Mansell, Burns cleared his throat and continued.

'Anyway, let's recognise where the problem lies here. The Chief Constable is squeezing both the Assistant CCs and then that means that balls belonging to yours truly are on the block for overspending.'

Mansell interrupted. 'With respect, you know my views on this. I just want to catch a killer.'

'I know, I know, and I sympathise,' said Burns, not sounding at all sympathetic. 'But this is more than a general chat, Len. I'm telling you to really keep an eye on the spend on this. Don't go throwing money about on hundreds of hours of overtime if it's not necessary. Don't be spending a fortune at Huntingdon or Wetherby, whichever lab they use, to speed up forensic reports. Just be careful, that's all I'm saying.'

'So if the budget runs out as we're about to make an arrest we call it off and say, "Sorry, public, a nutter's on the street because the cash ran out"?' He sounded angry; he was *angry*.

'There's no point getting ratty, Len, I'm just mentioning it so there's no hassle down the line.'

Mansell got up, despite not having been dismissed. 'Thanks for the tip, sir.' he said curtly. He turned and left.

Downstairs he met Rogers outside his room. 'Right, Tom,' he said, 'I've listened to all the bullshit I'm going to on this case, now let's get down to work and nail this bastard!'

Jeff couldn't help but wonder what sort of happy crew night it had been. A strange one that's for sure. Put aside meeting the girl of his dreams and witnessing a murder and what sort of night had it been?

It had started in the usual fashion, for about ten minutes, until Baz and Mike announced that they were only out for a few hours. There was something about their visits to the pub and pub/club that was fragmented, and there had been no Indian at the end of it all. It would be very easy to overlook all this after the other rather heavy events of the evening, but hey, we are talking about an institution here – the Famous Five and all that.

He had a nagging feeling that the night had been significant in happy crew terms. Not, surely not, the end of an era?

When was the last time they hadn't put in a full night? They all knew the rules, groovy gang night was a full night, anything else and you called off.

Strewth! The thought was looming large that the gang was going to fall apart. He supposed that it had to end eventually, and yes, they'd had a very good run, but it was still a shocking fact that he had really believed the five of them would go for daft nights out forever.

The thought added to his already sombre mood, all he needed now was to ring Jayne and find that she had blown him out, that her apparent willingness to see him again was a horrible trick to humiliate him – or in this case, sadden him. He held her diary page and dialled the number.

Jayne answered with an airy, 'Hello, Jayne here.'

'Hi, it's Jeff, from last night. Do you remember me?' Stupid question, he scolded himself; it was only last night.

'Hi Jeff, how are you doing? Sorry I had to rush off last night, my friend had an early start this morning.'

'That's okay, the reason I'm ringing is to tell you that I'll ring you Monday. I know that that sounds daft but I had a bit of an incident last night and I can't really talk to you today, and probably not tomorrow.'

'Oh!' was all Jayne said, and Jeff felt a surge of panic.

He was going to lose her before he started if he didn't explain, so against the wishes of the police, he blurted out, 'Jayne, you won't believe this, but I saw that murder last night, coming over the brickie, saw the man doing it! That poor girl! I think he saw me, then I ran home, so the police have been quizzing me and I'm not supposed to talk to anybody, so don't tell anybody. And when I get the chance tomorrow I'll talk to you properly, if that's okay... do you think that it'll be okay?'

He was breathless and all he could think of was that it must have sounded like a confession to being involved in a murder and, oh God, she'll think he's a nutter and...

'Are you all right, then? It must have been horrible?'

He was so relieved at her acceptance of the story and her apparent concern that he could have screamed down the phone, 'Thank you, oh thank you so much!' Instead he said calmly, 'Fine thanks, but you could say it took the edge off the night.'

She agreed and said, 'I won't keep you, then; thanks for ring- ing. I'm in Monday all evening if you get the chance, don't worry if you don't.'

He said 'Bye' and put the phone down, but started worrying aloud. 'Don't mind if you don't get the chance.' Was this the flick? Was this a polite, 'Don't bother, thanks, I'm not getting involved with someone like you'?

He thought about ringing her back but couldn't think of a sensible excuse so he wandered into the lounge to mope some more. He wished it was Monday evening.

He made another call to Toddy, and gave him a brief rundown on the events and also swore him to secrecy. He didn't think he was doing much wrong telling his girlfriend-to-be (he hoped), and his best mate, but he felt a little guilty when his mother appeared at his elbow and said, 'That Mr Rogers said not to ring anybody.'

'I know, Mum, but I trust Toddy and… Jayne.'

'Who's Jayne?'

'Er, a nice girl I met last night… I'm going to see her again so thought I'd better tell her about it. She's really nice,' he added, a little unnecessarily, he thought.

His mother looked at him closely. He sensed that he was about to be interrogated for the second time that day, this time about his well-being and a potential girlfriend, so he changed the subject.

'Can I ask you a question, Mum?' he began. Without waiting for acquiescence, he asked, 'Why is it that half the world now says, "You know what I mean" all the time?' We were talking about it last night. People at work, in pubs, anywhere and everywhere seem to say it. People say, "I went to the pub last night, you know what I mean?" …or, "I had chips for tea, you know what I mean?" It's driving me potty. Have you noticed it?'

Mrs Sanders pondered for a moment and replied, 'You know, I haven't specially, but now that you've mentioned it, I'll look out for it. Just another example of sloppy grammar and standards, I suppose. Does somebody famous say it? Is it a catchphrase or something?'

'Don't think so, but it really bugs me. Thanks anyway.'

Jeff retreated to his bedroom. His mum meant well but she did annoy him at times, still being unable to realise that as a twenty-eight-year-old accountant with a responsible job that he did not need wet-nursing every day.

If only he wasn't at home. Still, he was close now to having enough saved to get a property. It had been a long haul back from the debacle of Beth but the end was in sight.

Who knows, the next house could be his marital home, with Jayne perhaps. He laughed a little laugh at his premature thoughts, and then remembered the night before and lost his smile.

The meeting with DS Rogers had gone well, he thought, even if it was a little early at seven thirty, and he had not minded the trip to the brickie. Mind you, that Mansell guy looked a bit tough, wouldn't want to cross him... Now the police artist was at the door and being ushered in by his father, who was calling him.

This could be a long weekend, he thought; but at least on Monday he had Jayne to look forward to.

Chapter Ten

The little boy cowered in the corner of the dirty room. Litter surrounded him – empty food packets and wrappers, empty cans and old newspapers.

His mother stood before him, eyes wide and blazing. She hissed at him through gritted teeth, 'Don't you ever bother me again, ever, *ever!*' She raised her hand and slapped it down onto his bare left leg. The crack echoed around the sparsely furnished room. Tears welled in his terrified eyes but he didn't cry, despite the wobbling of his bottom lip. 'Never, ever again!' she shouted.

His crime had been to ask his mother for some tea because he was hungry. She had been busy with her nails, and when he asked again and tugged at her sleeve she smudged a finger and went berserk. This reaction was typical of the last couple of months. It was September 1963, the boy having been four in August. It was two years since the death of his grandmother. After that terrible tragedy there had been many people who doubted the ability or desire of the young mother to care for her infant. However, despite various meetings with social workers, nobody could prove that it was not going to be for the child's benefit to stay with his mother. The young woman had been very convincing throughout the autumn of 1961. She'd told people who asked everything that they wanted to hear. 'I love my baby, I'll raise him as, as good a boy I can, in memory of my mother who was devoted to him.'

One social worker felt that the girl's statements did not ring true, and his research suggested that it had been the grandmother who had held the family together; but like others, he couldn't prove anything.

After a few weeks the meetings and visits became less frequent, but the girl was still on her guard in case of unannounced visits, which still happened occasionally. After the third spot check in as many months, the Head of the Social Service Unit decided that the mother had proved herself. The baby was always clean, healthy and well fed, and the mother gave every impression of being a good parent.

So her deviousness worked and she was left alone. She immediately set about selling the house, which was now hers. It had no mortgage because her father's life assurance had paid for this when the cancer claimed him. She had also known where her mother's nest egg was, hidden in a shoebox buried under old blankets in the unused spare wardrobe. She was delighted to find over one thousand pounds salted away there, the result of daily scrimping and saving by a woman dedicated to providing for the future of her daughter and grandson.

The house sold quickly and she received a cheque for over five thousand pounds. This was a fortune, and she could have bought a more modest property and still had plenty left over. However, as part of her plan, she moved to a dingy bedsit in the poorest part of town. She knew that this was correct punishment for the pair of them for her mother's death. Through her father's strict financial sense there was also life assurance paid out on her mother's death, so she had a bulging bank balance.

She cut herself off from her friends, hardly seeing Mandy or Gemma for months. She did not make them welcome at the bedsit and after an initial spell of frequent visits, they got sick of visiting the dingy, unappetising place. They could not comprehend the move or the way in which their friend had changed – for the worse in all respects. They knew that she had suffered a terrible loss, but she had also undergone a complete personality change.

They tried to help but it was just too much like hard work and soon the contact with mother and child was minimal.

If pushed, the mother would admit that there had been great temptations in those first dark days in late 1961. It would have been very easy to give up the baby, shout 'Help' and receive lots of support. But she knew that that would be an insult to her mother. She had known at the first news of the death that her mission was now simply mapped ahead of her: punish the child. Short of killing him, and she had considered this, no punishment would be enough to recompense that horrible death, but it would go some way towards it.

The first element of punishment that you decided upon was to find a method that was the most effective, or vicious, depending on the perspective of the onlooker. She decided to ensure that her child would have no love. As he had caused the removal of the one love from her life, so she would remove love from his. This was easy to enact. No contact, no cuddles, no sweet nothings, no shared moments. The only contact was that born of necessity.

She tried no feeding and no changing of clothes, but this did not work, she felt, because it only led to tantrums that were difficult to control. She reined back on these policies. She also realised that the time would come when he would have to mix with other children, and then there was school. She did not want him standing out as either starving or filthy, did not want suspicions raised.

So now, at the age of four, the child was very quiet, did not have a great vocabulary and knew heartache and terror. There was none of the usual excited chatter or the thirst for knowledge. He had no imaginary friends. There was a battered old television set which he would spend many hours in front of, fascinated by the moving images. He also knew that to sit quietly in that spot meant that he could not be physically or verbally abused for wrongdoings, perceived or otherwise.

He had no friends, did not attend pre-school classes and saw no neighbours. He was taken to the shops once a week and always stared in wonderment when on those adventures at the bright, noisy, exciting world that existed beyond his confinement at home, populated by other children and their doting families. He was too young to comprehend the nature of the differences between his mother and the others, but something made an impression on him that there was a difference.

She took no interest in anything, except of course ensuring that Sam's existence was anything but comfortable.

Earlier that year she had been listening to some ponce on the radio going on about a crap jazz musician called Miles Davis who she thought played real drivel. So she had got up to turn the dial or switch it to off. Before she had got to the radio there had been a knock at the door and she had opened it to find two smartly dressed gentlemen there.

For a second she had almost panicked, thinking, My God, a surprise visit and the place is a tip! Shit, I'm in trouble here! But her fears were allayed when the elder of the two thrust a hand forward to grab hers and said, 'Morning! My name is Bill Smethwick, I am your Labour candidate in the election next week. Can I rely on your vote?'

She had taken Mr Smethwick aback by laughing at him, releasing her hand from his and slamming the door in his face.

Outside the door Mr Smethwick had said to his colleague, 'Mark that down as a "don't know".'

Inside the room Ruth Eastman was laughing and laughing.

At the age of five the boy started school. His mother had contemplated keeping him away from the school system but reckoned that the authorities would track him down eventually. So off he went into the school on that sunny September day. Within weeks the teacher who took Sam's class was puzzled by young Master Eastman. There were signs that he was alert but he was desperately quiet, didn't seem to respond to books, and did not interact at all with other children. After six weeks the school approached the mother and gently suggested that maybe the boy was ill, possibly deaf. He was given lots of tests but nothing was found. When the School Inspector visited the bedsit the mother was waiting for him. She had anticipated the visit and had smartened the place up. It was clean, if a little empty, and she had bought some second-hand children's books to scatter around. The Inspector saw nothing wrong. She played the dutiful mother beautifully.

The school, medical and local authorities soon lost interest and put their puzzlement down to overreaction. The child, they had to admit, did not appear distressed, and certainly showed no signs of physical ill-treatment.

One day she met him at the school gates and walked him home in a tense silence. The walk was always quiet; she never showed an interest in his day, but there was a tension that he could sense. Once they got home she pushed him to the floor.

'Do you remember this morning when you were washing yourself in the bathroom?' she demanded.

'Yes, Mummy,' said a little voice. He knew from the tone of her voice that he was in trouble and that the night could be very unpleasant, but he did not know why.

'I want to know why you left the dirty water in the sink.'

'I don't know, Mummy,' said a pitiful voice.

'Let's go and see!' she said as she yanked him from the floor.

She propelled him through the door and he stumbled in to the basin. 'Ow!' he cried. She ignored him. He stepped obediently onto the pile of old papers that lay in front of the washbasin. Tonight he realised that there were more papers than usual in the bundle and whereas his head normally just cleared the rim of the basin, tonight it was his chest that was in that position.

He looked at his mother, wondering what was going on. He looked down at the water in the bowl and did not think that it was very dirty, if that was her point.

His mother placed a hand behind his head and rammed it down into the bowl. He nearly fell off the papers but she steadied him with her spare hand. She held his face under the water. He struggled and gurgled and spluttered but she held him there. She dragged him back out of the water after about fifteen seconds. He coughed and cried at the same time, the water blocking his nose and throat. He gasped for air and was coughing again when she repeated the act. His arms and legs thrashed around but she pressed against him keeping him in place. She pulled him back and he retched, once, twice and then vomited into the basin. Water, mucus and vomit spurted from his nose and he choked again.

She splashed his face into the disgusting basin for a brief second then again pulled him back. This time she let go of him and walked silently back to the main room and put the TV on. She heard him hit the bathroom floor with a thump and felt a grim satisfaction as he struggled for breath just a few feet away.

After a long, noisy period, during which he was sick again, he appeared in the bathroom doorway.

'Sorry, Mummy!' he cried, big tears rolling down his cheeks.

'Go to your room,' she ordered, without looking at him.

After he had wandered forlornly to his little room, she went to the area called the kitchen and brought a pail and cloth. She cleaned up the bathroom. No need to make a fuss, she thought, I'll just remind him tomorrow of the mess he made.

The boy had shuffled like an old man to his bed, and sobbing, quietly pulled off, with a struggle, his wet clothes. He used his vest to wipe his face and nose. He dressed himself in a dry pair of underpants and a clean T-shirt and sat on the bed. He thought of going to see his mummy but decided against it. He slept badly.

At breakfast, when he came to the table he looked at his mother with big, sad eyes. She looked at him without compassion and said 'You will learn that when I tell you to do something simple, you do it, right? To save me having to repeat myself!'

The boy whispered, 'Yes, Mummy.'

'Your wonderful grandmother would not have approved of your bad behaviour, you know, she really wouldn't; and she so wanted to be proud of you.'

'I know, Mummy, I'm sorry,' whimpered the boy.

She sat munching toast listening without interest to the radio news that more Soviet dogs and rabbits had been launched into space. The boy ate bread. She looked at him and thought, Last night was a good one. He gets the message; no marks, temporary physical suffering. I need a few more like that. I'm getting there, Momma, I'm learning, and you will be avenged, I promise you that.'

The demons buzzed in her head. You haven't really started have you, not really? You realise don't you that in time you will have to destroy him, as surely as he destroyed your mother and by the same deed destroyed you. The boy did not understand why his mother smiled and said aloud, 'Yes.'

Chapter Eleven

Westmain had awoken with a start, his eyes snapping open as if on a timer, and for a moment he wasn't sure where he was. Then he remembered, the lovely Blue Marlin. He smiled at the name. Where did they get it from? He looked at the items at his bedside and he considered his night's work. He was proud of it, having overcome the various obstacles strewn before him. He decided that today was a day for really getting to grips with a strategy, a detailed plan for the future. So far his actions had been rather haphazard, too random; now it should be laid down, the numbers, the times and places. He was obviously good at it, and God was surely backing him all the way; but as the years rolled by there was increasingly a need to be a little more organised.

So, starting today he was going to sort it out. First, breakfast, then a bus home. Then he would write down the detailed plan, and of course he would have to consider what to do, if anything, with the man who saw him. Was there anything to be concerned about? He was hardly going to say, 'Yes, Officer, I saw Sam Westmain of 11, The Bank, Topside Park, Bishop Auckland,' was he? So why had God chosen to throw him into the picture? Just for the fun of seeing if Sam would panic, do something really stupid? It seemed a little excessive for a few minutes' pleasure. Or was the Lord going in a different direction? Like testing his acumen in choosing his next step? Yes, this was it, wasn't it – a challenge being thrown down to deal with this man.

Delighted that he had cracked this first puzzle so easily, Westmain jumped off the bed with a gleeful bound. The room was stifling, the management's view being 'rather boil the buggers than let them freeze to death', and the good news was that his clothing was virtually dry. He dressed and went down for breakfast. Conversation with the waiter was restricted to choice of menu, and there was only one guest attending breakfast who was hidden behind the sports pages of the *Daily Express*.

Breakfast was better than he expected, not as greasy as antici-pated and he was soon on his way back to the room. He went to the toilet and whilst washing his hands took the opportunity to rinse the bowl again. He did the same to the bath but there had been no suggestion of its previous horrible contents.

He picked up his weapons and placed them in their allotted spaces inside his mac. He rubbed the top of the bedside table with his finger, removing an imagined bloodstain. He checked the room and bathroom once more before going to the reception, where he settled his bill in cash. No point leaving a credit card trail, he thought.

His journey home on the bus was uneventful and he arrived at his house mid-morning and in a very good mood.

He showered and changed and put his clothes from the night before into the washing machine. He ate a snack of cheese and biscuits and then he went to a bureau in his bedroom and pulled out a brand new pack of large-sized writing paper. He took the pad to the dining table and picked up a pen from a nearby unit. He sat himself down and said aloud, 'Now then, where to start?'

He sat there for some time, appearing to be in some sort of daze or trance. He was motionless, staring unblinking at the blank sheet before him. Then, as if somebody had flicked a switch to activate him, he leaned forward and started to write. He had decided to write down a little history first, because he thought, to write a five-year plan needed a little background to explain it. He was going to start in his childhood, but he moved on to his teenage years and then, before putting pen to paper, switched to the death of his mother. Wasn't that truly the start of all this, when God had first spoken to him, confirming His plans for him?

He started to lay down his story, as he recalled it, always detailing the conversations and discussions that took place with the Almighty. He started neatly, taking care of the layout and grammar. He had decided at the outset that it may as well be done properly, as this could well become his mission statement. Out it poured on to the paper, page after page.

It always stayed in chronological order, but more and more random thoughts, ideas and opinions crept into the script. The structured start gave way to a continuous passage that contained no breaks. The writing became progressively more scratchy and disjointed, as if to reflect the thoughts being expressed. The narrative became full of bile and invective and the themes evoked became more extreme. It became a diatribe against womankind.

The planning started at page thirty-six, the writing having covered the 1975 death of his mother, the 1978 murder in London, and from 1990 to date, killings in Darlington, Sunderland, Manchester and Stockton. The plan covered the years to 2004. He detailed places and number of victims, ten in all, and he explained why it was perfectly justifiable.

There was a gleam of madness in his eyes as he worked. He wrote so furiously that beads of perspiration formed at his temples, even though the room was cold. The physical effort to get the words down quickly took its toll and after four hours of writing he slumped back in the chair, his right wrist aching madly. He rubbed his forehead as if to take away a pain, and he shook his wrist and hand to try to loosen the grip of the dull ache.

He did not read the forty-nine pages. He did not need to, as he knew that it was a wonderful piece of work needing no further attention. He felt that it was a revolutionary document, novel in its content. He nodded his approval at the plan; all he had to do was deliver the actions. God would be pleased. He turned to page thirty-six where he could decipher his words – just – and he laughed at his struggle. He read the opening point of his plan, nodded, then leaned back in his chair. He laughed, quietly at first, then it rose to a roaring cackle. He wept tears of laughter and joy, revelling in the beauty of his plan and the knowledge that God would embrace him further for these bold moves he had taken.

He calmed a little, still chuckling, and read again the opening lines of page thirty-six. It began, 'The Plan. One: Meet God's challenge. Kill the witness.'

He threw his head back and roared again. He spoke aloud, in his most theatrical fashion, 'If you compare yourself with others, you may become vain or bitter, for always there will be greater and lesser persons than yourself.'

This was the one bit of his beloved text that he had actually proved to be wrong. There were no greater persons than himself, he and God were the dream ticket.

When he had calmed down he realised that it was late afternoon, so he went to collect his P-registration Escort at the nearby garage. He was pleased to find that it was ready and that the bill was only for £57, a little better than expected.

He listened to the radio and watched the television news. They reported the grisly murder in nearby Stockton, but said nothing of significance. He watched a policeman read a statement but it too revealed nothing.

What a good day he was having…

Chapter Twelve

The Sunday morning was grey, cold and uninviting, with the sort of bitter wind that bit at your flesh no matter how many layers of protection you wore. It depressed even further the mood of Dorothy and Gerald Sanders. They were both in their late sixties and Gerald was long retired. He had had a long and enjoyable career of some thirty-seven years in the Health Service, culminating in his final post of Senior Administrator at the local general hospital. Dorothy had never worked, being one of the old school who believed that a woman's place was rightfully at home looking after house, home and family. She was a God-fearing woman who liked the order and routine of her life. Shopping days, ironing days, coffee mornings were all regulated and nothing had disturbed this way of life for a long, long time. And now this trauma had descended upon them – a shock to the spirit of the Sanders household.

The phlegmatic Gerald accepted Jeff's misadventure in his usual stolid way. 'What will be, will be,' was his standard response to any event that was out of the norm.

Dorothy could not take it in, not properly. She had got through Saturday in a daze and found refuge in making tea, coffee and meals for the stream of police visits. That nice Mr Rogers and his colleagues, that rather grumpy police artist. She remained pale, some thirty-three hours after the news had broken. Gerald was worried about her, but thought the quiet, unfussy policy was the right one. Gerald was very much an archetypal Englishman. He was loath to show or share emotion, especially when a stiff upper lip might suffice.

Dorothy had received another shock on Saturday, when, in the presence of her husband and a police artist, her son had blurted out, 'God, I hope they catch the bastard!'

Jeff had immediately flushed pink, as if he had not realised that he was speaking aloud and said, 'Sorry, Mum.'

The apology was for the blasphemy but his mother was taken aback by the 'bastard'. Throughout Jeff's twenty-eight years she had rarely heard her little boy swear. Only a grand total of a few 'bloodys, an odd 'crap' and a few 'shits'. Not a lot at all, so an aggressive 'bastard' was quite something. Not that it wasn't allowable in the circumstances. She had long ago instigated the house rules that bad language was a sign of weakness and indiscipline and was very unnecessary. This one occasion was all right, so long as it didn't happen again.

Gerald put his cup down and asked his wife, 'Should we go and see how he is?'

Dorothy looked at the kitchen clock and said, 'Possibly. Nine fifteen is very late for him isn't it?'

'Don't want to fuss of course, and I'm sure he needs the rest, but just to check that... you know... that he's all right,' Gerald finished lamely. Dorothy knew how his pride wouldn't allow her husband to drop his guard but she could see that he was hurting for his son.

'I'll go,' she said, and touched him on the shoulder as she passed him.

She went up the stairs quietly, not wishing to disturb Jeff, but then realised that she was going for the purpose of checking to see if he needed disturbing. She knocked gently on the bedroom door. Then again, a little loudly, she heard nothing so pushed open the door. The room was well lit because the curtains had not been fully drawn. Jeff was a crumpled heap buried under a duvet and blanket.

Mrs Sanders leant over the tousled head that poked out of the duvet and whispered, 'Jeff, dear.' Nothing stirred. She touched the duvet at about the point where she guessed Jeff's shoulder might be. She rocked it gently and said 'Jeff' a little louder. Still no movement and suddenly Dorothy Sanders' heart thumped hard. 'Jeff!' she barked, no longer worrying about niceties. The mound moved and Mrs Sanders exhaled loudly, not realising that she had been holding her breath.

Just for a second there, just a second, she had thought... Well, she didn't know what she had thought, except that it wasn't pleasant.

Something was emerging from the depths of the bedclothes. More hair, an arm, then Jeff's crumpled face, squinting in the light.

'What time is it, Mum?'

'About 9.20 love. There's no rush, we were just… checking.'

'I'm okay,' he said, but then the memories flooded back. He muttered 'Shit' under his breath and Dorothy chose to ignore it.

'Cup of tea?' she enquired, and he answered, sleepily, 'That would be great. Thanks.'

He stretched his body then drew his legs high up to his midriff. For that couple of seconds, hearing his mother's voice had actually cleared his head, and that seemed to exaggerate the pain of it when the memory rushed back: the girl, the man, those eyes…

Screwing his body and eyes up as tight as possible did not remove the image from his mind's eye. Yesterday had gone fine, considering, but what did today hold in store? More of the same, he guessed.

When he got up at ten o'clock, having enjoyed the tea that his mother brought him, he felt surprisingly well. It wasn't as if he was expecting a leg to fall off, but nothing was really happening. It was, in a strange way, almost disappointing. He had seen the police doctor yesterday who had given him the all clear but warned that there was a chance of delayed shock, but if that was the case then it wasn't just delayed, it was flipping held up.

He had been advised by DS Rogers not to contact anybody over the weekend. 'A bit early,' he said; and there was a strict warning not to talk to any press people who might be fishing around. Only the police, and the killer, knew of Jeff's involvement, said Rogers, so it was a huge surprise when Jeff picked up the regular Sunday paper and read the front headline:

MONSTER STRIKES – HAS HE KILLED BEFORE?

The sub-head read, *Mystery witness may hold key*. Jeff read the story, which did not give away a lot of detail but did refer to the alleged involvement of a witness who might have crucial evidence.

'Have you seen this, Dad?' Jeff's tone revealed his surprise.

'Yes, most of it is from the police statement that we saw on the news last night, but the "witness" bit is a little surprising.'

Jeff briefly wondered about Jayne and Toddy but dismissed the thought.

'Do you think I should ring anybody, DS Rogers or whatever?'

'Could maybe ring Rogers – do no harm, I suppose.'

Jeff found the card that Rogers had left on the coffee table in the lounge and rang the number. As he dialled he thought, Fool, it's Sunday, he'll be off. But he was proved wrong as a voice said, 'Rogers.'

Jeff exchanged pleasantries then asked if the detective had seen the papers. Rogers admitted that he had and apologised for the reference to a witness, reassuring Jeff that an enquiry was already under way to trace the source. Jeff himself had to admit that he did not quite know why he was ringing and was sorry for wasting DS Rogers' time. Rogers said, 'No problem,' and rang off. He was not having a good morning. Mansell had rung him at seven o'clock, full of ire, and demanding that by the time he got to the station at ten he wanted to know the cause of the leak regarding the existence of a witness. When he arrived at nine, Rogers could tell him nothing; at ten it was no different.

Rogers reran the videotape of the mini press conference given the previous day, checking that there was definitely no hint of anything said there that could lead to speculation about a witness. He saw nothing that could have done that. The statement was well prepared by Jenny Spears, giving nothing away, and was read precisely, with no adlibs by Simon Burns. The room that he, Mansell and Jenny sat in behind a small table, was not really big enough to accommodate the scrum of media folk who flocked to the conference.

The media had had a field day since the news broke in the early hours of Saturday morning. They all had plenty to keep them occupied; their biggest problem was deciding what to concentrate on. Television crews, journalists and radio interviewers swarmed into Stockton-on-Tees, and each of them had their views on where to focus their first strikes. Some chose the brickie, and shots of the tape, tents and characters in white were common through Saturday.

Wendy Fell's family home was targeted, and the police request at the home's gates for respect and compassion were largely ignored. Cameras were trained on every window. Their neighbours were contacted, each being asked their opinions of Wendy and her character: 'Was she good, ever in trouble?' 'Like the boys, did she?' 'Do drugs, do you think?' She had only had her flat a fortnight so the neighbours there did not know her.

Some of the more experienced hacks hung around the police officers, who themselves milled around the various locations involved. These older guys knew that once the initial flurry of reports covering the obvious had died down, the media would be left with little to say other than a regurgitation of the same few skimpy details. The best way for a reporter to get beyond the carefully released 'official' information was to get an informal inside track. And the best way to do that was from the horse's mouth, in this case the police or their associates.

One such hack was a grizzled old man called George Edwards who had worked on newspapers all his life. In his heyday, in the Sixties and Seventies, as a young ambitious twenty-something, he had made a big reputation for himself in London. He covered the showbiz side of life for a number of years, always seeming to get that big exclusive, whether it be film, rock or television stars. He moved from showbiz to another media-friendly environment, politics, and proved many sceptics wrong who said a light-hearted affiliation with flaky celebrities was no grounding for the heavyweight world of politics. George thought it was perfect training. After all, weren't both spheres of life populated by egomaniacs driven by sex, drugs, lies and greed?

He worked freelance for over ten years, often catching breaking news before the world realised something had broken. He was much in demand, so much so that the pressure began to mount. He became a victim of his own success and ambitious editors around the capital demanded more and more important stories of a more shocking and salacious nature. George simply could not fulfil the demand and then one day he cracked. He had a physical and mental breakdown and was hospitalised for five months. When he returned to the fray some six months later he was a shell of his former self, and when this was noted by all around him, he was dropped like a hot potato.

His career drifted and he worked around the provinces before spending a period in Scotland. For the last couple of years he had been an employee of the *North-Eastern Evening Gazette*, based in Middlesborough, and the editor gave him a fairly broad remit to report on 'issues of the day'.

Well, today's issue was a local murder, and George's experience told him to be at the brickie at eight o'clock on the Saturday morning. He ignored the obvious areas, the entrances at both sides, but wandered along the fence on the town side. He was not thinking of going over the fence; no, that was for the younger breed. But he had an idea that some time soon, some of his colleagues would try this and a young policeman would be along to sort the situation. Like a predator stalking a straggler from the herd of passing antelope, George would focus on a young officer and intercept him. He would give it his best shot to extract any details at all that were not currently in the public domain.

As luck would have it, fortune smiled on George that morning. As he was strolling along the fence an ambulance man was leaving his vehicle just in front of the reporter. Very nonchalantly, George moved quickly to the man's side and casually said, 'Morning! Nasty business, eh?'

The ambulance man was disarmed by George's easy manner and replied, 'Sure is, very messy.'

'Have you been to see her. Must be tough for you,' continued George, turning to look at the brickie over his shoulder. The paramedic couldn't see the gleam in George's eye and was happy to relate his harrowing tale.

'You could say that. Got called out hours ago and I had to go to see the body, as senior man in the team.'

George picked up on the man's attitude and said, 'Typical, you always get the shitty jobs when you're in charge.'

'Yeah, and this was messy. She'd had her throat cut, and at first I'd have said nearly had her head cut off,' he hesitated, the vision fresh in his mind.

'Just hope they catch the bastard!' volunteered George, 'Though you never know, do you?' This was the clever prompt that worked.

'Got a good chance, I'd say, I was just over there a while ago and I heard them say that they'd have to talk again to the witness.'

George forced himself to remain outwardly calm but inside his journalistic instinct was jumping wildly. Very calmly he said, 'Witness, eh? That would be a breakthrough. Wonder if it's somebody useful, or just a sozzled old tramp with Alzheimer's?'

'No, seemed a pretty good lead, young lad I think.'

George decided not to push any harder for fear of turning this wonderful source against him. He just said, 'God, I hope so! See you.' Then he wandered off as if he had taken no real note of the little chat. He had taken note all right, and was back in his car five minutes later. He had to decide what to do with the news: report it to his employers or sell it to one of the big boys. He struggled with the decision until vanity got the better of him and he said, 'Sod it! I can still deliver the big scoop.'

He used his mobile to contact an old friend in London who was a senior man at a big national operation. After a minute of catching up, George suggested that he had headline-making news from the scene of the Stockton murder. He would not divulge the details until the price was right, and that was duly negotiated. The money was nice, but what meant most to George was the bargaining power that he once again had. It had been a long time; too long.

At the Saturday news conference itself, which George did not attend, some of the local reporters were pleased to hear that Chief Superintendent Simon Burns would be leading it. If it had just been Jenny Spears it would have been a two-minute reading of a bald statement. With Burns you would get the statement but then questions and answers. Not that there was going to be any startling revelation of detail in the Q&A session, but it would help mark a few pointers for the coming days' stories.

And so it proved. The statement came and went, Burns having first expressed on behalf of the Force their condolences to the Fell family.

Then he invited questions. A wave of noise hit him and he raised a hand to command silence. 'Gentleman, please. You'll have to raise your hands and I will select you. Thank you.'

The hands shot up all over the room and Jenny Spears thought, What a tosser! He gets off on this power trip, thinks he's a sodding headmaster now. 'I will select you.' For Christ's sake!

He had made his first selection. A spotty youth asked, 'You say in your statement that this man is very dangerous... Do you have any reason to believe that he has killed before?'

'Not at this stage, but of course we cannot rule it out.'

Without being selected, Jim Johnson from the BBC crew shouted, 'Not even with recent Darlington or Sunderland murders?'

Burns was annoyed at the lack of respect and also the highly speculative question and gave Jim a withering look. 'As I say, no link has been made to any other enquiries, past or present; it is early days yet.'

The original questioner belied his adolescent complexion with an astute point that met the approval of his colleagues and rivals around the room. 'So the implication, DI Burns, is that once these early days are over that you will confirm a link?'

Burns was irritated more by the 'DI' than the question but tried to hide his annoyance.

'That's not what I said. Please don't twist my words or we are wasting our time. I am trying to help you here.'

At the back of the room two local journalists were whispering. One said, 'Ooh, get her!' The other sniggered, 'Christ that's hit an early nerve.'

Another selection asked, 'Do you have any leads?'

This was safer ground for Burns and his voice relaxed a little. 'The forensic team are doing their usual professional job and we are hopeful that they will generate some clues.'

The raised arm in the blue anorak was selected and when Mansell saw that it belonged to Gerry Goldberg, he glanced at Jenny, who acknowledged his glance with a tiny smile. They both knew that Goldberg, who was based in Newcastle, hated Burns because of a formal reprimand that Burns had issued against him when the two had clashed over a personal attack written by

Goldberg over the involvement of Burns with known drug dealers. Burns defended his position, claiming that the two men in question were valuable informants, but some mud had stuck.

Goldberg did not disappoint Mansell or Jenny.

'With respect, sir,' he started, and Burns groaned inwardly when he realised who it was. He had been a little blinded by the television lights and in the sea of waving arms had not recognised his rival. Goldberg continued, '...Why are you conducting this conference? May I ask where the Chief Constable or his two Assistants are?'

Titters rippled around the room and Mansell coughed to cover a laugh. Jenny stifled a giggle.

Burns was livid and made little attempt to cover it.

'Mr Goldberg, that is highly irrelevant for the purposes of this conference. I believe that you have shown the greatest disrespect for Wendy Fell and her family. I trust that others have more appropriate questions and do not wish to waste our time.'

Burns was clearly rattled and a lady in the audience bent to Goldberg's ear and said, 'Good shot, Gerry!'

Mansell knew that Burns had correctly tried to enlist the physical presence of his superiors but was thwarted in each case. Chief Constable Marion was on a family holiday in Florida, Assistant Chief Constable Barry Schuster was in bed with gastric influenza, and Assistant Chief Constable Ellen was at a family funeral in Scotland.

The questions continued for a few more minutes, Burns fending them off before they returned to the same ground regarding the possibility of a serial killer. At this stage, Jenny thought that Burns should sit down, but he seemed happy to keep on talking. She took the initiative and lent forward to the microphone in front of her.

'Excuse me, sir, I think we should now conclude the conference.' Without waiting for Burns to respond, she said to the room at large, 'Thank you, gentlemen,' and stood up.

Mansell followed and thought, Brave girl, very brave.

As Burns, Mansell and Jenny trooped off to a side room, Burns remarked to Jenny, 'You should have possibly left that decision to me, young lady, but I think you were correct; they were becoming repetitive.'

Mansell smiled, and Jenny breathed a sigh of relief, having expected Burns to roast her.

Mansell and Burns talked about the last fifteen minutes. Burns spoke first. 'Can you believe that little sod, Goldberg? Insolent little prick, who does he think he is?'

Mansell muttered, 'Yes, he has got a nerve.' They turned to the case and tried to plot a course through what was going to be a testing few weeks, possibly months.

The squad got together at three o'clock and covered what Burns had been told about with respect to the possibly connected murders of A, B and C. The team of senior detectives had listened attentively as Burns outlined that there was no firm link yet but there were plenty of loose ends that hinted at the possibility. The main function of the meeting had been achieved. This was to allocate areas of work within teams and to see a timetable over the next few days for communicating findings, suspicions, evidence or leads.

Mansell and Burns had discussed at six o'clock whether, should their fears of another murder in the series be proved correct, they could suppress the news and avoid firstly a media frenzy, which could jeopardise their investigations, and secondly possible public panic. They agreed that because Darlington, Sunderland and Manchester were incidents dated 1990, 1992 and 1997 respectively, the impact, despite media headlines proclaiming another Ripper, had been somewhat diluted. Could they expect the same again? They decided 'No', because Manchester was relatively fresh in the mind and because the connection of four murders carried too much weight. They accepted that the media were going to be all over this if it went the way they anticipated, and agreed that Jenny Spears would have to be closely involved with all available information so she could feed it to the piranhas and sharks in an orderly and controlled way.

Burns concluded the meeting with some advice regarding how it would be good for both of them if the thing could be resolved, and suggested that surely a witness was going to be a massive help.

Mansell said through slightly gritted teeth, 'Yes, I know that, and I will do my best.'

Mansell then returned to his desk and sat for a moment in contemplation. What did the star witness tell them? That the killer was 'average': average height, weight, colour, face, no distinguishing features. Well, that narrows it down to about ten million he thought wryly.

This case had a feel about it, mused Mansell, a bad feel. A feeling that perhaps the police were second best to a cold-blooded killer who had possibly murdered at least four girls, butchered them, and who showed no signs of pattern or routine. He could strike anywhere, any time. Mansell had seen plenty of blood and guts over the years – plenty – and nothing fazed him in that area. The only thing that ever scared him was the psycho, the madman; the person who did not think in rational, normal terms, but who heard voices and felt he was doing no wrong in carrying out vile acts. These people were often strangely cunning, and could lead the most peculiar double lives. They'd be a devoted family member, work colleague or friend for the vast majority of the time but then, with a full moon or some other trigger, off they would go to maim, kill or desecrate. They also always seemed to be lucky, often avoiding detection through narrow escapes and good fortune. These cases were far scarier than the routine stuff of a Friday night when you could be facing a 6'3" skinhead with a broken bottle. Even pissed or drugged, this guy would have some sense, some logic or conscience in there somewhere. The psycho wouldn't, and that always worried Mansell.

He was right to worry about Sam Westmain.

Chapter Thirteen

Sam Westmain bought three morning papers that Sunday, all from different newsagents of course, to avoid any suspicion. One local, two national. They were unanimous in their choice of lead stories, the only difference being the wording of the banner headlines. The local one went with, THIRD NORTH-EAST GIRL KILLED – IS THERE A LINK? The national broadsheet gave the story equal billing with ECONOMIC CRISIS IN AMERICA and read, GIRL SLAIN, POLICE ISSUE WARNING; while the favourite national tabloid, in its usual unsubtle fashion, had *We link latest killing to two others. Exclusive insight into new ripper* under a stark headline, RIPPER STRIKES AGAIN.

He read all three versions of the story very carefully, digesting every detail to glean from them any information that the police might have. Despite the common theme, the three stories were surprisingly different on the details.

The local version centred on the home from which the girl came. Neighbours past and present had been interviewed, and as so often seemed to be the case of murder victims, everybody appeared to concur that she was a lively, happy-go-lucky girl, nice to her neighbours, and a family girl at heart who would be sorely missed. Which was it, he wondered? Did neighbours and family lie at times like this to either protect the girl's character or family, did they say these things in order that some of the nice things said reflected on themselves? Or was it a simple fact of life that violent death only became nice girls? Would he ever read of a murdered girl, 'She deserved it, miserable bitch, she was rude, arrogant, a lying thieving drug taker. Good riddance!'

He supposed not. Anyway, the local press had targeted her happy home life, given extremely detailed description of the locale of the death, and then speculated on the possible link with two other North-East murders in the last nine years.

Although they made it clear that there was no official linking of the three deaths, they suggested that three girls of a similar age, killed within thirty miles of each other, all without an associated arrest, was a little too coincidental. There was no mention of any witness, for which, later that day, the journalist responsible for the piece was severely reprimanded by his furious editor.

The tabloid implied that there was an official link between Helena, Donna and Wendy. 'Police are baffled by their own inability to close the net on a killer who has now struck at least three times,' they declared. They ran a whole page inside on an article written by a criminal psychologist who laid out her list of personality traits, physical traits and the nature of the murderer's environment. This was based on the 'evidence' of... well, there was no real evidence, just a murder in Sunderland of Donna Mills, aged twenty-one, on 14 June 1992; a murder in Darlington of Helena Stockley, aged twenty-five, on 20 February 1990; and now the murder in Stockton-on-Tees of Wendy Fell, aged twenty-two. What evidence? Well, the police had plenty but the newspapers were only guessing.

The psychologist's profile suggested a man between twenty-five and forty-five, insecure and lacking confidence, possibly unattractive, living either alone or possibly with parents; a bit of a loner, working in a factory or other such manual occupation. Somebody may be protecting him. Probably a sexual deviant.

The broadsheet was the only paper to refer to a possible witness, George Edwards having made his call. When the broadsheet journalists had started checking the story, they asked questions of the police officers regarding the witness, stating it as fact that there was one, rather than speculating, and they got the desired reaction. Firstly there were angry and puzzled reactions, as if to say 'How the hell do you know that?' Secondly came a stonewalling and a tense reiteration of, 'No comment.'

These simply confirmed the existence of the witness. A lack of witness would have been met with, 'Don't talk stupid, fuck off!' So their article discussed a mystery witness, probably in hiding or in police safe custody. This person could unlock the three mysterious and vicious deaths over the recent past.

The paper also announced that there would be a news conference at 4.30 later that day, to be attended by the parents of the murdered girl.

Sam read and reread the articles. Basically nothing new, nothing to be concerned over. The witness story was interesting because it was only a matter of a day or two before his identify was revealed, no way could they keep it secret. Their only hope was to have kept his existence quiet – and that didn't last long did it!

What was he going to do when he found out who the witness was and where he lived? Ignore him? Threaten him? Meet and kill him? He didn't kill men, no purpose to that, but now he had his plan to stick to. Maybe after every two or three, God was going to chuck a spanner in the works, just to keep it interesting. Okay, let's view it as that, a test. No need to get too carried away, just bide your time, see what develops.

He watched the lunchtime TV news with interest. It ran the story of the murder again, having given it a lot of coverage the previous day, being fresh after the night of the killing. Today's main coverage centred on Saturday's news conference. It followed the now familiar route. A senior police officer first outlined the tragic, needless murder of a lovely girl. He dealt in facts: approximate time of death, death by cut throat, forensic groups working at scene, family devastated. In anticipation of a barrage of questions at a later stipulated question and answer session, he announced two things that he thought would take a little sting out of the journalists' onslaught. Firstly, he said, 'Yes, the police are investigating the possibility' (he stressed the word 'possibility') 'of a link with two other deaths, that of Helen Stockley and Donna Mills. There is nothing concrete to confirm a link, only that they were in the North-East, and they were women. The causes of death were similar but not identical.'

This was indeed true. Not all three were identical, but two were, those of Stockley and Fell. The third was death by blood loss. What he did not mention was that all three girls had been stabbed in the back prior to death.

The evening news was much more interesting, detailing the conference at four thirty with Wendy's parents.

'Please respect their distress at this difficult time,' the policeman instructed.

Mr and Mrs Fell shuffled in, assisted by another police officer. They looked at the floor all the way from the door to the podium where the microphones were placed. The battery of journalists and photographers were both seated and standing and they were alert to the fact that the emotionally charged atmosphere had suddenly risen a degree or two.

Mrs Fell was fifty-four, and was usually a brisk, bright lady. Today, she stooped as she walked as if somebody was physically pushing down on her shoulders. When she looked up, fleetingly, at the podium, and as the cameras flashed, hardened journalists sitting in the first three or four rows of seats, people who'd seen it all before, felt pangs of sympathy for Mrs Fell. Her face was a combination of grey skin and red blotches. Although nobody in the room had ever seen her before, they all sensed that this woman normally looked greatly different from this. She looked ill, very ill. By contrast Mr Fell outwardly looked okay. He had a sad air, for sure, but there was an almost expressionless, blank stare on his face. Bottling it up, thought more than one person. Could crack at any time.

The journalists often behaved like hounds in a pack, which they proved to be with the police officers just a few moments later; but for now they did indeed show respect and restraint. It was very quiet, although the cameras still flashed.

Jenny Smith of the BBC leaned to Sammy Jones of *The Times* and whispered, 'Christ, why's she doing this? She looks like death. She'll never get through it…'

A police officer stood up and held up a hand as if using magic to stop, at a stroke, all the cameras.

'Please, gentlemen, please. Mrs Fell has a prepared statement that she would like to read. Please respect her and allow her to complete this statement before taking further pictures. I know that you'll respect her feelings at this very difficult time, thank you.'

A lone flashbulb popped and heads swivelled to stare at the miscreant. He had the humility to blush, and he mouthed silently, 'Sorry.' Everything went very quiet and still.

Mrs Fell looked at the officer to receive acknowledgement that she could start. She received a nod and cleared her throat in almost theatrical fashion. She did what members of the public mistakenly often did, leaning forward unnecessarily to the two microphones in front of her. She read in quiet, clear monotones. The flatness of her tone reflected the numbness that she was experiencing.

'On Friday night last, the beautiful daughter of loving parents was taken from us... cruelly taken, violently taken. We can only guess the terror that she...' Mrs Fell paused, swallowed hard and blinked three times quickly... 'Sorry,' she said, and she picked it up again. 'That she suffered in her last moments. We are here, Wendy's father and I, to appeal directly to the person who did this. We could sit and call you names, giving you epithets like animal, monster, madman and so forth, but we will not do that. As you are a person with feelings and rational emotions, we appeal, indeed we plead with you, to give yourself up. You will surely be punished, we cannot pretend otherwise, but you will also be given help. Specific, direct help that you so obviously need. Please do it.

'If there is anybody out there who is harbouring this person, then please try and persuade him to give himself up, for help... So that this doesn't happen again. Nobody should ever again have to suffer with the same pain that...' Her face crumpled along with the 'I and my husband' but she managed to squeak, '...have had to suffer. Thank you.'

Her husband was sobbing silently, still looking at the floor. She was trying to control her bottom lip and losing the battle. It quivered violently and big tear-drops ran from both eyes down her cheeks. She stood up, and only two or three cameras clicked. Some journalists wiped away tears and the police officer looked a little flushed. He ushered the two distraught parents out of the room, then returned moments later.

'I'll think you'll agree, ladies and gentlemen, that that was a very brave appearance by Mr and Mrs Fell. I personally thank you for being respectful. I will now take questions from the floor.'

As if they were still stunned, the journalist met with a second's silence. But then they remembered why they were there. Questions were shouted from all sides.

'Okay, okay, please just raise your hands and I'll select you.'

The following ten minutes were trying for all concerned. The police were frustrated that the questions focussed almost solely on the areas that really had been dealt with, namely the witness and the possibility of a mass murderer on the loose. The journalists were annoyed because they knew that there was more that the police were not releasing and could not prise more information from them. The police finally acknowledged that there was possibly more but the journalists couldn't really expect them to jeopardise the case could they? The police brought the conference to a slightly premature end after nine rather pointless minutes. They would claim that they had held a news conference what more could they do? The press would argue that it was a conference without news.

On the TV bulletins, the cameras homed in on Mrs Fell's face and the anguish that she so plainly was suffering. The fact that her husband was dying inside was almost a more powerful image than the pictures of Mrs Fell who was so clearly dying on the outside. Sam Westmain watched the bulletin impassively. Not a flicker crossed his face, until Mrs Fell broke down. Then there was a reaction. He smiled.

Chapter Fourteen

Monday, 11 January was a cold day in the North-East of England. A hard frost covered rooftops, gardens and cars. The North Yorkshire Moors had a significant snowfall and the bitter northerly wind dragged with it frequent squally wintry showers over the whole region.

DI Mansell shivered as he walked from his Volvo to the back entrance to the station. He was in a grim mood for his instincts told him that he was in for a very tough day. Not only was it the day to pull together the case reports to date, and not only did he have to report to his superiors, but he had to meet the supervising officers in charge of A, B and C cases. On top of that the media machine would be up to full speed after a couple of days of getting organised. They were not going to make his life easy.

Rogers was already at his desk busily writing notes onto a big pad of paper.

'Morning, Tom.'

'Morning, sir,' replied Rogers respectfully.

Rogers asked what Mansell had lined up for the day, knowing that Mansell would have given this some thought overnight. Mansell's response was very unexpected.

'Do you think that Sanders is safe?'

'Don't you?' said Rogers in surprise.

'Just wondering… The guy's going to be thinking of what Sanders saw. A good ID and he's had it. He's also very dangerous, maybe literally a madman, so I just thought it was possible.'

'Do you want us to put a man on him?'

'No, probably not just yet, but I wouldn't dismiss it in the coming weeks. Let's see how it goes.'

Mansell went to his room and took off his overcoat and sat behind his desk. He did not like the preparation of reports, filing, administration and office duties, but fully appreciated the necessity of quality paperwork for communicating information properly. Rogers knocked at his door and stepped into the small, neat room.

'Do you have a timetable then, sir?' Rogers asked again, not having had an earlier response. This time he did get the expected analysis, and typed sheet diarising the day. He carefully read through it.

Eight	Door-to-door reports
Nine	CCTV reports
Ten	Transport reports
Eleven	Forensics. Weapon. Wounds
Twelve	Chief Super
One	Durham/North/Manchester
Two	
Three	
Four	
Five	Profile/Mr Warren
Six	Media

Under the times there were also six typed questions.

1. Serial?
2. Patterns?
3. Family Appeal?
4. Reconstruction?
5. DNA Screening?
6. Press Release?

He looked to Mansell and asked whether he had decided which Rogers should cover.

'Yes, Door-to-doors, CCTV and transport are all yours; use the team any way you like. I'll talk to forensics and medical, then brief the Super before the meeting with other forces. I want to see Tim Warren this evening for his first profiling, then I want you and me to go through the media coverage to see whether we can use it to our advantage. Okay?'

The 'Okay?' was rhetorical, Rogers knew that, and even the potentially very late end to his working day did not deter him.

'No problems,' he said generously.

He took a photocopy of Mansell's list and returned the original. Mansell was on the telephone to his secretary telling her that he wanted the times confirming for the meetings with Chief Superintendent Burns and the officers from the other forces. The meetings had been provisionally arranged the evening before and his secretary soon confirmed them. Mansell knew that Rogers and his colleagues would attack the reports available to them with gusto; he trusted them all, as good police officers, and he was not overly concerned about seeing the reports himself. The time that this trust released allowed him to spend some time detailing his approach to the afternoon meeting with half a dozen officers from other forces.

He had received by email synopses of the cases, which were now so very relevant, but it was the detailed files and intimate case knowledge that he desperately needed. He knew that A, B and C were the work of one man and he was sure that he was going to be given detailed reports which suggested avenues of interest, possible similarities, links or patterns. However, he also knew that the three murders, for all the details that they threw up, were very much unresolved, and that decent police work and computer assistance had yielded nothing of great use. He hoped that his case might just trigger something in the other officers that computers, forensics or reports could not do. He believed in gut instincts and especially the instincts of senior detectives.

He had initially thought that he would jot down a few questions for the meeting but now decided to do something a little different. He took his Black Cross pen, a birthday present from his colleagues, and wrote down a list of the ways that he thought they would catch this man, together with an estimation of the likelihood of each. He intended to then ask the other officers of their assessments and then, between them, prioritise the list in order of joint preference. This he thought would lead to a concentration of effort on the agreed best lines of enquiry. He was of course assuming that this girl was D, but his reliable instincts told him that there was no doubt.

He listed his ideas.

1. Gives himself up
2. Kills himself
3. Is turned in by family, friend, colleague
4. Photofit identifies him
5. Makes a mistake
6. Forensics/DNA nail him
7. Detection traces him

His assessment of likelihood read:

1. Very unlikely
2. Possible – See Mr Warren
3. Need to work on this – Use Media?
4. Chance – Work on Sanders
5. Possible, takes chances
6. Unlikely – Will convict when found
7. Possible

After writing it quickly, Mansell looked at his list carefully. So, subconsciously he seemed to be thinking that they needed help from the killer's associates, or maybe an accurate profile, in order to track him down. He did not discount the possibility of tracking the man down through excellent police work, either by pure detective work or sophisticated forensic or laboratory-driven analysis, but he felt that this work was going to be needed after a capture, to prove this man's guilt.

Mansell was a great fan of profiling. He had used it many, many years ago when it was often viewed suspiciously, as being airy-fairy, not strictly kosher. He was convinced that people's characters were a massive factor in any crime whatsoever, and he enjoyed the interaction with witnesses, victims and perpetrators of crime. In more recent times, psychiatric and psychological profiling had become commonplace and were important tools in many investigations. Mansell studied the work and writing of John Douglas, the Senior FBI Investigator who had been the inspiration for the character Jack Crawford in the famous film *Silence of the Lambs*. The methods and work of the Behavioral Science and Investigative Support Units based at FBI Headquarters in Quantico, Virginia, were a source of inspiration for Mansell, and he often reread John Douglas's various books.

Mansell had learned many truths, as he saw them, from these books, ranging from snippets that were interesting to fundamental methods of detection which he tried to apply to all cases. He had already considered the application of some of his principles to this case over the last couple of days. He would not suggest that a killer could be tracked down solely from profiling but he did think that such work was as valuable as fingerprints or DNA. For example, he knew that the FBI work strongly suggested that a weapon being involved in a case such as his meant that rape was not the motivation behind the horrible outcome. Strangulation suggested rape, not cut throats and knife wounds in the back. In fact, 99.9% of crimes were motivated by one of five driving factors: anger, greed, jealousy, profit or revenge. The trick was to identify which factor would fit the crime under investigation. One idea that he always looked at was that to know the offender you had to look at the crime, not the other way around. 'Behaviour reflects personality,' said the FBI and Mansell believed them. He knew that he would be referring to *Mindhunter* and *Journey into Darkness* over the coming weeks.

He sat at his desk for quite some time, not writing, not on the telephone, just thinking. It would be easy to run around like a headless chicken, chasing people, reports, going visiting and holding meetings, but Mansell believed in genuine quiet thinking time. After an hour or so he got up from his desk. He had decided on lines of questions for colleagues, for Jeff Sanders, visiting senior officers and Mr Tim Warren the criminal psychologist.

A few miles from the police station in a neat semi-detached home, Mr Roland Fell sat at the breakfast table at one end of the large kitchen. He sat alone and the *Daily Mail* lay unopened on a nearby work surface. He stared numbly at the big packet of cornflakes, unaware that the mug at his fingertips contained cold coffee. He could not accept that his girl, his only daughter, was dead. Not only that she was dead, but that she had been murdered. Not only murdered, not a single blow to the head in an extreme domestic dispute, but a horrible, brutal, deliberate act involving pain, suffering and fear. Tears welled in his eyes as he thought of the terror that Wendy must have felt those last few minutes. He was brought from his distant, disturbed thoughts with the sound of heavy plodding on the stairs.

Marie Fell appeared at the kitchen door and the sight of her brought Roland to his feet. His broken heart snapped into a hundred pieces at the sight of his distraught wife. She was a horrid greyish, yellow colour and her normally bright features were dull and sunken. She raised her lowered eyes as if by a huge effort and her eyes echoed the pain that she was suffering.

They did not speak, Mr Fell just reached out his hand to gently take his wife's. He guided her to a chair at the table and she slumped down on to it. They sat in silence and the husband got an unpleasant surprise when he put the cold coffee to his lips.

'Ugh!' he said. 'Stone cold!' The words cut him and his wife to the quick, reminding them in a flash of the body of their daughter. 'Sorry,' he added. 'Do you want a coffee, luv?'

'Yes, please,' she said flatly.

He busied himself with the coffee, occasionally glancing at his wife, who sat motionless at the table.

When he brought the coffee back to the table he sat down by his wife and took both her hands in his own. 'Darling, can we talk?' he asked, almost in a whisper.

She slowly took one hand from his and scratched the side of her head. 'Talk about what?' she asked, as if half asleep.

'Well, what they mentioned yesterday. Doing another one of those appeal things on the telly.'

'I can't do that. No, I couldn't, really couldn't.' She moved her head slowly from side to side as if convincing herself that she was right in her assessment. 'Just couldn't,' she repeated.

They fell silent again, both swamped with anguish and pain. After a few minutes Mr Fell spoke quietly. 'Do you think I should do it?' Marie looked at him with damp eyes. 'Don't know, Roly, do you think you could?'

'I don't know, but if it helped to catch the… the… bastard… bastard who did this… then I would have to do it.'

After an uncomfortable silence, Marie asked, 'What time's your Alfie coming round?'

'About nine, and he's bringing Doreen, I think.'

'That'll be nice,' said Marie.

Marie Fell knew that her husband was a strong man, but she also knew that he was a devoted, doting father and she was not at all sure that his spirit and strength could survive the battering that their loss was giving them.

The telephone rang and Roland moved to it slowly. The reluctance visible in his manner and his gait was brought about by the fear that the telephone was about to bring him yet more horrendous news. He answered the call with a feeble 'Yes?'

It was Chief Superintendent Burns. He enquired about the well-being of Roland and Marie. He was told that they were doing all right, but Roland's monotone voice suggested otherwise. He asked, as diplomatically as possible, whether Mr and Mrs Fell had had the opportunity to discuss the possibility of making a further television appeal. He was making the call more out of routine necessity than in genuine hope of a positive response, so he was surprised to hear Mr Fell say, albeit in a fragile voice, 'Yes, we have, and I'm going to do it. My wife will not be there.'

The police officer was delighted because he knew the impact that the first appeal had had, and a second could dramatically improve their chances of an early result. For an unprofessional moment he wanted to shout 'Yes!' but said instead, 'Well, Mr Fell, we can talk about it later today, but if you do go through with this difficult action it could assist our work considerably.'

He promised to ring later to discuss details and said his good-byes. Mr Fell put the phone down and stood by the telephone table. He felt as if he had just made a momentous decision that was both good and bad; would be of use but would hurt, would release some hidden pain but would bring its own tensions. He sighed.

Rogers was having a very mixed morning. The first bit of good news was that his colleagues had worked well on Saturday and Sunday and the three areas of reports that Mansell had mentioned were available.

He picked up the file, which was full of individual door-to-door reports, and saw that Detective Constable Williams had summarised the reports' main points. There was nothing of particular interest; nobody in the streets in the immediate vicinity of the brickie had seen anything up to the point Jeff Sanders had been spotted running to his home. The lack of any suspicious sightings of people or vehicles suggested to Rogers that maybe their man had not visited that side of the brickie. That would lead their investigations back to the town side.

He picked up the CCTV file. It simply listed all the places from where the videotapes had been picked up. It was a long list and covered the council video cameras, pubs, shops and a garage. Three covered the High Street and immediate area. He was surprised that only a couple of the nearby industrial estate units had cameras. A constable and a detective sergeant were assigned to scrutinise every second of every tape covering the period between six o'clock and midnight. It was going to be a long, laborious exercise.

The transport report covered enquiries made so far to taxi firms, bus companies and the railway station. The taxi and bus details ran to dozens of pages and he was glad that he would be able to delegate the task of reading every page looking for the proverbial needle in the haystack.

The report from the station was a lot briefer, only four pages. It covered the timetable of all trains passing through the station from ten o'clock to one in the morning. Attached was a statement from the two members of staff who had been present during those hours. Sandra James had closed up the little café at ten thirty, and referred to the couple of people who had been in the coffee shop at around ten. An old lady and a young backpacker did not interest Rogers.

The member of railway staff who did have something of interest to say was Will Davies who had been effectively Station Manager from six o'clock until two in the morning. His statement made reference to the few people whom he could remember, and Rogers was very encouraged to see reference to 'old lady' and 'backpacker'. Of the others who were mentioned, one particularly caught Rogers' attention. A man had been observed at around midnight, alone, with no luggage. He was apparently very wet.

Rogers immediately asked himself several questions: Why so wet, why no luggage, going where? He noted that the man in question was thought to have boarded the Doncaster to Newcastle train, and Rogers decided to act on this immediately. He called over DC John Dankins and told him to go to the station and talk to Will Davies, and also to find out if there was a conductor on the 12.30 to Newcastle. If there was, then he too would need interviewing.

Rogers went back to the CCTV file and was pleased to see that a colleague had been diligent and included the railway station for CCTV tape pickup. He smiled at the thought that crossed his mind which was: It would be great if CCTV had the station guy, and Sanders confirmed he was the man, and then they went to his stop and found him just like that!

His curiosity was significant enough for him to call over to DS Henry Hugill. 'Hen, where are the CCTV tapes?'

Hugill called back, 'Tommy Rees is keeping them upstairs. I think Tommy and Carole are going through them later today.'

'Thanks, Hen,' said Rogers. He then dialled the extension of Tommy Rees.

'Rees,' came the prompt response.

'Hi, Tommy, It's Tom Rogers. Just looking at transport reports for Friday night and I've noticed the railway station report mentions a guy, late on, who I'd like to look at. Have you got the station tape handy?'

'Should think so, Tom. Is that a hot lead or what?'

'Not desperately, just fancied a gander at this guy, see if he even comes close to Sanders' description.'

'Okay, I'll dig it out and give you a shout.'

'No problem, I'll come up now. See you in a minute.'

'Okay, I'll set it up.'

Rogers neatly rearranged the files and reports on his desk before setting off to go to Rees's room. On his way through the room he checked with a couple of the younger officers to ensure that they were focussed on their tasks in hand. They all gave him reassurances and he could feel confident that he had a good crew around him on this case.

As he walked into the room that Tommy Rees and Carole Walker occupied, Tommy was bending down to the video, inserting a tape. He glanced over his shoulder, saying, 'Won't be a sec, Tom.'

Carole was not in the room so Rogers sat in her chair. Rees stood back and pushed the appropriate buttons on the remote control. The television screen came to life with a snowstorm of white on a black background.

'Won't take a second,' said Rees. The seconds passed and he muttered something like, 'Silly sods haven't rewound it, probably.' He went back to the video and ejected the tape. He studied the tape in his hands and said, 'Hmm, looks okay – should be working.' He inserted it back into the machine and once again pushed the buttons. The same snowy screen appeared on the TV screen.

'Got the right video channel, Tom?' asked Rogers innocently.

'Yeah, I think I managed that,' was the curt reply; but he did check to make sure. He pushed the fast forward button and the snowy scene became a swirling blizzard.

'Either this is the wrong tape, or some tit has not had it running.'

'Can you follow that up Tom, please?' asked Rogers politely, 'I could do with knowing.'

'I'll get back to you,' Rees answered, with a distinct sound of irritation in his voice.

Rogers went back to his desk, annoyed at the prospect of a lead being obstructed in this way. He allocated the transport reports to two officers whom he thought would be careful enough not to miss the needle, should there even be one in that particular haystack, and then he turned back to the door-to-door reports. He personally wanted to review these because in his experience a lot of serious crimes were committed by local people, and neighbours often had something of use to say regarding the wild, dangerous man at number thirty-two, or the shy, reclusive, strange young man at number nineteen.

Mansell was upstairs with Chief Superintendent Burns. The senior officer had called Mansell to his office and when Mansell got there he was a little surprised to find the police surgeon and the senior forensics officer already there.

'Come in, Len,' welcomed Chief Superintendent Burns.

Mansell went to the empty chair positioned at the corner of a huge walnut desk. He nodded to the two gentlemen already seated by the desk and said simply, 'Morning.'

'Len, I've called you up because Philip and Joe here have come to me with some disturbing news.'

Mansell jumped in, almost involuntarily, 'He's struck before, then. It is serial?'

'That's what I can confirm, yes.' The Chief was not pleased with the interruption.

'Philip here has seen the case notes of A, B and C and the stab wounds are very consistent in size, type, angle, everything. The others were mutilated, of course, but if our man hadn't been disturbed here I'm sure it would have been the same again. What ties it up of course are forensics. Fingerprints are the same in all cases. You can add a D to the list, I'm afraid.'

'I've got Durham, Northumbria and Manchester guys coming for one o'clock, and you're all welcome to attend; it might be useful,' volunteered Mansell.

Gonzalez and Burrows both nodded and said that they would be there. The Chief looked at the diary on his desk.

'Hmm, already got a meeting with Head of Finance, discussing budgets for 1999, I think. I suppose I could cancel.'

'No need to, sir, I can report back to you after the meeting,' said Mansell, half expecting an insistence that the Chief attend the big meeting; but Burns said, 'Okay, that would be a help. Bugger to tie down, you know, this finance guy.'

They talked for a few more minutes and in that time Mansell requested a full report from both the surgeon and forensics officers that proved conclusively the links between A, B and C and now D. Mansell was pleased to hear the news that a further public appeal was possibly to take place; from his knowledge of profiling and psychological matters he knew that a killer could be profoundly affected by the sight of his victim's family begging for help and for the killer to give himself up.

They discussed the possibility of conducting a massive DNA screening exercise but agreed that this was not the appropriate time. The surgeon and forensics expert both suggested that with more time they would be able to provide a reasonable picture from DNA samples available to them, and Mansell was encouraged by this. If they could prove a physical outline, to which he could attach a mental profile, then this together would narrow the field of suspects.

The meeting broke up and Mansell had just got back to his room when his secretary told him that senior officers from Durham and Northumbria were waiting for him in Reception. He went to greet them, surprised that it was already 12.45. They moved into a conference room and made the necessary introductions. They exchanged pleasantries and Mansell explained that the officers from Manchester were expected any minute. Mansell rang the front desk and asked the girl there to page Joe Barrow and Philip Gonzalez. A minute later both men came to the room and as they were shaking hands the phone rang to advise that two gentlemen from Manchester had arrived. They were shown in, and the nine men sat around the well-polished oak table.

Mansell immediately got down to business. He quickly, but comprehensively, described the sequence of events from the first call just after midnight Friday night, to Sanders' statement, the press conferences and the media coverage. Then he went in to some detail on the various reports to date. Firstly he confirmed that officers were sifting through initial reports covering door-to-door enquiries, transport means and CCTV footage. He then turned to forensic and medical reports to hand. Although busy presenting his summary of the position, Mansell could feel the heightening of attention when he turned to these areas. He detailed the wounds suffered by Wendy Fell and noticed one or two heads nod in confirmation that they had heard similar details before. He then announced that the same fingerprints were on the body that had been found on girls murdered in Manchester, Sunderland and Durham.

'I have copies of your files, thanks for that, but obviously what I was hoping for today was a chat with yourselves – who know about this guy – to see if you can tell me anything which may not be in the bald facts of the files.'

Chief Superintendent Morris from Northumbria Force spoke first.

'These gentlemen and myself have met before with a similar aim, and I'm afraid that everything that we have come up with is indeed in the files. It's certainly a strange case in that we know a lot about this man, his blood type, elements of DNA, fingerprints, shoe size and other issues, but we collectively don't think we have come close to him. No pattern that the computers can give us, no occupation that the profilers can pinpoint, no obvious mode of transport. Would you agree, gentlemen?'

Several men nodded and Detective Sergeant Jewell of the Durham Force spoke.

'I'm afraid that that is correct. Hopefully, when you feed the data from the weekend into the computers then maybe something will click, but I'm not sure that we can add too much.'

Mansell was a little disappointed and surprised at what he perceived to be a defeatist attitude; he had been expecting a little more aggression and determination. He did not want his disappointment to show, so he said, 'I appreciate that, gentlemen, I think what I'd like to ask you is more to do with gut feelings than facts, which as you say are detailed in the files. If I could ask you to comment on what you feel this guy's about... if you can, suggest, how you think we're going to catch him.'

He looked around the table, expecting a rush of comment and ideas but for a few seconds nothing was forthcoming. He was puzzled because all police officers, junior or senior, usually loved to expound their personal theories and views on any case that you could put to them. Why the goddamn reluctance now?

DS Jewell spoke again. 'He seems either to be the world's luckiest man or just incredibly brilliant at planning, timing and execution. Like Friday, he's even been seen now, and yet I bet that somehow that doesn't lead anywhere. Personally, to answer your points, I think that he's not the classic loner, but that he's mature and wise. I think that his motivation is not sexual per se, although he gets kicks from the act of killing. The mutilation is a statement of his hate of either women generally or young women specifically. Jilted perhaps, but that hardly narrows it down. I think that he's clever and cool and takes risks because he feels safe and secure, either because he's confident of his planning or because of some protection that he's given by his demons or whatever. The randomness is a massive problem, but it's certain that he will kill again.

'As to catching him, he needs to drop a bollock, big time, or we need some huge slice of luck. It strikes me that good detective work simply isn't enough, for some reason. All our Forces' – he waved a hand at his fellow officers around the table – 'have worked long and hard on these cases. Good work, but it's got us nowhere positive.'

He stopped abruptly, as if the negative aspects to his comments were a little too strong.

Mansell appreciated the input but was taken aback by the pessimistic tone of the words. He looked at the other officers and asked, 'Do these sentiments coincide with your feelings about this case?'

'Pretty much,' concurred Detective Superintendent Wellesley from Manchester. 'We have explored every avenue on our case, done all the cross-linking with the other cases, taken literally thousands of statements and followed up hundreds of leads and – zilch. Like a gentlemen said earlier we don't believe that we've got close to this person. Very frustrating, I can tell you.'

He didn't have to tell Mansell, he could see it for himself. All hopes of an exciting brainstorming session at which they agreed where to look for this man, his potential haunts and how to track him down, were well and truly extinguished.

They talked for another half an hour but Mansell did not glean much from this further conversation, and he decided to wrap up the meeting.

'I thank you all very much for taking time out today, I really do appreciate it. As you know, the links between A, B and C have been well suppressed to date, and that has allowed you to conduct your cases without too much media intrusion, and has also minimised the chances of any copycat killings. Now, however, the option to suppress is removed; there are too many questions being asked and it would be extremely naïve of us to believe that the media will let it go. I'd appreciate your input into whether you agree that we should openly declare that we have a serial killer.'

'Yes, I'd agree totally,' said a detective from Newcastle. 'Hit the media hard, big coverage, try to flush him out – and it gives the media nowhere to go.'

'That's what I'm thinking,' said Mansell, grateful that the meeting had yielded at least one positive comment. Nobody dissented from the view expressed.

It was agreed that Mansell would forward his files to the other forces by the end of the week, and each senior officer promised to react to it immediately, each taking a personal interest from the receipt of the file.

Mansell was satisfied that the meeting had ended on a slightly more positive note and left the room determined to produce a thorough file that would give his colleagues the best possible chance of making some important connection or breakthrough.

After the handshakes and farewells, Mansell strolled back to his room, speaking to no one. His initial instinct about this crime had pretty well been confirmed over the last couple of hours. It was one of those cases – the exceptional, the very difficult, the frightening. Frightening, because as all police officers knew, the most challenging case you could face was the one where the criminal was not logical in his selection process, but acted without mercy, sentiment or any sign of human emotional frailty. Add in a motivation that was strong and not open to logical debate and you have every policeman's worst nightmare.

Trying to catch a madman – that's what Mansell decided he was trying to do.

Chapter Fifteen

The media machine really clicked into life on the Monday morning. The coverage on Saturday and Sunday had been intense for sure, but as both media and police knew, it was usually the third morning that was the big one. By then the investigative reporters had done forty-eight hours sniffing and had always dug up new, varied and exciting leads. The sequence of coverage was not set in stone but followed a well-established pattern. Day one: shock horror; day two: reasonably detailed facts but lots of speculation; day three: interview with family, friends, authoritative sources, criminologists, psychiatrists, the public, etc., etc.; day four: a passing mention down the news agenda, thereafter, forgotten unless a dramatic development or revelation came to the fore.

So day three arrived and the media did not disappoint.

Wendy Fell's image was everywhere, from recent holiday snaps to school photographs, the latter being used to emphasise the sweet innocence of the victim of such a hideous crime. Teachers from the same era as the photograph appeared on television and in print to state unequivocally that Wendy was remembered as a good student, a popular girl who had a lovely sense of humour and a kind nature. Such a tragedy.

Chief Superintendent Burns was reported as confirming that Wendy had been found at Stockton on Friday night on a patch of common ground near the path that crossed from town to suburbs, known locally as the 'brickie'. She had been out for a quiet drink in town with two close friends, one of whom left her at around 11.15 when she went to go to a nightclub; and the other at about 11.30 when she left Wendy to go to a party. The time of the girl's departure from the High Street was confirmed at 11.40 by closed-circuit television footage.

The two friends were interviewed. Suzie was calm and collected but Geraldine could only manage a few words before the lump in her throat leapt to her mouth and blocked her words.

Suzie confirmed the teacher's assessment of Wendy. 'She was always full of fun, but she was very bright and hard working too,' making the point as if to suggest a sense of fun and conscientious attitude were usually mutually exclusive. 'She was going to be a vet and she would have been good at that,' Suzie stated as fact.

Neighbours of her parents spoke well of Wendy, telling tales of good deeds, a friendly smile and their expectation that she would go far.

Family members, mainly uncles and aunts, spoke movingly of the lovely girl who was a loving daughter. Their tragic loss was doubly hard to accept because Wendy was such a paragon of virtue. Who could do such a wicked deed? And her being so happy, having just got a new job and a new flat.

Who indeed? And that was where the media efficiency glowed. As an impartial observer, you had to be impressed by the depth of the coverage that third morning.

Aerial shots of the brickie and route to town were highlighted, with circled areas noting Wendy's home and the point where she was murdered. Dots emphasised the route she had taken from town. All options of the murderer's route before and after the murder were considered, with road maps, train and bus timetables detailed and analysed.

Experienced specialists explained the type of man who could and would do such a thing, and listed what he may have been thinking, his nature, his possible employment.

The links were made strongly with previous murders. Locations, times, victim profiles were splayed across the column inches, and suddenly there was unanimity that there was a serial killer on the loose. The case was strongly made in terms such as 'There is a serial killer…' But the evidence was less than conclusive, upon close inspection. Several papers showed old photographs of previous victims and numbered them one, two and three, warning that number four was only a matter of time.

Senior police officers had reacted quickly to the reporting, worried that it could lead to a public panic which would only hinder the enquiry. Whilst public assistance was needed, they did not want to be swamped by thousands of suggestions that 'the man next door is worth looking at, his eyebrows are too close together'. So on day three they launched an appeal on television and radio for concrete help.

'Anybody who saw Wendy and her friends in the pubs in Stockton that night, we would like to hear from you. You may be able to tell us something of significance. Anybody who saw Wendy walking the half mile or so from the High Street to the brickie, please contact us. You may well have noticed Wendy because it was a wet, miserable night and not too many people were about on foot that evening.'

The broadcast emphasised that Wendy had not accepted a lift, as far as the police were aware, which served to emphasise how sensible she was; she was not one to forget the message drummed into her over the years: 'Never accept a lift off a stranger.'

'We are working presently on the basis that the killer had local knowledge so we urgently need help in tracing everybody who was in the same pubs as Wendy on Friday.'

The public expressed concerns that one, a serial killer was not established as being out there; and two, he could be living amongst them. Many members of the public also referred to the sad spectacle of the day before of Mr and Mrs Fell's press statement, saying their strain had really struck a chord.

One of the pub landlords thought he knew Wendy as being among the regular faces and confirmed that everybody else was right – she was nice, what a waste.

The vicar of the parish church had offered prayers for Wendy on Sunday and now, on Monday, proffered the view that every murder was a crime against God, the community and humanity; made worse, he concluded, when the victim was so well thought of.

Some reports referred to the supposed witness and the possibilities that this could create; other reports detailed that the witness was a man in his twenties who lived near the brickie and had seen the murder.

Police tried to deflect questions regarding the identity of the witness by hinting that they were looking at other unsolved murders which had certain similarities, particularly in respect of the weapons used, but they could not shake the media hounds off the track.

Later editions of local newspapers talked of the 'screwdriver killer' and the 'blade killer', not really sure of the more significant title.

Police officers had a tough day fending off accusations of withholding information about a known serial killer, not warning the public, and of being partially responsible for the death of Wendy Fell. They expected the line of enquiry, but that did not make it easy to cope with, especially when certain elements of the media revelled in rubbing the police's noses in the dirt.

On the evening news, as if to mark a crescendo of media intensity, Wendy Fell's father appealed again in front of the cameras. It was not a formal news conference and it took the police by surprise. Mr Fell had simply marched out of his front door at 6.15 and said to the assembled throng, 'I wish to say something.'

The news bulletin had broken into an item covering the latest crisis in the Balkans to take Mr Fell's statement.

'Although still at a loss to explain how we no longer have Wendy, my head insists it is true, though my heart refuses to believe it.' He swallowed hard. 'I know that everybody has heard it all before, I know I have; the plaudits and praise and almost unbelievable universal acknowledgement of goodness, attributed, it seems, to almost every victim of murder. Although I'm biased, I believe those fine words to be true of Wendy; but that's not why I am here. I want to say please catch the killer of my daughter. He hasn't to be found because she was perfect. Perfection, beauty, loveliness do not come into it. What does matter is that she was a daughter; she was a life.'

His voice broke a little at 'was', but he composed himself.

'My request, my appeal, is to all parents, no matter what age, no matter what relationship is held with those sons and daughters.

Just take a minute, literally one minute, and imagine your flesh and blood is dead. Just like that: dead. Not ill, very ill, terminally ill; just dead. Gone forever. Just imagine…'

He paused, and the assembled microphones and camera seemed somehow to hold their breath. This was dynamite.

Mr Fell continued. 'Not even "just dead", but horribly slain. Stabbed in the back, stabbed in the leg, beaten… and then her throat cut. Please imagine that.'

He drifted away, obviously imagining precisely that, and his eyes filled with tears. The media personnel buzzed messages down lines of communication, television directors barking back, 'Stay with him! He's on a roll, there's more to come!'

Nobody spoke to Mr Fell, each reporter fearful of the conse-quences of breaking his concentration and flow of information. The police who were watching the little drama unfold, live on camera, cursed, but knew that it was now impossible to stop.

Mr Fell continued. 'So you see it's more than the standard nightmare that people would associate with the loss of a child. Far worse, because nightmares fade away in the morning light. This, for us, is the end of our lives, because not only have we lost our light, but we'll never be able to live with the knowledge that Wendy died in pain and fear. Our lives are over; my appeal is made so that nobody else has to suffer such a fate. The fate that has befallen me and my family is, indeed, truly a fate worse than death. I know; I wish I was dead.' He took a moment, then sighed a deep sigh as if the strain of his speech had drained his energy. 'So all I ask is that whoever out there knows anything, whether it appears trivial or insignificant, please contact the police. Not for me or my wife, or even Wendy, but for the other parents out there who must not be allowed to be tortured this way; I beg you. Thank you for your time.'

He turned back to his driveway and walked slowly to the front door. The questions flew thick and fast, louder and louder, but Mr Fell never turned back.

The seven o'clock news led with Mr Fell's speech, and a mav-erick criminal psychiatrist, already on the programme to air his opinion that the killer probably worshipped the devil and believed his victims were sensible sacrifices, was asked to explain Mr Fell's mental state and the real message in his words. The professor lapped it up.

The nine o'clock news devoted fifteen minutes of its available thirty to the murder of Wendy Fell, the existence of a serial killer, and her father's speech. Just when the police observing felt that the time was being spent repeating earlier coverage, there was another twist to the saga. Three young men had come forward having seen Mr Fell's plea. They remembered driving along the road leading past the brickie, at around midnight on Friday night. They had seen a man and a woman kissing, somewhere near the brickie they thought, and bashfully had to admit that they had shouted some corny joke to the amorous couple. And no, it had not been obscene. And yes, now they thought about it, the description of Wendy, her physical appearance and clothes, did not sound dissimilar to what they remembered of the girl they'd seen sucking face.

The reporter who had pushed the microphone under the noses of the three young men could barely conceal his glee. 'What a breakthrough!' he crowed. 'Either this courting couple needs to be traced to eliminate them from possible enquiries, or to be interviewed for something that surely they heard or saw, being so close to the murder scene at the right time. Or…' he paused for effect, '…maybe these young men saw Wendy and a *boyfriend*. A boyfriend who perhaps snapped for some reason that we can only speculate on. This appears to be a significant breakthrough, and I am sure that the police will react accordingly.' He almost smiled at the end of his report, so delighted was he with the scoop.

The ten o'clock news headlined the three young men and questioned, 'Who were this couple, so close in time and location to the brutal slaying of Wendy Fell?'

The newsroom was almost overwhelmed with angles on the Wendy Fell murder and scrubbed interviews with neighbours, family and forensic experts. Instead they covered Mr Fell, the three youths and then managed to grab Suzie, Wendy's friend, at 10.25. She was quizzed about Wendy's boyfriends, past and present. But the girl appeared genuinely puzzled by the line of questioning. Sure, Wendy had had boyfriends, but none for a while, and all the exes that she could think of had parted on good terms. She knew that Wendy had no current boyfriend and most definitely had no male company on Friday.

The reporter was a little disappointed that Suzie had not said in dramatic fashion, 'Yes, Wendy said she was going to meet John Smith, an old flame, at midnight on the brickie.' The rapidly changing events of the last few hours had given him hope that anything was possible.

The news concluded with a summary of the murder enquiry developments and finished on Mr Fell's last few words.

The fourth morning broke the rules, because it was meant to be the time to move on to fresh stories. Today the media blazoned even more headlines, pictures and reports about the previous day's developments in the murder enquiry.

A whole page was devoted in one tabloid to Wendy's friends who analysed Wendy's love life over the past five years. They also picked up on the injuries detailed by Mr Fell and tearfully expressed how horror was now heaped upon horror at their disclosure.

'How could such a happy, normal night out end so horribly?' one of them said weepily to the cameras.

Another tabloid offered £20,000 for information leading to the capture of this 'monster in our midst'.

Mansell saw Burns early that morning and advised him of two things. Of all the detective work and reports disseminated so far the most significant thing to report was that the CCTV at the railway station had not been switched on.

'Good equipment in working order, good tape, just not switched on. Can you believe it? Apparently they hadn't been using it for a while, they'd just got out of the habit.'

'Why so angry, Len?' enquired Burns, genuinely puzzled.

'Just that we've got reports of a guy at about the right time who might be worth a look at.'

'Well, the train can't have had too many stops. Get the tapes from the other stations.'

'Already requested them, sir,' said Mansell respectfully, pleased that at least Burns had indicated an inkling of a policeman's thought processes.

'The more important matter, sir, is that we agreed yesterday, with all other forces, given that we know this guy's a serial, that we tell the press. Declare it, get it over with. Is that okay with you?'

Burns thought for a minute, annoyed that this significant matter had been decided in his absence. Then he realised that he had been unobtainable for hours with the finance guys, so he let it go.

'Fine, I'll organise that with Jenny.'

Burns and Spears organised another conference for the media, at two o'clock, and the experienced hacks guessed what was coming.

They were all surprised, however, when Burns announced that regrettably they had to add a Manchester murder to the list. Their man had killed at least four times.

There had been a lot of demands for questions, but Jenny Spears had spoken, saying, 'I'm sure that you will all agree that our enquiries are at an early stage, we need all our officers to be actively involved in the necessary detective work, so we will hold a further conference in a few days.

'I can repeat the request on behalf of Chief Superintendent Burns that we urgently require anybody with any information whatsoever relating to any of these crimes to come forward.

'Finally, to clear up one point which I am sure will be raised. The previously connected cases were not divulged to the public for reasons of security. Thank you for your patience.'

She abruptly turned and stood by Burns as if waiting for him to escort her out of the stuffy room. He looked a little startled by her presence above him and he jumped up and walked out.

Sam Westmain had watched the new bulletins, read the papers and listened to the radio throughout Monday and Tuesday.

He had scoffed at the various reports on wonderful Wendy, and felt no emotion at Mr Fell's speech. After two profiles given by so called experts on the Monday he had gone to his journal and written,

They know nothing. They speculate, guess and assume but they know nothing. Maybe it's you, Lord, clouding their judgement; maybe they are simply inefficient. They know nothing.

He had just watched a late bulletin on the Tuesday night and it occurred to him that this was his time. Everybody was talking about him, everybody knew of him. They would never know him because they would never catch him, but he was in people's lives. They were hearing his statement, admiring his work.

Maybe he should emphasise his abilities; maybe he should make a particularly grand gesture. Maybe he should kill a *man*.

Chapter Sixteen

His seventh year was not a good one.

A simple punishment was carried out in the summer of 1966, when he was not allowed to watch the World Cup Final. Football was one of the few things that he had an interest in and a little later that year the boy developed a stammer. One day it just appeared when he said to his mother, 'M–m–m–Mam, c–c–can I have some b–b–br–bread?'

His mother looked at him suspiciously and asked, 'You taking the piss?'

'No, M–M–Mam, my w–w–words are s–s–st–st–stuck.'

She looked at him with a grin then a smile, then a laugh. 'Are you sure you're not kidding?'

'N–n–no Mam!

'It's God, you know, he's punishing you for being so naughty, so nasty and so evil. He was always going to get you, you know.'

'I d–d–don't like it, Mu–Mu–Mummy!' he choked, tears welling.

'Tough shit! Tell God,' was the callous reply.

He had the stammer for nearly three years, and then one day it just went. He woke up near his tenth birthday and he spoke a sentence without a stutter. His mother had said, 'Don't get carried away, God'll think of something else.'

He went to his room and wept into his pillow. His life at school had always been tough because he was so obviously different from all his classmates, but the time since the stammer developed had been almost unbearable. Children can be devilishly cruel and his disability was mercilessly taunted. Now that it had gone, all he wanted was someone to share his relief, his escape; but there was nobody.

From that day on he would wake and immediately say a sentence, anything at all that came into his head, like, 'The sun is shining today.' 'It is a cold morning,' or 'It is Saturday and I'm off.' Absolutely anything would do, but every morning he had to check that his dreaded stammer had not returned.

Having proved to himself that he was stutter-free, he would spend an anxious few seconds tensing different parts of his body, toes, feet, legs, stomach, hands, arms, eyes, just to make sure that that was not the day when God had decided to render him paralysed, infirm, blind or whatever. He knew that it was only a matter of time before some horrible affliction was visited upon him, because his mother had told him it would happen, and she was always right. Like the times she had told him that because he was worthless, because he had been the cause of so much pain in his short life, he would make no friends at school. That had been true.

When he was ten he had discovered 'Desiderata' at school, a short poem by Max Ehrmann. He thought it was beautiful, even if he didn't understand half of it, so he decided to memorise it. He didn't tell his mother about it. Every morning he would recite a couple of lines and try and try to add another, and after only a few weeks he was word perfect.

He decided to adopt the first few lines as a way of life, because the teacher had said it meant 'be nice', and that agreed with what his mother said he had to be.

> Go placidly amid the noise and the haste, and remember what peace there may be in silence. As far as possible, without surrender, be on good terms with all persons.

Strangely, and for no obvious reason other than that he tried so desperately hard to be good every day, God did not punish him heavily. There were only minor reprimands now and again. Like when, in the middle of winter, Mummy said that God had taken all the electricity and they lived by two candles for a week, eating cold food and washing in cold water. Like that time God put tiny, tiny bits of glass in his food and he cut his tongue badly, and it bled for two hours. Or that time when he must have been nasty because God did get upset. He knew He was mad because his mother had come into his bedroom early one morning when he was twelve and sat on the end of his bed. She'd looked serious.

'What is it, Mam?' he asked. They were his first words of the day, and he said a mental thank you for no stutter. He didn't have time to flex his muscles as he listened intently to his mother.

'God has spoken to me during the night, Sam.'

He got a shock at the words because his mother very rarely called him by his name. What was going on?

She spoke softly, another unusual occurrence, and her soft tone added to the weight and menace of her words.

'He came to me and spoke to me. He said that although you have tried hard He cannot forget your early days, like Grandma and all that. He told me how to punish you.'

His head reeled. What had he done? This really was unfair, he had tried so hard, it was just bloody unfair…

'Don't, Mummy, please don't,' he pleaded.

'It's not me, it's God telling me.'

He imagined the beating to come and quivered under the sheets. To his amazement, his mother stood up from the bed and undid the cord at the waist of her tatty grey dressing gown. She slipped off the gown and stood before him, naked. He stared goggle-eyed at her body, eyes fixed first on her breasts and then moving down to her pubic hair.

She moved closer to him and pulled back the covers. He lay in a T-shirt and underpants and she leant over him and pulled his underpants down. He shrieked, 'What are you doing?' But as he tried to raise himself off the bed she pushed him hard in the chest, knocking him flat. She yanked his pants down his legs and over his feet.

She told him, 'Move over, and don't forget that it's God who told me what to do.' He shuffled to his left and she slid into bed next to him. He was totally bewildered and lay there uncertain of what he could or should do. His mother's breasts pushed into his chest as she turned to him. He felt a strange sensation shiver through his body. The mixed senses he was experiencing went into overdrive when his mother cupped a hand around his testicles and started massaging them gently.

'What does God want, Mummy?' he asked in a pathetic, confused voice.

'He's told me to perform an act with you, then you'll have to live with it the rest of your life, always remembering it whenever you have bad thoughts about girls.'

Oh God! Now it made sense… This was all because he had seen Beverley Thomas at school and got excited about her, thinking about kissing her and stuff. Beverley was in the class above his, probably thirteen, and absolutely gorgeous, but now this was happening because of those nasty thoughts.

She was rubbing his penis now and he was fully erect. She kissed the top of his head and her breasts moved against his body. She moved her hand to take his hand, and she picked it up and placed it on her vagina. She pushed his fingers into her lips and gently started to masturbate using his fingers. She moaned and moved her hand back to his swollen penis. His hand moved involuntarily between her legs. Then she swung her leg over his and pulled the head of his penis into her moist opening. She moaned as she sunk her vagina over his penis and slowly fucked him. He lay rigid, unmoving, but gave a little grunt as he climaxed and ejaculated into his mother. As she felt him come into her she rushed to orgasm, emitting a great 'Aaaawwww!' It scared him, making him think he'd hurt her. Then she pulled off him and said, 'God will be pleased that you did not make a fuss. Good boy.'

She left the room and he was left to his overwhelming thoughts.

It was only now sinking in what he had just done. All the whispering and sniggering at school by his contemporaries, it was nearly always about sex, and although he was rarely party to the chatter he got the drift that it involved pictures of naked women or talk of touching, kissing, playing with or doing things to girlfriends or fantasies. But never mothers. He realised with a jolt that God had issued a peculiar but effective punishment, and he knew that it was going to work when the feeling of guilt and shame swept over him like a tidal wave.

And so at sixteen he had formed the simplest of plans. Knowing his mother's routine, knowing her sleepy, yawning traipse down the stairs at eight o'clock every morning for her first slurping of coffee and slopping cereal, all he had to do was trip her at the top of the stairs. He had thought about pushing her, but reckoned that she might react to his approach, so decided that a simple tripping device was called for.

A trip to a fishing tackle shop on the far side of town procured some very fine fishing line. He tested it when she was out at the shops, tying it to the top baluster of the stairs' handrail and stretching it tightly across to the nearest handle, which was on the bathroom door. No good; it raised the line too high. He found that the only thing he could do was to bang a nail into the floor along the landing near the skirting board next to the bathroom door. The line could then be stretched tightly enough to take the weight of a foot kicking against it. He obviously did not want the line snapping at the impact of a leg hitting it, or the nail lifting from the floor, but his tests satisfied him that it would work. He was delighted at how invisible the line was against the background of the green patterned carpet. He was so happy with the test results that he decided to do it the next morning.

He set his radio alarm for 6 a.m., setting the volume low. He arose quietly and crept on to the landing. He listened at her bedroom door and could hear her breathing heavily in her sleep. Probably drunk or drugged, he thought, without rancour. He had prepared a hole in the floor the day before, so now he inserted his six-inch nail, sinking it so that only one inch showed above the carpet. He tied the fishing line tightly around the nail, tugging at it to ensure it was held fast. He then stretched the line to the baluster at the top of the stairs. He fastened the line around the baluster and again pulled hard to confirm that the knots would not untangle. He revisited the nail. Wearing his heaviest shoes, he pushed it down with his foot. The nail sank a little further, but he knew that it was not going to budge with a kick at the line.

He stood back and decided that you could not really glance and see the line, you had to really look for it, and his mother would certainly not be doing that. He went back to his room and stood just inside the door. He stood there for an hour then realised that he was very cold so went to his wardrobe and pulled on a jumper and a pair of baggy jogging bottoms. He returned to his place by the door, listening for any hint of movement in his mother's room. At 7.55, right on cue, he heard her shuffling around, probably looking for misplaced slippers. Just after 8 a.m., she emerged, as always bleary-eyed and appearing as if another hour in bed was needed. It usually was, and she often felt even worse than she looked, but she had got into a totally addictive routine of coffee and cereal at 8 a.m. It was weird, and even she could not possibly explain the illogicality of the dreary wander to her breakfast.

Her grey dressing gown hanging loosely around her held so much significance for Sam that he was glad she was wearing it on this special morning. His door was slightly ajar, and as he peeped out through the tiny crack he saw her take a couple of shuffling steps to the top of the stairs. He wanted to shout, 'Go on, go on!' But he held his breath, because she hesitated. For a moment, blind panic threatened to overwhelm him, thinking that she had seen the line, but he realised with huge relief that she was just emitting an enormous yawn. She had not got it completely out of her system as she stepped forward. Her cry of surprise registered that she had struck the line and he watched in delighted awe as she moved – as if in slow motion – forward into nothingness. Her arms flailed but she was grasping at air and she was soon bouncing and tumbling, face first, down the stairs. She made a lot of noise going down those stairs, crashing, banging, a couple of shouts, then finally a thud and silence. No moans or groans; nothing.

He quickly followed her down the stairs, noticing immediately a few flecks of blood on the banister, wall and treads. She lay grotesquely twisted at the bottom of the stairs. Her left arm was almost behind her, horribly dislocated, and she lay half on her back, half on her side.

He stepped over her and his initial thought was, That's gone even better than I hoped for. Her eyes were closed and there was a lot of blood on the bottom stair near the back of her head. Her right leg had a big gash in it just below the knee.

Is she dead? he wondered, curious but not at all remorseful at the prospect that he might, as planned, have killed her. He knelt down beside her and said calmly, 'Mother dear, oh Mother dear, are you there?'

Her eyelids flickered briefly but they did not open. He put his ear to her mouth and could sense a little breath. He picked up her limp wrist and patiently waited for a pulse. One duly arrived, but it was weak and erratic. He stared at her and asked, 'Mother, can you hear me?' and giggled, because the words reminded him of a comedy show that he had once heard on the radio.

Her eyes flickered and this time they opened. 'What...?' she whispered.

He then spoke in a slow, deliberate voice, as if talking to an old relative who was deaf or confused.

'You've had a nasty fall, you fell over some fishing line.' He enjoyed her bewildered expression.

'Wha'? What... fish line?'

'Yes, dear Mother, fishing line, which I put there.' He was slightly disappointed that there was no response to this confession.

'Wakey, wakey!' he said as he noticed her eyes closing, and for good measure he slapped her cheek. He spoke in that voice again.

'You see, I'm going to kill you.'

'What did you say?' she slurred.

'I'm going to kill you.' He was happy to repeat it.

'Like *this*,' he said, and he grabbed both her ears in his hands and pulled her head from the floor. There was a soggy squelching sound as the head left a pool of sticky blood. He bent towards her and with their noses almost touching he said with a hiss, 'Die, you fucking bitch!' He recognised the fear in her eyes and revelled in it, adding, 'And there will be more.'

In her final moments she knew that she had created a monster.

He rammed her head into the floor and she moaned.

'Bitch,' he spat. He pulled her head up and again thumped it down into the floor. And again, and then for a fourth time. This time there was more of a splattering noise, rather than the previous more solid thumps. He held her ears still and a little more gingerly pulled her head from the spreading mess on the carpet. He looked a little closer at the back of her head and smiled at the mess he saw. Crushed skull, blood and matter mangled together in a deadly mix. If she had been alive to see his smile she would have found it terrifying, evil.

He marvelled at the clinical, unemotional pleasure that he had derived from the previous few minutes and the control that he had exerted over his actions and feelings.

His heart was possibly beating a little harder and there may have been a bead of perspiration on his brow, but hey, this was his first murder, give a guy a break!

He stood up and considered his options. First thing would be to retrieve the line and nail, cover up his nail hole then dispose of the line. He did this first, pocketing the line.

'Now how could she have quite so much head damage?' he asked aloud. He worked out that if she'd gone arse over tit right at the top of the stairs, making her somersault her way to the bottom, then in theory she could have cracked her head about five times. In which case all he needed to do was emphasise the nature of the fall with a little evidence.

He scooped up a palm full of blood off the carpet and went up the stairs. He calculated the earliest point where her head could have connected with wall or stair and he deposited some blood accordingly. He repeated this twice more. Then, for the next chosen spot, he picked from his mother's skull some bone and brain matter. He dropped this on to the second stair from the foot.

He checked his handiwork and thought it looked convincing. He thought about the line and decided to hide it in his bedroom now and dispose of it later. He walked very carefully upstairs, avoiding the original blood trail and the one that he had laid. He hid the line in an old shoebox at the back of his wardrobe; it already containing knick-knacks and bits of accumulated junk.

He was splattered with blood but that could easily be explained by him having cradled his beloved mother's head as he heroically comforted the dying woman.

He called the emergency services, adding a tremor to his voice, garbling his message about a fall, the shock, the blood. He screamed and told them to hurry.

The ambulance crew found him in a distressed state when he opened the door. He was apparently hysterical, screaming, 'Save her! Somebody save my mother! But it was too late, she had suffered a terrible fall. The ambulance men, hardened as they were, were nauseated at finding the woman, brains partly scattered over the bottom of the stairs.

'What a mess!' one of them muttered.

They felt a great sympathy for the young lad, he was obviously in terrible shock and denial and they comforted him the best they could. When the police arrived a few minutes later, the senior ambulance man had a quiet word with the first officer through the door. He explained the scene and said, 'The lad's in trouble, we'll give him a shot and I think we'd better trace his doctor. How the hell you get over that I'll never know. What a thing to witness!'

The paramedic and the police officer both shook their heads. 'Wasn't life sometimes just too cruel.'

Chapter Seventeen

He had gone to work on the Monday morning, arriving just before nine. The salon was already open, the boss and a couple of the girls already busy with their first appointments of the day. He gave them all a cheery greeting.

'Morning, Sorry! Morning, girls!'

He received a nod from Stig 'Sorry' Sorensen, and the girls said, 'Hi, Sam,' and 'Morning, Sam.'

'Everybody all right?' he enquired generally.

'Apart from having a nutter on the streets, smashing,' squeaked Alice in her falsetto voice.

'Yeah, just what were you doing Friday night, Sam?' asked Sorry with a smile.

'That's not funny at all,' said Suzie angrily. 'A girl died and it could have been any of us.'

Sorry's immediate retort was going to be a jocular, 'No such luck.' But he sensed the atmosphere and volunteered a meek, 'Sorry.' No point in having them up in arms; quality and quantity would definitely suffer.

'Yeah, bad news, isn't it,' said Sam. 'You're not safe anywhere.'

'You're not kidding!' piped Alice. 'The sooner they get him the better! Nobody's safe.'

Some are safer than others, thought Sam to himself wryly.

The girls continued to discuss the murder and as the other staff arrived the same points were revisited and discussed anew.

Sam busied himself with preparing his station. He was in no great hurry; his first appointment was at 9.20. He sorted his equipment and materials. There was always something to track down that had been borrowed.

Sorry sighed; the girls were prepared to discuss the murder with every new client and he was already bored with it. Every further conversation added a new rumour, a new twist. Chinese whispers in action, he mused, marvelling how in the first half an hour of business, general opinions on a nasty crime had moved into specific details of weapons, motives, physical descriptions and mental profile.

'I heard that he was a big bloke and he raped her then cut her throat and then cut her breasts off.'

'Yeah, I know a lad who works with a lad where the police drink and he heard that he was trying to cut her head off, cos that's what he's done before, but that witness stopped him.'

And so forth. Every new line being dissected, and what was dismissed as poppycock at a quarter past nine was now, half an hour later, being repeated as fact.

As the morning wore on and Sorry's frustration grew at the whole overblown event, he took a chance with a break from appointments to move from girl to girl, saying quietly, 'You know, I think that the story is a little gory for some of our clientele. Can we lay off it a bit, please?'

He mentioned that some of the blue-rinse brigade could not be expected to appreciate Shell, Lisa, Tracey or whoever, expounding their theories on why Wendy Fell had had innards strewn around the brickie or had her tits cut off to be used as ornamental bowls, or how the witness saw the bastard cutting her fanny out to use as a hairpiece. Enough!

He was not sure whether he had got the message across, but it struck him that maybe he was making a valid point, and it wasn't just his boredom factor at issue here.

He looked to the reception area where two elderly ladies sat patiently enjoying the complimentary coffee and biscuits.

They were used to chat and gossip at the salon, Christ, that was part of the attraction and pleasure of their visit, but he knew that this was different. It was too local, too pertinent to the girls who visited pubs here in Bishop Auckland and often over in Stockton. It was too damn personal, and that was why there was such an edge to the girls' chatter. There was an intensity and fervour that was not usually there.

He went to Sam and said, 'Keep it light, Sam, we've got to change the record.'

'No problem, boss,' Sam replied.

As the morning wore on, it became apparent to Sorry, Sam and the girls, that the murder and all its ramifications were indeed all the customers wanted to talk about, blue rinses and all. However, Sorry noted that because the customers were driving the conversations and it was them making the wild observations, his employees' stance had now changed and they appeared a lot more reluctant to get involved in gory speculation.

Sam's customers also raised the subject and Sam entered the conversation the same way each time with the question, 'What do you think could drive somebody to do such a thing?' He didn't keep a detailed log but by the end of the day, having dealt with fourteen clients, he guessed that eight had said mental illness or basic madness; two had said devil worship; two said a grudge against women and/or, prostitutes; one suggested an inadequate sex drive or inability to become erect; and one clever one, old Mrs Witherspoon, retired postmistress, thought maybe a horrible childhood could have been partly responsible. He enjoyed hearing that, and he went home at five thirty, satisfied that it had been a good day.

He enjoyed his work anyway, but to be talked about all day long, albeit anonymously, was indeed a pleasure. He recorded it so in his journal. He looked up at the text on his study wall and selected a passage which he read slowly, with feeling: 'Enjoy your achievements as well as your plans. Keep interested in your own career, however humble; it is a real possession in the changing fortunes of time.'

He really did believe in his career as a hairdresser, having worked at the salon since he was thirty-one, previously having had a quick succession of jobs ranging from office clerk at an insur-ance office (which he had hated), to production line manager at a local factory (which he had loved, bossing those girls all day long). He had lost that job when two girls claimed that he had intimi-dated them one night in the staff car park. He protested his innocence, of course, sticking to his story that he was only joking, but mud stuck and he couldn't stay on in that atmosphere. The fact that he had set out that winter's evening to scare the shit out of two bolshie shop steward types was irrelevant, he thought. He left his home town after that and stuck a pin in a map to see where he should go to. The pin duly struck next to Bishop Auckland, County Durham. He knew nothing of Bishop Auckland, although he had a vague recollection it had something to do with football way back in time.

He moved to Bishop Auckland in the summer of 1989, when he was thirty. He rented some acceptable lodgings and set out to find a job. He had decided to stay in an employment that involved women, but had also learnt his lesson from the factory. Acts of revenge against enemies would have to be much more subtle in future and then realised that this was God's way of conveying a message to him. God was saying, 'Don't be subtle, get out there and get one back.'

He had got excited because he knew that he and God were eventually going to work together to carry out a 'plan', and he thought that maybe this was the start. He bought himself a macintosh and stitched into the inside lining some Velcro tape. He then purchased some tools from a local DIY store and put a little tape around the handles. They fitted snugly and easily into his coat lining.

He went prowling every few nights for months but nothing came of it. He felt like an inexperienced hunter who was disturbing his intended prey.

He lost interest for a long time, realising that he must have misinterpreted God's message.

He decided one morning to write down the pros and cons of all possible jobs and then spent four hours mulling over every occupation where there could be interaction with women – with him in some position of power, of course. Then he wrote down in two columns all the good and bad aspects. He ended up with a list of six, which he then applied even more critical criteria to, and he then had a shorter list of two. They were not two jobs that he would have contemplated had not his selection process been responsible. Senior hairdresser and manager of a tele-sales office were his choices. Hairdresser was written first, so he applied next day to every salon in the town, applying for any position whatsoever. Among his replies was one from 'Fringe Benefits'. Having attended two other interviews and not been impressed by the salon or owner, he arrived one day at Fringe Benefits.

Stig 'Sorry' Sorensen had been surprised to find that the applicant, Sam Westmain, was a male, assuming Sam was Samantha. He was also surprised that this male Sam was thirty years old and about to be thirty-one. Sorry knew that he couldn't turn Sam away from the salon but was sure that he was too old to learn, wouldn't fit in with the girls, and was just too damn male for the old dears who liked a chat with the trendy young things. He was wrong on all counts. The interview had gone well for both parties. Sam felt comfortable at this salon and liked the look of Sorry, even though he could see that he was surprised at his gender. Sam's enthusiasm was very pleasing to Sorry and, as they talked, Sorry started to think, Maybe this fella could be an ally – it's been me and the girls too long.

The interview, which became a chat along common themes, cleverly manipulated by Sam, was concluded with Sorry saying, in his lilting Danish accent, 'What the hell, let's give it a go.'

Sam started immediately and proved to be an excellent trainee. He spent two years watching, observing and attending the right night-school classes at a nearby college. During his third year he took exams and passed with flying colours.

The girls at the salon had taken to him from day one. He was courteous, respectful, and despite his more worldly experiences, lorded it over nobody. He was prepared to bide his time. He never made a play for any of them despite their obvious (too obvious) attractiveness; and much as he enjoyed their skimpy outfits and acreage of flesh, he did nothing to dispel the much touted rumour that he was gay.

The customers appeared to appreciate the alternative available to them, to escape occasionally from the dizzy chatter of an excited young female and to talk about more serious matters with a mature man.

Sorry was delighted that his hunch had paid off and he enjoyed being able to discuss 'the big match', cars and his problems with women, rather than the usual staple topics of soap operas, boyfriends and diets. He also presumed Sam to be gay, not because he did not chase his colleagues but because Sam never mentioned girlfriends, girls and conquests, other than in nudge-

nudge, wink-wink terms. 'Score at the weekend, Sam?' Sorry would ask with a smile.

'Big, blonde and beautiful,' Sam would reply, with a wink.

He never gave details and Sorry simply assumed that there was no detail to give. Sorry never saw any evidence; nothing was ever presented to make a case, so it was noted as 'fantasy'. Sorry was not bothered, after all, he, a raging heterosexual, married with three kids, was known locally as a poof. So, so what? Sam was good to have around and his sexual proclivities were irrelevant to Sorry.

Sam knew soon after joining Fringe Benefits that it was a good move. The work was going to be easy. He would be a qualified hairdresser in a few years. He could be a valuable ally to Sorry and in so becoming, would gain power. Furthermore, to work so closely with the type of female that he was going to kill at an increasing rate over the coming years could only be beneficial.

There were currently three Fringe Benefits franchises in the North-East, with numerous others to come, and Sam reckoned that one day he would run one, with all the power that would give him. There were already plenty of branches around the country that he could possibly get seconded to.

He accepted God's challenge to try to understand this breed of person, women. Relished the fact that it was a hefty challenge, almost daunting. He saw women as very different from men. Humans together possibly, but hey, Eve had set the pattern as a mean, selfish, lying bitch, and womankind had followed.

He acknowledged that men could do cruel things, commit cruel deeds, say cruel hurtful words, fight wars and destroy life; but this was what they did as a reaction, usually provoked by a woman-driven act. On the other hand, women were intrinsically cruel, it was in their nature, their make-up. What did women contribute to the world, apart from babies? Did they make things, cure diseases, create beautiful art, change things for the better? No, no, no, fucking no!

So where were women in the grand scheme of things? Well, they weren't were they? God made sure of that. He knew that they would only invoke their cruel bitterness, their revenge for being so fucking inferior, in order to vent their wrath on weaker creatures: either a domineering wife treating a weak husband like a piece of shit, or a mother doing to her infant child the sort of things that his bitch mother had inflicted on him.

So, work with them, occasionally socialise with them, get to know them, the way their feeble minds worked. Learn what sweetness each killing would bring by understanding what he was removing from the face of the earth. One might start to calculate the full effect over the centuries of his anticipated thirty, forty or whatever killings. If he took a conservative thirty and assumed an average four daughters for every six mothers, and if those daughters had a similar ratio of daughters then, by heck, he was effectively removing dozens, even hundreds of pieces of evil! He likened it to diagnosing and treating cancer of the big toe. Deal with it now and you stop it spreading through foot, leg, stomach, chest and head.

He idly supposed that God would maybe stop him one day, saying 'Enough my son, your work is done.' Then he would reluctantly accept the command – but hell, wouldn't he be revered? The world would speak in reverential tones of Sam Westmain, his carefully delivered programme and his amazing contribution to his fellow beings. People would whisper, 'I know the Lord helped Sam, but hey, it was Sam who did it, Sam who led the way, showed women that we were not going to take any more!' Forthwith thousands would be prepared to follow Sam's example, taking inspiration from his great work.

Chapter Eighteen

Jeff had decided on Sunday night that he would go back to work on the Monday. The doctor he had seen had suggested a few days' rest, but Jeff had said that he wasn't tired and was over the shock, so what was the point? Jeff's mother had fussed around him all weekend but even she would have had to admit that he did appear, on the surface at least, to be surprisingly okay.

The police had advised him to keep a low profile on the Sunday, and not to speak to anyone, given the media speculation about the witness, but he had spoken to Jayne and Toddy on Saturday and felt a little guilty about it.

Toddy had rung on Sunday lunchtime. Jeff took the receiver from his mother just as she was explaining that her son was unavailable. Jeff asked Toddy his opinion about returning to work, and was pleased to hear Toddy say, 'Why the hell not? No point sitting at home festering.'

So on the Monday morning he had gone through his normal routine. Up at seven o'clock with Zoë Ball and Radio One; toilet, shower, dressed; a breakfast of toast and marmalade, two cups of coffee, brushed teeth and ready to go. Today was different only in that his mother kept popping up during his routine. Was he all right, how did he feel, if he felt funny at work would he come straight home? Promise? She was actually at the door as he left and she moved quickly to give him a peck on the cheek as he went past, saying, 'See you soon, take care.'

If he had been setting off to war, setting off for his first day at school or perhaps emigrating, he could have appreciated the gesture. As it was, he wiped his cheek with the back of his hand as if it was dirty and said, 'Flipping heck, Mother, I'm only going to work!'

'I know, I know, I just worry.' It wasn't an unexpected reply.

'Well, don't!' he snapped back, immediately regretting his tone. He marched to the car thinking, Sodding hell, as if I haven't got enough to worry about without Mother slobbering all over me! Well okay, that's a slight exaggeration, and damn it she does mean well; but strewth! What would the lads say if they knew that my mother had kissed me?

He drove the five miles to work thinking about what it was going to be like. The police had said that if he told everybody about Friday night then, although they were no doubt discreet people, the news would be in the press within days, if not hours. If he chose not to tell them then they had to admit that he was fuelling the media speculation and also postponing the 'inevitable'. Disclosure of his role was going to be revealed at some stage and might be seen by colleagues to have been less than open. Jeff appreciated that the police had left the choice to him, not pushing him in either direction.

Throughout Sunday he had only thought about how he would be able to concentrate on his work, and had decided that yes, having to worry about sets of accounts, audit programmes and tax computations would be a welcome distraction from the images and thoughts currently clogging his mind. So now he was still debating whether to tell or not.

On the one hand he could do it now, bit of fuss, get it over with, deal with the press and let it blow over. As the police and he both realised he would be tracked down pretty soon anyway by the bloodhounds of the media. *Blood* sprang into his mind and he quickly re-addressed his dilemma. So, given that the 'mysterious witness' would soon be less than mysterious, what was the point in delaying? On top of that he couldn't guarantee not to let something slip in conversation and he didn't want to have to lie about any of this. His mind was made up; he would announce his sensational news.

As he pulled into the office car park he decided to go and see Henry Leighton, the senior partner. Henry would be in; he always arrived on the dot of eight thirty to spend half an hour flicking through *The Times* and organising his day. He was a very approachable man – avuncular, really – and although highly respected for his professional skills and manner, was loved for his human touch. He had never forgotten his days as a junior and as he had risen through the ranks over thirty years he had never treated his colleagues and staff any differently from the way he had wanted to be treated as an articled clerk himself.

Jeff parked his car and entered through the big double doors. He flicked the name tag on the wall chart that declared 'JS In' and went to his room. He realised that he must be distracted because he had left his briefcase at home, something he normally never did. 'All that kissing stuff…' he muttered. If pushed he might have struggled to explain why he did actually bring his briefcase to work every day; he certainly didn't always need it, but it was a strangely habitual, comfortable thing to do.

So today he had forgotten it, a small but significant tell-tale sign that he had things on his mind.'

He hung up his coat and went straight to Henry's room. It was just along a brightly lit corridor and bore his name on the door, *Mr Henry Leighton, FCA, Senior Partner.* Jeff knocked twice briskly and waited.

Henry's voice was clear and loud. 'Come in!'

Jeff opened the door, stepped inside and turned and deliberately shut the door, quietly, behind him.

'Morning, sir,' he said respectfully.

'Morning, Jeff. How are you?'

'Fine, thank you, sir. Could I please have a word?'

'Of course. Take a seat.'

'Thank you.' Jeff settled into a comfortable chair.

Henry's avuncular manner could sometimes mask the fact that he was a very astute judge of character and technically very sharp. His judgement at this moment was that despite the few words exchanged there was something bothering Jeffrey. Personal rather than professional, he thought.

As Jeff hesitated, Henry helped him by prompting with a gentle 'Something the matter, Jeff? You look a little tired.'

Jeff replied, 'Actually, yes, sir.' Then he told his boss the story of Friday night. He tried to keep calm relating the story, but couldn't help rushing through the actual sighting of Westmain and Wendy.

Astute he may have been, but Henry could not have anticipated this. Girlfriend trouble (like that time with Bethany); money worries, even family strife; but not this. Taken aback as he was, he did not convey a great deal of emotion; just a quiet, 'Goodness me! What a shocking tragedy and shock for yourself.'

In his capacity as sounding board over the years, Henry had thought that he had seen it all: stories of the deaths of loved ones – young and old; boyfriend trouble (once with a forty-two-year-old man); stories of depression and admission of criminal acts, but this was certainly a new one.

'How are you now, Jeff? Anything we can do?'

'I'm okay, I think, I'll just get on with it, I've got the pine factory audit to get out today.'

Henry was impressed with the conscientious attitude but wondered if it was masking some buried shock. He also knew that there was an unasked question waiting to be answered: What to do now?

Henry volunteered the answer. 'If I was you, Jeff, (And I'm glad I'm not, he thought) I would get everyone together and tell them; or I could do that for you. Then it's over as far as the office is concerned. Tell individuals and the stories will spread, get lost in translation and then that will be messy. What do you think?'

Jeff's mind was made up by Henry's comments and he blurted, 'Yes please, sir.'

Henry could see that Jeff was strung out so he took the initiative. 'Right, let's do it now.'

He rang his secretary and asked her to page the office to request everybody to go immediately to the boardroom. Forget opening the post, drop everything; everybody, please.

Henry said that they could give everybody a couple of minutes to assemble and asked if Jeff wanted to be there himself.

'Difficult, sir, because I don't want to give the impression that I'm hiding.' Jeff also thought, but didn't say it, And what if I go and I start blubbing?

'It's entirely your choice; but whatever, I'll do all the talking.'

'Thanks, I think I had better be there.'

They set off a minute later and Jeff suddenly felt very nervous. Thank God he had had the sense to go to Henry, he thought, and congratulated himself.

Henry led the way into the boardroom, which was just big enough to accommodate all thirty-four office members. Sixteen were seated around the splendid oval table, with all the remainder scattered around the edges of the room. The staff fell silent as Henry took his place at the head of the table, a couple of juniors shuffling aside to give him space. Everybody looked quizzically at Jeff, then Henry, then back to Jeff. What was going on. Had Jeff been sacked, caught stealing, what the hell was this about? One or two looked around to see if any absentees could offer a clue but the four missing persons were all accountable; Sandra, a junior, was on a training course; Gerry, a senior, and Lucy, an assistant, had gone straight to an audit in Durham; and old Pamela, the payroll clerk, was still recovering from a hysterectomy.

When Henry asked if everybody was in attendance and that the telephones were temporarily switched to the answering service, he was told that Mr Sanchez had not come down yet. Just as he was about to be summoned, Joseph Sanchez burst into the room. He looked flustered and said to Henry, 'Sorry, had a client on the phone.'

All eyes were on him and for a horrible moment Joseph felt that the meeting was aimed at him, but Henry put him at ease with, 'Don't worry, Joey, nice to see somebody doing some work around here.'

Everybody relaxed a little. Both the words and the manner in which they were spoken suggested that Henry was not angry, and that this was not therefore some collective bollocking.

'I'm sorry to have to drag you from your desks but there is a need for a little chat this morning. As you will all know, there was a horrific murder in Stockton on Friday night.'

People stiffened in anticipation; Henry was talking about the murder. Christ, what was to be revealed?

'You will also have read or heard references to a witness who saw something of the crime. I can tell you that press stories of the witness's involvement have been exaggerated, but it is no secret that somebody was in the vicinity of the crime scene.'

One or two people who thought that Henry had entered the room with Jeff were suddenly enlightened. They stared at Jeff, but he looked down at the table.

'I have to advise you that the witness was Jeffrey here.'

There was gasps from around the room and Jeff flushed red. Nobody spoke; nobody even whispered.

'Jeff's decided to let you all know this for several very good reasons. One, he feels that it will come out anyway in time. Two he wants you, his colleagues, to be fully informed. Three, by advising you in this way he trusts that you will neither bother him with it, or worse, talk to the media about it; and finally, he knows he can rely on your confidentiality. Thank you very much for your attention, I hope you all have a good day.' Henry nodded to Jeff and Jeff smiled a weak smile in thanks.

Nobody moved and for a moment Henry thought that he was going to have to say, 'Shoo, go back to work!' Luckily, somebody opened the door and everybody filed out. Henry and Jeff were left, and Jeff said, 'I just want to say thank you, sir, for helping me through that.'

'No problem, Jeff, and if you need any further help in this matter, just give me a call.'

As the staff moved back to their rooms, some said, still surprised, 'Well, I never expected that.' Others said, 'Poor Jeff,' while others revelled in the sensational news.

Henry went back to his desk and sat for a moment, resting his chin on his hands, elbows on the desk. He admitted to himself, almost sheepishly, that he would love to ask Jeffrey, 'Just what did you see exactly? Describe it graphically.' But he pulled himself together and told himself, Don't be so unprofessional.

Jeff sat down in his chair with a thump, and let out a big sigh. That's better! Now get on with some work. There was a knock at his door, but before he could say anything it was pushed quickly open and Harry Dean entered. Jeff groaned inwardly; Harry was last person he wanted to see. Harry had a big cheesy grin on his face which Jeff felt like walking over and wiping off.

'So,' said Harry, 'I'll see you later and you can fill me in on the juicy bits, eh?'

Jeff couldn't believe his ears. Even for Harry Dean this was crassness in the extreme. 'Didn't you hear Henry?' he asked angrily.

'Yeah, yeah, words, words, words, blah, blah! But don't tell me you don't want to tell us what the psycho was doing to her?'

Jeff's hackles rose and his temples throbbed.

'What I want to tell you, you skinny twat, is what Henry said and which is not blah fucking blah, but is the truth. Bother me again about this and I will probably smash your ugly fucking face in!'

Harry was stunned, totally gobsmacked. His mouth remained slightly ajar, his smile frozen in a sickly line across his face.

'S–s sorry,' he stammered. 'I did–did didn't realise.' He turned and rushed out of the room.

Jeff stared at the door for a second then threw his head back and let out a huge, raucous belly-deep laugh. He had needed that release and God, who better to be on the receiving end than Harry Dean! He had always wanted to tell him to get stuffed and now he had done it. Perfect! He turned to the files on his desk and grinned; this was turning into a really good day.

When Jeff got home that evening he was shattered. His workload was always onerous and he had barely stopped for a second all day. His own work schedule, assisting others, planning for meetings, fielding client queries, all made for a hectic but enjoyable timetable. After he had changed and gone to the kitchen for his tea, his father had asked, 'Good day, son?'

'Fine, thanks.' Jeff could have left it at that but he felt that he owed his father a little more, so he said, 'Work as usual, and Henry called a meeting this morning and told everybody about it. It cleared the air and they haven't bothered me, so it was a good move, I think.'

'Good, good,' said his father slowly, as if not entirely convinced.

At about six thirty the phone rang. It was Tom Rogers checking that Jeff was okay and that he had not remembered any further detail. Jeff confirmed that his was the case and he volunteered the news of the meeting at work. Rogers was non committal in his response, just saying, 'Right, I'll tell Mr Mansell.'

Jeff was about to settle down to read the morning paper when he remembered Jayne. When he had rung her on Saturday and told her about the events of Friday night, he had promised to ring her Monday evening to chat to her properly, as Saturday's conversation was understandably brief.

He rang her number and was delighted when she answered. They chatted for half an hour, and for somebody like Jeff to whom chit-chat did not come easily, this was some achievement. Further evidence, he thought, that my gut instincts about this girl are right. She's for me.

They arranged to meet the following night in a local pub – not exactly a throbbing centre of excitement, but certainly acceptable for a quiet first date.

Rogers had been instructed by Mansell to get Sanders out of the investigation as soon as possible, given that he was their first suspect.

Jeff had his fingerprints taken on the Sunday and they did not match.

The happy crew were interviewed Sunday and their stories gelled. The taxi driver who had dropped Jeff off at midnight confirmed the face, and his shoes – size nine – were bigger than the killer's size eights.

Rogers was pleased to ring Jeff on Tuesday to advise him of what Jeff already knew. 'You are not considered a suspect, so that's out of the way.'

Jeff never considered that he was 'in the way' but at least it was official, he supposed.

'It went brilliantly.' Both Jeff and Jayne were pleased to tell their friends as soon after the Tuesday as possible.

'He's so nice and kind and nice to talk to, and he's good-looking, you know… and he's got a good job, and he's so nice to me and…' Jayne pushed to her friends.

'Whoa girl! We get the message,' they laughed. 'He's nice!'

After a couple more dates over the next few days they introduced each other to their families on the Sunday.

Everybody agreed that they were good together. Both families were delighted that their offspring had each had found an obvious soulmate. Jayne's friends warmed to Jeff because he was a nice bloke, with no airs and graces, just down-to-earth – and not stunningly handsome, which might have got them a little jealous; and he obviously made Jayne happy. They were pleased for her.

Jeff's mates looked at Jayne closely the first few times they'd met her. Sure, they were all surprised to find that she was very good-looking. It wasn't apparent at first glance, but on a closer look she was different. She was very attractive, with a nice face, great figure. They were impressed and let Jeff know it in the usual manly way with light-hearted ribbing and banter.

'But does she go?' asked Toddy after his second meeting of Jayne.

'Does she take it up…?'

'Whoa there big boy!' said Jeff. 'This is the woman of my dreams you're talking about, not some floozy who wants a quick bit of rumpy and off.'

'Sorry, mate,' said Toddy, in mock-serious tones. 'I should have said, "Does your good lady wish to indulge with your good self in the act of lovemaking in order to consummate your obvious love etc., etc., blah de blah de blah?"'

'That's better,' said Jeff, grinning. 'Now piss off, I'm not telling you.'

Truth was, Jeff wasn't bothered about 'rumpy' as Toddy called it. This really was different and was even better than those early days with Beth when he had thought it could not get any better. This was a hundred times better and was incredible, exciting, invigorating love. Real, tangible, all-encompassing love. Marvellous!

So he had a bit of bad luck that gloomy Friday night, so what? He felt desperately for the girl, and God yes, that image was buried deep into his consciousness, but he had come out of it relatively unscathed. And now that he had Jayne – well, hell, the world wasn't just fine again, it was positively humungously friggin' fantastic!

Life was good and with Jayne around could only get better.

On Valentine's day Jeff had surprised Jayne with a simple yet wonderful night out. He had picked her up at six o'clock and they had gone to the cinema to see *Shakespeare in Love*. Jeff knew that Jayne was already a big fan of *Romeo and Juliet* so the film was ideal.

He had then taken her to a romantic Italian restaurant for a lovely meal and then they had visited a trendy wine bar for a drink at the end of the evening.

Jeff was not at all garrulous; in fact one of his favourite sayings was, 'I just hate people with verbal diarrhoea,' but in Jayne's company he found he couldn't stop chatting. He wanted to tell this girl so much, he wanted to learn so much about her, everything about her. They would occasionally have a night out or a trip somewhere when the chatting did not seem necessary, like when they went to Whitby at four o'clock in the morning to watch the fishermen bring their catches in, and saw the sunrise later at six.

Generally, though, they both gave the impression of trying to cram a long courtship into a matter of weeks, there was such an urgency about their inquisitiveness about the other.

They learned of each other's work, and families, pet hates and likes. Jeff was impressed that Jayne did not have much on her 'pet hate' list, but she did admit to a deep mistrust of women who had three or four gold earrings in each ear, a half-dozen gold necklaces, usually all tangled up, gold bracelets on both wrists and at least one ring on every ringer. She admitted, 'I always think it's so tacky, a vulgar display of a lack of wealth.'

One day, in a pub, such a lady was sitting at the next table. Jeff had quietly nudged Jayne and said, 'Don't look now but Mrs Tacky is sitting behind you.'

Jayne had eventually stolen a sly look and leaned over to Jeff and said, 'And how stupid does the silver watch look with all that gold plate around?'

One of the few other irritations to Jayne was what she called, 'the irresponsibility of daft, selfish, senseless parents, who do not think their child's name through properly'. She had reeled off quite a few examples and Jeff was a little surprised how passionate she was about it.

'You've got three or four obvious ways to cock up a child's life with their names. Daft combinations, combinations with connotations, initials, and the totally off the wall. For example...' (she's got into this, thought Jeff, just stand back and listen) '...Tommy Thomson, Stephen Stevenson; just daft. William Burns, Willie Burns; I ask you. Same as Richard Burns, Dick Burns; strewth! Thomas Ian Trent, TIT, or Nellie Olwen Brown, NOB. And then there's the absurd, like that guy last week who christened his baby after the entire Middlesborough football team…'

'Including the coaching staff,' added Jeff.

'Exactly!' finished Jayne, triumphantly. 'Out of their flipping trees!'

Jeff got on well with Annabel, Jayne's five-year-old sister, and Annabel enjoyed the couple of trips that they had taken her on. Jeff decided, and Jayne did not voice her disapproval, that there could be a lot more trips for Annabel in the future, but for now the time was precious with Jayne, alone.

A little later in the relationship and they both experienced the 'perfect night'.

That Saturday night they had eaten at an expensive, classy Italian restaurant and enjoyed the high standard of service, food and drink. They had got a taxi home and sat closely together on Jayne's sofa in front of the warming fire on the wintry night. They drank red wine from large goblets and held hands and kissed throughout their conversation.

At midnight Jayne had stood up and, with a beautiful smile on her face, pulled Jeff from the sofa. Without speaking she had led him to her bedroom. Her dim lighting added to the atmosphere.

They were both very relaxed, very ready for this. There had been almost no sexual contact over the previous three weeks, there was too much respect on both sides, too much hope for the future of the relationship to jeopardise it with a quick fumble or clumsy petting session.

Kissing had been allowed, but only nice kissing, not too heavy on tongues or slavering face-wetting. The rules were not written in stone but they were known.

So now was special. Jayne put a finger on Jeff's lips and said, 'Shh.'

She undid his shirt and slowly peeled it off him. He did not feel at all conscious that he was not in great shape. His feelings were not even of enormous sexual excitement; it went deeper than that. It was what he would later describe to himself as 'total pleasure in every possible sense of the phrase'.

She undid his belt and the zip on his trousers and once they had been removed, she then pulled down his boxer shorts to the floor. He was erect and she stroked his penis in one slow motion.

He said softly, 'Jayne...' But she again said, 'Shh!' and that same finger went to his lips.

She took his hands and placed them on her blouse and he undid her buttons. Once the blouse was removed he reached behind her and pulled down the zip on her skirt. He slowly drew it down her legs and she stepped out of it. He knelt down and pulled her tights down and she nimbly stepped out of them.

He moved even closer to her, his penis rubbing against her, and he undid her bra. He pulled it gently off her shoulders and her lovely breasts were exposed. The nipples were stiff and an involuntary moan of delight left his lips. She smiled.

He placed a finger in either side of her panties and drew them down. He knelt again to pull them over her feet and his face was only an inch or two from her pudenda.

He stood up and she took him by the hand to the bed. They lay together and started kissing. They touched and stroked and nibbled and every nerve end was alive with pleasure. He kissed her breasts and between her legs, she licked his penis, and then when they were both moist he entered her.

For the first time since they had entered the bedroom he felt a surge of nervousness. 'What if...?' But somebody smiled on him that night because he was able to perform manfully. They came to orgasm together, both crying out loudly.

After a moment's silence, Jeff said, 'Jayne, that was truly, honestly, the most amazing experience I have had in my entire life!'

'I'd have to agree with that... it was perfect,' Jayne murmured.

They held each other and fell asleep; there was no need to say any more.

They were awoken at two o'clock by the shrill ring of the phone. Jeff nudged Jayne and said, 'Who the heck is that going to be?'

Jayne padded into the lounge naked and said a sleepy, 'Hello.'

It was Mr Sanders, who was very sorry to bother Jayne, but she didn't know where Jeff was, did she?

She said she did and apologised for them not letting Jeff's parents know where he was. Mr Sanders apologised back, explaining, 'It isn't that Jeff can't stay wherever he wants, whenever he wants. It's just that we're worried when we don't know where he was, in case, you know...'

Jayne said she did know and said they were sorry for not ringing.

She crawled back into bed and snuggled up to Jeff. 'Just your dad checking up on you,' she said, laughing.

'Oh, shit! Sorry about that. They're a bit panicky after the trouble. Sorry.'

'No problem, I told him that you were safe with me, except that there was a danger that I could make love to you all night and you'd be a shell of your former self by breakfast.'

'What a way to go,' laughed Jeff, as he rolled on top of his love.

The next morning they had arisen together and Jayne had called Jeff to the lounge window. There was a beautiful orange sky rising in fire over the Cleveland Hills. They gazed at this holding hands.

In celebration of the night before they decided on Sunday morning to go for a run out.

They set off from Stockton and crossed the venerable old Victoria Bridge, still proudly displaying the World War II bomb damage, into Thornaby, the strange half-town that was crushed geographically and spiritually between Stockton and Middlesborough.

They marvelled at the sprawl of new buildings down by the river that had sprung up over recent times with Development Council monies. Attractive commercial and residential properties vied for space by the river and the tributary canals that ran off it. A minute later they were approaching the A66, one of the three main thoroughfares of Teesside. In the distance to the east the Cleveland Hills stood darkly. Roseberry Topping, the highest peak between Teesside and Moscow, stood silhouetted across the grey sky.

Jayne suggested that maybe they shouldn't bother with the seaside but should pull off the A66 and go to Teesside Retail Park instead, but Jeff did not rise to this genuine baiting and just said, 'Another day maybe.'

They soon joined the A19, the road which links York to Newcastle, cutting a swathe through Teesside. The signposts started early for Captain Cook's Birthplace Museum, Whitby, Redcar, Teesport and Yarm; Jeff always considered the contrasts of these places essential to the area. Popular fishing port, old-fashioned seaside resort, beautiful old town, and the 'natural' heartland – all within a few miles of one another.

The third major artery of Teesside, the A174, known as The Parkway, was soon upon them and they swung on to this heading for the coast. The slip road to the A174 gave the first indication of the approach of Wilton, the colossus of an industrial estate and chemical plant that was home to Teesside's biggest employer, ICI. The concrete, chrome and steel skyline soon appeared to the left but at the same time, on the right, the road took motorists past the Cleveland Hills. To climb these hills was to take in too the magnificent North Yorkshire Moors, and that was why Jeff loved this road. He thought its ten-mile length summed up the area. The massive, heavy, dirty industry that the area's forefathers had striven to create lay a few miles from magnificent beaches and wonderful fishing villages, all on the doorstep of superb country-side. When describing this area, Jeff would mention these aspects and throw in also the nearby magnificence of Durham Cathedral and York Minster, the superb leisure and shopping facilities, the inexpensive cost of living, and state his case that Teessiders would not swap homes for others anywhere in the country.

They passed sliproads to the suburban conurbations of Middlesbrough and the alternative (Moors) road to Whitby and Scarborough, and Jeff took this moment to expound his views of how strongly he felt about the proud heritage of the North-East, how he loved the down-to-earth, hard-working people; and how the area was so misunderstood – sometimes on purpose – by those outside the area who had never visited the marvellous coastline and beautiful moors, dales and parks.

To the left, the sun shone on Wilton, ICI, British Steel and over the Tees to the Billingham plants. Jayne pointed to the industry and said, 'Really great that,' but she appreciated what he meant. A few minutes later she asked, 'Are we nearly there, Dad, are we there?'

'Now, now,' said Jeff as if to a daughter. 'We'll soon be there for sweeties and candy floss; be patient.'

Steam and smoke blew and belched into the sky from the cooling towers to the left and Jeff wondered whether they belonged to ICI or Teesside Power Plant.

The suburbs of Dormanstown and Grangetown seemed submerged by the overwhelming scale of the industry. Elements of the industrial landscape always struck Jeff as resembling the world's largest Meccano set, such was the complexity of tangled metal, concrete, pipework and towers.

At the next roundabout they could see straight ahead the dark line of the North Sea. At the roundabout the exit signs covered Wilton, the power plant, stately homes and nature trails, again that eccentric mix of 'the good, the bad and the ugly', but all still the truth of Teesside. It rankled Teessiders that the national press never or rarely acknowledged this contradiction, that they only ever focussed on the smoking chimneys; but native Teessiders were never bitter for long. Despite the negative coverage, they knew the truth.

Road signs warned of deer as they passed Wilton Castle and golf course. They could still see on the left Wilton, now the headquarters of ICI and the hub of this industrial city with its own infrastructure.

At the next roundabout they left The Parkway, which would have taken them to seaside towns of Marske and Saltburn, and were soon in Redcar.

They came to a crossroads signposting the racecourse less than a mile to the right, Teesside Airport twenty-four miles to the left, and the seafront straight on. They crossed Corporation Road and Jeff said, 'Corporation Road, Number 962. It's up there with Victoria Road, Albert Road and Regent Street.'

They crossed a railway bridge and some scruffy wasteland; to the left British Steel chugged its fumes into the sky. The road cut through Cleveland Golf Course and there in front of them was the North Sea. As ever, there was an astonishing queue of huge tankers and cargo ships waiting, apparently patiently, to unload their goods at Teesport. They just sat there, never appearing to move. There were fourteen today.

They passed a depressed, tired amusement park, and Jeff cracked one of his favourite jokes. 'Jayne, did you hear about the clown who went to an industrial tribunal after being sacked by the circus?' She waited for the punchline and when Jeff said, 'He was claiming funfair dismissal,' she laughed loudly.

On the right was the Redcar Bowl, previously the Coatham Bowl, a small entertainment venue that accommodated either unknown, up-and-coming bands, or those who'd been famous and in the charts ten years or more earlier. Today it advertised a battle of the bands and a forthcoming boxing attraction.

They were soon at the seafront and the main promenade with its cafés, amusement arcades and small shops. Jeff felt that it was tacky but in a comfortable, reassuring way. It never changed; people continued to enjoy its pleasures, and what the hell, it was a nice enough distraction from work for a couple of hours.

The sun had broken through and this did show the chip shops and rock shops in their best possible light. The road was full of parked cars and they had travelled through the entertainment area without finding a parking spot. They passed the fishing boats lined up by the roadside, opposite the lifeboat station and museum. They then spotted a gap among the parked vehicles and pulled in.

There was a huge expanse of clean, debris-free beach, and the sea was still pulling away from the sand. They walked towards the shoreline, deliberately crossing some exposed rocks and their interesting rock pools.

A bitterly cold northerly wind was threatening to bring in dark, brooding clouds from the distant horizon.

They strolled hand in hand across the beach, initially moaning about the cold wind, but soon welcoming its harshness because it made them snuggle up as they walked.

'Delightful,' said Jayne as the wind whipped up the sand and the cold bit at their skin.

'You can't beat a bit of fresh air, can you?' shouted Jeff, and he exaggerated the struggle against the wind by leaning forward as if into a gale.

They walked and talked for half an hour, covering a couple of miles towards South Gare where the promontory and lighthouse stood proudly in the distance.

They stood for a second staring at the distant shapes and smoke of British Steel and Jeff said, 'Great isn't it?'

He said it with such feeling that Jayne looked at him, a little surprised. 'You mean that, don't you?'

'Certainly do. I think there's what you might call a savage beauty about sights like that. Especially when you have the contrast of the beautiful beach, the dunes and sea next to it.'

'I'm in love with a romantic,' said Jayne in genuine admiration.

'And I'm in love with the most wonderful girl I've every met, seen or heard of.'

They kissed, and when they broke apart, Jeff said 'Flipping heck! If that's what I get for a reference to savage beauty, I can't wait to see what I'll get for waxing lyrical about the stinky old Tees!'

As they walked back to the car a lady struggled past with a huge dog. 'Look at that,' joked Jeff, 'a genetically modified poodle!'

Jayne her tinkling laugh and said, 'You're not kidding, Annabel could ride that!'

They arrived at Jayne's shiny red R-reg Seat Ibiza and Jeff held her close as she looked for her keys in her handbag.

'I love you, Miss Gilmour,' he said.

'I love you back, Mr Sanders,' said Jayne.

On the way home they talked of holidays, of Nice where he had been, of Disneyworld where she had been. They started to plan their summer holiday. It was a perfect weekend.

Chapter Nineteen

He had never panicked, he really hadn't. He would argue that with anybody, absolutely anybody – even somebody skilled at arguing or debating. He had never ever panicked, not really. Sure, there had been quite a shock when those eyes had met his, but, hey, tell me the name of the individual who would not have felt a tremor of nervous tension at that moment and I'll show you one unnaturally cool customer. If he had gone soft, if he hadn't held his nerve, how could you explain how he had survived the night so easily and then had the presence of mind to sit and plan his next move? His 'next move' – so called because this was a weird game of human chess, with people moving around the board, sometimes dictated by him, sometimes by God. That night had gone to him, but God had made a late, interesting move with the introduction of Sanders. So he had stayed cool, formed a strategy, and today was the day for executing both the plan and Sanders himself.

He congratulated himself on his clever, simple plan, and now part one was in motion. As he waited at the bus stop he thought, Will good old Jeffrey Sanders be so collected when he looks up into the eyes of his worst nightmare? I think not...

The bus pulled up next to him, spewing filthy dark exhaust fumes. He climbed aboard slowly.

'Ninety pence, please,' he said in a flat voice, placing the correct change on the driver's counter. He thanked the squat, bald, ugly driver for his ticket and moved slowly down the bus. Within the first few steps he had weighed up the seating options open to him: gauche, spotty adolescent; weary old spinster; and a retired type, probably heading for the library for his two weekly detective novels. He'll do, he can be the one privileged to have me sit next to him. Privileged, because today was one of those special days again, and anyone crossing his path was surely in the presence of greatness.

He was soon in town (thank God for Sunday shopping), and he marched briskly to the huge DIY hypermarket. He wandered through the labyrinth of departments and eventually found the one he needed. The assistant he found was possibly more hindrance than help but the item he wanted was eventually purchased and parcelled up. He carried it out of the store but then re-entered to track down another item. This too took some locating but they did have what he wanted and the deal was soon done.

He then picked up a few groceries in town before heading home. The only reason that he took the bus was because he'd had to use the bus on the day that he first met Sanders. This was Westmain's little message to God that he wasn't at all fazed at the prospect of God placing more obstacles in his way. God had to be made to realise just who He was dealing with here.

That night, 21 February, as Jeff lay in that comfortable, pleasant pre-sleep doziness, his thoughts turned to the night that had so profoundly affected his life. They often did at this time of day, when he had nothing else to directly occupy his mind (except Jayne, of course, and the magical weekend they had just enjoyed). Although over six weeks ago it was not, unfortunately, difficult for Jeff to recollect with chilling efficiency the feelings, the emotions, the downright terror of that night.

The rain pattered prettily against the window, and Jeff wondered if it was the rain that brought back the memories into his crystal-clear focus. He found himself grinning, albeit a little wryly. Christ, I wouldn't want to go through that again, he admitted to himself, although the celebrity status had been kind of cool. If only he had proof, any kind of evidence, that the bastard in the mac was out of his life for good, forever. The police had said time and time again that this type of psychopath never 'interfered' with witnesses, passers-by or third parties; it simply was not their style. And he nearly believed them, but the nagging doubt remained: What if this nutter, his nutter, was different?

Be brave, for God's sake! What are you, man or mouse? he scolded himself. 'Squeak, squeak,' he said aloud and allowed himself a giggle. 'Fresh start tomorrow. Look ahead, not back. That's the new motto for Jeff. Good idea!'

He pulled the covers a little tighter and drew his knees towards his stomach. His eyes closed, his last conscious thought being that for some less than obvious reason, he suddenly felt as if a great weight had been lifted from his shoulders.

It was rather ironic that Jeff should have felt that way at that particular moment on that particular night, and he would have seen the twisted sick humour himself had someone gently tapped him on the shoulder and whispered, 'The man in the mac hasn't gone away, he's never been too far away, you know. Oh, and by the way, he's coming to see you, in fact he's coming soon. Tonight!'

It was true. Westmain had enjoyed a quiet day at home. Then, after an evening in front of the television, he'd treated himself to a Chinese takeaway for supper. After he had washed up and put the crockery away he got himself ready for his night. Neatly dressed, he then got his mac ready. Tonight it needed special attention because in addition to his constant companions, the screwdriver and Stanley knife, he'd had to add the items bought earlier that day: a glass cutter and a small sink plunger.

Once organised, he went to his car and set off for Stockton. He was soon there and had no difficulty finding the area in which Jeff lived, the media coverage being responsible for that. He used his *A to Z* to find the street, which had been disclosed in the press, but he did not know the exact number. The television coverage had often showed the house, which had no number on the door or gate; but the Georgian-style bay window appeared unique, and together with the little front garden pond he was sure that he would recognise it. He parked in a street a little along the main road from Jeff's and set off on his mission. It was a showery night, and at three 3.22 a.m. it was raining quite hard.

Must be something about me meeting Sanders that makes the skies cry, he told himself, as he looked hard at a house across the street.

Same windows, drive, garage… looks promising. He crossed to the gate and saw the telltale pond.

'Piece of cake,' he muttered as he quietly opened the gate just wide enough to allow him through. He went straight along the path between garage and house and looked at the back of the house. The rain splashed around him but he glanced at the moon, which was bright between dark clouds. He looked closely at the kitchen window and the patio doors and decided on the kitchen door, which had a window built into it. He enjoyed using his new toys. The plunger did its job perfectly, holding the glass in place as he easily, quickly and silently cut out a circle about ten inches in diameter. He placed the glass carefully outside the door, having to pull hard to release it from the plunger's grip.

He put his arm through the hole in the window and reached across to the kitchen window. He could comfortably handle the window latch and he pulled it open. The window was not far off the ground and he raised himself into the kitchen easily. He moved quietly, loving the sensation that enveloped him. It was sheer excitement, allied to that marvellous control that he exercised over his emotions. Those conflicting sensations alone would normally have granted him enormous satisfaction; but tonight, well, it was very special. He was doing something different, he was putting right a wrong done to him, he was winning this particular game of chess. He felt that it didn't get better, *couldn't* get better than this. Life was great.

Mrs Sanders tossed and turned, she always had been a light sleeper. Not exactly qualifying as an insomniac, she certainly came close. To exacerbate her usual problems, tonight she had the tiniest of tickly throats and every few minutes she would give a gentle, almost apologetic cough. It was so polite it was like listening to a sparrow coughing, quiet and squeaky. There was no way that it could disturb her husband lying next to her; he always slept heavily anyway and tonight he was snoring like a rattling engine.

At midnight she had managed to drop off to sleep but awoke at one, coughing. She had taken a glass of water to bed and lifted it from the bedside table. It helped alleviate the cough but she knew that the relief was only temporary. Sure enough, there it was again, ten minutes later. The minutes dragged on: fitful sleep, cough, drink, until just after 3.15, when the glass was empty. She lay there or a minute or two then decided that she would have to get a refill, no matter how cold it was outside her lovely snug bed. She listened to the rain for a while and then watched the patterns on the ceiling made by the street lights, finding every gap in the curtains. She liked the noise of the rain and was almost disappointed when she sensed that it was easing up.

Glass of water or cup of tea? That was the tricky choice. Water was more convenient, from the bathroom; but tea sounded appealing. She plumped for water. The kitchen would be freezing and once she had told herself not to get comfortable again she drew back the duvet and sheet and swung her legs from the warmth of the bed into the cool air. She hesitated for a second or two as she thought about the need for this excursion, but another gentle cough served to remind her. She rose from the bed and moved, as if on automatic pilot, to where she knew her fluffy pink slippers were. She slipped her feet into the slippers and took her plum-red dressing gown from the back of the bedroom door. She pulled the cord tight, as if that was going to bring instant warmth. It didn't, but she felt a little less cold and she shuffled to the landing. The lights from outside gave enough guidance for her to find her way across the landing to the bathroom. She was fumbling for the bathroom light cord when, with her fingers around the pull, she froze.

She had heard something, just something, unlocated, intangible, unknown, but something. There it was again, and this time it frightened her, a lot, because the noise could be identified by somebody who knew the house intimately. It was a creak, the creak on the third stair from the bottom. She felt very, very cold.

Maybe the house settling, she thought, unconvincingly. If it was somebody creeping up the stairs, then obviously the creak on stair eight would by now… She didn't finish the thought, as stair eight obligingly groaned right on cue. Her hand remained on the light cord, stuck in its position from the lack of brainwaves instructing it to move. Her brain was trying to cope with fear, terror and panic, and it wasn't coping too well.

Must be Jeff, she thought, but a voice said, 'He'd hardly be creeping up the stairs, would he?'

May be my imagination, she lied as she realised that she had not moved or breathed for ten seconds. She released her grasp of the cord and breathed out, then slowly turned around, as if to move quickly would alert somebody to her presence or would turn her to face something she did not want to see.

She stepped from the bathroom and with her hand over her mouth she peered over the landing rail onto the stairs. Her heart pounded and she knew inside that that was because she had definitely heard creaks at three and eight. Those boards had been loose for years, and now were physically and spiritually part of the household.

Her eyes were accustomed to the gloom and she gasped and took a step back when she saw the large dark shadow on the middle of the stairs move. It was a man, a man on her stairs, coming up the stairs. She screamed, one long piercing scream. It stopped as quickly as it had started and she squeaked, 'Jeff!' But someone ten feet away would have struggled to hear her as fear strangled her vocal chords.

The man appeared to take another step up the stairs and was now only four or five from the top; but then he stopped, and although she could not clearly see his features, there was an overwhelming sense, a vibe, that he was angry. He stepped up another stair and his face was caught in the light coming through the landing window. Cleanshaven, slim features and tidy was how she would remember him.

She thought he said something but she did not catch it and he turned and rapidly descended the stairs. As he got to the bottom of the stairs both Gerald and Jeffrey appeared from their rooms, both looking startled.

'Dorothy, what on earth is it?' asked her husband.

Jeff had awoken from a nice dream about Jayne and had taken a moment to register the scream as reality and not part of the background noise in his dream. But now, on the landing, he saw his mother, and although she was obviously scared stiff he presumed that she had seen a huge spider run across the carpet.

She really is hopeless, he thought. As if a spider's going to kill you.

He was about to gently mock her when she slumped against the wall, and with a wavering finger pointing down the stairs, said weakly, 'A man, there was a man on the stairs, he's just gone.'

Jeff and his father looked at each other and then down the stairs but just as they were about to suggest that Mrs Sanders had had a bad dream they heard the kitchen door slam shut.

Jeff raced down the stairs, jumping from the third bottom stair into the hall. He skidded on the rug that lay there and careered off a wall towards the kitchen. He did not hear his father shouting, 'Jeff, be careful!'

Gerald put his arms around Dorothy and cradled her head, saying, 'What happened, love? What did you see... are you all right?'

The sight of her menfolk had given a huge lift to Dorothy, but she was in shock and her words betrayed her confused state.

'Water, came for water, then I heard, on the stairs – you know, at the bottom – I heard the creaking, when I was getting the water, and then more creaks and then I came out and saw him standing there, coming up the stairs... and it was, it was when I was getting the water, he was just over there.'

His eyes followed hers and he shuddered when he realised how close his precious wife had been to the burglar.

'And then he ran off, did he?' enquired Gerald, thinking, 'Cowardly bastard, If I get hold of him...' His thoughts then snapped back to Jeff. God, he hoped he was all right. He realised that Dorothy was speaking again, very quietly, as if she was afraid of the words themselves. 'No, not straight away. He looked at me, and even took a step or two up the stairs. I think that's when I shouted, when I thought he was coming for me.'

Screamed rather than shouted, corrected Gerald in his head. Christ, you must have been terrified, poor old soul. Aloud, he said, 'Did you see him, Dorothy. Get a good look at him?'

'Yes, I think so, at the top there,' she said, pointing to the patch of light a couple of stairs from the landing. She pondered for a moment and then, as if asked a formal question by a police officer, she specified, 'Short neat hair, dark but not black; sharp features; smartly dressed, wearing a macintosh, I think.'

Gerald's blood ran cold. 'A macintosh, Dorothy? He was wearing a macintosh?' he shouted, panic-stricken.

'Yes, I'm sure it was. What on earth's the matter, Gerald?'

'Oh Lord, oh Lord! No, no!' wailed Gerald and he released his hold of Dorothy. 'Phone the police, use this phone!' He pointed to the extension on the landing, 'Get them here quickly, it's an emergency, I'm going to help Jeff.'

Gerald's manner scared her. He had transformed from a quiet rock of support to a scary character who was in a right state.

He rushed down the stairs as quick as his old legs would take him, the same thought thumping through his head. Burglars don't wear macs, they wear jackets or anoraks or something, but they don't wear macs. He turned into the kitchen. But we know somebody who does wear a mac, God yes, that bastard Jeff saw, he was wearing a mac... Oh God, let Jeff be okay, please, please.

Gerald saw in the kitchen that the back door window had been cut and, the door left ajar. He flicked the light on as he passed. At the back door he stopped and looked out into the garden. The showers had passed and there was a little moonlight as clouds scudded across the sky. He switched on the outside light and the near area was illuminated. He listened but heard nothing so he shouted as loud as he could, 'Jeff, where are you, Jeff?'

No reply was heard and he started to whimper, 'Please God, don't take our son, please, please.' Tears ran down his face and his nose started to dribble.

He walked slowly down the stone path that ran neatly down the middle of his garden, with flower beds, shrubs and trees some five yards away on each side. He peered left and right as he walked and shouted again, 'Jeff, son, where are you?'

Nothing was heard, just his own heavy breathing.

At the bottom of the garden was his little 'country garden', a mass of bushes and large sycamore tress that was better managed and organised than first impressions suggested.

In the middle of this was his shed, and behind that the six-foot fence that divided their garden from a neighbour's.

Through habit he had put his slippers and dressing gown on when he had got out of bed but he was fairly certain that Jeff only had on the T-shirt and boxer shorts and was barefooted.

'Jeff, Jeff' he shouted, with renewed urgency.

He was almost at the bottom of the path when his body stiffened. He thought that he had heard the faintest of noises, a murmur perhaps, or a moan. He strained his ears, suddenly very conscious of the shadows in the undergrowth, the cold and his obvious isolation.

'Jeff!' he shrieked, the tremor in his voice emphasising his emotions. His ears picked up what he was sure was a weak moan, and he looked hard in the direction that he guessed it came from, just past the shed. He moved quickly towards the spot. Where were the bloody police? Warding off a strong desire to turn and run back to the house, he asked in a quieter voice, 'Jeff, is that you?' Then he bent down to try and see under the bushes. The moon poked out between clouds and in the flash of moonlight he saw a naked foot.

'Nooo!' he wailed, 'Nooo!' He scrambled under the lowest twigs and branches and saw that Jeff was lying flat on his face, unmoving.

'Jeff, Jeff, Jeff!' he cried, pulling at his son. He ignored the scratches and cuts that the bushes inflicted on him and was not even conscious of the distant approach of a police siren. He dragged Jeff out on to the path and turned him over. He could make out the lad's features and he could see that his eyes were shut. He leant close to him and said, 'Son, can you hear me? Jeff son, can you hear?'

Tears dropped from his face onto Jeff's, and Gerald's nose ran messily down his face. He wiped his nose on a sleeve, an unthinkable act in any other circumstance, and stared at something he had just noticed. On Jeff's grey T-shirt, just above his shorts was a dark stain that Gerald just knew was not mud, or soil, or wet. He touched it with a finger and confirmed his worst fears: blood, dark and sticky and plentiful.

He started to pick Jeff up but Jeff's unconscious weight was too great for him. Gerald slumped to his knees on the grass by the path. He sobbed, 'Jeff, Jeff!' and received an enormous shock when Jeff answered, 'Dad?'

'Oh, thank God!' Gerald gasped. 'Thank God!'

'You okay, Dad?' mumbled Jeff.

'Fine, son, fine. Take it easy, we'll get you sorted.'

The police siren had arrived at the front of the house and Gerald shouted 'Help, out in the garden! Help!'

Two police officers appeared at the back door, Dorothy having guided them through the house, and they were soon at Jeff's side. One of them talked to Gerald, establishing the sequence of events, whilst his colleague radioed for an ambulance.

They tried to comfort Jeff and he became a little more lucid as the minutes passed. He recollected being surprised at the hole in the glass in the kitchen door, had rushed through the door and immediately cut his foot on some glass lying there. He had seen the man going into the bushes at the bottom of the garden. He had raced to the spot where the man had disappeared, but as he reached them the man had leapt out at him. They had fought, crashed back into the bushes and struggled in the clinging branches and foliage. That was all he could remember.

What he did not recall was that when they had tumbled onto the ground beneath the bushes Westmain had uttered a loud grunt, disproportionate to the impact of the fall, caused by a screwdriver slicing across his side. Jeff wrestled with Westmain and grabbed at his body, his head, his clothes. There was no room to swing punches so it was jabbing blows and kicking only. Westmain had pushed Jeff's head down towards the ground but felt that his injury was weakening him. Westmain knew that he was in trouble, so in a last burst of energy he whacked his knee into Jeff's chin. The blow knocked Jeff out. Westmain scrambled out of the bushes, dizziness buzzing around his senses. He moved to the fence, turning as he heard Jeff's father shouting from the house. His hand went to his side and he winced at both the sharp pain and the knowledge that one of his weapons had sunk into his side when he had been knocked to the ground.

He scrambled up the fence and fell over it clumsily, giving a yelp of pain. He saw stars before his eyes, and they were not those in the sky. The realisation kicked him between the eyes that he had had Sanders at his mercy and had let him off the hook. 'Damn it!' he spat, angry at the thought and angry at God's apparent victory.

He made his way through the garden, hearing cries of 'Jeff, Jeff!' behind him. He was soon back on a street and he got his bearings before moving back to the main road on which Jeff's house was situated. He was moving briskly towards where his car was parked when he heard the approach of a police siren. He crouched behind a gatepost as the car sped past. He was soon at his car and he climbed in with a groan. His side hurt like hell and he knew that he was soaked in perspiration and blood from the wound.

He gathered his thoughts, trying to exert his prowess at cool concentration in any situation. He was soon driving safely back to the sanctuary of his home.

The ambulance arrived and Jeff was stretchered to it. Gerald had gone to Dorothy, who was standing very still at the kitchen door, and told her that he was going to hospital with Jeff. Dorothy had protested that she was going too and after a muted debate Gerald agreed that they should drive there together. They informed both the ambulance crew and the policemen and established exactly where Jeff was being taken.

They quickly dressed, not speaking. In the car, Dorothy asked, 'What was it about the mac, Gerry?'

He glanced at her, unsure whether she really did not know or was just asking for confirmation.

'It reminded me of the mac that the man Jeff saw was supposed to be wearing.'

She gasped. 'I hadn't realised,' she said, and fell silent for a moment. 'Was it him?' she asked.

'I don't know, I really don't; Jeff didn't say.'

They said no more, Gerald thinking of the only other time in his life when he had felt anything similar to the fear that he was experiencing tonight. It was a hot day near Monte Cassino in Northern Italy, in 1944. He was in the Tank Corps and they were advancing on a German stronghold. All hell had broken loose, with explosions, smoke and fear crashing and swilling in equal measures. The whoosh of an incoming bazooka rocket gave no time to react. Their tank was knocked out in a huge explosion. One comrade was dead, another fatally wounded. Gerald had struggled out, his left leg badly injured. He scrambled down the side of the tank and dashed into nearby bushes. He lay there for some time, unsure of the state of the battle, the positions of allies and foes. He lay there petrified, scared by the explosions, terrified of being discovered and afraid of the damage to his leg.

The fear of that experience flooded back. Maybe it was lying under the bushes that had triggered it, but he did not welcome it, as it was making him feel sick; and that was war, an allowable excuse for fear and hate.

They were soon at the main entrance of the hospital and parked nearby. They scurried in and went to the admissions desk. The lady there was expecting them and directed them to a room just down the corridor. They knocked at the door of Room 36, still polite, and entered in trepidation. The sight that greeted them was probably beyond their greatest hopes. Jeff was sitting up in bed, attended by a doctor and a nurse. His T-shirt had gone and he grinned a little grin as his parents entered. 'Hi, Mum. Hi, Dad, are you both okay?' he asked.

His mother flung herself on him, kissing his head and crying the words, 'Thank God, thank God.'

Mr Sanders Senior stood stiffly by the bed, upper lip fighting its designated firmness, bottom lip visibly quivering. He could not hold back and broke with years of tradition by holding Jeff's hand, allowing his emotions for once to show through. The British way was not appropriate at this moment.

Dorothy Sanders asked, 'Jeff, was it that man again?' But before Jeff could consider the question, Gerald blurted out, 'How are you injured?' He moved around the bed looking at Jeff's torso, where he could see no mark.

Jeff smiled 'Not my wound, Dad. It was the other guy's blood.'

The doctor confirmed this. 'That's right, Jeff's got a nasty knock on his chin, rattled a few teeth and had a bit of concussion, but nothing worse. We'll keep him in for a day or so but there should be no long-term effects.'

Jeff suddenly sat forward with a start and exclaimed, 'What do you mean, Mum, "that man"?' He looked at his mother, but before she could answer he turned to his father and said, 'How did you know, Dad? How did you know?'

'Don't know, Jeff. It was just that mother saw his mac; it could have been just a coincidence.'

Jeff was staring into the distance, racking his brain in order to recollect any clear image he had had of the burglar. He hadn't seen him at all until he had lunged out of the bushes. *Out of the bushes.*

'My God! you're right, it was a mac, the same mac. My God!' He fell back to the pillows that were plumped behind him. 'My God!'

He knew it was his man because he had seen his face and heard those words that Westmain had spoken, but he hadn't recognised the mac. Jeff contemplated the horrible truth: that his man had come for him, had been in his house. He thought it through and suddenly said to his father, 'His wound. Dad, he must have fallen on his own weapon. Jeez...'

Gerald and Dorothy stood together, uncertain of what to say. The medical staff were not too sure of what was being discussed.

Jeff sat there, semi-naked, with pinpricks and scratches caused by the bushes visible, but it was in his head where the pain was. The police had promised that serial killers did not visit witnesses; it was not their style. Well, this bastard obviously did not know the rules. He had visited Jeff and his family, armed and prepared to kill. And now he was injured and probably even more dangerous. Jeff tried to suppress a growing worry but it burst free.

The serial killer obviously thought Jeff was a problem; he obviously thought that this was personal.

Chapter Twenty

Over the weeks the investigation had covered a lot of ground. Hundreds of statements were taken from persons who were in the same pubs as Wendy, people who had just been on the streets at the same time and her family and friends.

The door-to-door statements gave no insight to the crime other than confirming Jeff's running from the brickie to his home.

The transport leads led nowhere other than the CCTV video from Durham Station.

Mansell had received this on the Wednesday after the murder and sat down to watch it with Rogers.

The time on the footage recorded 9 January 1999 – 12.54 a.m. as the 12.50 to Newcastle pulled in.

One man alighted the platform. A man in a macintosh. Unfortunately that was about all it told them: a man in a mac. It was dark, he was only on the platform a few seconds, and he was quite a distance from the camera.

Mansell had called Jeff on the Thursday and asked him to call in to the police station after work, if that was all right.

Jeff arrived at 5.40 and asked for Mansell at the desk. He was ushered by a helpful desk clerk to Mansell's room where Mansell greeted him cordially before leading him to the video room.

Mansell explained the video and played it for Jeff.

Jeff studied it hard, and asked for it to be replayed. Mansell obliged, and waited patiently.

Jeff asked if it could be paused as the man left the train, and Mansell froze it at that spot.

Jeff leaned towards the screen and looked hard.

'There's no way, unfortunately, that I can say for sure, not at all, but I have to say that it's not unlike him. Same sort of average size; dark, short hair; and the mac looks similar. But I can't see his face in any detail so I can't say more. Sorry.'

'That's okay. Thanks, Jeff,' said Mansell. 'It gives us a lead, the timing's certainly possible.'

Jeff went home wondering if it was a reasonable lead or not.

Mansell had got to work. He reckoned that the man would have had to run to get to the station at twelve thirty when the train arrived, so took it that he must have got a taxi – if it was him at all, of course.

He tracked down the taxi list of the drivers who had operated around Stockton that night and got DC Wilson to chase them up for a specific fare of a single guy, after midnight, to the station.

He had also received the name of the conductor of the specific train, and requested DS Reece to visit him, when he could fit it in, over the next couple of days.

That Saturday, he received responses to both lines of enquiry. Lol Kennedy was the taxi driver from ABC who had given a man a ride to the station at about twelve twenty the night in question.

Lol remembered the fare as ordinary; gave him a reasonable tip, if he remembered correctly. No, the guy didn't say where he was going, where he had been, anything. No conversation as he recalled. Thought the guy looked pretty soaked, but that's all. Vaguely remembered a mac but couldn't be sure.

DS Reece reported to Mansell on the afternoon of his meeting with Gary Peterson, the conductor on the train.

'Gary', said DS Reece, 'was not the brightest spark I've come across recently. I doubt if he knows what he did yesterday, never mind a late night fare a week ago. He has no idea about anybody on that train. Sorry, boss.'

Mansell and Rogers met to discuss their next move on this suspect.

'We'll try and get it enhanced at the labs, but I'm not sure that his face is ever really exposed to the camera. Worth a try though. How about releasing it to *Crimestoppers*?'

Crimestoppers was a facility available to the police whereby they highlighted a local crime, usually with CCTV footage, on local television, in a couple of minutes' slot around the evening news.

'Yeah, will do, might just strike a chord somewhere.'

So they did that the following week. The pictures had not been enhanced so they knew it was a long shot hoping somebody could recognise a fleeting outline – and maybe that mac.

It duly appeared over two nights on Wednesday 20th and Thursday 21st. There was a mixed response to the hotline number given with the footage. Thirty-seven calls were received. Two were wrong numbers (incredibly); three were total cranks, one of whom rang every *Crimestoppers* appeal number; and the rest were genuine attempts to help. They were all followed up, but none led anywhere.

Mansell was disappointed, but not surprised; it always had been a speculative attempt for public assistance.

He considered further options. They could publish a print of the video image, but it would be even more fuzzy. They could go to *Crimewatch*, the national BBC TV monthly programme, which was very popular; who knows, he might get to meet its attractive presenter. Or they could begin making enquiries at Durham – but where to start?

He also received videotape from the CCTV system at the Durham Station car park but it showed nothing, although this in itself suggested that maybe the mystery man had taken another taxi, or perhaps he lived within walking distance of the station.

Taxi firms were contacted in Durham but nobody had any record of a fare at 12.50 on the Saturday morning.

Mansell took the problem to Burns and requested funds for an extension of the budget to accommodate door-to-door enquiries within a half mile radius of Durham Station.

Mansell was frustrated, but again, not overwhelmingly surprised, when Burns said, 'Sorry, Len, only way to do that is to divert funds from other areas of the enquiry. I've been slapped down on the numbers again, and got internal auditors coming from up north in a couple of weeks, never mind the consultants who arrive on Tuesday to re-establish case budgets, cash flows and the rest of the unfathomable shit that I spend half my life wading through!'

Mansell was surprised at the anger in Burns' voice, for he had always thought that Burns enjoyed playing with those big numbers, enjoyed the power.

So Durham, for now, was abandoned.

So now Mansell was getting ready for work at 6 a.m., with a typical Monday morning attitude, and was on automatic pilot. He had dragged himself from his warm, comfortable bed and the arms of his wife, Ellen, at the first sound of the radio alarm. He sleepwalked to the en suite bathroom, tugged at the light cord and blinked in the harsh light of a three-bulb spotlight.

He peed noisily, as if the excessive splashing was going to wake him. It didn't. He washed in the cold water, loosely cursing the knackered heating timer that he just couldn't find the time to sort out. The cold water on his face did shake him from his lethargy, and his thought processes kicked in. He thought in staccato fashion, as if formulating a list of bullet points.

Rogers for an update on house-to-house, Alan for CCTV again; Tom to chase the forensics; see Sanders again; pull transport reports together; read the reports on the Darlington murder; go and see…'

His train or thought was broken by the shrill ring of the telephone in the bedroom. He moved quickly to the bedroom, carrying a towel with him to mop the dripping water off his face. He was known as a gruff man – a rough-edged diamond, some might concede; but at home Ellen knew a different man. For example, as now, he would always hurry to minimise a ringing phone if Ellen was still asleep. If Ellen was awake before he left for work, he would always bring her a cup of tea and a bite of breakfast also if she fancied some.

If pushed, really pushed, he would concede that he truly loved his wife. He respected her, he needed her. He adored her in the true sense of the word. He knew that without her he would be nothing, not a copper, not a man. So he deliberately did as much as he could to make her life enjoyable and comfortable.

So now he got to the telephone before more than a couple of rings had trilled their call. As it was 6.11, on a cold wintry morning, he knew that it was only a business call and so there was no need for any formality.

'Yes,' was all he said.

'Nige, it's Rogers.' The fact that there were no preliminaries, no 'How you doin'?' no 'Flipping freezing this a.m.,' alerted him, more than the timing of the call, that there was something serious afoot.

'Jeff Sanders had a visitor last night,' Tom hesitated, expecting questions, but Mansell simply said, 'Go on.'

'Local guys got a call about three thirty with a report of an incident at Moorland Street. Turns out to be Sanders', where he and his family disturbed an intruder. They chased him out of the house and there was a scuffle. Our boy Sanders got a bump on his head, nothing serious, and they're all in shock, but nobody seems damaged. The intruder got away but our fellas at the scene say there's blood and it's probably the intruder's.'

He paused for breath and Mansell took the chance to butt in. 'Has Sanders identified him, then?'

'Not exactly,' said Rogers hesitantly, knowing the reaction.

Mansell hissed through gritted teeth, 'What the fuck does that mean, Will? And, how come we're sitting here at six o'clock?'

'Local plods didn't twig it was *the* Sanders. That was only at about five o'clock when Andy caught a whisper of a strange incident and heard the name. I'm getting this information from him. He can't find out if the intruder has been identified by Jeff, but the father's description fits.'

'I'll be there in twenty minutes,' said Mansell and put the phone down noisily.

Ellen stirred and he immediately switched to devoted husband mode. His tone changed and he said, 'Sorry, love, got to dash; anything you want before I go?'

He knew he could ask because there was no way Ellen would ask for anything. One, it was too early; and two, if Ellen knew that he was in a rush she would never get in his way. She duly murmured from under the covers, 'No, ta... See you later.'

He kissed the top of her brow, the only bit exposed to the cold air. 'See you tonight,' he said gently, and went quietly downstairs. He had pulled on a grey suit and wore it with a cream shirt and a blue tie. Ellen had long stopped worrying about her husband's fashion sense, deciding it was simply easier for all concerned if he was allowed to get on with it; another reason why he respected her.

He carried his tie in one hand and his overcoat over the other arm as he marched down the frosty path, stopped at his R-reg Volvo and started looking for his keys. It was a car he took pride in when it was easier not to, but that was another gesture to normality. To do something like washing the car at the weekend made him and Ellen both feel as if they were part of the crowd, leading an ordinary life.

He tracked his keys down in his overcoat and jumped in. The Volvo started first time and he was soon away. At that hour the roads were usually quiet, and on the one real stretch of open road that he travelled on to work he always opened the throttle and enjoyed a quick burst of speed.

Today however, there was a thick blanket of fog, and that annoyed him, for it would add a few minutes to his journey.

It was the little things that irked him, or, in the most extreme cases, really pissed him off. Examples were many and varied but that foggy morning alone three things had increasingly wound him up.

He had stopped for petrol just outside his home and had inserted the nozzle having selected the green unleaded pump. He pulled the trigger and the dials spun, advising of price and volume. Then the pump clicked and stopped. Only a couple of pounds taken and he knew he had twenty pounds to go: pull, supply, click, pull, supply, click. His hackles rose. 'Jesus!' he muttered under his breath; then a few clicks later and he was done, but extremely annoyed.

On the main road there had been a hell of a lot of fog because of the nearby river and that's where the second frustration took place. He knew that warning signs had a function to play, warning of dangers ahead, but how come they never did actually warn in advance? Was there anything more frustrating than driving slowly through a pea souper and seeing, looming out of the stew, a bloody neon sign proclaiming in big red letters 'Fog'? Could anybody tell him what the bloody point was?

Finally that morning he had got stuck in misty roadworks. Three miles an hour, stop, crawl, stop. So which sadistic bastard decided to stick up the signs which said, 'Police Warning, Strict Speed Limit of 50 mph Through Roadworks'?

Life just took the piss sometimes didn't it?

He eventually got parked outside the station. He marched through the back door and down the corridors to his office. In the open area of the squad room, from where his room branched off, there were five or six officers busying themselves with reports, printouts, computer screens and telephones. He saw Rogers standing just outside their room. Rogers moved down the room to meet him, and started talking before Mansell could even greet him.

'Jeff Sanders is in hospital with concussion; his parents are both in hospital under observation for shock. The blood in the garden does not belong to any of them. Everything else is as I told you. Shall we go and see them now?'

'Yes. We've got to ID this guy. If it's our man, well, one thing is that he's obviously left a lot of clues behind; another is that he's changed his MO and is obviously scared of Sanders identifying him, which maybe makes him dangerous or careless, or both.'

They set off before Mansell had even gone to his room and they exchanged a couple of 'Hi's and 'Morning's with their colleagues as they went back out of the station.

The station was hardly the old-fashioned stereotype of a front desk, an office area and a few scruffy interview rooms and cells. This was effectively a modern office block: big, spacious, comfortable and air-conditioned. Mansell and Rogers benefited from this, as the doors into the car park opened automatically.

They went in Mansell's car, for no reason other than his was nearer the door. They talked a little as they drove, but there wasn't a lot they could discuss without knowing a lot more about what had happened at the Sanders' home. They were far too experienced to indulge in idle speculation so they fell silent. Mansell had confirmed that the local boys had the obvious angles covered, house-to-house, forensics etc. He trusted the local lads to do all the donkey work and they would be going to the scene themselves after the hospital visit.

They knew from Andy that all the Sanders family were in Ward 6, which they guessed was only because it was on the ground floor and the hospital staff presumably thought that the family would only be in for a short time. They followed a familiar path to the reception area, having visited this hospital many times over the years visiting both victims and perpetrators, both public and officers.

Rogers recognised the matronly lady on the desk and greeted her in cheery fashion. 'Morning, Jean! Early shift, eh?'

She smiled. 'Morning, Mr Rogers. How are you?'

'Fine, thanks… bit chilly. Come to see the Sanders family. Ward 6, I think, Jean.'

'Been expecting you, Mr Rogers. Yes, Ward 6 is right, all in Room B off the far end of the ward. Do you know where it is?'

'Not exactly… Down that way, is it?' he asked, pointing towards a nearby set of double doors.

'No, turn left just short of those doors, then straight on… Can't miss it.'

Mansell was already in motion as Rogers said his thanks and set off. They soon found Ward 6, and Mansell spotted the two rooms marked 6A and 6B.

He got to the door first and knocked firmly. He was itching to get inside but experience told him to wait for a response. He heard a voice but couldn't make out either what was said or who was saying it; not that this was going to make any difference. He had observed the correct etiquette and the mumbled noise from behind the door was the equivalent of somebody screaming, 'For Christ's sake get in here now!' He opened the door and stepped in purposefully, Rogers a pace behind him.

Mansell quickly took in the situation inside the room. Jeff Sanders was lying in the only bed in the room, apparently asleep, hopefully not unconscious. No, he had concussion, that's all. Jeff's father was rising out of a chair to meet him; Mrs Sanders was sitting in the room's second chair, looking very weary and grey.

Jeff's father was offering his hand to Mansell, saying, 'Good morning, can I help you?' He had seen that these two fellows were not of the medical profession and could sense that they carried some weight. And then he recognised Rogers.

'Morning, sir,' said Mansell. 'You'll probably remember Detective Sergeant Tom Rogers, I'm Inspector Len Mansell.'

'Of course,' said Mr Sanders, embarrassed that he hadn't recognised Rogers immediately. 'How are you both?'

'We're fine, thank you. More importantly, how are all of you?'

Mr Sanders ran a hand across his furrowed brow as if all the memories of the night before had hit him hard. Rogers worried for a second that Mr Sanders was going to faint and he quickly said, 'Take your seat, please sir.'

He indicated the chair and Mr Sanders gratefully plumped down into it.

Rogers then turned to the lady. 'And how are you, Mrs Sanders? Terrible shock for you…?'

She nodded weakly, and Mansell noticed the look that passed across her husband's face. Shit, thought Mansell. She's in a bad way, and his concern for her is going to slow us down here.

He turned to Jeff in the bed. 'So what's this young fellow been up to then? Playing hero?'

He tried to make it a light comment but Mrs Sanders did not hear it that way. She let out a noisy sob then seemed to bite her lip and swallow the next sob.

Mr Sanders reached across and patted her forearm, which rested on the chair arm. He said gently, 'Okay, pet, okay. No need to get upset again. He'll be fine, just a bump on the head – nothing to worry about, the doctor's said.'

Both Mansell and Rogers were surprised to hear Mrs Sanders speak; they were both thinking that she was going to be of no use whatsoever today.

'I know, Gerald, I know, but when you think what could have happened…' Her voice tailed off and the tears welled in her eyes.

The door opened without warning and a grey-haired man wearing a white lab coat appeared. There was little room in which to manoeuvre so he stayed by the door. He looked at Rogers and spoke in a voice that betrayed his irritation. 'Gentlemen, I've just heard that you were here. I'm a little disappointed that you didn't see fit to consult with myself or any other medical staff before barging into a room occupied by three patients. You have no idea of their conditions, and seeing you, unannounced, is going to do none of them any good whatsoever. I would prefer it if you left immediately.'

Mansell was not a patient man at the best of times, and having been quietly irritated at the prospect of getting nowhere fast in the immediate future with the Sanders clan, this instruction from a jumped-up Doctor Kildare lookalike was always going to needle him.

'And you are…?' he asked.

'I am Mr Wittam, Senior Consultant Neurosurgeon to this hospital. I was here last night, having just performed a delicate operation, when Mr Sanders here –' he indicated Jeff '– was brought in. I gave him the once-over and diagnosed the concussion. In my expert opinion he needs the whole of the day today just to rest. No questions, no stress. Mr and Mrs Sanders here –' he waved dismissively in their direction '– are also in traumatic shock, and also could do with a break from intensive questioning.'

He looked at Rogers smugly, as if his words would send the two men running away. His manner and words often had that effect on junior staff and even colleagues. Rogers laughed inside, knowing precisely what was going to happen. He guessed that this guy was a bully, an arrogant prat who nobody would every warm to. It was payback time. He turned to Mansell and waited.

Mansell was in what the lads in his team called 'Triple M'. 'Oh God', they would say in mock-serious tones, 'Nige's gone triple M!' It stood for 'Mean, Moody, Magnificent', and it happened when Mansell vented his frustration or anger by way of a Churchillian-type speech that terrified opponents or recipients and inspired colleagues.

Mansell's tone was icy cold as he moved a step nearer Mr Wittam. He stared hard into his eyes.

'When we arrived there were no doctors around. If we've upset anybody we're sorry,' he said. His tone suggested anything but sorrow. 'However, Mr Wittam, I should possibly clarify a couple of points.' Wittam was about to speak but Mansell drove on. 'Firstly, we are the officers who are conducting a murder enquiry – the Wendy Fell case that you may have heard of. Jeff Sanders was a key witness in that case. The murderer in that case has killed before and will almost certainly attempt to kill again… a serial killer if you will. He's a particularly unpleasant serial killer who picks young women and appears to enjoy the task of slaughtering them. There would appear to be a good chance that the intruder at Mr Sanders' home last night was this murderer, whom we are all so keen to bring to justice. I apologise again for breaking medical etiquette, but I am sure that you know that we would not add to any of these good people's discomfort at this time. Similarly, I am sure that you appreciate that we too are professionals and have a job to do. You would never wish to knowingly obstruct our aims to get the job done, particularly in such a serious matter as this. We will leave you now to take care of your patients and we will come back this afternoon. Thank you very much indeed for your time.'

He turned to Mr and Mrs Sanders and said, 'Glad to see that you're okay. I'm sure Jeff will be fine. We'll see you later; bye for now.'

He managed to get past Wittam and achieve the double affect of giving the Sanders family the impression of making a dignified exit whilst letting Wittam believe that he was being pushed out of the way.

Rogers turned to the Sanders. 'See you soon. Goodbye.'

He smiled at Wittam as he passed him. 'Mr Wittam,' he said. Wittam stood there, in common parlance, gobsmacked.

Back in the car, Rogers and Mansell discussed the previous half an hour. Their conclusion, swiftly reached, was that it was going to take a little time, a frustrating time, to get any useful information from any of the Sanders clan. They went back to the station and busied themselves with a myriad of relatively minor tasks, organising paperwork and men and suchlike. Both were somewhat distracted, knowing that their best chance of any significant breakthrough at this moment in time lay with a concussed young man, a doddery old man and an elderly lady who was in a state of shock.

They ensured that top priority was given to the Moorland Road break-in, at the same time trying to keep it low-key within the station and definitely away from the press.

Time passed slowly until three o'clock, which was the hour they had settled on for a revisit. Rogers instructed Gloria, the Station's senior secretary, to contact good old Mr Wittam and check with him that it was okay to visit Sanders. Rogers gave

Gloria a knowing wink when he said, 'He shouldn't be too much trouble; Nige triple M'd him this morning.'

He was right. When Gloria eventually got through to Mr Wittam, who was grabbing some late lunch, he started to make the expected noises regarding how he would prefer to have his patients left undisturbed, and so on. When Gloria said that Mr Mansell was very anxious to meet the family again because every minute lost was another minute between the police and the perpetrator (a lie she often used), then Mr Wittam said 'Okay,' he would reluctantly sanction a few minutes between patients and police.

Mansell and Rogers followed the familiar path to the room where all three Sanders remained, checking in at the front desk as usual. They knocked politely at the door of Room B, Ward 6, and as they'd done earlier, waited for a response from within. They heard Mr Sanders say, 'Come in,' and they exchanged a quick glance before entering. 'Good luck was needed here; fingers crossed for a breakthrough, anything to get them somewhere on this case…

They exchanged pleasantries with Mr and Mrs Sanders before turning to Jeff, who was sitting propped up in bed, eyes wide open and looking alert. The two officers were relieved more than anything that Jeff was awake; they had not been enamoured of the prospect of trying to glean information from his elderly parents.

'So, young man, we meet again,' said Rogers with a friendly grin. He was delighted to see a broad smile on Jeff's face.

'Yeah, making a habit of this, Mr Rogers.' The smile vanished as Jeff glanced at his parents. The emotional pain of their involvement was etched on his face. Mansell responded in kind by adopting a more serious tone.

'Nasty business all round, and we're obviously keen to crack on. Are you okay to answer a few questions? …I'm DI Mansell, by the way,' he reminded him.

'No problem, fire away,' said Jeff in a determined fashion.

'First thing is the obvious one, Jeff,' Mansell said. 'Was it the same guy?'

The room fell very quiet, so quiet that everyone in it heard the crash of a distant trolley somewhere at the far end of the ward.

Nobody spoke. Jeff looked at his parents and then across to Rogers. He looked back to Mansell.

'It certainly was,' was all he said, but it was enough for both Mansell and Rogers to feel a rush of adrenaline.

'Right!' was Mansell's brisk response. He didn't even bother to cross-question Jeff with, 'Are you sure,' so positive was the young man's statement. Privately, Mansell was thinking, Thank God for that! Would have been a right kick in the balls if it hadn't been.

'Just tell us what happened, then.'

Mr and Mrs Sanders sat in the same seats as they had occupied that morning; Rogers and Mansell flanked the bed. Rogers took out his notebook and pen and stood poised to write.

'Well, there was nothing different or unusual about the night until I heard Mum screaming. I didn't know what time it was, didn't check or anything. I just got out of bed and went to the landing, in the dark. I didn't put a light on at first, I just went to her. Then she pointed to the stairs and said a man had just gone down them.'

Rogers couldn't help himself. He burst into the conversation with, 'And you saw who it was there and then?'

'No, not at all. I just heard the kitchen door slam. I ran into the kitchen, went out of the back door, cut my foot and saw a man go into the bushes at the bottom of the garden.'

Mansell shot a look across at Rogers which Rogers interpreted as 'shut up', so he did.

Jeff had stopped, unsure of whether he was going to be asked further questions.

'Go on,' said Mansell.

He paused, and as if asked what he was feeling at that point, he volunteered, 'I wasn't really thinking about it too clearly, but I know that I was crapping myself.'

Rogers looked at Mrs Sanders and was aware of how desperately fragile she looked. She was looking in Jeff's general direction, but somehow did not seem at all focussed. She had a vacant expression, and a fixed stare on her face; a perfect example, he thought, of 'the lights are on but nobody's home'. He was aware also that Mr Sanders was much more together than this morning and he seemed to be listening attentively to Jeff's story.

'I probably wasn't far behind him, really, as he went through the kitchen to the back door. I didn't know what I'd do if I caught him, it was just instinctive to chase him. It was probably because he had scared Mum that I'd got sort of angry. Maybe I wasn't that close to him, I don't know, but when I got to the garden I saw a full moon through the clouds and it seemed very light. I went down the path towards the bottom of the garden. I was thinking that he must have gone over a side fence when I just got the feeling that he was still in our garden, at the bottom near the shed. I don't know why I thought that, whether I'd heard or seen something. I don't know. I know that my feet were absolutely freezing and hurting from the cut. I got to the bushes near the shed and it was then that I started thinking I should go back in to call for you. Maybe the cold was knocking some sense into me.' He smiled, but it was a thin smile as if it was very difficult to extract any level of humour from the memories of the night. 'I was just about to turn back to the house when he came out of the bushes,' he stated.

Rogers bit his tongue as his voice nearly burst again. 'And then did you see him?'

Jeff had apparently read his thoughts, as he said, 'I still didn't see him, as he just jumped on me – just a blur really. He knocked me down and I took quite a whack. We struggled a bit and I was scared stiff he'd have a knife or something, so I tried to keep hold of his arms and wrists to keep his hands away from me. Next thing I knew I was pushing him into the bushes and I sort of fell on top of him. We were getting scratched to bits by the branches...' he ran a finger along a scratch down the length of his left cheek '...and neither of us could get a good grip of the other cos there was no space. I seemed to wind him or something, cos I heard him give a couple of loud grunts or groans and then for a second I thought that he had collapsed, and then I heard Dad shout from the back door. Then he seemed to get loads of energy from somewhere cos he just jumped off the floor. I think he whacked me in the ba—, er, groin, then he kicked me or kneed me in the head, which is when I must have blacked out. Next thing I knew I was in here.'

He stopped and exhaled a sigh, as if tired by the telling of the story.

Mansell and Rogers both knew that there was a question to be asked and Mansell duly asked it.

'Scary stuff, Jeff. Just one thing, when did you see that it was the same guy?'

'I got the feeling in the fighting, and because it was bright I got a few looks at him and it started to sink in then that it was him; I don't know why it hadn't crossed my mind until then. When I thought it might be him it scared me a lot more and I know that I got an adrenaline rush. I remember that.'

He paused, so Rogers interjected, 'So you definitely identified him in the struggle?'

'No, couldn't say for certain; more a feeling than a definite sighting.'

Like drawing teeth, thought Rogers, as he pressed again. He tried to make it sound like an innocent, throwaway remark as he continued, 'It's just that I thought you had said a little earlier that it was definitely him. Now you don't seem quite so certain.'

He wasn't expecting the answer that Jeff gave when he said, 'Oh, I know it was him Mr Rogers, because he told me.'

Mansell and Rogers blinked in surprise. Mansell said incredulously, 'He *told* you?'

'Yeah, as he got that last energy surge he said – and he was gasping as he said it – "You seeing me with young Wendy was a nuisance, and now you've hurt me. I'll see you again." He said it as he kicked me down below and as he was leaving the bushes. I know that he kicked me in the head then, but I'm not wrong; that's what he said.'

Mrs Sanders' eyes were full of tears; Mr Sanders looked close to tears and Jeff appeared to be exhausted from his efforts. Rogers and Mansell were happy in the knowledge that everything that could be gleaned through detective work and forensics at the Sanders household would not just be aimed at catching an intruder but aimed at the capture of a deranged and dangerous serial killer.

Chapter Twenty-One

He thought, as he wrestled on the freezing ground with Jeffrey Sanders, that this was a fight to the death. He had panicked when he had seen Jeff only a few feet away outside the bushes where he shivered, hunched down on his haunches. He hadn't thought clearly enough to use a knife; everything had been too rushed since that damn woman had screamed and scared the shit out of him on the stairs.

He had leapt at Jeff and the struggle that followed was fierce, adrenaline pumping on both sides. When they tumbled back into the bushes there had been another brief scratching, pummelling thrash before he got an enormous shock as he felt one of his blades dig into his side. He had gasped and suddenly stopped all movement. He flexed a muscle on his side and the pain surging through him there confirmed his initial assessment. One of his own weapons had pierced his flesh. He knew that he was in desperate straits here, and to exacerbate it he heard a distant voice calling from inside the house. He summoned all his strength and, preparing for the pain, he gritted his teeth and thrust Jeff's body away from his own. He swung a hug flailing punch, catching his hand on branches which diminished the force of the blow; but it still carried some venom as it connected with Jeff's testicles. Jeff grunted as he rolled away from Westmain. For a split second Westmain thought of finding a weapon and finishing Jeff off but the combination of the pain in his side and the growing volume of the calls of Jeff's father told him he had to leave now.

He moved towards Jeff and spoke as he moved, saying, 'You've been a nuisance to me,' and added, 'I'll see you again!' Then he grabbed Jeff's head and raised his knee to it. It connected with a thump and Jeff fell back with a loud 'Ugh!' Westmain scrambled out of the thicket, turned to the shed, went behind it and glanced back to Mr Sanders near the house, peering into the bushes shouting, 'Jeff, Jeff!'

He hauled himself over the high fence. The pain dug deep into his guts but he pushed it as far away as possible. He tried desperately to gather his thoughts. Get your bearings, for God's sake, get back to the car. He knew that he would have to go left and left again through the garden that he now stood in, and then past the Sanders' neighbour's house, to get back to the street that Sanders lived on. From there it was only a matter of getting to the car before the police filled the area. He headed for the house and soon saw a path that ran down the side of it. He went through a little waist-high gate, wincing at the pain shooting through his body. He held a hand to his side and he was conscious that his fingers were becoming sticky with blood.

He thought to himself, I'm injured here, possibly badly, but I'm still thinking, still functioning. He gained strength from his realisation that even a wound couldn't stop him. Just another obstacle and twist in the greater plan that God had for him.

He was soon on the street and he looked left and right. Nothing moved; there was no noise. He heard a distant cry, presumably Sanders' father finding Jeff.

He moved swiftly down the street away from Sanders' home and turned into the first street that he came to. His car was parked neatly some thirty yards down this street, in between two houses so as not to have either householder looking and wondering.

He went to the car, found his keys and got in. That really hurt, he thought, as he sat down with a heavy bump into his seat. He drove away sensibly, not wanting to rush and arouse suspicion, and was soon out of the area. In twenty-five minutes he was parked in his drive. He moved stiffly to the front door, let himself in and went as quickly as he could to the bathroom. He winced as he took each item of clothing off; the slightest movement was now hurting like hell. He saw that the inside of his mac was blood-soaked, and when he took his shirt off he noticed that a large crimson stain had spread down one side of the material. He was not panicking; in fact he felt quite detached about this and he would have said that at this point his major sensation was one of curiosity. He looked at the wound in his side and saw a two-inch long slash in his well-toned abdomen. He gingerly poked at it and blood oozed out, but he reckoned that, painful as it was, it was not life-threatening. It was a nasty cut, that was all; he wasn't sure whether from a protruding Stanley knife blade or from a gouging screwdriver. He washed the wound, and once it was clean he could see that his diagnosis was correct: a cut that technically might have needed stitches but in the circumstances would have to be tended by himself. The blood was not flowing from it, so it couldn't be that bad. He put a big plaster over it and then put some cotton wool and tape over the area. It felt pretty uncomfortable so he went and sat down on his bed. He sat there quietly, not wanting to move, in order to allow the wound to settle down. He then considered the night's events.

His first thought was, God is really making this difficult, isn't He? First the Almighty brings Sanders into the equation that Friday night and now, when Sam has taken the initiative to do something about it, He goes and chucks another spanner in the works in the form of Mrs Sanders.

'Charming! Whose side are you on?' asked Sam aloud.

Okay, so tonight was a wash-out, but there was time. He wasn't in the habit of making idle threats and his assertion to Sanders that 'he'd see him soon' would be carried out.

He left the bed and grimaced as the wound shot pain through his body. He told himself to ignore it as he took his journal from the bureau. He wrote down the night's events and at the end of the entry added, *Sanders/God 2, Me 0, half-time*. He laughed at his little joke.

Before he fell asleep he silently mouthed the truth from his favourite text. No matter what the circumstances, no matter where or when, 'Desiderata' always told the truth. Tonight was easy.

> Nurture strength of spirit to shield you in sudden misfortune.
> But do not distress yourself with dark imaginings. Many fears are
> born of fatigue and loneliness. Beyond a wholesome discipline,
> be gentle with yourself.[2]

So true; he had to dismiss the most fleeting of thoughts that God maybe wasn't really on his side, and he would have to be gentle with his wound. 'Desiderata' was always so truthful.

The next day he sat in the café at lunchtime and thought about the names that he had seen in print that morning for the first time in a long while.

1990 – Darlington   – Helena Stockley
1992 – Sunderland   – Donna Mills
1997 – Manchester   – Laura Bull

To these he added,

1978 – London   – Joyce Lindsay

The first had been in 1975 – his mother; and now there was Wendy Fell. These were the six women that he had killed to date. The press speculation was such that it was impossible to ignore the names, they were being bandied about on television, radio and in the press.

He cast his mind back to London in 1978, when he had gone for a weekend break. There had been no malice aforethought whatsoever when he had met a girl called Joyce at the bar near London University. He liked student areas and watering holes, the atmosphere was lively and there were loads of attractive women. He liked the look of attractive women, even though he knew that he could never get close to them. He had wanted to have sex with quite a few whose paths he had crossed between 1975 and 1977, but never forming any sort of relationship always blocked his dreams. He would imagine taking them to his flat, or pretend to himself that he had had them on the back seat of his car.

He had a vague idea, which he had never made concrete, that he had to make use of women for a couple of years, to sow some oats as a man should do, and then after that time span, well, he was aware that there was a greater plan at hand; but the oat-sowing never took place.

So that night in London had been the start of the plan being put into action. The night had gone okay, pleasant chat, filling in a few background details. But as the night grew late Joyce had got more and more drunk and her manner changed for the worse. She started a tirade at about eleven o'clock against men, useless fumbling men who screwed you then dumped you; they were all the same. Sam did not want to hear this so he said, 'Thanks for the company,' and left the pub. He was standing at the kerbside unsure whether to walk or hail a taxi when Joyce stumbled out into the street.

She saw him and went straight to his side. 'Did I upset you? I'm sorry, I'm sorry! I didn't mean to moan on, I'm sure you are different.'

'Oh, I'm different all right,' he said, 'I know how to treat a woman in the manner that she deserves.'

'Oh, that's sweet, it really is. Can we go somewhere?'

'Let's walk,' he said. 'It's a nice enough night.'

They had walked a half-mile from the pub when he stopped, took Joyce in his arms and kissed her passionately but not in an overpowering way.

She said, 'Umm, lovely, maybe you are different.'

'Here, this is a short cut to my hotel, let's go down here.'

He took her by the hand and led her down a dingy, unlit alley. A few yards into the alley a further alley broke away, very dark and full of menace. He turned into it and stumbled over a bottle, kicking it against a wall, where it smashed.

'Where's your hotel, did you say?' asked Joyce, the surroundings awakening her senses.

He heard God say, 'Go on, then... If you are really serious about helping Me to sort out the bitches who inhabit my world, do something! Did you like it when she berated you?'

He felt as if he was watching somebody else. He felt no emotion as he shoved Joyce against a wall. She cried out and began to scream but he grabbed her with both arms and threw her down to the dirty ground. She was winded, and before she could scream again he had reached down to the broken bottle. He picked it up and turned the girl. He was not thinking of this actions; nothing was considered, he just did it. He rained blows down on her, across her face, onto her head and against her arms as she held them up to protect herself.

She soon fell silent and he raised himself up, puffing with the exertion. As he looked down at the body he had quoted, 'Avoid loud and aggressive persons; they are vexatious to the spirit.'

God spoke again. 'So you've done one thing, but is that really enough? I think you have got to make a bolder statement, don't you? What are you really trying to say here? Isn't it that women should not be allowed to dominate, to hold sway just because they produce babies?'

'You're right,' Sam said aloud. He pulled up Joyce's wet jumper, exposing a trim stomach, then he pulled down her skirt to below her knees. Her white panties were inviting but the fleeting thought was quickly pushed aside. He pulled them down to expose a triangle that an hour earlier might have been deemed the target for the night. Now it was targeted for other purposes.

He drew the jagged edge of the bottle across her stomach and in the dim light could see the blackness of the oozing blood. Then he started to cut around her pubic hair with the bottle. The broken edges were not easy to work with and it took him a time to finish cutting out large chunks of flesh. After a period of some twenty minutes he was satisfied that he had made the statement that God had led him to.

He knew that he was a mess and stepped back to the first alley where it was a little lighter. He knew that he was spattered with blood and his hands felt very sticky. He walked slowly to the end of the alley where the street lights illuminated the entrance. He saw the bloodstains on his jacket and took it off, wrapping it into a bundle. His jeans were messy but he didn't think that they were too noticeable. He carried the jacket in both hands and hurried back to the hotel where he was staying. The lobby was well lit, but he scurried past the reception desk and into a lift. He was relieved to find it stayed empty. He was soon back in his room and standing in the bathroom. He quickly got cleaned up, only thinking, Wash this, do that, careful with that. Once satisfied that he was clean there was a moment when he thought, Well, I've just killed a woman. Will I get caught?

He smiled because he knew that although there had been no planning, no taking care of contingencies and the whole thing had been spontaneous, God had really directed it and he, Sam, was only an instrument on this occasion; because he knew that now it had started, he would have to take the lead for all those to follow.

The media coverage was intense because of the nature of the frenzied attack and the horrible mutilations that he been inflicted on the girl's corpse. Inevitably because of the circumstances and location, the media had fun speculating on a new 'Jack the Ripper', but as usual the interest waned after a few days.

Sam had returned home to Leicester, triumphant that his plan was up and running. He took no notice of the various reported sighting of himself and Joyce; he felt God's protection wrap around him.

Sam had been offered a place in care after the tragic death of his mother, but as he was sixteen he was allowed to stay with family or friends. He had neither, but a neighbour took pity on him, especially in view of the nature of his mother's horrible accident, and took him in. He lived with the elderly couple for a year, but after his seventeenth birthday he announced one day that he was leaving to go into digs. He thanked them for their kindness and moved out.

He had found some digs in an old part of town and although they were less than salubrious, they offered anonymity.

Sam needed a job and eventually got one as a junior clerk in the administration office of a large supermarket. He found the work easy, he was good with numbers, and he intended to progress through the ranks over a couple of years. All the while he was trying to establish some contact with God for a detailed explanation of the plan, which he knew deep inside he had to follow. He had been told all his life by his mother that God was punishing him, through her, for the death of his saintly, perfect grandmother; but each time that he heard this he would hear a contradictory message – from God Himself, no less – saying, 'Don't listen, you are the victim of an unbalanced mind. Your mother is evil and once you have been released from her power then you will be rewarded by assisting Me in a glorious plan that I need someone to help Me with.'

The problem was that he had never received any details of the plan, even after he killed his mother. But he was prepared to wait; no point rushing God, He was a busy person.

Then Joyce Lindsay happened and the plan was becoming clearer. He sat at home after his weekend in London and wrote down in a diary *The Plan*. He then outlined in a few sentences his thoughts on what the plan was going to entail and why. Basically, this amounts to *Removing women who had yet to breed, for the purposes of stopping future motherhood and its terrible possibilities*, as he put it.

The first thing he did was to change his name by deed poll to 'Westmain'.

Over the following months he thought of the options open to him to action the plan: go on a spree and kill one a night over a number of weeks; kill one a month; or kill totally randomly over a number of years. He decided on the third option. So he planned and he jotted his thoughts down in his diary, and then one day he awoke and God said, 'Do one tonight.'

So he had donned the macintosh that he had already adapted for the purpose and carefully inserted an array of weapons.

He really believed that he would simply walk into town, meet a girl, take her somewhere and kill her. But it didn't happen like that. For some reason the opportunities never presented themselves. He went out many times with the intention of carrying out his next stage but he couldn't make the appropriate contact. Even when he met a girl and struck up a conversation, the night always seemed to end with her getting a taxi home, staying with friends or giving him the elbow. He tried pubs and clubs but it just did not happen.

He was frustrated but not disillusioned. He realised that God had given him the first one on a plate and was now making him earn the second one; a challenge, if you like. He welcomed it.

His twenty-first birthday passed and he was still fully committed to the plan when disaster struck. He went to work one fine Thursday morning late in 1980 when he was confronted by the office manageress. Apparently a significant amount of money was missing from the safe and he was one of the keyholders. Did he have anything to say? He didn't, but after two days of the enquiry and questions the finger of suspicion fell back on him. The management informed the police that they had been tipped off by an employee that Sam Westmain had bragged about stealing the money, that he'd said nobody was bright enough in the office to even notice. He defended himself vehemently but the police believed him guilty. No charges were ever brought as there was simply no evidence, but he was asked to resign his post.

He suspected a jealous colleague, Marie Windsor, who had been overlooked for the senior post that Sam had been given at twenty-one. She deserved it, being older than him, she thought, and did not hide the fact. Sam would have been interested to hear some time later that Marie Windsor was found stealing goods from the storeroom, and in a panic attack at the police station confessed to several other criminal acts, including framing Sam Westmain a few years earlier. She had borrowed his keys from the staffroom for a brief but effective five minutes one sunny day.

After losing his job Sam was devastated, if nothing else the episode had proved yet again the worth of his bible:

> Exercise caution in your business affairs, for the world is full of trickery; But let this not blind you to what virtue there is; many persons strive for high ideals, and everywhere life is full of heroism.

He believed the only heroic thing he knew of was his own courage, so he decided to adopt a high ideal; he would spread his wings.

He then decided to go to France to seek pastures new, to cleanse himself of the reek of corruption and disappointment that enveloped him in his home town.

Paris was a nightmare. He found squalid digs with the intention of finding work and moving up in the world, but it didn't happen. He ran out of ideas, money and hope and ended up begging at the major tourist spots. He eked out a living but knew that he had to get home. He scraped enough money for the ferry crossing and hitchhiked to London in 1983. He went to a hostel and stayed a few nights, only to end up on the streets again. Then he decided that he wasn't going to be beaten. His plan was never forgotten, and in the dirty old rucksack that travelled everywhere with him was his diary, where he laid down his thoughts and plans.

One night he was squatting in a derelict old building when a young couple came in through the entrance that had once been the back door. Sam was slumped behind a wall and they had no notion that he was there. They were giggling a lot and he suspected that there were on drugs, but he listened with interest as they disrobed and found a piece of unlittered ground to lie on. They had urgent, writhing sex and as he listened his mind drifted back to the days with his mother when he was forced to stay in the same room as her while she performed sexual acts on yet another temporary boyfriend. He would be told to watch as the man would screw her in various positions, her head often turning to him and her mocking expression driving him to distraction. He remembered the pain of those many occasions and felt tears burn his eyes when he realised that it had gone very quiet. He peeped out from behind the wall and saw that the room was empty. A used condom lay on the floor and he picked it up. It was sticky but he held it for a while enjoying the sense that it gave him, the thought of where it had just been thrilling him.

He felt as good as he had for a long time, the memories of his mother relighting some embers long cold. He resolved there and then to sort himself out, telling himself that he had passed the recent challenge, by surviving. He knew that the spark was back. All he had to do was get a job, get a home, get organised and then he felt sure that God would be back with him again.

Over the next few weeks he searched fruitlessly for an opening but then got a break when he was hired by a restaurant as a dogsbody in the kitchen. It was a start, and over the following months and then years, he moved through progressive jobs, always improving his lot, and all intentionally short term to allow him to move around retaining his anonymity. He felt that this was somehow important.

He started going to church regularly and believed that it was a good way to say 'Sorry' to God for whatever he had done that had upset him all those years ago. He couldn't think of what he had done, but accepted the years of punishment.

One evening in 1986, he was in church when the statue of Jesus told him to start his plan again. The next day, Sam went out to find somebody. Nothing happened, nor on the next day, nor the next or over the following month. He was in church after several fruitless attempts to find someone when God said, 'I've given you time but I now need to tell you, you're doing it wrong. Don't just sit in a bar and hope to get lucky; follow them on the streets – it's much more likely to lead you somewhere.'

So he did this the following night and, lo and behold, it nearly worked. He had wandered around the streets some distance from the busy thoroughfares of the town centre when he saw a young woman strolling down the pavement towards him. He tensed in anticipation and as she passed him he grabbed her, putting one hand over her mouth to stifle the screams. He dragged her into the driveway of a house they were passing and threw her on to the lawn. He jumped on top of her and slapped her face. She lay quivering in the moonlight, he sitting astride her.

'Listen, bitch! This is not about sex, it's about you and your type and the cruelty you inflict.'

He reached inside his coat and pulled out a Stanley knife. The girl's eyes were wide with terror. 'What's your name?' he demanded.

'Edie,' she whispered, and was amazed when he suddenly changed his manner completely.

He stared at her then leaned forward and said, 'Don't move!' Then he jumped up from her and was gone.

She never knew that the only thing that saved her from a terrible death was the sharing of a name with a lady who had died in a very unpleasant accident some twenty-five years earlier.

Sam was surprised to find that he couldn't kill because of the sound of his grandmother's name, but was delighted with the success of walking the streets.

He decided to move away from the London area, as the girl had given the police a not unreasonable description of himself. So he moved back to Leicester. He never felt settled there, despite it being an area he knew, and he realised that the city was haunted by both memories of his mother and her very presence.

He had a couple of jobs over two years, first as an insurance office clerk and then obtaining a promising production line management post; but that ended in tears, so one day he went home to his little flat and pulled an atlas of England from a shelf. He stuck a pin in the map, having spun it around a couple of times whilst keeping his eyes tightly shut, and looked down to see the pin embedded next to Bishop Auckland, County Durham.

The day after he arrived in Bishop Auckland he visited a local church. As he prayed, God said, 'All right, you have proven your worth to Me, I will make you fitter and stronger; the plan starts now.'

Over the following nine years he had killed, including Wendy Fell, four girls. Just before Wendy Fell, God had told him that it was time to step up the frequency. One every couple of years was to become one every six months; or at least that had been the plan until Jeffrey Sanders had stuck his nose in. That would have to be sorted, quickly, because he had a date with destiny and the date was now.

Chapter Twenty-Two

By anybody's standards it would have to be said that Doris and George Wilkinson were an eccentric couple. To an unknowing third party they would, at first meeting, appear to be seriously potty; to the knowing family they were dear, jolly, wonderful, funny and potty. Only three people really knew that they were very ordinary, sane people who had somehow decided many, many years ago to perpetrate an act of eccentricity. Those three were Doris, George and Dorothy – Jeff's mother, and Doris's sister.

What had started as a little joke between themselves in the Sixties had, at first unconsciously, and then consciously become a full-blown act that they simply got used to doing whenever in anybody's company other than their own. They even sat down one night in 1968 and planned what and how to do it. Admittedly they had smoked a little marijuana that day.

'Let's just be mad for six months and kid everybody that we're loopy,' said Doris.

'No probs, we can do that,' said George with a huge grin. 'The aim has got to be to get everybody we know to accept in six months' time that we've lost it. Nutty but nice, eh, Doris?'

So, in the years that followed they kept it up, honing their act to perfection. They believed that it was their way to enrich people's lives and they believed that they were always in control. The truth was that they had indeed gone the way of the Colditz man, a little anyway. They were now a little mad, genuinely eccentric, but as Doris would always say, 'What's the harm?'

She called George 'Mr S' for his spoonerisms, she was called in turn by him 'Mrs M' for Malaprop. When they used these names in public, people occasionally debated what they stood for, and indeed occasionally enquired this of Doris and George but they just smiled their happy smiles and said, 'That's our little secret, you'll have to guess.'

People guessed 'Mr Sexy', 'Mr Super', 'Mr Sensational', but never got close. Mrs M was 'Mrs Marvellous', 'Mrs Magic', 'Mrs Magnificent', but never got close.

In 1986 George acquired a hearing aid from a car boot sale. After a serious amount of disinfectant soap and bleach to clean it, he took to wearing it occasionally. He'd fiddle with it and say, 'Damn thing, never seems to work properly!' and people would tut-tut sympathetically at the traumas of the ageing process.

Doris had developed her 'I'll just blurt out' quite nicely. It had become a blurting out that usually had a gentle sexual content. Nothing too sensational, nothing too explicit. She would just say, whilst watching the television with friends, for example, 'Look at the knockers on that!' in an excited voice, whilst watching *Baywatch* or similar girlie shows.

And so it was that Doris and George were everybody's favourite relatives. You always left Doris and George having had a good laugh. People went away feeling good because although much of the laughter was gained from their afflictions (deafness and oncoming senility), it wasn't cruel laughter because they laughed too, and somehow there was just this feeling that their afflictions weren't being endured, they were somehow being enjoyed. Nobody could explain it (well Dorothy could, but didn't), but everybody felt the same. They were lovely company, lovely people and meeting them was always pleasurable.

So now, as they sat soberly in Jeff's lounge with his mother and father in attendance, it was a shock to see them and not be laughing. What was an even greater shock was listening to what they were saying about the last thirty years of pretence.

Doris was saying, 'So, somehow with your murder, Jeff, and then the intruder the other night somehow it has put everything into perspective and our messing about does not seem appropriate any more, now that you are in danger. So we are coming clean and telling you all about it and apologising for kidding you all these years.'

Jeff's father said, 'I don't believe it, I just don't believe it!'

Jeff asked, 'You're not kidding us now, are you, Aunt Doris, just to cheer us up?'

'No, son, this is the truth; we are frauds, but we are stopping as of now.'

They discussed the ways that the two of them had managed to maintain the pretences for so long and Doris and George were forced to confess that they didn't rightly know, it just sort of evolved.

After they had gone, Jeff turned to his parents and said, 'I don't believe it. Just when you think it can't get any worse… this! Who would have believed it?'

The news that his favourite Auntie and Uncle had been deceiving them all for so long hit him hard. Any other time and the revelation may have been greeted with hoots of laughter and congratulatory back-slapping for a job well done. In today's circumstances, though, it felt like another nail in his coffin of misery.

Jeff went to his room, lay face down on his bed and thought about things. If it wasn't for Jayne, well things would be pretty damn bleak. Things seemed to be stacking up against him. The murder; the impending end of the happy crew; the break-in and all its possible sinister implications; his parents being half scared to death, and now Doris and George confessing to being bogus deceivers, nutters who had been laughing at them all this time.

He thought he'd had a break when he had only been kept in hospital for a day with mild concussion. Jeff knew that he was a million miles from perfect. He sincerely believed that his greatest strength was that he knew his weaknesses, all of them. He could say, hand on heart, that he did try to eradicate his weaknesses but he'd equally have to admit that, hey, the spirit is willing, the flesh is weak; and that more often than not his best intentions fell short of achieving their goal. At least he tried.

He would have to admit to two things in particular that he wasn't proud of. Sure he was weak in bad language, bad deeds, bad thoughts etc., but wasn't that just general stuff that all human flesh fell prey to? No, two specifics that he'd have to admit to were one, nose-picking, and two, his sexual fetish.

He just could not lick nose-picking. 'Lick' was not a good term, and he'd never done that, but God yes, constant nose-picking. His only saving grace was that he never did it in public, unlike some people, who appeared to take great delight doing it in cars, restaurants and the street, ramming a digit to its hilt up into a nasal orifice and raking about. At least Jeff was private, but he couldn't understand how or why he should take so much gratification from raking about in both nostrils, often when there was nothing in there. But when he did trace some miscreant dust and muck particles that had gathered together to form snot, oh, the joy of locating, catching and extracting the bogey! If he saw, as he often did in public toilets, a bogey skilfully flung to a wall where it stayed as if superglued to the tiles, always above the urinal to which he marched, he would feel nauseous. If – God forbid! – he should ever find on his hand somebody else's bogey, albeit a small, neat, hard one, he would almost certainly vomit there and then. But if he found a stringy bogey up a nostril at home he'd squeeze it, pull it, roll it, enjoy it. Weird! And, like any true addict, he couldn't stop. He wasn't aware of any national – or indeed, international – clinic for bogey chasers, so he guessed he was stuck with it. He'd look at a freshly extracted bogey as if it was an old friend, staring at it with a slight smile.

His other concern, his fetish, really wasn't that bad. It wasn't as if he wrapped his testicles in cling film, smeared Branston Pickle over his nether regions and shouted, 'Slappa my thighs!' His weakness was very tame by any comparisons he was sure, but he was a little concerned that it was something he couldn't really control. He loved the smell, the perfumed smell, of women. It could be the actual perfume, it could be hairspray or deodorant, but he just loved feminine smell. If he was aware that a woman in his company had that lovely cologne smell he would make a point of passing her as often as possible. He had found himself a couple of times standing behind a particular target and sniffing – very nearly sniffing the woman directly. It was harmless, wasn't it? It wasn't as if he was touching or anything. He wasn't convinced, and thought he should stop it, but like other weaknesses, like going on a diet, words were cheaper than actions.

Despite all this however, Jeff felt that he was generally okay, nothing special, not virtuous, but 'okay'. He was respectful of his family, friends and colleagues, honest. Jeez, he was even kind to animals! So why was he being picked out for this run of bad luck?

He decided to watch a bit of television and saw his father in his usual chair as he entered the lounge.

Jeff loved his father deeply, far more than he could tell him, theirs not being that sort of open 'touchy-feely' relationship, as Toddy would have put it. Jeff was proud of his father's high moral standards, his work ethic and the love he gave to his family. Jeff said in rare moments of openness, usually to associates or even strangers, 'I've got the best dad in the world; he simply couldn't be better.'

Even as a youngster Jeff had appreciated that the family were never going to be wealthy, but it had never bothered him. He was always provided for, had been brought up to appreciate the value of material things; not their price, and never felt cheated that his family had never had the best car, best foreign holiday or latest gadget. So what?

His father had worked for the local Health Authority for some thirty-seven years, usually in administrative roles, ending his days there in 1990 as a sixty-five-year-old senior authoritative figure at the General in Stockton. He had worked in various hospitals over the years, at Durham, Sunderland and Northallerton but had always lived in Stockton.

And so now Jeff felt it deeply when he saw the pain etched on his father's face.

They were sitting together in the lounge, quietly, when Mr Sanders put his *Times* down onto the nearby coffee table. He turned to Jeff and asked, 'Have you got a second, son?'

As Jeff was staring blankly at the television screen as an old, old episode of *Bonanza* played again, he said, 'You could say that, Little Joe is bound to get better. What is it, Dad?'

'This business with this man, I know that you've been through this a dozen times with the police, but are you absolutely sure that there's nothing, not even the tiniest thing that you haven't mentioned, anything, that just might help?' He paused and looked at Jeff with a pained expression. 'It's just that, that, well, I think it'd be better if he was caught, that's all.'

Jeff was shocked, and saddened, to see that his father was scared; that was something he'd never seen or experienced before.

'They'll get him, Dad, don't worry. If I think of anything I'll tell them, but I don't think there will be.'

Nobody spoke; then Jeff's father said, as if he had been asked, 'Because I can't stop thinking about the other night and what might have happened to your mother if she had been... if he had been... I just can't stop.'

Jeff hadn't realised just how shaken his father was and he felt compelled to go to him. He knelt by his father's chair and put a hand on the old man's arm.

'It'll be okay, Dad, honest it will. We've just got to be grateful that nothing did happen. He won't bother us again.'

The last few words were spoken with as much conviction as he could muster, but Jeff wasn't sure if they would convince his dad.

'Okay, son, just me being a fuddy-duddy. Bit of a shock, that's all; you're right, there's no real harm done. Sorry.'

Bloody hell! thought Jeff. Dad apologising to me – that's all I need, a guilt trip about that! Aloud, he said, 'Nothing to be sorry for, Dad, so long as you and Mum are okay.'

He patted his dad's arm and left the room, emotions jangling. He went to his bedroom and sat at the desk.

He suddenly felt very sorry for himself and he put his face into his hands. A feeling was welling in his stomach and he didn't like it. He tried to focus on Jayne, his one source of happiness at this time. He felt a surge in his spirits as he thought of seeing her again soon but then the dark images crowded in again. The killer, Wendy Fell, his sad, old dad. The feelings in his guts rose through his system and attacked his tear glands.

He wept, crying for his parents, for Doris and George, for himself.

Most of all he wept for the future, for he knew that this wasn't yet over.

Chapter Twenty-Three

The alley was dark, very dark, and very quiet. Deep shadows and shades of dark mixed in a gloomy, eerie patchwork of scary possibilities. Like a scene from an American cop show, the high walls of the alley were lined with boxes, crates and black plastic refuse sacks. The only visible breaks in the walls were made by an occasional back door. They led to a couple of restaurants, one or two commercial properties, a wholesaler and a small mini-market. There was the odd recess also, dotted here and there along the length of that oh so uninviting black tunnel.

What the hell Jeff was doing there he just did not know. His scrambled thoughts only told him that a night out with his darling Jayne had somehow gone horribly wrong, that there had been a serious (first) bust-up, at the Chinese restaurant. A few details drifted back into his consciousness, like Jayne theatrically throwing her napkin down on the table and storming off. What did not drift back was the cause of her disappearing act. What had happened? Had he sneezed in her food, cracked a dirty joke. What, what, what?

He knew that he had grudgingly settled the bill, unhappy at paying for two largely untouched meals. Although he had paid the amount quickly, by the time that he stepped out into the snow flurries there was no sign of her. He had to decide quickly which way to go, a simple choice between left or right. She could have gone either way because they had come by taxi and there were ranks in both directions. He chose left, for no particular reason, and started to jog along the pavement. The road ahead of him curved to the left and as he rounded the bend he got the chance to scan the area ahead of him. He slowed to a brisk walk and eagerly looked to both sides of the street. It was well lit and he knew within a few seconds that Jayne was not down there ahead of him. Now he had a problem, because he didn't think that he had time to backtrack and get to the rank in the other direction before Jayne would have had time to get a taxi. At least, not back along the main road. He looked to his left, a little way ahead. He saw the entrance to what looked like either a little side street, or maybe an alley. He estimated that if it turned back on itself a little, then it should effectively be a short cut to the area where he thought Jayne might be heading.

So that's why he was now in the alley, staring down it, wondering if this was wise. He had gone a few yards into the alley and was soon plunged into Stygian darkness. The alley seemed to stretch farther ahead of him than he would have imagined, and indeed farther than he wished. And was that a dead end that he could just about see in the distance, illuminated thinly by a light from an upstairs window?

He had hesitated but now moved on with purpose because his normally reliable sense of direction told him that the end of the alley had to bring him somewhere near the locale where Jayne just might be. The light, noise and life of the main street was soon behind him like a distant memory, and an inner sense made him hesitate again. He felt as if he was very, very isolated, a hundred miles from civilisation, from life, from safety. He stood still in his silent, dark environment. He shivered and looked up into the narrow strip of sky above his head. The wispy snowflakes still fluttered around him aimlessly, making no impression on the cold ground. The strangest thing that struck Jeff was that the point where he had entered the alley was now almost out of sight, just a pinprick of light. Had he really walked that far? It certainly didn't feel like it. The question that popped into his head was, If he had come this far, how come he wasn't out the other end and had broken out onto a street full of activity?

He strained his eyes one way then the other, wondering whether he should abandon his original intention and head back to where he had started. Back or forward? Back seemed sensible somehow, the route suggested by the head. The heart, however, reminded him of the Jayne factor, and this proved too powerful a force to ignore. He set off again, determined to find her and right whatever wrong had been perpetrated. What the hell had they fallen out for?

He kept his head down, one to avoid the blowing snow and two to keep his eyes on the wet ground, watching for alley debris, potholes, puddles or the dreaded dog dirt. It wasn't easy to see where he was walking as the dark and shadows seemed to shift beneath and around him. There was litter scattered around, and he kicked the occasional empty tin can and shook the odd paper product from his feet.

He was thinking of Jayne and straining to identify the 'problem' when his attention was snapped back to his immediate surroundings. The thought present at the forefront of his mind slapped him sharply: This is not a good place to be. It was the first time in the few minutes – or eternity – since he had entered the dark passage, that such a strong negative feeling had enveloped him. What had precipitated this sense? Did it really matter? His feeble attempts to raise the query of Jayne's early and unhappy departure from the restaurant were swept aside by the demons of the dark. They were now whispering, 'Forget that, forget Jayne; this is now not good, not comfortable. This is scary, isn't it, Jeff? Scary and dangerous. Have you seen the recesses coming up? What do you think could be lurking there?'

He had slowed to a very slow stroll. He looked over his shoulder but the dark and thickening snow blotted out sight of anything beyond the first few yards. He had a horrible flash of a crazed axeman bursting into view and hurtling towards him, but there was nothing. The heavier snow served to muffle further any possible noise, and he thought that it was so quiet that he could actually hear the snow landing. Why was there no distant traffic noise?

He looked ahead again and let out a little involuntary 'Phew!' as he saw nothing in sight. The end of the alley was discernible, and although it looked a bit like a dead end he felt sure that it would offer a left turn out onto his targeted street. The moment appeared to have passed so he took a couple of bigger, quicker strides. The demons were not impressed. 'Stop, stop, you fool, it's coming! It's coming! Run away!' they screamed.

What's coming? What is going on? he wondered, and a rising well of panic rumbled in the pit of his stomach. And then it hit him with a thud, so hard a blow that it stopped him in his tracks.

'Oh shit!' he said aloud. The thought that rushed his brain was terrifying in its obviousness: What if *he*, is here? Why hadn't he thought that at the entrance? But surely he couldn't be here, how on earth could he be? How could he be so stupid to come into such a dangerous place... this tunnel of fear? He shook his head and gave his right cheek a sharp slap. Aloud, he said, 'Get a grip for Christ's sake, get a grip!'

Hearing the words seemed to galvanise him and he decided to jog a little way. He broke into a gentle jog, not wanting to risk falling at any greater speed. Moving quicker triggered another wave of fear, telling him that he was now running away from something, from somebody.

He slipped on snowy patches and tripped over an old fruit crate. He kicked a bottle which smashed noisily into an unseen wall. Then he met the closing wall at the end of the alley. He could see that he had been correct in guessing a T-junction and he was offered the choice of turning left or right. The quickest way out to sanctuary was going to be the chosen way; he would catch up with Jayne later.

He heard something which chilled his blood and made him stop again. He was a few feet from the junction and he had heard a noise. He couldn't identify it, just a scraping noise, and worse still he could not tell which side of the turn it had come from. His choices were limited, and the demon voices did not help, 'Now you're screwed! Go for it, run around one corner and run, run, run!'

He leaned forward slowly, his heart thumping so loud that he put his hand to his wet jacket as if to quieten it. God, he was scared, and all the fears of his recent encounters came back to say 'Hello', and turn his legs to rubber.

He thought for a second that fear was going to turn him into stone, so that he could not lean any further forward, but he gritted his teeth and forced himself into a position where he could just see around the two corners. He quickly glanced left and right and received conflicting news. The immediate good news was that there was no obvious sign of anybody in the near or far distance. So what about that noise? He ignored it. The bad news was that the cursory glances gave the strong impression that neither way offered an immediate release back to bright lights and security. He looked harder; to the left was another alley similar to the one he had just come along, with no lights at all. To the right, a few distant blurred lights appeared in the alley walls, possibly upstairs rooms of eateries. Maybe he should just knock at a random door and go through the surprised kitchen of some Chinese takeaway. The thought of an early escape from this horrible place lifted his spirits and he decided to move on. He would go right, because its pale distant lights called him like a siren to a wallowing ship.

'What about that noise?' asked a demon, a little less effectively than before. In a clear, determined fashion he answered it. 'Nothing, just a combination of me clattering rubbish and a vivid imagination.'

For a moment he actually believed that and he almost felt happy, such was the release of positive chemicals into his system. Only for a moment, though, because he recognised a movement some ten yards in front of him that he knew was not whirling snow, or shadows or moonbeams filtering through the snow clouds. It was definitely something physical... moving. Before the spindly fingers of fear had squeezed the life from his heart, Jeff saw a cat dart across the alley.

He emitted a snorting, laughing sound that conveyed the heights of the mixed emotions that he had endured in such a short period of time. 'A frigging cat, I don't believe it!' he said in a loud voice, and he quickly walked to the spot where he had seen it run. All his fears seemed to have instantly evaporated, and the demon who was asking, 'Could a cat have made that noise?' was drowned out by positive thoughts.

'Here, puss, puss, puss!' he called. He knelt in the wet by some bin bags and clicked his fingers. 'Here, puss, puss! Come on, kitty.'

He didn't want to touch the rubbish bags for fear of encountering particularly nasty filth, or maybe some broken glass or other equally dangerous objects, but he was keen to see the cause of his fears. He was looking behind the second litter bag, looking into what he realised was a previously unnoticed recess in the alley wall, when he spotted something that struck him as very unusual for a wet, cold, dark alley in the middle of nowhere, where the only companionship and alleviator of fears was a disappearing cat. He looked in disbelief at a shiny, new-looking expensive brown shoe. He was still wondering about it when the other shoe, with an accompanying leg, was placed next to it.

Jeff recoiled in shock and horror, his hands splashing on the wet ground as he scrambled across the alley floor. His head spun and he was frightened. His panicky movements never allowed him to regain his balance and he fell back off his heels into the wall on the other side of the concrete corridor. Before he could get to his feet the owner of the brown shoes had stepped from the recess and moved over to stand above him. Jeff looked up, eyes wide, and then blinked as snowflakes pricked his vision. The man's definitions became clear and Jeff retched as terror rose from his guts to his throat.

Jeff stared again into the face of a serial killer. His serial killer. *His* killer?

Jeff felt his bladder and bowels heave as his orifices screamed 'Open up and let the packages go!' That same cold hand that had gripped him that cold Friday night several weeks earlier was evident again, tugging at a heavy stomach and pinching his breath. He could not speak and could barely breathe; he was only conscious that his head and heart pounded and that his very worst nightmare was being visited upon him. Adrenaline and other chemicals flowed through the same channels and veins adding to his panic and confusion. 'Run, fight, hide, beg!' he was told. Too many instructions led him to do nothing. He just cowered and stared.

'So we meet again,' said the man, through tight lips. 'How very opportune for me.'

The trapdoor remained shut on Jeff's throat; it had the effect of containing both words and vomit. His palms were wet, not just with snow but also with sweat, and their clamminess was in stark contrast to his mouth, from which every droplet of saliva had been removed.

The man bent towards Jeff, and Jeff half raised a hand in readiness for an anticipated blow. It never came as the man spoke.

'I could talk to you, but I don't think I really want to. You have caused me problems and for that you are to be punished.'

As if by pushing a hidden button, the words had the effect of releasing Jeff from his inertia and he started to pull himself up. He thought that he had been quick, but the man was quicker. He was strong too, as Jeff would soon appreciate, when the man grabbed Jeff by the shoulders and smashed him effortlessly back down to the ground.

A little dazed, Jeff shook his head in order to clear his thoughts, but all thoughts were suspended as Jeff saw the man open his mac and reach inside it. Jeff suddenly knew that this was the same mac as the one worn on the night of their first ever, memorable, meeting.

The man drew from his coat a long-bladed knife. 'You hurt me that night; you know that, don't you?' he asked Jeff.

Jeff couldn't take it in that he was not being asked a rhetorical question and shouted 'Ouch!' when the man kicked him hard on the left shin.

'You do know that, don't you?' he was asked again, this time in a more aggressive manner.

For the first time in his life Jeff stammered 'D–d–d–don't kn–know.'

'I don't believe you, Jeffrey,' said the man. His voice, in direct contrast to Jeff's, was controlled and clear.

The man closed in on Jeff and was now only a foot or two away from him. Jeff could see the man's eyes burning angrily. His words and tone reflected his ire. 'I'll do whatever I want, you snivelling little shit!' he hissed at Jeff. 'Don't you dare to tell me what to do, you pathetic, weak-kneed bastard.'

The man's spiteful assessment of Jeff stirred an emotion other than terror. It was Jeff's turn to feel anger nibble at his innards. Anger at the words, anger at this miserable situation, maybe anger at the way his innards were shredded with fear.

Jeff moved quickly again, only this time he stayed low, launching himself at the man's legs. He did not give himself time to worry about the man plunging the knife into his back. The surprise and venom of Jeff's attack took the man unawares and he was knocked backwards. Unfortunately, he did not fall over, just staggered a little, then a slip; then he regained his balance and composure and looked down at Jeff wrapped around his legs.

In a blur of movement and strength he hauled Jeff to his feet, spun him around and whipped a steely left arm around his neck. His other arm yanked Jeff's right arm behind his back and Jeff yelped in pain. Jeff's left arm hung down redundant. What could it do?

Jeff's anger was replaced by that now familiar sickening pull of terror. His eyes pricked with tears of helplessness and he defiantly croaked, 'You bastard!'

'Not true, Mr Sanders. You do tell lies, don't you?'

He drew the knife to Jeff's throat and every muscle in Jeff's body tensed for that final moment.

'No more,' said the man. But then, as Jeff felt his attacker's hand grip the knife tighter for its desperate deadly deed, the man added, 'Or maybe just one more thing…' Jeff's head swam. What game was this now?

'Your girlfriend looked really pissed off tonight, Jeffrey. What on earth did you do?'

It was not only the unexpectedness of the question but also the way it brought memories of the Chinese meal flooding back that made Jeff gasp. The night had been going great, with a highlight when Jeff had pondered too long over his choice of the main course. The menus were extremely large and Jeff had rested his menu over the candle that the waiter had lit upon their arrival at the table. He was just considering the final shortlist – king prawns in black bean sauce, Singapore fried rice or beef with cashew nuts – when he noticed wisps of smoke circulating around the edges of the big menu. He was idly wondering what this meant when Jayne shrieked, too loudly for a posh restaurant, 'You're on fire, you're on fire!'

He turned the booklet over to see an ugly black stain and a little flame scorching the back. A lot of smoke drifted from the crinkled burnt offering. 'Shit!' he gasped, and beat the menu on the table.

Bits of charred plastic spun lazily into the air and smoke was blown on to neighbouring tables. A waiter rushed over and took the menu off Jeff. He ran off to the kitchen holding the smouldering item dramatically at arm's length. The strange scene was made more surreal when a second waiter approached their table and, with pen and pad in hand, asked politely, 'Are you now ready to order?'

Jeff and Jayne looked at each other, Jayne with her mouth open in surprise and Jeff still stunned at the discovery of his flaming menu. Then they both howled with laughter. They didn't just titter, or giggle, but both roared. People around the restaurant looked across at them, some openly, some furtively. Some tutted, others joined in the laughter. The waiter carried out his duties to the letter and waited… and waited. It had taken some time for Jeff and Jayne to settle down and finally Jeff had regained his composure.

He started to say, 'King prawns in black be—' but never finished the sentence. He choked and coughed as his attempted stifling of the next guffaw nearly cut off the air in his windpipe. Jayne was squeaking, a sure sign that it would be a few minutes before she could recover. Jeff waved the waiter away, sobbing, 'Sorry!' between convulsions of tearful laughter.

When they had settled, some five minutes later, they studiously avoided eye contact with each other, fearing another attack of uncontrollable hysterics. The food was carefully ordered and an apology proffered by Jeff for both the destroyed menu and the consequential reaction.

'Probably spit in the food now!' said Jeff and Jayne had wrinkled her nose.

If the conversation had then turned to the weather, the latest storyline in *Eastenders* or the latest defeat of the local football teams then it might have been continued to be a nice night. Jeff however continued on the food theme.

'Mind you,' he had said, 'A bit of spit would probably add to the special taste of Pekinese or Alsatian or whatever the hell is the main ingredient.'

Jayne was not impressed, 'Okay, Jeff, that'll do, thank you very much.'

He did not read the warning signs that Jayne flashed at him: eyes that said, 'Enough,' and a pursed mouth that shouted, 'Do not go down this avenue!'

So he ploughed on.

'Everybody knows it's true; the only question is which class at Cruft's is missing a few best of breed.'

He chuckled, but Jayne did not join him. She said, 'You know I don't like stuff like that about animals. Please stop!'

Jeff sounded a little crestfallen as he said, 'Sorry, J.' But a moment later he continued. 'It's just that you can't beat a bit of poodle chow mein, especially if it is topped with fillet of chop suey pussy!' He laughed again and did not pick up on the distress etched on Jayne's face.

Now she was angry. 'Don't mention it again or I'll be off,' she said. 'I mean it, Jeff, I hate talk like that.'

He just said 'Sorry' contritely and they both fell silent. The food duly arrived and they both picked up their utensils. They looked at each other and Jayne said, 'Mm, this looks lovely!'

Jeff grinned and said, loudly, 'Woof, woof!'

Jayne then stunned him by roughly pulling away from the table and throwing her napkin on to her full plate.

He knew that she was not joking, but added fuel to the fire with a comment guaranteed to upset Jayne at the best of times, never mind at this precise moment. 'They're only bloody animals, for God's sake!' he protested.

'I warned you!' she said, and a single tear swelled in her left eye.

'Sit down, don't be silly!' said Jeff, irritated by her militancy.

'I warned you,' she repeated, and then spun around and went to the door. She dragged her coat from the coat stand and stormed out. Jeff was conscious that people were looking at him for the second time that night, only this time nobody was laughing. He didn't know what to do, so in order to buy some thinking time he'd eaten a few mouthfuls of the excellent food. He knew that he would have to swallow his pride along with his king prawns and catch up with his beloved. So he neatly placed his knife and fork on his plate and went to the payment point as quietly as possible.

He had then found himself on the pavement outside, and that's when his real problems had started.

The man was talking again. 'Here's a last thought for you, young Jeffrey Sanders. I know where she lives, your Jayne, and

I'm going to see her soon, very soon. I'm going to enjoy meeting her and whatever we get up to, consider this. It's all your fault!'

Jeff had never felt pain and anguish as he did at that moment. Not Jayne, please God, not Jayne If only he could get away from this madman, if only…

The knife was drawn across his throat. His blood oozed at first and then spurted out into the winter's night.

The man threw his head back and laughed, then louder again. His terrifying maniacal laugh sounded deafening in the silent alley. Jeff slumped to the floor, oozing life but clinging to it. He stared along the ground, the few frozen snowflakes around him turning pink. Jeff could not move, only thinking, Why is he laughing so loud?

Just as he felt that he was about to die, Jayne knelt down next to him. She was smiling, and she gently placed a hand on his wet head.

Jeff screamed, 'Run, run! There's the killer, just behind you!' But the only noise that he made was a gurgling rattle of blood and spittle. He should have known better; after all, you can't expect to talk with no vocal chords, can you?

Jeff shook as the horror of the situation tortured him. How could she not see him, standing so close, laughing so loudly?

Jayne was standing up and the man was suddenly at her side, smiling down at Jeff. Jeff rolled his eyes as far as he could and from the corner of his eye could see that Jayne was holding the man's hand. He just couldn't understand what he was seeing. He tried to say, 'Jayne, Jayne, for God's sake! It's him, it's him!'

Jeff wriggled in a pathetic attempt to raise himself and the man and Jayne both laughed at him.

In slow motion, Jeff saw the man reach inside his mac again. God, no, no! Please spare her. The pain in Jeff's heart far exceeded that caused by his fatal wound. *Ruuunnn!* he screamed.

Jayne was still motionless and smiling when the man plunged a screwdriver into her face. She was not smiling when he repeated the action, and again. Jayne fell to the ground, dead. The perpetrator of the hideous act knelt down to Jeff. Jeff could smell his putrid breath as he spoke to him, inches from his face.

'There you go, Jeffrey, job done!'

Jeff sat bolt upright, screaming. He was immediately conscious that he was soaked in sweat. It felt like he was sitting in a shallow bath. He was also breathing hard, as if he had just finished some heavy exercise.

He put his wet hands to his face and rubbed both cheeks and forehead. He was shocked at the layer of perspiration that covered his face like a mask.

He pushed the soaked bedclothes back and felt very cold when the night air wrapped itself around his wet body. Christ, that was too vivid a nightmare... far too real! He shivered and he was not sure whether it was the perspiration, the cold night air or remains of fear that had caused it.

The memory of Jayne's face in the nightmare was fresh in his mind's eye as the bedroom door was flung open, making him jump off the bed. The light snapped on and Jeff's heart moved back to its allotted place when he saw his father in the doorway.

'All right, Jeff?' he asked, a tremor in his voice betraying the emotion he was feeling having heard his son's scream.

'Fine thanks, Dad. Sorry, bad dream.'

Gerald Sanders looked at his son curiously, not fully believing that he was 'fine'. Far from it, he thought.

Jeff was thinking of Jayne, and the same thoughts were going around his head, over and over. If ever anything happened to Jayne, anything, ever... But no, that was too much to contemplate.

Not Jayne.

Chapter Twenty-Four

Jayne loved his sense of humour. 'Not at all like an accountant,' she teased. She also welcomed the fact that he had no fashion sense whatsoever; she would take that as a challenge.

She reassured him about his weight. 'It really doesn't matter Jeff, a couple of pounds, so what.' But she noticed that he was on his exercise bike quite often. She also told him that the scar under his chin, received when Toddy hooked him whilst fishing when they were nine years old, was endearing rather than ugly. 'It adds character,' she had told him firmly.

He had told her about Beth, and that he had only qualified as a Certified Accountant at twenty-five because she had knocked him off track; but Jayne said that that was something to be proud of, not something to explain about as if embarrassed.

She had laughed when he told her that he would go potty if he ever saw her eating nuts from a bowl on a bar or table in a pub. 'I read that if you took any of these bowls and tested them you would find an average of thirty-seven specimens of urine on them. Think about it! Please don't do it, Jayne.'

He hated buzzwords, phrases or acronyms, usually imported from America, so she would tease him by dropping them into their conversations.

'Heard a rumour about getting downsized today, might just be the CEO winding us up,' she would say. She liked the way he accepted being teased.

She would get the giggles when she watched Jeff attempting to swallow a headache tablet as he had to go through the most exaggerated action. Pill pushed right to the back of the mouth, huge swig of water, a shake of the head like a pelican swallowing a fish, the pulling of a funny face... and then, hopefully but not always, it was gone.

She hadn't tired, so far, of his constant use of the phrase, 'Ain't it the truth,' sometimes said in the voice of the cowardly lion in

The Wizard of Oz, a film that they both unashamedly adored and watched together often.

He entertained her with his quirky ways, like the day he said 'I think it's time that I explained the four "S"s and the five "and"s.

'What on earth are you talking about?' she asked.

'Happy days equals four "S"s. That is to say, in a happy state of bliss with the one you love, you should always start the day with four "S"s: a shit, a shave, a shower and a shag, though not necessarily in that order. Heaven! And the five "and"s goes like this: Give me a sentence with five sequential "and"s and have it make sense.'

'Don't be silly, it can't be done,' she'd said, knowing full well that he was be about to prove her wrong.

He said, 'There was a new sign being painted for a pub called The Dog and Gun, but when the landlord received the sign he was annoyed and said, "That's no good, it's all wrong. The gaps are just not the same between *Dog* and *and*, and *and* and *Gun*. Please change it immediately."' Jeff fell silent and looked at Jayne.

'Five "and"s,' she said. 'What a smart ass!'

He loved words, and verbal trivia, and he asked her one evening how many letters she thought were in the longest English word in the world. She guessed sixty, and really did not believe him when he said, 'No, nineteen hundred.' She said, 'Go on, then, what's the punchline?' But he said, 'No punchline, I've got it at home somewhere, I'll show you.' And he duly did later that night.

They enjoyed a nice meal one evening at the end of March at the nearby Chinese, and he had one of his 'moments'. To be fair, he had only said to Jayne across his crispy duck, 'Now don't get excited, and I'm not making a fuss, am I, but I've just seen a guy in a car, who stopped over the road for a few minutes, and he really, really looked like you-know-who. As much as any of the other imaginary sightings, anyway.'

Jayne was grateful that at least he was now starting to joke about it; the 'you-know-you' and 'imaginary sightings' were very encouraging, she thought.

'Is he still there?' she enquired innocently.

'No, as I say, he just stopped a few minutes, seemed to be staring at us whilst he sat there, and then went off. No problem. How's the king prawns?'

She was delighted that he seemed to be getting back to his old self; things could only get better.

They finished their meal and Jayne drove Jeff home. She had a coffee with him in the kitchen and then kissed him goodnight.

'Goodnight, darling,' she purred, 'Love you, see you tomorrow.'

She hesitated at the front door, looked at him and thought, It's been a tough five weeks since the break-in, but I think he's really coming through it.

She blew him a kiss, which was reciprocated, and then she was gone.

Shortly afterwards, Jayne walked slowly up the frosty path towards her front door. It was a beautiful night, crystal clear, and the night sky twinkled with a mass of stars. It was the sort of night, she thought, as she paused to look up into the sky, that if you were in a good mood made you feel even better, because it was so pure, so awesome. Mind you, in a bad mood you would just say that it was bloody freezing! It was a wonderful night for Jayne, and she could not help smiling as she hesitated at the door to find her door key. She looked again at the nearly full moon and muttered, 'Superb!' There even seemed to be less than usual light pollution, that horrible all-invasive orange glow from town and suburbia. Tonight there was just a black sky littered with lunar and stellar reflections.

She dreamily opened her door and pulled hard at the Yale key which was getting a bit sticky lately. As she entered the small hallway, she smiled again, this time recollecting Jeff's joke about the man with one leg who tells his girlfriend that... well. She smiled.

Jeff was great, really special, and she knew, really knew deep down that she never wanted to lose him, ever.

She wandered into the living area from which the little kitchen sprouted. She went to the kitchen and flicked the kettle on, checking the water level indicator first. She always did this, religiously, ever since the incident last year when she had turned the (admittedly old) kettle on, without water in it. The resultant mini fire had not been serious, as she had been on the spot to immediately smother it with a tea towel, but she did not need a second lesson in good habits.

The rooms in Jayne's flat were all very dimly lit, deliberately so because she just loved candlelight and thought that gaudy neon just wasn't the same. Consequently, until she had pottered around the place lighting up the fifteen or so candles, the place was positively gloomy. She put the kettle on because she fancied an Earl Grey tea, with milk. Instead of busying herself around the flat whilst waiting for the kettle to boil, she leaned back against the kitchen units and thought of all the things that she could imagine about Jeff, all the reasons why she loved him.

She loved his dreams of wanting one day to be able to play a musical instrument. 'Any flipping thing, a recorder would do,' he'd said. And to speak a foreign language. 'I should go to France, cos when we were in Nice we realised that the schools must have brilliant language departments because the kids all spoke great French – ho, ho!'

She loved the way they talked like excited teenagers about life, God, the moon and the stars, as if star-struck for the very first time.

She loved the way he could be such a clumsy oaf, like when he had knocked over the display of Easter eggs at Safeway, and his sense of silly humour like today at Marks and Spencer, when he kept peeping from behind displays sticking his tongue out at her.

The kettle boiled and she took her tea into the living area. She placed the mug carefully on a coaster on the little teak table that was her constant companion by her favourite chair. The truth was that she only had two chairs as she did not want to clutter the place, but of the two this was by far her favourite.

She thought about sitting down but decided to go and put on her Winnie the Pooh pyjamas first, before returning to sit with the book that she was currently engrossed in. She was an avid reader, usually devouring a book a fortnight, and she had a wide and varied taste in subject matter. Romances, crime, factual – pretty much anything was in her range. Currently it was a scary thriller which had been amongst the many tomes bought for her at

Christmas. Her only criticism was that the author was extremely graphic in detailing the 'romantic' scenes. Is there really a need? she wondered, as it does seem to be a little gratuitous, and ultimately... She stopped her train of thought. Moaning again, prude girl, she chided herself. She shivered.

She undressed quickly because it was very cold in her bedroom. Too cold? She moved to the radiator behind the door and found, as she expected, that the radiator was hot. How so cold? She neatly folded her skirt and blouse and placed them on the stool next to the small vanity table. She pulled on her jim-jams and shivered again. Can definitely get a second day out of the skirt and blouse, she thought idly as she pushed the stool a little more neatly under the table. She carried her underwear to the wicker linen basket that stood quietly in a corner by the window. It was decorated with a bright, almost garish pink ribbon, and she made a mental note to wash the ribbon over the weekend.

She shook herself a little, trying to remove the cold that kept seeking to envelop her. She picked up her book from the bedside table and wandered into the living area. She could no longer ignore the cold; she had to address the reason for it. The heating was on, and although it was a very cold night, her flat normally retained the warmth generated by its heating system.

Surely I didn't leave a window open. No, I haven't opened a window for a couple of weeks. Definitely been ages since I... Her thoughts froze, and not because of the temperature, when she saw the nearby curtain flutter gently away from the window before settling again.

How on earth has that...? But before finishing the thought she lifted her face into the air, sniffing like an animal that had just caught a scent. She stood very still, sniffing. She had definitely caught a whiff or two or something flowery, perhaps sweet, a faint hint of an odour that should not be in her room. She lowered her face, curious but not unduly alarmed, when she reached for the curtain. She drew it back and gasped at what she saw. There, in the middle of the pane of glass was a neat round hole, about six inches in diameter.

She let go of the curtain and took a step back, her head reeling, her mind trying to grasp spinning thoughts.

It's not been caused by vandalism, too neat, no debris. Where's the glass? Must be burglary... Have I been burgled? She spun around and glanced around the room. There was no sign of any disturbance; the television and stereo system were still in place. She moved to the bureau that contained her passbooks and jewellery boxes, but they too were in their allotted places.

She was puzzled and drifted back to her bedroom, where again close inspection told her that everything was as it should be. Except the temperature.

Was it a disturbed burglar, or some particularly strange joke? She stood at the door between bedroom and living area and thought hard. The first thing to do was ring Jeff; maybe he would have an explanation. She moved to the telephone mounted on the wall and reached for it. She was calm; puzzled but not frightened. She tapped Jeff's number but the phone made no noise at all. She put the receiver back into the mounting then picked it up again. No dialling tone greeted her. No buzzing, beeps... no sound. She repeated the actions because sometimes if you were a little quick off the mark you did not catch the dialling tone. She did everything slowly, conscious that suddenly her heart was thumping in her chest. Now she raised the phone slowly to her ear, not wanting to hear that horrible silence and all its implications. No sound was heard, and for an abstract moment she felt that she was going to bang her fingers down on the phone unit, saying 'Operator, operator!' as she'd seen in countless American films. She did not do this, but instead pushed the receiver tighter to her ear as if maybe she had simply not heard the sound she sought. Still nothing, so she quietly placed the phone back to the wall.

Could be a coincidence, she speculated, not believing that there was the slightest chance of any coincidence with the window and the phone. For the first time since she had arrived home she felt fear. Quietly, insidiously and effectively it nibbled away at her sense of security. She cursed herself for not having charged her mobile the previous day and looked again at the phone on the wall, as if her glare would force it into action, but it did nothing. Her gaze drifted down the phone to the cable leading from the unit down the wall.

'You idiot,' she said aloud, realising that she must have, at some time, knocked the connection loose from its fitting by the skirting board. 'That's why there is nothing.'

She moved to the wall and bent down, ready to insert the little white fitting into its socket. Her hand hovered in mid-air as her eyes locked onto something truly horrific. The cable was cut, some ten inches above the skirting board, the fitting below resting correctly in its socket. The cut end of the line curled away from the wall.

She raised herself slowly, her body feeling very heavy and lethargic. Cut wires mean somebody has been here, right here, tonight. The adrenaline kicked in and she was told by all her senses to run, take flight. She grabbed her coat and shoved her feet into her comfortable old slippers. At the door she put her hand to the bolt at the top of the door and saw how much her hands was shaking.

Her head was screaming, *Get out, get out*, and she fumbled for her keys in her coat pocket. Then, that smell again, something like… Her eyes bulged as the gloved hand wrapped around her mouth. She was slammed into the door, just turning her head enough to avoid having her nose broken, but still receiving a painful blow to the side of her head. Her left hand was grabbed and her arm was pulled behind her. She winced and uttered a yelp of pain. The initial contact, together with the shock of being thrown against the door, had rendered her defenceless. She was dragged backwards and she inhaled a nostril full of that strong smell.

Her legs were turning to jelly and could not support her but she was being held by her assailant. She felt a trickle of warm liquid down her legs.

A voice hissed through gritted teeth, 'You know who I am, don't you, Jayne dear?'

It had not crossed her mind that any intruder may be known to her. She had supposed in the previous few moments that she was being burgled. Now, just now, the terrifying realisation dawned on her of just who was with her in her flat.

'Don't you?' Westmain asked angrily.

She couldn't speak because of the hand clamped tightly to her mouth, so she nodded in tiny movements.

'Don't make a sound, or I'll kill you,' he snarled into her ear. She shook her head to acknowledge the instruction. With his lips touching her ear he said quietly, almost in a whisper, 'I just want to have a little chat.' He surprised her when he released her and said in a louder voice, in an almost conversational tone, 'Been waiting for ages. Not too comfortable in the cupboard there.' He pointed to Jayne's only significant storage cupboard, which housed her vacuum cleaner and the like.

She had not turned around to face him but he reached her left shoulder and spun her around. She did not want to look at this monster, but he placed a hand under her chin and lifted her head roughly.

'Look at me!' he said, and when she still averted her eyes he cracked a hand across her face. Her head snapped to one side and then she looked at him, eyes welling with tears.

'That's better,' he said in a pleasant tone that gave no hint of the circumstances.

'You'll see, it's not personal at all between me and you; obvious, I suppose, as we've never met. We do of course have a mutual acquaintance in young Mr Sanders.' He hesitated, as if losing his concentration, and he muttered, 'Good old Jeff,' before returning from his distant place to once again focus on Jayne.

'Different kettle of fish, me and Jeff. We've had something going on since that night in January. Are you listening, Jayne dear?'

She could not manage to bring a word to her lips so she nodded.

'Good. I just want to explain, you see. He's never let go, that's been the problem. He really has been a pain in the arse; he's really screwed up all my plans. At first I thought, naturally, that it was God chucking me another curve ball, like the car, like... like those early disappointments. But I came to realise that God was not directing the actions of this little prick. He had put him there, sure, but Jeffrey took it on from then himself. Free will and all that I suppose. Do you understand?'

Jayne had no idea what he was talking about but nodded in agreement.

'Good,' he stated simply.

Jayne was terrified but was recovering from the first wave of shocks and she heard herself whisper, 'He's done nothing.'

A big grin spread over the face of Westmain and it struck Jayne that he was most definitely, absolutely certifiably mad.

'Done nothing? Good grief, he's been a proverbial thorn in the side!' He laughed a humourless 'Ha!' and said, more aggressively, 'He's never been out of the press! He didn't play the game at his house, and he talks to the police all the time.'

'It's not his fault, they won't leave him alone.'

'Enough!' he barked, the order hitting Jayne like another slap. 'I've been watching you for a long time now, I know all about you and lover boy, and he has no excuses. Actually,' he continued, looking at her slyly, 'I've been about this close to you once or twice. At the Flying Firkin, and last week in the Lord's Tavern. Oh, and a few days ago in Safeway. You never see me, do you? Funny, that.'

She shivered at the idea of him being so close to them, stalking them, and then she thought, Shit! It's *him* that is that smell, I knew I had smelt it before… aftershave or something.

He seemed to have drifted off to other thoughts and she felt herself, almost unwillingly, leap towards the door. She actually had the door open a fraction before a vicious kick slammed it shut. The next kick was delivered to her calves and she screamed. He grabbed both her shoulders and picked her off the floor. She shouted, 'You bastard, you fucking bastard!' but he didn't hear her as he flung her into her favourite chair. She hit it hard with a sickening thud and the wind was knocked out of her. She had her hands on the floor and he came over to her and stamped viciously on her left hand. The little air in her body left it with a squeal as bones crunched in her hand and fingers.

'Bitch!' he hissed. 'And I thought we were getting on so well.'

She wanted to scream but the noise stuck in her throat. Her hand was in agony and there were shooting pains in her legs from the kick. She closed her eyes and prayed. *God, please help me, please.* She kept thinking, What to do? Fight, talk to him, do nothing?

But that was the only thought, going around and around, and no answers were provided.

He was mumbling on, saying, 'I've been told, "Speak your truth quietly and clearly; and listen to others, even to the dull and ignorant; they too have their story." If I listened to you or the others, there would be no story, nothing of consequence anyway. Now I do have a story, long and interesting – but hey, we don't have all night.'

Jayne continued to pray.

'He hasn't looked after you, has he, your lover boy? Maybe he didn't take me seriously, what do you think?'

She shook her head weakly, dazed and stunned by the heavy fall and the pain in her hand.

'Like two warring stallions... no, that's an exaggeration... like two cunning chess players, plotting moves and counter-moves. Head to head, trying to outdo the other; him slaughtering me in the press: "Wild animal" ...I won't forget! And me trying to deal with him in a finite way.' He grinned again, 'So who is your money on, lovely Jayne?'

She did not respond at first, but then chose her words carefully as she gambled on another tack. 'I'll talk to him, tell him to stop it.'

He looked surprised and nodded slowly, 'Yeah, that could do it I suppose, point out the error of his ways maybe?'

She nodded, more enthusiastically.

'Hmm, interesting, do you think that he would accept my victory?'

'Of course. He knows that you've won.'

Jayne's spirit was raised. He seemed genuinely interested in the offer, and she stifled a cry that burst into her throat from the pain in her hand. She swallowed it, not wanting anything to disturb the moment. If only she could reason with him, if she could make him believe that he had beaten Jeff, if only... She realised that he was talking, or more precisely, mumbling. She strained to catch the words.

'...Only ever been women, and the world will recognise the justification, total justification; but Sanders, well, he was going to make it women six, men one. But he wouldn't play the game, would he, no, he would not.'

He was looking at her with eyes that were not focussed on her, but which darted back and forth. He continued to talk under his breath as if debating with himself or trying to explain something to the demons within.

'I'm not bitter about that failure, really I'm not, not even the wound; but it wouldn't be right, would it, to have such a hollow victory? Just words? What about making him suffer, what about taking something from him? If not his life, something almost as precious.'

His words were now garbled, rapid and very quiet and Jayne could not hear them to make any sense of them.

'His pain, kill him... Stop the girl, his girl... him and her... Do it, do it, of course you'll do it! Came to do it... don't listen... God's playing... Right, right, right!' His focus cleared and he uttered a long, loud, guttural, 'All right, I hear you!'

He chuckled, and spoke to Jayne as if they were friends in a pub.

'So I've had a chat and thought about your idea, and I'm afraid that it's not acceptable, if that's okay. No hard feelings?' he asked, smiling.

Jayne's blood ran cold at his nonchalant manner and for a sickening second even imagined that he would offer her a handshake. She believed that there had to be a key which could unlock this terror, a word or an action which could unsettle him or assuage him, something to allow her further time to escape this nightmare.

'Please let me explain,' she began, but before she could continue, a loud, heaving sob escaped her lips. If asked she could not have identified the source of, or reason behind the cry. Was it fear, physical pain, emotions churning, or thoughts of her loved ones? Or all the above? A second, gulping sob followed, and she squeezed her eyes tight in a huge effort to stifle any more.

Westmain smiled a wicked smile and asked patronisingly, 'Something the matter, Jayne dear?'

She did not answer but listened carefully as he again spoke, apparently making a speech that was not necessarily addressed to her.

'So really, all I am doing is getting back on track, that's all it is. And anyway,' he said, staring at Jayne, 'you and lover boy were getting so chummy that you could have been knocked up any day, and we can't have that now, can we?'

He laughed at his little joke and Jayne sensed a change in his mood; she felt that the uncertainty a little earlier had been fully removed and that he was now clear as to his next move. He stepped forward and Jayne shouted, 'No!'

'Now don't be difficult,' he said, holding out a hand as if in a gesture of friendship.

'Fuck you!' she retorted, her anger rising.

He laughed, a loud, cackling noise and Jayne felt as if plugs had been removed from her feet and all hope had run out of them. She prayed again.

'There's probably some people out there, Jayne, who'd want to make the comparison of my deeds with the likes of Sutcliffe, Nielsen or Fred West – you know, because of it being women; but that would be so, so wrong. You see, those three were mad, horrible men with sick, twisted views. They had no good cause to do what they did; they were evil bastards.'

If Jayne had listened to these last few words she might have found a hint of gallows humour in his assertion that they were mad and by implication he was a fully paid-up member of the sensible party. She was not listening because she was begging God for help. She was reminding the Lord that she had been a good person throughout her lifetime. She confessed to being less than perfect, to have occasionally fallen short of His, and indeed her, standards; but really, she was good, and had always loved God. He would know that of course. *Make him go away, make him go away*, she pleaded. Her heart said that God might be listening, so she kept on begging. Her head sent other thoughts shooting through her body, all very contradictory, none of them helpful: fight, panic, scream, go weak with fear, go stiff with fear... She pushed these confusing thoughts away and tried desperately to make contact with God.

Her nemesis continued. 'You see, they did their thing for all the wrong reasons. Greed for Nielsen, a sexual gratification for West and sexual rationale for Sutcliffe, prostitutes and all that. Nobody should die for those reasons; that's obscene. But of course, that's why they got caught. Nobody –' he pointed heavenwards '– looked after them… unlike me,' he remarked, grinning.

He remembered those dark, justifying days and shook his head a little. 'God says it's okay, and anyway, what's six or seven women in the scheme of things?'

Jayne did not pick up on the 'or seven'.

He moved quickly, unexpectedly, his steely grip throwing her easily into her chair. He was suddenly astride her and he slapped her saying, 'No noise, none.'

She was desperate and she switched her pleading from the Almighty to a more real, more tangible power.

'You don't need to hurt me,' she said, as calmly as she could. 'You've won.'

For a fraction of a second she thought that she saw something in his eyes, but in a moment it was gone. The sneer on his lips dashed her hopes.

'You are attractive, aren't you? I hadn't really noticed before. Maybe I should fuck you, to sort of emphasise my win. Not that that's my style – but hey, this is unusual, isn't it?'

She started to recoil but he casually yanked her back to face him.

'Only kidding! That would be like joining those evil swine I mentioned earlier. Not good form.'

She remembered some of the reports of Westmain's earlier victims and in particular the graphic details regarding the mutilation that he had carried out on them after he had killed them. How he had ripped out organs and genitalia. She wept, silently at first and then with great shuddering howls.

'No, I'm not like the rest, I'm on a special, hallowed, mission. It's just that your boyfriend has created an unwelcome distraction. It will be funny, won't it, to see his face when he hears the news, and knows that he is responsible for it! Yeah…' he added distractedly, 'that will be funny.'

Jayne sobbed and his mood swung again when he leaned close to her and shouted, 'Won't it be so very bloody funny?'

Spittle sprayed her face but she barely noticed.

She tried to talk to God, but He either wasn't in or His line was down (cut wires?); so she chose the one last option open to her. She lunged at him, grabbing his hair with both hands, ignoring the wretched pain in her broken bones and pulling him towards her advancing face. She bit into his nose and enjoyed a fleeting moment as he cried out in pain and surprise. But he was simply too strong, pushing her off, his face contorted with rage and his nose bloodied across the bridge.

He wrapped his hands around her throat. As he had opened the window earlier he had decided that strangulation was perfect for tonight because it was so very personal. It would really hit home to Jeffrey Sanders that not only had his beloved died, but she had stared into her killer's face as he slowly squeezed the life from her. He was sure that Sanders would appreciate the little subtlety.

So he squeezed tightly, then harder, and then harder again. His face was now a mask of complete normality, showing no emotion.

Jayne's eyes bulged, and she started to fight. She could not scream but began a defiant, croaked invective.

'You... evil... bast... ard,' she gasped as she pulled at his hair and pummelled his head. She tried to scratch his face but he turned his head down and away, exposing only the top of his head. She dug into his scalp but he seemed oblivious to the pain.

Her nails were embedded in his scalp when she died. Her eyes remained open and she looked strangely peaceful. Her sphincter had opened and the not inconsequential contents of her bowels ran out. That lovely meal with Jeff soaked through her pants, through Winnie the Pooh and on to her beloved chair.

Apart from the conscious efforts to target his weak spots with her nails and fists, Jayne's last mortal considerations were of Jeff, her parents and God's failure to act.

He pulled away from her and said, 'Ow, ow, ow!' as he put his hands to his head. It felt very raw where she had attacked, but at least it wasn't going to be visible to the world. The nose was possibly a bit more difficult but he could think of something.

He set to work on her, then stopped, relishing the sudden thought that there was an array of extra tools only a couple of yards away in the kitchen. Once he had finished, the area around the chair where Jayne sat propped up was a hideous mess. So was he, but he cleaned himself up in the bathroom.

He thought about leaving a note saying 'What a pleasure this has been'. But decided that that was an unnecessary touch of melodrama.

He took a last look around the place, thinking what a nice flat it was. He felt that it was bad luck on Jayne's behalf to have been Sanders' girlfriend, but hey, he knew all about bad luck.

He moved slowly towards the door and hesitated for a second.

He left a moment or two later, walked briskly down the frosty path and then along the few hundred yards to where he was parked.

As he drove off he considered that he had had a satisfying night. That glass cutter was proving a good investment, he had enjoyed the banter with Jayne; her death was another on his belt for his mission, but it would also cripple Sanders.

'Pretty damn good,' he said aloud, laughing. He put the radio on and was soon singing along to The Corrs latest smash hit. Now there's three girls I'd like to meet, he thought lustily.

He contemplated having a bite to eat – maybe a Kentucky, which would be a little ironic perhaps. Eating bird having recently pulled the head off a budgie… a petty act, perhaps, and he was not even sure why he did it.

Wonder if it was female, he mused, and roared with laughter at his joke.

Chapter Twenty-Five

In 1996, four of the happy crew (Jonno couldn't make it because of work commitments) had gone to Nice for a summer holiday.

There had been a particular day on that holiday which they all remembered but had not spoken of since. It was a day that they had decided to spend on the beach at Nice doing absolutely nothing. It was near the end of the fortnight and they had done the obvious touristy things for the previous ten or eleven days. They had done Nice, the sights, the shops, bars and the excellent city museum. They had strolled along the Promenade des Anglais and ogled the glorious examples of female pulchritude on show. They'd had a couple of mornings when the beer intake from the night before had not been too heavy and they had jogged along the promenade to the harbour.

They had visited Monaco twice, once to do Monaco and the second time to see Monte-Carlo itself. They had taken the train to St Tropez and they had done the pedaloes, paragliding and swimming.

The 'empty' day had arrived. Over their continental breakfast it had been decided to take four chairs from the promenade down on to the shingle beach, and concentrate hard on doing nothing. They duly took their metal chairs, which were freely available, onto the Ruhl Plage public beach.

'Are we capable of a quiet day, do you think?'

'Why the hell not? A day of contemplation and serious thought,' said Jeff, not smiling.

'Christ, I thought that this was meant to be a holiday,' said Toddy, but his grin betrayed his serious tone.

'Let's go for it,' said Mike. 'We could do with a rest.'

'So are we not going swimming or anything?' asked Baz, a little less convinced than the others by the notion of a complete day of rest.

'No swimming, no nothing, we sit down, get lathered up in suncream and we just sunbathe. We think, read or talk. It'll be good for you – therapeutic, probably.'

'Talk about what?' asked Baz who did not understand quite what was going on. This did not strike him as the sort of thing four young heterosexual English blokes did on a foreign holiday. It all seemed a bit wimpish.

'Talk about anything or nothing, it doesn't matter. Footy, women, lack of women, life, dreams, anything. I don't know, make it up as we go. Jeez, it can't be that difficult!'

They chatted about it a little longer, voted on the idea and got a four–nil vote, Baz just giving in. So they packed their bags with the necessities and set off.

They picked a spot near the promenade wall, sat down and got organised. After the last of the suncream was applied they all sat back and there was total silence for few seconds. It was a strange, slightly uncomfortable silence, as if everybody was waiting for someone to do something, make the first move. Then Toddy said in a loud deep voice, 'Well, gents, this is marvellous entertainment isn't it, just marvellous.'

They laughed, but it had broken the ice and Jeff asked, 'So who would want to live here?'

Discussion followed covering the merits, pros and cons of a life in the South of France as compared to Teesside, but the argument was not as one-sided as might have been imagined. It lead to other chats dealing with geography, travel, race and religion and the talk flowed easily and comfortably.

The sun beat down from a cloudless sky, and the heat was intense, despite the sea breeze. The shingle and stone beach seemed to reflect the sun's rays, rather than absorb them as sand would do, and it gave further effect to the feeling that they were sitting on a barbecue or grill. The four lads were accustomed to the heat after both a hot ten days on holiday and also a rare hot summer at home. They all wallowed in the almost painful intensity of the Mediterranean sun.

The beach was busy, but being so vast was not overcrowded. There were all sorts of people enjoying the sun: young, old, families, locals and tourists. There was a gentle atmosphere and a happy feeling, as befitted a beautiful place on a beautiful day on the aptly named Côte d'Azure.

So they sat and watched the world go by, occasionally passing comments on a particular beauty or somebody strikingly eccentric. The first-day novelty of topless girls had soon faded, Toddy commenting, 'It was like a kid being allowed unlimited access to a sweet shop. After a while he just wouldn't bother, would he?'

Not that they did not enjoy the sight of firm, shapely tanned breasts passing by, it was just that the 'nudge-nudge' factor had gone.

Jeff in particular was in a very contemplative mood that day. He sat and looked across the Baie des Anges from the airport in the west to the headland of Villefranche in the east. He had never felt so relaxed. A few yachts were dotted along the horizon and a large ferry occasionally slipped in or out of the port to the east of the town. There was the happy noise of children playing and the lovely crunch of people strolling along the stones, together with the gentle swish of waves against the fringe of the beach and he could not imagine happier sounds. So who needs Beth, he thought.

A couple of vendors plied their meandering trade along the beach, one selling ice creams, the other watermelons. They were kept busy and it took them three quarters of an hour to cover the sections of beach that they had targeted.

A couple of fishermen fished off the beach and two tiny fishing boats bobbed not far offshore, possibly anchored there. Pigeons and seagulls scoured the beach for scraps. Some got lucky and fed on the natural debris and occasional kindness of the human intruders.

Jeff took all this in, trying to absorb the moment, its sights and sounds and more importantly that wonderful feeling of happiness. He nudged Mike who sat next to him when an old lady, presumably local, marched across the stones to a spot just a few yards from where they sat. She was dressed in a long skirt, flip-flop sandals and a cardigan that looked overly warm. She had a rolled-up beach mat tucked under one arm and she selected a precise spot before plonking the mat down and unrolling it. She picked up the bright pink towel that had been inside the mat and shook it before neatly laying it on the mat.

'About one hundred and ten and as fit as a lop,' said Jeff, grinning.

'Just looks a hundred and ten, probably thirty-six, it's just the sun that's dried her out and made her wrinkly.'

They laughed and Toddy cast a lazy glance across to the woman, remarking, 'About thirty-seven, I'd say, and God yes, that *is* wrinkly.'

Baz did not look up. He was desperate for a swim, a walk, anything involving movement. He was in a bit of a huff that his objections had been so overwhelmingly crushed.

The old lady pulled her skirt down to reveal dark bathing shorts. Her cardigan was discarded to reveal a black swimming top. She folded her clothes before striding to the sea. She waded in without hesitation and turned onto her back. She did a gentle backstroke and splashed quietly away from the shore. She fell and rose with the swell of the sea. There were no waves at all until the water reached the beach where it shelved quite sharply, and even then the water flopped almost apologetically onto the stones. The lady was soon a long way from the beach.

'Do you think she's happy?' asked Jeff.

'Who, the old crone? Yeah, she must be, what's she got to be unhappy about?'

'So what's life about?' asked Mike abruptly.

'Now there's a question…'

'Isn't that what today's about – the big questions, philosophising, whatever?'

'What do you think, Baz, do you want to discuss the meaning of life?'

'Piss off, I'm having a kip,' snapped Baz.

'Ooh, get her!' said Toddy.

'So, ignoring misery guts, what do we philosophers think of life? You first, Jeff.'

Jeff could have dismissed this with a quip but he was prepared to go along with it. 'I think it's about counting your blessings. I've got a theory that…'

'Whoa, hang on everybody,' Toddy said, loudly enough for a few people nearby to hear. 'Jeff's got a theory. Wait for it, wait for it!'

'Thanks, mate, my theory is a simple one.'

'Bit like yourself, then,' said Toddy.

Mike laughed but said, 'Give him a break or we'll never hear the sodding thing.'

'Okay, okay, continue, Monsieur, s'il vous plaît.'

'*D'accord!* here it is. I reckon…' He hesitated, looking at Toddy and waiting for another interruption, but Toddy sealed his lips with a pretend zip. '…I reckon that everybody, absolutely everybody, has something, and nobody has everything.' He stopped and looked at both Toddy and Mike. They looked at him, waiting for a sensible response and both burst out laughing.

'You what? Everybody has somebody and nobody has nothing?' asked Mike.

'No, pillock, everybody has something, and nobody has everything.'

'Very profound… What's it mean?'

'Well,' Jeff started to explain patiently, 'when you see sick kids in hospital with horrible diseases – leukaemia or something – it always strikes me that they are so cheerful, almost happy. They are so grateful for small mercies; they appreciate every act of kindness and seem to have a great *joie de vivre*, whatever the circumstances.'

'Good phrase for here,' interjected Mike.

Jeff carried on. 'So, when you think that they must be totally miserable, they prove you wrong by showing the opposite. They have hope and spirit and… stuff,' he finished lamely.

'That was quite poetic until "stuff",' said Toddy. 'I want to hear the other bit.'

'Which bit?' queried Mike.

'You know, the kids have proved that everyone has something. But what about "nobody has everything"?'

'Well that's easy. Who do people think has everything? Richard Branson, film stars, top footballers, TV celebrities, rich people, whoever. But they don't, do they? They have the material things, but six houses, ten cars and gorgeous tottie isn't everything, is it?'

Jeff expected a wave of comment but was surprised when the only comment was, 'Go on,' from Mike.

'Well, there's always a price, isn't there?' Jeff explained, 'There's the pressure of maintaining that lifestyle, of continuing to be successful. Whatever line of work it needs effort to keep it going, whether it's business, football or rock stardom. You can always lose your touch, your form or your voice. Then there's the enormous media pressure; they're always watching, waiting for you to fail, spreading lies and innuendo that you can't defend. There's stress with family and friends, dysfunctional families and all the rest.'

'Yeah, right, life's a bitch when you're a multi-millionaire, and there's gorgeous groupies wanting to shag you!'

'Wanting to sell their stories, blackmail you, tell the wife.'

'...Houses in LA, Nice, Sydney...'

'All with mortgages, staff who nick the antiques, stalked by murderous loonies and hunted by paparazzi.'

'...Yachts and helicopters...'

'That breakdown... need maintenance; that can be sabotaged.'

'Okay, okay, we get the picture. Would you rather be a penniless tramp?'

'Course not, but the point is, nobody has everything. It's all relative. Somebody could get as much depression out of the fact that they've had to sell their third home in Monte-Carlo to raise some cash as the bloke who has to increase his mortgage by two thousand pounds on his pokey terrace in Sunderland to pay some bills. It's all relative.'

'Not convinced,' said Toddy.

'I know, but you're a philistine, aren't you?'

They laughed and Jeff passed them the large bottle of Diet Coke. Away to the right a large plane left the ground and swung out to sea, leaving a distant smoky trail behind it. Two helicopters were just visible on the horizon, too far to identify as private, military or coastguard.

The old lady was coming back up the beach. She crunched up to the two showers that stood to the left of her mat and, unflinching, turned on the cold water and stepped under it.

'Fit as a lop,' said Toddy, 'but what is a lop?'

'A twig, isn't it?' said Mike.

'No idea, but I wish I had one.'

'Anyway, that's one little theory. What's yours, Toddy?'

Toddy, the constant joker, the least serious minded of the four, took a second to reflect on the question. He ran a hand through his mop of tousled fair hair. His response surprised them all.

'I'd have to say that it's a list of hopes. Yeah, a list of hopes.'

'Such as?'

'Well, to find somebody to love me, somebody that I love back. To settle down and have a family. To stay healthy, with a happy and healthy family. To stay close to my mates, to be loyal to them. To be successful without ever becoming desperate about it. Overall, to be happy, because to achieve that means all the other things take care of themselves. And that's the easy stuff.'

'Wow!' said Jeff, genuinely taken aback. 'What a serious list for one so daft.'

'I have my moments,' said Toddy, smiling modestly.

'To settle down with someone who loves you... What, like Debbie?'

Debbie had been Toddy's longest relationship, nearly six months, until she was found to be two-timing him.

'No, somebody who loves me,' said Toddy good-humouredly.

Jeff knew that Debbie was not the great love that she had been portrayed as. Toddy's bedding of four women in four weeks as compensation after the break-up testified to the fact.

'I'm talking about someone who provides real, real love. The sort that wrenches your guts, where it's almost tangible.'

They talked on the subject for quite some time and inevitably the subject of Beth cropped up. Jeff admitted that it had been real love and tried to describe the pain he'd experienced when they had split up.

Baz never really joined in but the other three opened their hearts about love, aspirations and dreams. They established that they all shared Toddy's wish list, and on a lower level of desires Jeff wanted to learn a foreign language, while Toddy would love to write a novel and wanted to sit with a special girlfriend in front of the Taj Mahal.

They got into pet hates about themselves, how they hoped to become better people and how they handled other people's opinions of them. They dealt with many deeply personal matters. The conversations continued through lunch, which Baz brought from the McDonald's just over the Promenade des Anglais.

They tried to involve Baz, but the longer the day wore on the less inclined he was to participate, even in grunts.

'What a miserable sod,' said Mike at one point after Baz ignored a polite question.

'Better than being a prick talking about girlie shit,' retorted Baz.

'Hey, we've been bonding,' said Toddy in a deep, mock-macho voice.

'Bond off, you poof!' retorted Baz gruffly; but he smiled for the first time in about three hours.

In mid-afternoon it was somehow decided that they had chatted enough, and a walk around town was called for, including stops at local hostelries. They did this, the chat reverting to type-football, women they'd like to meet and do things to, and what it was going to be like going home in a few days' time.

That morning's discussions were not mentioned that evening, or the next day or indeed ever again. No reference was ever made to the issues exposed, laid bare and discussed that day. They had bonded as Toddy had joked and they individually all felt satisfied with themselves for the honesty. But somehow, maybe Baz was right, they felt a little uncomfortable about being perhaps a tad too open.

It wasn't really manly, certainly not British, to be so open, was it?

Jeff relived every moment, every word of that morning as he now lay on his bed. The talk of real, deep love and being happy seemed very relevant now as he lay here contemplating life itself and the possibility of suicide. How could anybody be expected to get through this? How? The pain inside was worse than a cancer, he felt sharp pain, aching pain, and nausea. He could have believed it if somebody had shown him an X-ray of a burrowing animal gnawing at his guts, chewing his organs, scraping the flesh. He could really feel the physical pain. The pain in his head was bad enough, but the ache in his heart and stomach were ten times worse. There were times that he thought that his heart was going to either burst, or stop and he would have welcomed either option.

He had been on his bed for two days since the police had delivered the dreadful news. It was several hours after the terrible moment before Jeff really took in that Jayne was not only dead, but killed by his man. His nightmare. He had cried all night, sometimes sobbing aloud, sometimes crying silently. The same thoughts raced through his head over and over again, Why was this happening? How could Jayne be dead? His beloved, lovely Jayne?

At midnight he was sick – the consequence of shock and distress – and he felt that his heart was literally breaking in the early hours of the morning. He had not slept and rejected all approaches from his distraught parents. He had lain on his bed for several hours now, unmoving, his head spinning with images of Jayne, once happy, then so suddenly slaughtered in such a horrible fashion. The police had given him no specific details, just that she had been strangled and mutilated; and yes, it was almost certainly the killer that Jeff had seen.

He cried out 'No, no!' a couple of times, but his parents fortunately did not hear him.

How could he have had the incredible good fortune to have found Jayne, and what evil forces now dictated that she be taken away, so cruelly? It was real love all right. It was that tangible stuff which Toddy had spoken of in Nice; the sort of deep, aching love that meant that the merest thought of her, the sound of her voice or sight of her in the distance made his heart leap, his pulse quicken and a smile spread across his face.

Nobody could now seriously believe that he could ever recover from this – even partially recover. He was sure that some unknowing prick who had never experienced that real love, the real article, would soon be saying, 'Honest Jeff, time is a great healer.' And he was equally certain that his reaction would include either a mouthful of invective or a short sharp punch, or both. He did not want to hear that crap from anyone.

Would these pains, this overwhelming feeling of guilt ever go? He doubted it very much, very much indeed. He tried to gather rational thoughts, tried to contemplate what lay ahead of him, but images of his parents, Jayne's family, his mates, colleagues and the media got very confused in his mind's eye. He twisted over on the bed, burying his face in the pillow, trying to blot all thoughts out, but they would not go away. He saw the face of Westmain and he was laughing, and Jeff screamed into his pillow 'Nooo!' and punched the headboard hard.

How they had got it so wrong in Nice was beyond him. God, how totally fucking naïve they had been! Yes, they were a few years younger, but Christ, all that bollocks about hopes, dreams and love! What a pile of shit! How had none of them punctured their pathetic happy balloon with an acknowledgement that fate and devils and wickedness also existed, and that these fuckers perpetrated evil acts. Like allowing his man to exist, and allowing him to do what he had done to his Jayne. A picture of Mr and Mrs Fell, Wendy's mother and father, flashed into his head and he emitted a loud, rattling sob for her now, having an inkling of what they had suffered.

The doctor had visited him late last night and left some tranquillisers to aid sleep and Jeff now looked at the small brown bottle by his bedside. He thought of taking the lot, there and then, but images of his family and friends held him back, on the brink of total despair.

He took a tablet, desperate to sleep, praying that it would offer some comfort from this living hell, this torture that was his waking hours.

He did drift off to sleep but his dreams were troubled ones. His mother came to see him on the beach at Nice, saying, 'Jeff, dear, everybody thinks losing a loved one is the end, but it's not, life goes on and time is a great healer. Isn't it hot here?'

He told her to fuck off and she walked into the sea, fully clothed, and swam off into the distance.

Toddy and Mike walked up to him in the same spot, and Toddy said, 'No probs, mate, just chalk it up as another Beth, a Debbie, no probs! Plenty more fish in the sea.' Then he laughed, pointing at the fishing boats bobbing gently on the sea. Jeff told him to fuck off, and they suddenly weren't there.

Then Jayne walked up to him and he leapt up from his chair to greet her, but she held out her hand in a 'stop' motion and she spoke to him softly. 'I'm dead, Jeff, killed by the madman. He strangled me.' Jeff could see her bruised throat. She was only wearing a bikini and now Jeff saw that there were marks all over her body, cuts and abrasions. He dragged his eyes from her marks and looked at her lovely, smiling face.

'It is lovely here,' she said, 'we could have had a holiday here, just the two of us.'

He started to speak, to tell her he loved her more than the world but she reached out and put a finger on his lips. 'Hush,' she said, 'I know you love me, and it really is not your fault. Nobody can control such a madman. Be at rest, my love; remember me.'

He slumped back into his chair and closed his eyes for a second. When he opened them, he shaded his eyes, for despite his sunglasses, it was very bright. He saw, some ten yards in front of him, walking towards him, seven people. From left to right he recognised them, one by one: Mother, Father, Toddy, Mike, the old crone from Nice, Jayne (beloved Jayne) and, chillingly, the killer. He was smiling and he stopped on the shingle as the other six continued. They stopped just short of his seat and then Jayne moved to his chair and kissed him; a beautiful, heart-churning kiss.

'Nothing's impossible,' she whispered, 'you will get through this. I promise you, I really do.'

He looked at her with renewed hope and a love almost too intense but then the killer's face appeared over her shoulder, grinning.

'No fucking chance!' he said.

Jeff awoke with a start, unsure of whether he had just cried out or screamed, but aware that the pillow was very wet, either with tears or sweat.

Nothing's impossible. How he hated that phrase! When he was seven he had been on holiday in Weymouth and had cut his foot on a piece of glass. Go back now, find the glass, prove it's the same piece. That's impossible. When he was twelve he fell off a wall at school and cut his hand. Find the plaster that the teacher applied to that wound. That's impossible. In Nice, four years ago, there had been a girl who walked into a bar one night where Jeff and his friends sat. Jeff thought she was the most beautiful girl he had ever seen. She had one drink, alone, then walked out; end of story, goodnight Vienna. Find her and prove it was her, get her to recollect Jeff. That's impossible.

But if you want something seriously difficult, something really fucking impossible, then get somebody to tell Jeffrey Sanders that he will get through this – this utter nightmare, devoid of hope – and he will respond by climbing the nearest high point and screaming to all and sundry, 'Don't ever tell me that again, ever! This is the fact, plain and simple, this is impossible, and don't tell me it's not!'

Just let somebody do it.

Chapter Twenty-Six

He had collected teddy bears from the age of twenty when he had found one, in good condition, in a street. From the condition it appeared that it had not been abandoned but had been lost or forgotten by a careless child. He took it home, and called it 'Edie' after his grandmother, despite not being sure whether teddy bears were all supposed to be male.

Over the years he had picked up a further twenty-six teddies, never deliberately seeking them out, just buying them when he chanced upon one that he particularly liked the look of. He continued to give them female names.

He had them neatly arranged in order of size on a shelf unit in his bedroom, and he often took them down, dusted them and carefully replaced them.

He presumed that it was a deep need for childhood things, things that he had missed out on, that kept him interested, but he did not analyse it too closely.

He had bought a new one that morning, nothing special really. It had cost him £49.99 at the shop that sold old things down by the river. It was a small one so it went near the end of the arrangement on the left.

He named it Jayne.

Now he had more pressing matters to deal with.

There was a bit in his bible that said, 'Take kindly the counsel of the years, gracefully surrendering the things of youth.' He knew that this was to do with his hair loss, and wise old Sorry saying, 'It's hardly noticeable, Sam, forget it.'

But it wasn't that easy. Westmain had for some time thought it ironic that he should be employed at a hairdresser's and be suffering from premature baldness. He had first noticed the problem some ten months earlier when he had spent some time on a nearby beach on an unseasonally hot day. The next morning he had found that the top of his head was sore, and upon inspection had found that his head was sunburnt, and sunburnt because the hair was thin. Shock horror! It had never been noticeable before. What was happening? From that day forward he monitored the situation daily and there was no question after a month or so that he was losing hair. Strands appeared in the bath or shower, or on his pillow in the morning, and the bald patch on the top of his head felt more obvious as the weeks passed. He decided early on that he had to do something about this, so he started researching the facts known about baldness. He dismissed very early on in his researching the myths about bald men being a) virile b) sexy to women. He simply did not want to be bald if he could help it, and he was going to do his best to help it.

He found the address of the Institute of Trichologists and wrote to them requesting fact sheets about the condition, their research into finding a cure and all the options open to him. He was pleased to receive a prompt reply which gave him lots of information. He carefully read every word in the literature provided, including the complex scientific data. He then read it all again, this time making his own notes and lists. He noted that it was a medical fact that baldness was not linked to increased testosterone or virility – which he had already dismissed; and also that it was a myth that too much shampooing causes baldness. Damage could be caused by excessive blow-drying or heat treatment, so he decided to cut down on that. Vigorous brushing with a soft brush was recommended by certain experts to stimulate hair growth, so he put this on his agenda.

It was of no comfort that hair loss (they seemed to avoid the word 'bald', he thought) affected around about eight million men in the United Kingdom alone, and that every man would experience it at some time. One particular article made great fuss of the emotional turmoil that men suffered through hair loss, the feelings of being unattractive, the stigma etc., but this did not interest him as this was not his reaction to those departing hairs. He simply felt that it was not right, that it was a bit of an insult to the way that he looked after his body.

Waffle about successful hair-challenged personalities did not convince him either. Sean Connery, Yul Brynner, Ross Kemp or André Agassi did not strike him as relevant to his circumstances.

One salient fact did grab his attention, and that was that the most common kind of hair loss is male pattern baldness, androgenic alopecia, a genetic disorder that can be inherited from either parent. More proof, he thought, that my bitch mother plagues my life, even from the grave. He read that the inherited gene reacts badly to the androgen range of hormones, such as testosterone, and causes the problem. He jotted down some of the almost indecipherable technical terms, such as 'Dihydrotestosterone' and '5 Alpha Reductase', for he intended to look further into every aspect of this curse.

The statistics regarding the age factor in baldness were interesting but of no direct use, he decided, because he was going to correct the condition over the next few months. The facts that 40% of men aged thirty-five have noticeable hair loss, rising to 90% in elderly men, struck him that men were not attempting to deal with it.

Such was his confidence in his own abilities that he was sure that he could sort out this problem quickly, even though institutes spending huge amounts of money could not.

He was a little concerned that alopecia areata, a loss of a patch, could develop into alopecia totalis, total loss. Shock or stress was attributed to this development and he considered for a minute whether his first observation of loss coincided with any particular event. He could not make a connection, and didn't even consider the stress of being a serial killer as a possible influence.

So he knew of all the possible causes, but what of the possible solutions? He soon noted that of the various 'remedies', the majority appeared to suggest that they could slow down the loss but not necessarily reverse the trend. He wrote down, 'Minoxidil (Regaine)' when he read that this was a treatment that you could buy at a chemist and apply to your scalp, even though the *British Medical Journal* in September 1998 had cast doubts on the success rate of this product.

He was not surprised to read that American scientists had developed an alternative, more radical treatment, not yet available in Britain. Finasteride was originally used to treat prostate problems, but because it prevents testosterone from being turned into DHT, it could cure baldness. The bad news, of course, was multifold. Firstly it took months to work and the recommended course was two years. The side effects included erectile problems, and the interference with the development of genitals in male foetuses. Great! he thought. A nice head of hair, not a stiffy in sight and a possible son and heir with no cock!

There was a lot of documentation dealing with hair transplants, its expense, timescale and possible outcomes, and he was not impressed. The grafts involved also sounded painful.

He dismissed the concept of hairpieces, he had seen too many at work to believe that they were a serious alternative.

He saw that the scientists at Columbia University in New York had recently made a breakthrough in gene research and he guessed that the final solution was probably only a few years away. That, however, was too long a wait for him and he needed to do something now. He wrote to a couple of other tricology centres but received very similar material to that which he already held.

He visited chemists and bought a couple of recommended products but did not expect any great result from them.

He had decided after a couple of months to approach his boss at the salon. Stig 'Sorry' Sorensen was Danish by birth and had lived in England since the age of twelve. He was a friendly man who would always take time to listen to staff, whether they were grumbling about him, colleagues or clients or putting forward a sensible idea for the salon. Sam duly followed Sorry into the staff restroom one day and asked if he could have a word. Sorry willingly said Yes. He knew that Sam would not be bothering him with a trivial matter of internal politics.

'I've got an idea boss and wanted to run it by you, if that's okay?'

'Fire away, Sam.' Sorry smiled, as he poured himself a coffee. 'Fancy one?' he offered.

'No thanks. What it was, I was wondering whether you had ever considered selling products that dealt with hair loss?'

Sorry was not expecting this, and laughed as he replied, 'Hair restorer and baldy creams, you mean? No, I can't say I have. Do you think I should?'

Sam was ready to put forward his case and went into a well-prepared speech explaining how he had come upon an article about it and had been intrigued by the statistics describing how common a problem it was. From there he had determined that there was a potentially huge market for reputable products in this field. He quoted facts and figures, and he referred to fictitious friends and family who had, he said, expressed interest in the availability of such products. Sorry was not laughing now, for Sam's speech struck a chord. The Head Office of the national franchise network of Fringe Benefits had recently been issuing strong directives about the need to increase profitability, direct sales and the submission of commercially sound ideas. The ideas proposed by Sam fitted the bill perfectly.

Sorry asked Sam many enthusiastic questions, and the well-researched Sam provided the right answers to achieve his aim. The result was that Sorry immediately prepared a fax outlining his ideas on a new product range and sent it off some twenty minutes later to Head Office in Derby.

Only a week had passed when Sorry took Sam aside from a client and excitedly told him that a senior rep from Head Office was coming tomorrow to discuss his fax.

A week later, and workmen arrived to construct a shelf unit next to the one that already stood near the reception desk. A day later, and a delivery arrived of a dozen large boxes. Eleven boxes held bottles, in all sizes, of hair products that were aimed at arresting baldness. The final box contained signs, leaflets and posters that explained the figures, the problems and the cures of hair loss.

Sam was absolutely delighted to hear that amongst the products was a revolutionary Swedish product, Kenjaal, which Head Office declared to be the best possible hair loss product on the European market. The accompanying publicity blurb declared that Kenjaal blocked the effect of DHT and promoted regrowth. 'Regrowth' was the critical word and Sam was intrigued. Sorry was proud to announce that only the three franchise salons in the North-East were being allowed to promote Kenjaal, as supplies were short, so new was it on the UK market.

Sam said that he could provide the first sales for Sorry's targets as Sam's friend Steve, a payroll manager aged thirty-seven, was waiting in hungry anticipation for such a product. Neither the cost, £24 per bottle, or the stated side effects of strong odour or greasy look, were going to deter Steve, said Sam happily. Sorry was delighted to pass over the first sale from the new range.

Sam used Kenjaal over the coming weeks and was surprised and very pleased to see that he thought there was an improvement to the tiny patch atop his head. Sorry was a little disappointed that sales were not massive in those early months. Sorry had not taken account of the reticence factor that affected men who might desire the product but lacked the nerve to buy it in a place populated by mainly nubile young females. The less dramatic products sold all right, the ones that promised no miracles but hinted that they could thicken your existing hair. Maybe people felt that these products did not admit the seriousness of the problem; maybe it was just the cost. Over the first couple of months Sam's friend, Steve, was the biggest buyer of Kenjaal.

As 1999 moved into March, Head Office advised Sorry that he had failed his targets for Kenjaal specifically and the whole range generally, and the products were going to be withdrawn. Sorry was frustrated that the items had not sold better but he knew that he had made an impression at Head Office for the initial suggestion, so it had not been a futile exercise.

As Sam went about his business, dealing with the young, old, glamorous and decidedly not so glamorous, Sorry came across to him.

'Just a word, Sam.'

Sam made his apologies to the old lady who was getting her regular monthly perm and moved to Sorry's side.

'Just thought I'd let you know that HQ have pulled the plug on the baldy range, the whole lot. It just hasn't come off. But never mind, it was worth a go. You'd better let Steve know, cos we'll be getting no more Kenjaal.'

Sam was taken aback and for a second fought to regain his composure as an inner voice tried to shout, 'You fucking prick! How dare you take it away from me? It frigging *works*, for Christ's sake!' He said instead, 'Thanks for the tip, boss, I'll let him know.'

Sam calmed down and rationalised that if he had to he would buy direct from the manufacturer. No worries, he would get hold of the stuff somehow.

That night at home Sam scoured the publicity literature that had accompanied the initial delivery of Kenjaal. It had referred to a complimentary article that had appeared in *Hair*, the hairdressing industry magazine. In there he found an address of the main supplier in the UK, based in Reading, and he wrote a letter that night requesting supplies.

Perhaps he wouldn't have written the letter if he had realised that fifty miles away in Wetherby, at the Police Forensics Laboratory, there lay on a desk a file headed, 'Murder: Jayne Gilmour 7/3/99'. In the section of the file marked 'Materials', there was a lot of analysis detailing fibres found on Jayne's body and in her apartment. Hairs found in the same locale were listed and there was a chemical analysis of material found under Jayne's fingernails. Attached to this particular page was a supplementary report provided to Wetherby by the helpful chemists and analysts at Procter & Gamble laboratories. On both the forensic summary and on the Procter & Gamble analysis there was an interesting word. It would not have meant an awful lot to members of the public, or even indeed to the forensic scientists; it would mean a great deal to Sam Westmain. The word was 'Kenjaal'.

Chapter Twenty-Seven

Four weeks later on 24 April a family gathering was to take place at Jeff's house at four o'clock on the Saturday, for 'Sunday tea', that great northern institution. It might be the modern age of computers, world travel and the Internet, but megabytes and gigabytes did not impinge on the bites of ham sandwiches, scones and cuppas of a northern family Sunday tea.

This wasn't a mega event, when all the cousins also descended; they were becoming less frequent. The last major gathering had been for the matriarchal Grandma's 100th last September. There had been thirty-one at that gathering, and it had been an excellent function at a Sunderland restaurant.

This was to be an adults only, fourteen in all, a sympathetic show of solidarity for Jeff and his traumas. He couldn't have wanted this less if somebody had said the penalty for saying no was to remove his testicles with a blunt knife.

It had come about because of communication channel problems and breakdowns. Jeff's mother had said on the telephone to her other sister, Maude, that Jeff would appreciate a bit of support at this difficult time. Maude had said yes, people showing love and support around him would no doubt go a long way to getting him through this. Maude rang Gerry to say that Jeff had indicated that he wanted people around him. Gerry called Sophie and said that the family klaxon was booming for a gathering. Sophie and Angie decided the date, and the next thing Jeff's mother knew was that family from all over the North-East were ringing to confirm their anticipated arrival time on Saturday 24th! Even Jeff's mother was given the impression that greater forces were at work here, and that somehow Jeff had willed this party. Jeff didn't get to hear of the event until the Thursday beforehand and after some weak protestations he simply couldn't be bothered to argue. He just convinced himself that he would be able to get out of it on Saturday.

So Saturday arrived and the day wore on. Lunch was a per-functory affair, as gatherings for tea dictated, because you couldn't have two big meals in a day. That was proof of the extinction of one northern myth – that to function properly you needed four square meals a day. That hadn't been true since the demise of coalmining, shipbuilding and other heavy industries.

So dinner time had passed (it was still called dinner time up here) and four o'clock loomed. Jeff had come out of his room at eleven thirty, mooched around aimlessly for half an hour, walked around the garden for ten minutes, then sat down for his fish fingers and mash at twelve fifteen – early because of the function. He had gone back to his room at one o'clock where he lay on his bed watching omnibus editions of soap operas.

The chat between Jeff and his parents was minimal. What was there to say? As he had headed for his room at one o'clock his mother had said, 'You don't have to get changed if you don't want to.'

This, as much as anything, showed the depths of Dorothy's sympathy for Jeff. She had never, ever said, '…if you don't want to.' Being smart for a gathering was de rigueur. But not today. Jeff had grunted 'Okay', but he wasn't really taking any of it in.

At three thirty his mother knocked gently on the door and waited politely for a mumbled, 'Come in.'

'Time to come down, son,' she said gently. Her heart was breaking at her son's plight but she was determined to put a brave face on it. Recognising his disinterest and disenchantment, she said (again a first), 'Just show your face. You haven't got to stay all night.' And this with Jeff as 'Guest of Honour'!

'Okay, Mam,' he said, and robot-like went to his wardrobe for a clean T-shirt. Better make that a jumper to hide the bulges, he thought as he looked at the shelves and rails in the wardrobe.

This physical act of getting ready, minimal though the effort was, seemed to galvanise him into mental action and dragged him from his lethargy. So Auntie Mary and Uncle Bob coming, are they? Well at least that'll be a laugh, and God knows I could do with one. The thought passed through his subconscious without registering.

He walked into the lounge at four o'clock just as the blue Nissan belonging to Gerry and Maude pulled up. Always punctual, Gerry believed that to be late for anything, anywhere, was an insult to the person, destination or event to which you were travelling. No excuses could or would be tolerated by Gerry for tardiness; traffic, weather or a plague of frogs were all irrelevant per Gerry, as you could and should always anticipate the unforeseeable. If you arrive in the vicinity of your target early, simply sit and wait until the appointed hour.

As each car brought its passengers to the front gate, Jeff felt the tension mounting. As each family member entered the house the sombre atmosphere seemed to become bleaker as if everybody brought with them another lump of gloom to add to an ever-burgeoning pile. When Doris and George arrived there would have usually been cries of 'They're here, they're coming!' Then, upon their entry into the house there would be laughter simply at their arrival. Today was very different. They entered the house quietly, George shaking Jeff's hand, as had all the men, and Doris following the pattern set by earlier arrivals and giving Jeff a big hug. Talk was quiet, everybody enquiring of everybody's health.

One or two people asked Jeff how he was, despite his appearance, which spoke volumes. 'Okay,' was his only response.

After half an hour, with everybody there, Jeff suddenly stood up and to no one in particular said, 'I'm very sorry, and I appreciate you all coming, but I'm afraid I have to go.'

He left the room in a hurry, unable to hold back the tears. As he ran up the stairs he could barely see where he was going, so full were his eyes.

In the lounge several of the ladies dabbed their eyes and even a couple of the gentlemen had to blow their noses and cough a little.

'Tragedy, absolute tragedy!' people were muttering, and everybody knew that the get-together was a mistake: well intentioned, but a mistake.

Then Mrs Sanders did something very brave. She stood up and in the loudest, most confident voice that she could muster, she announced, 'Right, this is a tragedy, but we can't change that. There's a time for grieving and there will be plenty of it, but today, let's talk and let's be satisfied that we are all together, that the love we share will get us through this. I'm not saying, "Let's have a party and pretend nothing's happened," but let's make the most of our coming together.'

'Well said, luv,' said Mr Sanders.

He got out of his chair and asked who wanted a cup of tea. That always helped the English through a crisis and soon the room was full of chatter. The death of Jayne and Jeff's misery were never far from the conversation but plenty of other topics were raised and discussed. There were even a few laughs.

The 'leek war' between allotments which were run by Aunt Sylvie and Uncle Tom and their nearest rival, old Jim Smethwick, was hilariously chronicled, with disguised leek growers peering over hedges, sneakily taking measurements at midnight and taking videos of feeding methods from hideouts.

The tale of Aunt Doris's bunion and the way it was destroying her shoes and ability to tango was funny, and there was an interesting tale of Gerry studying chemistry, through the Open University.

It would have been a normal, enjoyable gathering if it had not been for the shadow cast by murder most foul.

Jeff lay on his bed and heard the hum of voices. He recognised his mother talking and wondered what she was saying; he assumed that she was making his excuses. He heard the chatter pick up and even heard a couple of laughs. He rolled over, then back again, unable to get comfortable, to find any release from the physical aches that he was suffering, brought on by the anguish of Jayne's death.

He stood up, walked to the window, then sat down at his table. He stood up again, then lay down on the bed. He sat up, banged his head with the palms of both hands, and then stood up again. It was no use, he was going to explode if he didn't get out, so he ran downstairs and went through the front door into the cool air.

He walked to the gate and then started to gently jog down the street. He wasn't sure why, only that he needed to move, to go somewhere, to do something physical. He had gone a few yards when he had to spit the saliva from his mouth. He enjoyed the sound as it left his mouth. He only jogged slowly but he was soon gasping, his chest heaving, but he was determined to keep going.

His legs felt fine, it was just the rest of him that was struggling. He had gone about half a mile and the spitting was frequent when he felt a stabbing pain in his left calf. No point in wrecking his leg, he realised, so he slowed to a walk. He decided that he would start jogging regularly once the next few days were out of the way.

If he could have anticipated what was to be faced over the coming few weeks, he might well have kept on jogging, on and on and on, until he either fell dead to the ground or simply ran off the edge of the world. But he didn't know what was in store, so he eventually turned and went home.

On the way, he dwelt on the memories of that Wednesday, some twelve days earlier, that had been the day of Jayne's funeral. The police had kept her body for over two weeks, but once it had been released the funeral was quickly organised. Jeff could not think of the words to describe the day. He just used the word 'bad' a lot.

To hear what Westmain had done to Jayne, how he had strangled and then mutilated her was almost too much, literally, to bear. He had thought of suicide, frequently, from the first moment that the police had broken the news to him.

It was only because a doctor, whom he didn't know, told him that some people would kill themselves in this situation, but it really would be a cowardly, selfish act, that he didn't do it.

He had not been to work since Jayne's death and didn't expect to ever go again. He wished he could just have a massive heart attack, that wouldn't be selfish and it would finish off what was left of his heart, which certainly could not be much.

'Please God, just do it,' he said to the sky as he trudged home, crying.

The next morning, around eleven, Jeff heard the telephone ring, but didn't leave his chair; he had no energy, mental or physical for anything. He heard someone answer it, but did not listen to the conversation. A moment later his mother came into the room and said, in that gentle fashion of hers, 'Jeffrey dear, it's for you.'

He looked up at her, disinterested, but saw an extraordinary look on her face.

'What on earth is it, Mum?' She looked shocked and his only thought was, Another disaster.

Of all the things that he might have speculated his mother would say, he'd never have put on the long list the two words she uttered.

'It's Beth.'

'Beth?' he queried, not understanding. 'Beth who?'

'Your Beth, Beth Middleton.'

He stared at her as if she was mad and she had to prompt him 'Go on, Jeffrey, she's waiting.'

He shuffled into the hall as if pole-axed and said flatly into the receiver, 'Hello.'

'Hello, Jeff, it's Beth.'

He did not know what to say.

'Are you there, Jeff?'

He shook himself and forced a reply.

'Yeah, sorry, you, er, I wasn't expecting to hear from you.' His mind was racing. Beth? Why the hell was she ringing him?

'I don't want to disturb you or anything, it's just that... that I've heard the recent news and I just wanted to say, I was thinking of you, that's all.'

'Well, right, thanks, thanks for ringing. It's nice to hear from you.' He immediately regretted the words, for he did not believe them to be true.

'I don't know what I could, or should say, so I'll say that I'm very, very sorry.' She paused as if for a response but got none. She said softly, 'You know I'll always love you, don't you?'

'Yeah, suppose so,' he answered, again, not fully believing his words.

'That's it, then. I'm thinking of you. Take care, bye.' Then she was gone.

He stood with the phone in his hand for a full minute before replacing it. His mother appeared from the lounge and asked 'Everything all right, dear?'

He mumbled, 'Fine,' and she got the message from his demeanour that further enquiries would not be a good idea.

He went upstairs and sat on the end of his bed. *Beth*, could you believe it, after all this time...

He and Beth had met at a club in 1991, when both were twenty-one. It had been a slow courtship, casual at first, dates being fitted in around happy crew ventures, football and other pleasant pastimes, but over months it had become a real affair. At twenty-three they had bought a house together and had plans to get engaged.

At twenty-four, Beth had announced one night that she was seeing somebody else and they would have to split up, sell the house and move on. He had thought she'd been behaving oddly for a while but this bombshell devastated him. In a highly weakened emotional state he let Beth organise all the financial arrangements of their 'divorce'. He had immediately moved back to his parents, and she had stitched him up good and proper. He'd ended up having to plough money into the house which somehow had negative equity. He let her keep the house and came away with an old car, a few personal possessions and no savings. He just couldn't believe it; not Beth.

He had not enjoyed moving back in with his parents, who were equally shocked, but knew he had no choice. She had seemed such a nice girl, they said. He'd felt so too; he had loved her passionately. It took him a long time to get himself together both socially and at work and he had failed to sit his final professional exams that summer. It had set him back twelve months at work; several years financially.

It was about the same time that Gerry disappeared from the happy crew scene and there was some speculation that he had been seeing Beth behind Jeff's back, but nothing was ever proved.

Beth's new man had never materialised, as far as Jeff heard, so wondered if it had all been a con from the start. But he found that very hard to swallow, as they had been so happy for so long.

He heard that she had soon moved out after their separation, Beth had sold up and left the area. She'd gone to Manchester to do marketing or something similar.

He had heard nothing from her since, until today. He felt very confused. What was the purpose of her call? To wind him up? Surely not. To try to get back with him? Surely not. To remind him that she loved him? Maybe, but that just added to the mystery of why she had left him all those years ago.

Jeff sat on his bed, dazed at yet another twist in his sad life that he simply did not comprehend.

Would he ever find the truth behind the story of Beth's departure from his life?

The truth was that she had been having a routine medical examination when the tests revealed cancer. She had not told Jeff, and when it was diagnosed as probably short-term and terminal, she had decided to act fast. She did not want Jeff to suffer seeing her die, she loved him so much.

So she had arranged to stay at an expensive treatment centre in Bristol that had an excellent record in saving 'terminal' patients, about nine per cent, she heard. If they couldn't save you, then at least they made your last days comfortable and you died fighting.

She had nobody to turn to, having only a small family and no parents. She had despised herself for 'stealing' Jeff's money with the house deal, but she'd decided that she would rather he hated her forever rather than watch her die a horrible death.

She invented the mysterious 'Other man', booked herself in the clinic and left.

She became one of the nine per cent. She went through hellish treatment but after two intensive years came through the course and into full remission. She had contacted friends and mentioned Manchester but said that her guilt was too strong to see them again. She stayed in Bristol and forged a successful career as a journalist on the major local newspaper; but she never forgot Jeff. She often thought of going back, but presumed that he would have a wife by now and did not want to upset that.

Then she had seen his story in the newspaper and felt she had to contact him. He obviously wasn't married, although the description of the sweetheart who was killed suggested their relationship was strong.

Beth meant it when she had said she loved him, she always had, and she now sat in her beautiful apartment overlooking the river, weeping over lost opportunities.

At the same time, two hundred and eighty miles away, the love of her life wept too.

Chapter Twenty-Eight

'So what the hell have we got? Where the hell are we?' asked Mansell of Rogers, who sat on an adjacent bar stool. It was 9 p.m. in The Toadstool and they had just left the Station after a fourteen-hour day. Another one. They had decided that a couple of pints, away from the noise, interruptions and atmosphere of the squad room, would be beneficial.

'Bit of lateral thinking needed, Will, maybe we can't see the wood for the trees.'

So over their pints of Carlsberg lager, Mansell repeated his question. 'I mean, really got?'

Rogers was prepared to go through this exercise because he had seen it done before by Mansell, and it had produced a result thanks to the clarity brought to the investigation by the pub session.

'Let's talk facts, boss. He's done at least five: Darlo, Sunderland, Manchester, Stockton, Stockton again, and probably old London as well, so six. All women, all under forty, no sexual attack, but mutilation to all but Stockton number one, and that was only because he was disturbed.

'They're spread over a number of years, different locales, similar weapons, screwdriver type or sharp knife. Not the same time of day, week, month or year. Not lunar. No links between girls, physically, career wise or dress code. None of the girls were prostitutes.

'We know his blood group, DNA patterns, shoe size, type of shoe and his physical appearance. We know he had a nasty wound of some description, though I wouldn't put too much store by that. We have psychological and psychiatric profiles, so all in all we know him physically, mentally and emotionally, and yet...'

'And yet we don't know the bastard's name! He might as well be you, Will.'

'Yep, it's a bugger all right, we're about as close to catching him as finding Santa Claus in June. What are we missing? There's got to be something that is the key. Some small detail?'

Mansell knew that Rogers was really making these comments to himself so said nothing. Rogers took a swig of lager then asked, 'What is the most useful info we've got? What do you think, sir?'

Mansell considered the question for a moment and then answered, 'I would say the eyewitness report, because if he saw him again then that's it. That's better than blood groups and maybe even the DNA, which the courts don't understand. They do understand someone like Sanders standing up, pointing and saying, "That's him, that's the man I saw killing a girl."'

Rogers said, 'I agree, so how about we see Sanders in case there's some tiny detail we've missed?'

'How about reading his statement again, word by word, to see if there's any detail which we've overlooked?'

'Fine by me, how about now?' Rogers offered generously.

'No, thanks anyway. Tomorrow will do nicely.'

They discussed the possibility of carrying out an enormous DNA screening exercise but knew that the budget would not carry it, never mind the fuss the civil rights groups would make. Mansell made a caustic remark suggesting that civil rights activists would rather have a maniac on the streets who denied young women the right to live than upset a few namby-pamby types who had something to hide.

'So you reckon we should focus on one factor – Sanders – for now?'

'Yeah,' said Mansell distractedly, obviously thinking hard about it. He came out of his ruminations and said, 'We have to find that key, Will, just have to. He's going to do another one, I just know he is.'

They drank up and went back to their cars parked behind the pub.

'See you first thing, sir.'

'Goodnight, Will,' Mansell said wearily and set off home.

His head was buzzing with thoughts, but not ideas, and he couldn't help wondering if he was losing his edge. How could they know so much and not feel that they were close? Was it his fault? Was he misleading the case, missing some clearly signposted avenue of exploration? He didn't think so, but maybe…

He thought Rogers' suggestion of revisiting the Sanders lad a good one; at least that had come out of tonight. He was not enamoured of the thought of again going through all the tapes from CCTVs in the area, but if need be he would do it.

When Mansell got home he took a few minutes out to sit with Ellen and have a coffee. He hated not spending more time with her, a consequence of his total devotion to his job, particularly when involved in a case like this.

He soon made his apologies and went to the room he called his 'den', a third bedroom they didn't need.

He had shelves and cabinets packed tightly into the room and in the corner stood a spartan table with a lamp on it. He sat down for a moment deciding what to do next and decided that profiling was his best bet.

As a fan of the Behavioral Science and Investigative Support Units at Quantico, the FBI headquarters in Virginia, he knew of their work, had studied it and believed in it, but his enthusiasm over the years had often fallen on deaf ears. Sure, they were slowly catching on in this country. Hadn't Rogers earlier that night said that 'they had profiles, both psychological and psychiatric? But Mansell truly felt they were only scratching the surface in this fascinating subject.

He pulled down off one of the shelves a couple of the books written by John Douglas, ex-head of the specialist FBI department and flicked them open. He didn't know what to expect; divine inspiration, perhaps, but it didn't happen. He knew life wasn't that kind.

He had made many markers in these books over the years and he turned to some of them now.

He started to jot a few notes down, then began to read more and more. The more he read, the more he wrote. At four in the morning he sat back, exhausted but he felt that in the short few hours he had gained a valuable insight into the killer.

Why the hell hadn't he done this simple exercise earlier? He could only suggest to himself that he had been diverted by the profiles presented to him, but he felt that this was a lame excuse and he cursed himself for missing the obvious route. He directed some of his anger and frustration at the senior guys – some civil servants, not police officers, who thought profiling was an 'American thing' and that it wasn't real police work. 'Damn it!' he said aloud, before switching off the lamp and trudging wearily to bed.

His last waking thought was about the news that had broken earlier that morning that the computer guys had confirmed a sixth murder by their man, way back in 1978 in London. They had got a shock receiving the news, not so much that he had killed before, that possibility always existed in their mind; but the date was a nasty surprise.

'Are we tracking someone who has been killing for twenty years?' asked a shaken Rogers.

'Christ, I sincerely hope not,' Mansell had said with feeling.

Mansell fell asleep wondering if he was dealing with one of the greatest mass murderers of all time.

Mansell arrived at the Station the next morning at 6.30 a.m., Rogers not far behind him at 6.50. Rogers grinned as he approached his colleague.

'Couldn't sleep, eh?'

'Yeah, that's right. So excited that I didn't go to bed,' said Mansell gruffly.

'So what's the starting point? Tapes or statements, forensics or what?'

'Actually, I've already dug out – like we said – the Sanders statement, because that's the best, most real evidence we've got. A direct witness. A copy is on your desk. I checked through it...'

'And?'

Mansell looked a little rueful, 'Zip so far,' he admitted, 'but my guts tell me that there's something, just something.'

Mansell surprised Rogers by changing tack.

'First, Will, I'd like to run something by you. You know I've always harped on about the FBI profiling techniques and how I don't think that our lads have quite got the hang of it?' He didn't wait for an answer. 'Well, I dug out the John Douglas books last night and tried to nick some of his and the FBI's ideas. And guess what – my profile is fairly detailed but different from the official ones that we've been using.'

'How different?' asked Rogers, intrigued.

'Well, following FBI ideas I reckon the following.'

He pulled a sheaf of pages from a briefcase and Rogers thought, How the hell did he find time to do that little lot?

'One, our man is not doing this for sexual gratification; it's definitely anger.

'Two, the mutilation after death is not torture for torture's sake; it's doing something, achieving something. Given what he mutilates, I'd say he's glad that these women will never breed, never create more women.

'Three, he doesn't stage them for anybody's attention. It isn't necessary for him to humiliate them, he's done his job with the mutilation.

'Four, because of the blitz attack and wounds to the back, he can't get a woman for himself, can't face them on a one-to-one basis. His confidence has been shattered. I don't think he's ugly or handicapped or whatever, because then I think he'd have to humiliate them. No, I think he's had some traumatic childhood experience with a domineering woman, mother, aunt or guardian, and this is payback for that.

'Five, the FBI would say he works with women. He wants to know them wants to understand them, so he may well work in a female-driven environment: a big clerical office, travel agent's, production line, hairdresser's – something like that.

'Six, the FBI talk of "stressors", that is the thing that triggers him off. Could be anything, big or small, but – and it's a big but – there will always be stressors, so that means he could go off at any time.

'Seven, his childhood will have been so horrible that he may attach himself to childhood things. He may hang around play-grounds, parks, funfairs etc., places where kids have fun, kids' shops maybe. It might be worth digging out files on any known "child observers".

'Eight, he works neatly and he enjoys it, so we're dealing with a cool customer. That can't be underestimated.

'Nine, despite visiting London and Manchester, he lives up here, he's in the North-East, he's settled down now.

'Ten, although physically strong, he's no giant, the shoes tell us that. So he works out, probably at home.

'Eleven, his work is over with the mutilation; he has no reason to revisit the scene of the crime or the victims' graves. Staking them out was a waste of time.

Twelve, because his work is over with the mutilation, it explains why he takes no trophies. There's no need; he's made his statement, done his job.

'Thirteen, unlucky for some…'

Rogers was highly impressed, and even more so at the injection of humour.

'He drives a car. It won't be a flash model – too ostentatious – but it will be a bright colour; that's him boasting that he's not afraid of anybody.

'Fourteen, and finally, he won't have a girlfriend, won't have had a girlfriend, won't have a stash of porn, won't have a record for sexual offences. This is not about sex, although the other profiles see it as that.'

Mansell took a deep breath and Rogers simply said, 'Wow! Impressive boss!'

'Just bear it in mind, Will, but let's stick to first things first, the Sanders statement.'

Rogers went to his desk and picked up a red lever arch file which contained the copy of Jeff's statement.

He sat down, lit a cigarette and started to reread the statement. He noticed that Mansell also was reading the statement at his desk a few feet away.

Rogers was conscious of a murmuring in the background and registered, without interest that Mansell was reading some of the statement aloud, albeit quietly.

He read a little more, struggling to bury the pressing thoughts that this was a waste of time and also that he could quote most of this statement word perfect, so many times had he pored over it.

He was suddenly aware that Mansell had gone very quiet. He glanced up and could see that Mansell was not reading further. 'Anything, Nige?' he asked, without any real hope.

Mansell didn't answer directly but just started reading from the statement.

> 'I saw a man kneeling over a girl, who was lying on the floor, on the ground.'
>
> 'Please describe the man's appearance.'
>
> 'He looked over at me, because I must have made a noise or something and I saw him quite well because he wasn't far away. He looked about thirty-something, not over-big. He wasn't fat or skinny – sort of fit, I suppose. He didn't have any specially noticeable features like a big nose or anything. I couldn't see the colour of his eyes or hair, though I noticed that his hair was slick with the rain.'

Mansell stopped, and stared down again at the statement, with an expression that Rogers couldn't quite place.

'Did I miss something, Nige?' asked Rogers.

'Oh, umm, probably not,' replied Mansell. 'It's just that I'm struck by the words, "I noticed that his hair was slick with the rain."'

'Still don't get it. Sorry,' said Rogers, feeling a bit thick.

'I just wondered, what if his hair wasn't slick with rain?'

'But it had been, or was, pissing down, wasn't it?' asked Rogers, turning back to the statement to confirm the fact.

'Yeah, tanking down. But what if his hair was gelled down?'

'Well, what if it was?'

'I'm just thinking of that lab report that said that under the Gilmour girl's fingers was an as yet unidentified gel.'

Rogers was already turning to a blue file on his desk that contained all technical matters related to the case.

'Just a sec,' he said, and then quickly produced a copy of the report. He flicked through it and ran his finger down a particular page. He read,

> Under three of the victim's fingernails we found a gel-like substance. The constituent parts include chemicals associated with hair products but as yet (18/4/99) we have not specifically identified the substance to any particular brand name. The sample has been forwarded to the laboratory at Procter & Gamble whom we

feel will soon be able to identify the product in question. We are unable to suggest that this sample will be of particular significance; it may be a product used by the victim as a matter of routine.

'What do you think?' asked Rogers.

'I don't know,' replied Mansell. But both of them were feeling the first little stirrings that usually meant only one thing: a lead, a break.

'Nothing to get too excited about,' observed Mansell flatly, but for the first time in many, many days he felt that there was some excitement in the case... just maybe.

Rogers looked at his watch: 7.20, not too early to contact Ged Lawrence, the author of the lab report. He rang through to the girl on the switchboard.

'Hi, Jeanie, it's Tom Rogers. Get me Ged Lawrence, the lab guy, please.'

A minute later, the phone rang and Rogers picked up. 'Rogers!' he barked.

'Mr Lawrence for you,' said Jeannie.

'Hi, Ged. Tom Rogers here.'

'Hi, Tom. How you doing?'

'Great, thanks. Sorry to bother you so early, but it's the Gilmour case.'

Ged Lawrence presumed it was and he really wasn't bothered about the time. For his first call, seven thirtyish was quite civilised, as he was known to get calls around the clock. The only thing that ever bothered this rather placid character was the 3 a.m. call asking how a certain report was coming on from some prick of a detective who thought the world revolved around his case and his career.

He also liked Tom Rogers, who struck him as a very decent sort, unlike that arrogant bastard he worked alongside, Mansell.

'What can I do for you, Tom?'

'Nothing special, Ged,' said Rogers casually, 'just a loose end, really.'

'Fire away,' said Ged, curious why something not special had engendered a phone call so early and, more importantly, given an edge to Tom Rogers' voice which he recognised as a hint of excitement.

'Under the girl's fingernails, or at least a couple of them, there's a note in the report about tiny samples of a gel or something. Just wondered if you'd heard anything more about this?' There it was again, Ged thought, the casual 'Just wondered'.

'Yes, I remember that stuff. We just couldn't pin it down. Thought it was hair product at first, but it's like nothing we've seen. Then thought maybe a face cream or something similar, but couldn't match that either. Tried the usual tests but had to send it away. Went to Procter & Gamble, didn't it? Must admit, I haven't heard anything yet. I'll chase it up at the office.' He thought he'd play them at their own game, and asked, 'Anything in it, Tom?'

'Doubt it, Ged, just a loose end to tie up.'

Lying sod, thought Ged, he's on to something. But no matter, it wasn't his business and the detectives often wouldn't divulge things, even though it was the labs and forensic guys who broke a case.

Rogers thanked Lawrence and said he'd wait for his call at about nine, and Ged said it would be nearer ten by the time he'd got bounced around the various departments at Procter & Gamble.

'As soon as possible will be great,' said Rogers nonchalantly.

He dropped the receiver down on the handset and leaned back in his chair. 'Interesting,' he remarked to Mansell, with a little grin. 'They first thought it was hair product, but couldn't place it. Tried cream and stuff but still couldn't place it.'

Mansell cut in, 'Struck me that the lass wasn't the sort to use creams and stuff. Seemed a bit too clean-cut for that somehow.'

This was not exactly what he wanted to say, but Rogers knew exactly what he meant, adding, 'Not a lot in her room, if I remember rightly.'

'Not too bad, no,' confirmed Mansell.

'If it is hair product and our labs can't spot it, do you think that it could be a new product?' Rogers asked.

Mansell finished the thought, 'And if it's that new, then maybe it's only available at a few outlets?'

They fell silent for a moment.

'How come', mused Rogers, 'that this has been overlooked?'

'Just thinking about that. The problem's been that there was so much of the other stuff – blood, skin, shoes, DNA – that this little detail's been deemed unimportant. In some sodding cases where we had absolutely bugger all, the gel would have been our only lead and dealt with as priority.'

'Roll on ten o'clock,' said Rogers.

Between seven thirty and ten o'clock they busied themselves digging out the old High Street videotapes and scouring them, but as ever it was like looking for a needle in a haystack, without even knowing what the needle looked like.

The time dragged, but just as Rogers was about to contact Ged, at 10.10 the phone went on his extension. He snapped up the phone and barked, 'Yes?'

'Ged Lawrence for you,' said Jeannie.

'Yes, Ged,' said Rogers, as his heart beat just a bit faster.

'Good news,' said Ged, and Tom pulled the receiver a little closer to his ear, as if that would make this good news arrive quicker. He didn't say anything, so Ged continued.

'Finally got the right Procter & Gamble guy... told you it would take three departments.' He waited for a comment, but received none, so he continued.

'Apparently they bottomed it last week but the guy who traced it went on holiday on Wednesday. Tuscany – at this time of year would you believe?'

Silence from Rogers, so he pushed on, conscious that anything but the facts was not going to be well received.

'So he left it to his deputy, who herself didn't realise what it was, and now here it is.'

Rogers felt the hairs rising on the back of his neck. Christ, please let this be it, please!

'The gel sample found under three nails of Jayne Gilmour, murdered on 28/3/99, is a compound that has recently been released in the UK under the brand name "Kenjaal".'

He hesitated, and this time got a snapped response from Rogers. 'Yes, yes, and what the fuck's that?'

Ged smiled; this confirmed something he'd felt since breakfast, that this was significant.

'It's a new hair restorer, a new wonder product developed in Sweden and sold throughout Europe with almost guaranteed results. Oh, and if you didn't guess, it's a male product. Your man must be going bald.' He stopped again, quite enjoying the power that he knew he held over Rogers, and he waited for the reaction that he knew was coming. Rogers didn't disappoint him.

Trying to sound calm he asked, 'And how many outlets market this?'

Lawrence paused for effect, and then slowly said, 'Only one.' He heard Rogers emit a tiny gasp. 'Yeah, I thought that this would be called good news. The only places that stock Kenjaal around here are in a chain of eighteen hairdressing salons, but only three of the shops stock it. Goes under the name of Fringe Benefits; they're all in the North-East, I think that you've got a lead, Tom. Sorry that it didn't come a bit quicker.'

'Christ!' exclaimed Rogers as he thumped the phone down.

Mansell was standing only a few feet away, eyes bright, with an expectant look across his face.

'So?' was all he said.

'Hair product, new to the UK, only sold through three hairdressers in the North-East.'

'Three!' exclaimed Mansell.

Rogers had a big grin on his face. 'It gets better.'

'Better?' asked Mansell, 'You're kidding!'

'No, it's not just any old hair product, shampoo or something that could be sold to hundreds of thousands of punters.' He paused and with undisguised glee announced, 'It's for baldies, and how many baldies would buy this sort of stuff in such a public place?'

'Not many, I bet,' agreed Mansell. Thinking ahead, he said, 'Right, let's get cracking. Three guys get out to the three shops.'

'Three hairdressers,' corrected Rogers.

'Even better,' said Mansell, and hurried on. 'These places must have sales records or something, surely? If they don't, it shouldn't matter because it'll be their regulars who are going to be buying stuff, won't it? I mean, you don't wander in off the street to a hairdresser's for bald cream, do you? Give it to Jim, Andy and Tom. I want this doing now, not tomorrow, or later today; now.'

He sounded aggressive and in no mood for arguments, not that Rogers wanted to argue. He left his seat and went into the main body of the squad room where the resident crew of nine were seated at various scattered desks.

'Listen up, lads!' he bellowed. 'We've got a break!'

Everybody stopped what they were doing. Two who were on the telephone said to those on the other end, 'Excuse me for a minute, sir.' They didn't want to miss this news.

Rogers couldn't help but smile. 'Seems our man is worried about going bald. He uses a new product called Kenjaal, which is only available at three hairdressers' branches called Fringe Benefits.'

Andy Dale piped up, 'I know them, there's one in Stockton, one in Darlington and one in Bishop.' A couple of guys looked at him inquisitively, so he explained, 'I know because I use Stockton, and the girls talk of the other two branches.'

'That'll do for me,' said Rogers. He dealt out impromptu instructions. 'Andy, you take Stockton as you know the people. Jim you take Darlo; Tom, you take Bishop Auckland. Now. Find out who buys this stuff; there can't be many. Track them down this afternoon with a couple of guys each.' The expectant faces looked for more. 'That's it! What are you waiting for? Go, go, go!'

There was a flurry of activity as people stood up, picked up notepads, pens and pencils, jackets and coats. In a few moments the nine were six, and Rogers was satisfied that at last they were doing something positive.

Between the hours of twelve and one, Andy, Jim and Tom all checked in. Each had fairly short lists of names obtained from the manager of each shop. As suspected, wonder product though Kenjaal might be, the general public were slow to be seen being so vain that they were concerned about hair loss. Too closely associated with loss of virility etc., thought Mansell; but great news, the lists were short.

Six further squad members set off in pairs to join the three already in the field. There wasn't a single instance of anybody recalling a stranger walking into the shops to buy this particular product. Through appointment books and local knowledge, they were able to quickly pinpoint the few people in each case who were known to have bought Kenjaal.

Rogers and Mansell sat until three o'clock discussing how close they felt they were to a major breakthrough. Even allowing for the bias that desperation and frustration brought, they had to admit that the net had closed significantly in the last few hours. They considered the possible negatives. It could be that it was somebody from outside the area who used the stuff. What were the chances of that? Could Jayne Gilmour have come into contact with the stuff somewhere else, somehow? Possible, but she would surely have washed her hands, and thereby lost all traces, during the course of that fateful day.

No, all in all, their guy had to be a user of Kenjaal; and as there were so few names to deal with, well, they almost had him, didn't they?

They were close, of course they were, but they had missed a couple of rather important points. Firstly, they had only asked the three shop managers, Johnny at Stockton, Dan at Darlington and Sorry at Bishop Auckland for customers who'd bought Kenjaal. They had not asked for the names of staff who used the gelatinous substance in question, nor had the information been volunteered. So the name of Samuel Westmain did not appear on the lists. To add to the woes of the police (had they known it), was the fact that Sam had been in the shop when DS Tom Sturridge arrived at Bishop Auckland. He had contrived to involve himself in the conversation between Tom and Sorry. He had overheard the initial question from Tom, and had stepped forward and said, 'Sorry to interrupt, but I heard the question. That old Colin Dunmoody from West End, I'm sure he took some a while ago.'

'You know, I think you're right,' said Sorry.

'That's a good start,' chipped in Tom enthusiastically. 'Thanks, son,' he said cheerily to Sam.

Sam smiled his acknowledgement and said, 'No probs, anything to help.' He smiled again and went back to his station, forgetting to take the hairdryer that he was supposed to have been going for; but neither he, his client or Tom noticed.

Sam was thinking furiously while he fussed around Mrs Kolowski. She prattled on about the weather, the price of a loaf at

Mr Patel's, the rudeness of today's society and the commerciality of the Christmas past. He was able to listen, digest and respond to her sympathetically, without taking any notice at all of the conversation. He started thinking, I don't believe this. Frigging Kenjaal. That's going to be my downfall. Surely not! Maybe, just maybe, though, they would miss the point and get absolutely nowhere with their names and then let the lead go cold. Maybe… but shit! I can't really believe that… even the stupid police won't miss this lead. So what to do? What to do?

'Yes, sure, Mrs K, they have no respect, do they,' he mumbled, keeping time with the ongoing conversation.

The big question was, how much time did he have? Hours, weeks? He just couldn't tell could he. Shit! He laughed aloud as he joked with himself. He wouldn't care, but the fucking stuff has been so hard to get hold of from day one. Why did he bother?

He managed to chortle in response to the contention by Mrs K that kids today should be birched for being abusive to people in authority or old people.

He glanced up at the salon clock and saw that he was only about four hours from home. Stay calm, do nothing, wait till you get home and then sort it out…

He saw that the copper was still quizzing Sorry, and the pair were obviously working their way around all the girls, asking each one, no doubt, for any names to go on the list of suspects.

Would Sorry have the sense to ask? Or would the cop be the one to enquire whether he or his boss used it? When the pair came to his station, they stopped for a second and Sorry said, 'Anybody else you can think of who's bought that stuff?'

'Nope, been thinking about it, Sorry; can't say I can,' said Sam. He smiled an easy smile and they moved on.

Sam watched the detective eventually take his leave, clutching a valuable bit of paper which he was sure could only contain a handful of names at the most. Presuming that they were simultaneously visiting Darlington and Stockton, he estimated that they would have no more than about twenty or thirty names. When they'd eliminated those poor buggers – who were about to get the fright of their lives – what would the police do? He guessed that they would revisit the salons and surely someone would mention that he had taken a couple of months' worth of Kenjaal.

His thoughts were broken as the policeman returned to his side and said, 'Mr Sorensen tells me you had a friend – Steve, was it? – who used Kenjaal before your head office pulled the plug recently.'

'That's right. Flipping heck, I'd forgotten that! Yeah, he used the stuff. Said it was no good.' Sam provided Tom with a story saying Steve was abroad for a month and turned back to Mrs Kolowski.

So, was the game up? If it was, what were his options? He was going to have to give this some thought.

Chapter Twenty-Nine

Jeff went to bed on the Saturday night worried that he had made a serious mistake in letting Steve Nuttall at the office talk him into turning out for the office football team on the Sunday. 'Emergency,' Steve had said. 'There really is nobody else, Jeff.' Not much of a compliment, thought Jeff as he reluctantly said yes and then wondered if he'd ever find his boots.

Sunday morning brought with it scudding grey clouds and cold bursts of rain. The bitter northerly wind dampened his enthusiasm further. Great – that's all I need, a wind to freeze your nuts off and a heavy pitch, was all he could think as he drove to the Council-run area where eight pitches were laid out. He had suffered a moment of weaknesses where he seriously considered contracting flu, but once again his loyalty to the firm pulled him through. He had already changed into the strip that Steve had dropped off at his house on Saturday, having decided that to get changed at the field of play, literally on the field, would have been the height of folly. He had a vest and a T-shirt under his team top and an extra pair of regular socks under his football stockings. As he approached the recreation area, he glanced at the carrier bag on the passenger seat which contained his boots. Thank God feet don't get fat like chins or waistlines, he thought.

He pulled into the car park in good time for the kick-off at eleven o'clock, noticing a couple of cars that he recognised from the office. He saw the signposts that indicated the pitches and he followed the path to pitch five, where Steve had told him they were playing. It was very cold and he shivered, despite the layers under his strip, the strip itself and the jogging suit that he wore on top. Probably look like the sodding Michelin man, he said to himself as he approached pitch five and his teammates, who were already warming up.

He waved to Steve, who he was not surprised to see was already there, and spoke a few words to Darren Moore, a junior who was playing in midfield. He pulled his jogging suit off and immediately regretted it. Shit! Could have kept that on for another five minutes, you stupid sod, he chided himself.

He walked onto the pitch and said a few 'Hellos' then self-consciously jogged across the grass. He was literally trying to warm up but hoped that anybody watching would think he was limbering up. After he turned back towards his team, some inconsiderate sod thumped the ball towards him. It was his worst nightmare, a driven ball coming at his chest when he hadn't got himself sorted, physically or mentally. Instant choice, get hit or duck. He didn't duck, but took the ball full in the chest without any pretence at trying to control it. It thudded into him and bounced ten yards off him, making him gasp and emit an 'Ouch!'

Somebody shouted 'Nice control, Jeff!' but there was nothing more abusive. He rubbed his chest and moved towards his teammates. They had all arrived now, and Steve called them together for a team talk. It was hardly Churchillian, but Jeff was impressed by Steve's genuinely passionate speech about team spirit, playing for each other and for the reputation of the firm.

They took their places, Jeff having been handed the right back role. The nearest person to him was Tommy Mack, a very bright, partly qualified student whom the partners had great hopes for. He had not yet put his top on and Jeff shouted across to him, 'Christ, Tommy, how hard are you exactly?'

Tommy grinned and replied, puffing out his chest, 'Nipples like tent pegs, Jeff! It is a bit chilly, isn't it?'

A couple of the other lads laughed and Tommy pulled his top on.

Steve had told them that the opposition, although from a namby-pamby solicitor's office, had a reputation for being rather physical, so he'd warned his team not to be intimidated early on. These were not the words Jeff wanted to hear so it was with some apprehension that the accountants' right back moved forward as the referee blew his whistle to start the match. The regulars in the team were not at all perturbed because they would always choose solicitors over a team from a factory, store or garage. Those teams always contained at least a couple of evil nutters who existed only for Sunday mornings when they could kick the shit out of some poofs from a professional office. Despite Steve's pep talk, the regulars were quite relaxed about the odds of having lumps removed from various parts of their anatomy.

Jeff decided that he would have to keep moving in order to avoid frostbite, but he was aware that he did not want to exhaust himself just keeping warm and also that he could not run too far from his allotted position. So he ran forward a few yards then ran back again, then repeated the action. He did not care less if anybody noticed his movements and wondered if he was unwell. He got an early touch of the ball when it arrived by accident at his feet. He controlled it neatly but then spoilt his moment by attempting a long pass up the line to one of his forwards. He scuffed the ball only about ten feet to a litigation trainee who took a step forward and rifled a shot just wide of the post. Jeff was aware of some hard looks in his direction, and the keeper said, 'Steady, Jeff!' Steve shouted from his midfield position, 'No problem, Jeff, keep going!' and clapped his hands in encouragement.

The ball then spent a little time on Jeff's side of the pitch and he had to sprint a couple of times in quick succession. As he paused for breath, he recognised that his lungs had apparently collapsed and that, together with his looming heart attack, this did not augur well for the next seventy-five minutes. He could also taste thick saliva – or maybe blood – at the back of his throat, so he was very grateful for Steve and Tommy combining brilliantly to fashion a good chance for Paul Harrison, a manager, which resulted in a corner. Jeff did not go forward for the corner.

Unfortunately, the ball was whacked clear from the penalty box by a conveyancing senior and fell between Jeff and a qualified divorce lawyer. Now Lenny Rosyth was a very kind, sympathetic gentleman, who by his nature was ideally suited to emotional clients suffering the ordeal of matrimonial collapse. In the office this was certainly true; but once on a football pitch he was, to use commonly agreed parlance, a dirty bastard. He played up front and enjoyed any physical confrontations with aggressive defenders and now there was a loose ball to chase. Jeff was a clear favourite to reach this particular ball, but Lenny Rosyth did not believe in lost causes, neither on the pitch nor in the office. Jeff had poked the ball away when Mr Rosyth lunged in and Jeff's general lack of match fitness meant that he did not have the resources to react to the fast approaching weight of an aggressive lawyer. Lenny's raised boot caught Jeff in a crunching blow on his right knee. The resounding crack was heard all over the pitch like a gunshot. Both players said 'Ugh!' and lay in crumpled heaps on the cold, muddy pitch. The ball rolled apologetically over the touchline so the game came to a standstill. Several players ran to the prone bodies. The referee looked to the heavens before making his way wearily to Jeff's side. The ref had had a row with his kids at half past seven that morning – usual thing, untidy rooms – his wife was extremely premenstrual and he had a bad back. He just wanted to go to the pub, and now this; at best a delay, at worst a hospital job.

'What's the damage, Jeff?' asked Steve, fearing some bad news as that crack sounded a lot worse than your average knock, bump or scrape. Mr Matrimonial was wriggling around in the mud moaning, 'Ow, ow, frigging ow!' he didn't get a lot of sympathy from his team-mates; they had seen him do this before, clobber somebody then feign injury to avoid a booking, or worse, from the referee.

Big Johnny Devlin, Jeff's centre forward, hovered menacingly over Lenny, bending down towards him.

'You dirty twat, you had no chance of that ball!'

'Fuck off!' retorted Lenny, and the next instant saw Johnny grabbing Lenny around the throat. Other players then piled in, fortunately in order to pull colleagues apart rather than to indulge in a complete free-for-all.

The referee gave an audible groan and blew his whistle, shouting, 'Come on, lads, for God's sake, break it up! We've got a lad hurt here!'

Attention turned to Jeff, and Lenny decided that he had got away with it, so he got off the ground and hobbled away with a hugely exaggerated limp.

'Okay, son?' the ref asked Jeff, and was surprised at the relatively cheery response.

'Smashing, never felt better.'

A few of Jeff's colleagues picked up on the humour and indulged in banter in an attempt to relieve the tension of the moment.

Jeff was white, and it wasn't from the cold, which at the moment he'd forgotten. He shook his head and looked at the faces gazing down at him. 'Feels bad,' he said, to nobody in particular.

'Can you move it?' somebody asked, and Jeff concentrated on doing just that, but his right leg felt as if it weighed ten stone and he couldn't move it at all. He was conscious of a throbbing ache in his knee, but it wasn't the pain that he would have expected to accompany what his head told him was a serious injury.

The referee turned to Steve and said, 'Going by the sound of the crack and the fact he hasn't moved, I'd say he's taking no further part in this game, so you'd better get him off the pitch. Better think about hospital too.'

Jeff had hardly made a sound lying there, trying very hard to take it like a man. But as soon as Steve and Johnny started to pick him up he yelped like a wounded puppy. 'Steady lads,' he said bravely, wincing and screwing up his face in pain.

They carried him very gingerly to the side of the pitch, but the movement had triggered the not unexpected screaming agony. Hot pokers, needles and knives were the images that sprang to Jeff's mind, and he made several involuntary mewing noises. He was laid gently by the pitch and the referee said to Steve, 'This is definitely a hospital visit. Can you organise it?'

'We've got no subs, ref, that's why he's playing,' Steve said, pointing at Jeff.

The weather meant that there were only a couple of people watching the games this morning and they were currently engrossed in a needle match on pitch eight between a local cement factory and the nearby brick works. Despite the lack of obvious signs of injury to Jeff – no cut, no blood, hardly a mark – Jeff's demeanour, and that crack, spoke volumes.

'Going to call the game off, ref?' asked the lawyers' left back, hoping for an abandonment. He, like Jeff, was not a regular, and did not enjoy this cold, but the main motivation for his enquiry was that his girlfriend, Julie, had been on heat that morning, and he was very keen to get back to her as soon as possible. He was not surprised to hear the referee say, 'Up to the captains,' knowing that there was no way they would sanction abandonment.

'No thanks, ref,' said the solicitors' leader, a criminal lawyer by trade. 'We're happy to keep going.'

They turned to Steve, who in turn bent down to Jeff. 'Okay if we play on, Jeff?'

Jeff hesitated, wondering, And what the hell happens to me? But Steve read his thoughts and blurted, 'After we've got you sorted, of course.'

Jeff nodded and mumbled, 'No problem.'

He appreciated that they had even bothered to consult him.

Most of the players started to drift back to their positions, satisfied that the crisis was no longer their problem, but Steve was now left to deal with it.

'Need a car, don't we?' said the ref, stating the obvious, but his question prompted an unexpected response from the lawyers' left back.

'Look,' he said, 'I've got a car. If I take him it will even the numbers up. It's even, full back for full back, and my captain won't mind.'

Without waiting for the referee's consent, he called to his captain who was a few yards away. He explained his idea and the captain, said – grudgingly Steve thought – 'Suppose so, see you later.'

Will you bollocks! thought the left back. I'm dropping the gimp off at hospital, then I'm off to Julie for rampant nookie.

'Get back if you can, Danny,' instructed the captain, but Danny thought, Yeah right, a few minutes to hospital, drop off, back to Julie. In twenty-five minutes he should be in a warm comfortable bed with hot, attentive, oh-so-attentive Julie!

Steve, the referee and Danny carried Jeff painfully and in haphazard fashion to the car park. It was quite a trek across the vast playing area and they were panting when they arrived at Danny's Volkswagen. They bundled Jeff into the passenger seat and he cried out again in pain.

Steve and the ref both said, 'Good luck.' Then they thanked Danny, and Jeff gave them a sickly grin and a half-hearted thumbs up. Danny and Jeff would have been interested to hear the conversation taking place between Steve and the ref.

'Right,' the ref was saying, 'let's get on with it. First thing is to send that bastard off!'

'Send him off?' said Steve, surprised.

'Yeah, I've crossed swords with him before, that Rosyth, and seeing as I'm in a bad mood – sod it, he's going!'

Steve was taken aback at the rather unprofessional attitude of the ref, but hey, it was an amateur level and ten against nine gave them a chance, especially as the lawyers had no substitutes either, because of a training course being held in Durham.

Jeff would have gained some satisfaction from the retribution meted out by the ref. Danny would have been worried that he was going to get a rollicking later for the humanitarian gesture that now left his team in the lurch.

They had only moved a few yards when Danny braked hard.

'Ow,' shouted Jeff loudly.

'Sorry, mate,' Danny apologised. He beeped his horn and Steve and the ref looked back.

'You go on,' Steve said to the ref, and moved back towards the car park. He feared that something terrible had happened to Jeff and was therefore relieved when Danny stepped out of the car and shouted, 'Give my clothes to my team!' Then Danny jumped back in and set off.

It only took a few minutes to get to the General and Danny parked right outside the Accident and Emergency entrance. He ran in, firstly to give the impression of an emergency and, secondly, to try to shave vital seconds from the time between now and seeing Julie. He found a porter and they grabbed a wheel-chair. Jeff was soon in the waiting area being assessed by a young doctor.

Jeff was feeling distinctly queasy now, unsure whether it was caused by the pain taking its toll or shock setting in. He was sent to the X-ray department and was soon seen to. He was quietly impressed with the speed of the service, and everybody he saw was reassuringly professional. Most of those dealing with him asked about the football match, but by the time another doctor came to see him he could barely concentrate on the small talk, such was the pain.

The doctor explained that Jeff had ruptured his knee and that surgery was going to be needed, preferably later that day. Jeff groaned at the prospect and felt a wave of self-pity wash over him. The doctor told Jeff that he had to visit another patient but that a porter would take him to admissions shortly. The doctor left and Jeff felt very vulnerable. He was alone in a cubicle on a trolley, and, having had various people fussing over him since the crunching foul, he now felt lonely.

He unexpectedly burst into tears, not through the pain but because his train of thought had taken him from self-pity to cursing his luck to thoughts of the ultimate bad luck and Jayne. The pain of Jayne was all too vivid, and in his current vulnerable state it all flooded back and forced its way from him by way of tears. He sobbed loudly, tears pouring down his face, but he managed to drag himself back under control. The involuntary nature of the outburst had given him quite a shock, but he was grateful that he had been alone. He pulled himself together and wiped his face with both hands.

Somebody in a white coat entered his cubicle and without introduction started prodding his knee. Roughly, Jeff thought. He felt queasy again and said so, but the man said gruffly, 'It will pass.'

Jeff felt a bit miffed with this person, whoever he was, and was about to say something when the surgeon said, 'Right, I would say that there's serious damage here, let's get you into surgery now.'

Jeff was taken aback and the next half an hour was a blur. He gave lots of personal details, including his home telephone number so that his parents could be contacted. Various medical personnel buzzed around him. He felt a little panicky when he was given an anaesthetic and told that he was soon off to theatre, but the worries were minimised by the haste of it all. His final recollections before drifting into unconsciousness were of a pretty nurse, or doctor, smiling a lovely smile and asking, 'So what was the score when it happened?'

When he awoke he had the almost obligatory confusion about where he was, but then the memories returned. He was pleasantly surprised to find his parents sitting beside his bed, his father smiling, his mother looking a little weepy.

'Now then,' he said, and his father responded in kind with, 'Now then.'

'How are you feeling, dear? asked Mrs Sanders in a quiet voice.

'Don't know yet. Bit sick, I think.'

Someone appeared at the bedside and spoke to him in those first-person-plural terms that so rankled some patients.

'So how are we doing, then? Feeling okay?'

The surgeon explained that there was a fair bit of damage within the knee, bruising and tears, but that the surgery had repaired the obvious problems. It would be a few weeks, he said, before the whole knee settled down and they would know better then whether further internal work would be needed. At least a week in hospital for complete rest and observation was the conclusion.

Jeff talked to his parents for a while but soon tired, the effects of the anaesthetic still within his system dragging him down. They recognised this and said their goodbyes. It was four o'clock, his operation having taken an hour, and him having been in post-op for another hour. He asked his parents to ring a couple of friends and his office first thing in the morning, and closed his eyes as soon as they left his ward. There were three other men in beds on his ward and he was dreading any of them trying to strike up a conversation, so he decided to pretend to be asleep. He was soon not pretending.

The next morning, Jeff finished his acceptable breakfast and thought about the week ahead. He had never stayed any length of time in hospital before and was not looking forward to it: the food, the routine, the boredom. His spirits lifted when the pretty nurse from the day before came to look at his wound. She removed the bandages and was soon studying the long line of stitches around almost all of Jeff's kneecap.

'Hmm,' she said, 'looks rather swollen.'

Not surprising, thought Jeff. You're flipping gorgeous! But he regretted the idea as he felt a pang of guilt. The wound was neatly dressed and Jeff was alone with his thoughts. One of the older gentlemen in a bed opposite asked him what he was in for and soon all four of them were comparing medical notes.

For no reason at all, the notion that Jeff would be revealed as being the man in the recent media coverage popped into his head, and he thought, Hell, I'm a sitting duck here! Once they find out I'm going to get the third degree for a week. The idea was most unappealing.

A combination of negative thoughts crowded into Jeff's head. Stuck in a goldfish bowl, crap food, nosy neighbours... Can it get any worse?

Well, actually it could. The negativity of all that swirled around him led him inevitably back to Jayne, and her name and image struck his heart like a physical blow. Jayne, oh God, sweet Jayne. His eyes closed and two large salty tears ran down his face. He squeezed his eyes tighter shut as if that would either stop the tears or the ache in his heart. It did neither. Goddamn it, why her, why her? The same old question that he had asked countless times since that horrendous day. What he would do to see her walk into the ward right now. He would literally do without both legs if only she could be there. Just to see that devastating, heart-warming smile, to hear her voice.

The other men in the ward exchanged glances, knowing looks that said, 'Stay quiet a bit, the lad's obviously suffering.' But they had no idea that the pain that was crippling Jeff was not in his leg but in his heart. He clenched his fists at the painful memory and drifted back to his days and nights with Jayne.

After a while he came back to the present circumstances and sighed a heavy, sad sigh. Can't get worse, can it? he asked himself rhetorically. Well, actually it could.

If someone had complied a list of the visitors who were to attend his beside over the coming six days he would not have believed it. It would have read: Mr and Mrs Sanders, Mr Todd, Mr Horsham, Mr Leighton, Mr Nuttall, Mrs Doris Wilkinson, and a Mr Samuel Westmain.

Things definitely *could* get worse.

Chapter Thirty

The following weekend Toddy arrived at the hospital just after four o'clock and passed Mr and Mrs Sanders in the corridor on the way to Ward 44. He said hello and asked how they were, and they said fine, in the circumstances. He thought that they both looked tired. Mrs Sanders in particular was showing signs of the strain of recent months. They shuffled off and Toddy made his way to Jeff's room. He reached the door but before knocking, took a second to tell himself to watch what he talked about. Jokes and light-heartendess, yes; flippancy and insensitivity definitely not.

He knocked politely and waited for a response. This was some sort of sign of respect and was an unusual occurrence where irreverence was the normal order of things.

He heard Jeff shout come in and he swung through the door. 'Now then, mate, how're doing?' he asked with a smile.

'Okey-dokey, young Toddy. How are you?'

'Great, thanks. Just been to the flicks with Baz to see *Arlington Road*, cracking thriller with Jeff Thingy, what do you call him...?'

'Bridges... Yeah, I read the reviews. It sounded good.'

'Cracking twist at the end, one of the best I've seen for ages, I won't spoil it for you, in case you go to see it.'

'If I do it'll be a while, seeing as I'm stuck with this bloody thing,' Jeff said, pointing down to his bandaged leg.

'So how's it going? Is it getting there?'

'Yeah, to be honest I can walk on it okay now, and I could be home, I reckon, but they're keeping me in for observation.'

'So another few days, or what?'

'I'd think so – two or three at the most, I'd reckon. It's been a long week.'

'Stinks a bit still, doesn't it?' said Toddy, referring to the aroma of fresh paint that still lingered.

'Yeah, I'm sure that made me queasy on the first day or two.'

'No news, then. Oh, I just saw your ma and pa as I was coming in.'

'Nothing to report, and yes, I've had the pleasure of one hour of Mother going on and on and on and on. She means well, bless her, but Christ, she does go OTT. I had to give Dad the nod to take her away before I…' Jeff gulped and looked at Toddy, 'Sorry,' he said, lamely.

'Okay, Jeff.' Toddy realised that Jeff had been about to say, 'before I killed her', or maybe even worse, 'before I strangled her'.

'How you coping with the rest of it then?'

'Oh, you know, I have my moments, like that, when it comes rushing back.'

They fell silent for a few seconds.

'It really hurts, Toddy, it really does.'

'I can only imagine, Jeff. Hang in there; it will get better, but I wouldn't pretend that it will be soon.'

'Remember Nice?' Asked Jeff.

'Of course, cracking holiday.'

'Remember the infamous bonding session?'

'How could I forget, you soft tart. It was a lovely experience,' replied Toddy with a smile.

'Well, I remember saying then that everybody has something. I don't really believe that, sitting here. I can't explain it because I know I've got great family, you, the lads, work and everything else, but Christ, it feels as if I've been singled out or something for the worst run of bad luck the world has ever seen! I could take the Wendy Fell thing; I could cope with a break-in, and this knackered knee is nothing. But add to these things Jayne and it's just too much, it really is.'

He let go a snuffling whimper and Toddy reached out to put a hand on his friend's arm.

'I know, I know, but we'll help you through this, honest we will.'

'I'm sorry, I just… it just sort of hits me sometimes. I feel a right tit, sorry.'

'Tell you what,' said Toddy, trying to lighten the leaden atmosphere. 'If you say "sorry" once more I'm going to either kick you in the knee, or get your mother back. Your choice!'

316

'Hoof me, please, God, hoof me!'

They laughed and Toddy sensed that the moment had passed.

They started talking about an old friend called Lenny Andrews whom Toddy had bumped into the night before in a local bar, and that led them to reminisce about their childhood days when Lenny was an integral part of what could now be classed as the original happy crew. They dragged up stories of adventure and misadventure that they had not talked about for a long time, each enjoying the stories and memories themselves, but also enjoying the freedom from the thoughts that so occupied their minds at the present time.

They creased with laughter at the story when the three of them had spent one hot summer day digging a huge hole in the middle of a nearby field. They had dug for hours, the intention being to build an underground labyrinth of tunnels. In one day they had achieved the creation of a big hole, which they sat in, exhausted but satisfied, as dusk drew near. They sat in their hole and planned to come back the next day to take it further and to build the first tunnel. When the plans were complete they scrambled up the sides of the hole, which was now in near darkness, only to find that the field was full of cows, dozens of them. They were only eight and the cows looked menacing. They stayed in their hole.

When they had been found an hour later by search parties formed by their anxious parents, they explained that the cows were chasing them. The parents did not know whether to laugh, scold or hug, so they did all of these in succession.

At thirteen, the three of them had each bought a rail ticket for the summer holidays that allowed them to travel the North-East line from York to Edinburgh. On one excursion to Edinburgh, they had got separated near the Castle, and even when Lenny and Jeff finally bumped into each other they couldn't find Toddy.

They finally hailed a passing police car and told them their story. The police, to their credit, took it very seriously and involved a dozen officers in the area to try and find Toddy. Hours later, exhausted and frightened, Jeff and Lenny had conceded defeat and were trying to come to terms with the fact that their friend was kidnapped, dead or very lost. They were on the platform awaiting the last train home, wondering how the hell they could explain this to the parents, when along came Toddy, an attractive sixteen-year-old girl in tow.

'Where the frigging hell have you been, you stupid wanker?' was Jeff's furious question.

'Thought you'd have gone home by now... it's late, you know,' was the nonchalant reply.

The police officer who had waited with Jeff and Lenny stifled a smile. 'Your mates have been worried about you, laddie, they've been looking all over for you,' he said.

'I met Jenny at the Castle and we got talking, so we went for an ice cream, and then she took me to her house.'

Toddy was beaming and the police officer said, 'I think you owe your friends an apology, and what about your parents? Weren't they expecting you a while past?'

'I rang them about three o'clock when I knew I'd be late; I thought you'd have had the sense to do the same, or go home as planned.'

Jeff was fuming; Lenny just looked at the gorgeous Jenny and said, 'You lucky bastard!'

Police Constable McDonald laughed aloud and said, 'Have a good trip home lads, and hey,' he said to Jeff, 'don't kill him!'

To emphasise the luck to which Lenny referred, Jenny gave Toddy a huge, sloppy, delicious wet kiss, and said thanks for a wonderful time. Three erections took place simultaneously.

Once they had boarded the train, Lenny started to quiz Toddy, but Jeff refused to sit with him. However, as the train passed Dunbar a short while later, Jeff came to where the others were sitting and said, having calmed down, 'Go on then, you bastard! Tell me all about it.'

Toddy enjoyed relating again how Jenny had flirted with him, used and abused him, and how he had had the most wonderful experience of his life. His mate losing his virginity had certainly reduced Jeff's annoyance. And wasn't Jenny gorgeous? Jeff had to admit she was, and reiterated Lenny's earlier observation. 'You really are a lucky bastard!'

'What about the bogeyman?' Toddy asked Jeff. 'Scary or what?'

The reference was to a man whom Jeff and Toddy had encountered some two years ago when they'd caught the train one day to Newcastle.

They had taken their seats either side of a table on the Intercity 125, it not being too busy because it was midday and midweek. The man had got on the train at Durham and sat opposite them. He was a big person, big all over: tall, wide, deep, big everywhere. Even for a very large person he had a disproportionately large head and Jeff muttered across to Toddy, 'Jeff, it's melon-head.'

Huge, overbearing, unkempt eyebrows added to the menace that this Goliath exuded. He had enormous hands that, if they'd been painted yellow, would surely have looked like bunches of bananas hanging from the sleeves of his scruffy fawn jacket. He was horribly hairy too, black tufts spouting from ears and nostrils, the backs of his hands and no doubt, thought Toddy, out of his arse.

The two lads could not help looking across at him, exchanging glances and nods and winks as they both took in the spectacle.

Jeff leant across the table and whispered, 'So which zoo has the gorilla escaped from?'

'Yeah, and how did he find clothes that fit him?'

Then in horribly comical fashion the man giant stuck the little finger of his left hand up his nose, raked around and extracted something. He rolled an object like a marble in those huge rubbery fingers, discarded it and then searched for a replacement. At first it was funny in sick sort of way, but then it became plain out and out disgusting.

Toddy, looking out of the window had said aloud, 'For fuck's sake, there can only be brains left in there.'

Jeff was aware of the man looking across but had no desire to return the glare, not through any sort of guilt at Toddy's remark but because of the stomach-churning prospect of catching sight of another marble-sized bogey being rolled in the fingers of gorilla man.

The memory was vivid and their smiles were twisted with the 'yuk factor'.

They talked for hours until Toddy said, 'Got to go, I'm afraid, meeting a girl downtown whom I saw last week. Nothing special, but I don't want to stand her up.'

'Sure, thanks for everything. It's been good. I needed that.'

'No problems, Jeff. See you next day or two – at home, hopefully. Mind how you go.'

After Toddy had gone, Jeff sighed and lay back on his bed, tired from having continuous visitors since three o'clock. He looked at his watch: half past seven. He thought of Toddy's earlier question, 'Just when did you smash a mirror over a black cat's head whilst walking under a ladder?'

They had smiled, but the hurt couldn't be joked away. Well, most of it could, possibly, but not Jayne. He felt the sting of tears at the memory of her name, and decided to go to the bathroom to wash his face before settling down for a viewing of *Casualty* and *Match of the Day*. He reminisced for another couple of minutes about the days he and Toddy had shared as youngsters then swung his stiff legs on to the carpeted floor.

Toddy made his way back through the hospital and as he strolled through the corridors he noticed a drinks machine and got himself a Diet Coke. He pulled the tab and drank in great gulps.

He was in no great hurry. He had plenty of time to get to town to meet his date, and after talking to Jeff he somehow felt lethargic, sad perhaps, certainly introspective. How would I cope with all that Jeff's had? he wondered. With a struggle, probably, he answered.

He saw a small sign proclaiming, *This is a non-smoking hospital* and thought wryly that it should add, *Expect of course for all the medical staff who smoke like chimneys.*

He strolled through the hospital complex, in awe at the scale of it all. He had only visited such places a couple of times before, both for elderly relatives after minor operations, and he had forgotten about the vastness of it all.

No wonder stuff gets nicked and staff get assaulted. Just how come it's so deserted? Anybody could walk in, he thought to himself.

He saw the signs warning visitors, *Car Park Management Systems remind you of a £25 Clamping Fee.* But he felt certain that nobody would be checking his unticketed car at that time of night.

Just near the exit was an apparently abandoned wheelchair – as if, it seemed to him, somebody had miraculously risen from the chair and gone home.

He got to his car and again felt that sympathetic wave wash over him for the plight of his friend. He comforted himself with the thought that at least he had been able to provide a few laughs that afternoon. God knew Jeff needed them. He sat in his car with his engine running and smiled at the recollection of their dispute, around six o'clock, about the relative attractiveness of women. Jeff sided with Courtney Cox, Toddy chose Jennifer Anniston. Jeff preferred Agnetha, Toddy went for Frieda. Jeff contended ugly could be sexy, like Steffi Graff; Toddy said you might as well say Boris Becker's got nice legs, and so forth. He smiled again. Jeff was a really great mate, if only… if only… these last few weeks…

He reversed from his parking bay and he drove away. He paused at a tight corner to allow an incoming car to pass. The other driver did not acknowledge his courteous gesture and Toddy said aloud, 'Miserable git.'

It was arguable that the other driver was at least a miserable git. It could be argued that the other driver was a thoroughly nasty piece of work, for whom the term 'miserable git' was woefully inadequate.

The other driver was Samuel Westmain.

Chapter Thirty-One

'So. We didn't check the people at the salons who might have used this stuff, only the sodding punters who bought it?' said Mansell incredulously. 'We didn't check the frigging, bleeding obvious? I don't sodding believe it!'

He had been going through the reports of all the possible suspects who might have bought Kenjaal. He had been delighted to hear that every bottle of the stuff sold in the last two months had been accounted for. Because there had been no external advertising campaign, no members of the public at large had even been aware of this new wonder product. It pretty much involved regulars only, and they had been tracked down pretty quickly. Great. Then the bad news. The buyers of twenty-six bottles of Kenjaal in the period February to date all had good strong alibis for the night of Jayne Gilmour's murder. Family, friends, colleagues, taxi drivers, restaurant staff and the like, all vouched for the twenty-six suspects. Strictly, it was twenty-five, because one bottle was bought by a wife for her husband as a present. Some present, thought Mansell, on a par with buying the wife oven gloves or something.

He and Rogers had pored over the reports for a second time, and then Mansell had read them a third time. They had spotted a few loose ends in the reports and statements, but felt that there was nothing in there to get excited about. They talked to the officers who had taken the statements, and from those discussions they felt less sure than ever that there was going to be a breakthrough from these statements.

It was on this third reading that Mansell suddenly grabbed the pile of Darlington statements and scanned the cover sheet on the fat stack of paper. He ran through the names of the suspects and thumped the pile down. He grabbed the pile of Stockton-on-Tees statements and did the same. The same things followed and a frisson of excitement ran through him. He turned to the front of the Bishop Auckland pile and this time he muttered, 'I wonder, I wonder...' He shouted across to Rogers who was discussing something with Tom Allan at the far end of the room.

Rogers turned and something in Mansell's manner made him move quickly down the room. 'What is it, Nige?' he asked before he had got to his seat opposite his boss.

'These reports and statements,' he said, waving at the three piles, 'there's something I've just realised.' Before Rogers could ask, Mansell continued, 'I don't see statements from the staff or owners or managers or whatever they are.'

'Well, no,' Rogers started to explain. 'The brief was just for who bought...' He stopped, realising immediately what Mansell was about to say.

'Yeah, but surely there was a chance that staff or managers would have had a dip at the stuff? Don't tell me we didn't even ask!'

Rogers shook his head, looking crestfallen. 'Don't think so, Nige, got sidetracked by punters who might have bought it.'

'So we didn't check the bleeding staff at the salon?' Mansell's language began to deteriorate as he got more agitated at the thought that they had missed something, somehow blown an opportunity. 'Get your arses in gear and get back there now, for Christ's sake!'

Bodies scurried back out of the station and to the three salons.

At Stockton and Darlington, Andy and Jim quickly found that their visits were a waste of time. At Stockton, the only man on the payroll was the manager who was young, thick-haired and defined as 'virile'. He took umbrage when Andy suggested that maybe he, Johnny Slinger, could even contemplate good old Kenjaal. The girls also confirmed there that they were not likely to be going out with, shagging or using and abusing anybody that could be remotely interested in hair restorer/grower. At Darlington, Jim found that there were two men on the payroll. The manager said that he had no need for hair restorer, and his assistant was an athletically built 6'3" coloured gentleman, who, being a trendy twenty-two-year-old was as bald as a coot. Not a thread of hair here.

It was a similar ratio at Bishop Auckland salon. Only two guys on the wage records: Stig Sorensen and Sam Westmain. Tom was very careful to enquire of anybody else, part-timers, casual acquaintances and so on, who might possibly have used Kenjaal. There was nobody, and the manager stated immediately that the girls would never take any of the stuff for boyfriends. Tom was just thinking what a long shot this is when the manager nonchalantly volunteered, 'I don't see how it's important, but of course Sam used loads of the stuff until we stopped getting it recently.' Sorry added, 'Sam claimed it was for a friend, silly sod.'

Tom knew from the records that Sam must be Sam Westmain and if Tom remembered correctly, wasn't it Westmain who had mentioned a (fictitious?) friend who hadn't been tracked down yet? He tried to sound relatively unbothered as he asked, 'Sam – Sam Westmain, presumably – uses a lot does he?' He smiled a cheery smile, trying to convey that this was just two blokes engaged in a little gossip about a colleague or associate.

'Yeah, and it's not even as if he's that bad. Bit of a bald patch, but it's hardly spreading. Anyway, I don't really think that it works too well, although I shouldn't criticise a product, I suppose,' Sorry finished a little guiltily.

'Is Sam about today?' asked Tom, mentally crossing his fingers.

'No, he just worked this morning, you know, the guy you spoke to.'

'What can you tell me about him?' asked Tom.

'What's this about, then?' enquired Sorry. 'Is Sam a suspect, or what?'

'No, no, just eliminating everybody we can. You know how it is, loads of donkey work for ages then hopefully a breakthrough later.'

'Fair enough,' said Sorry, not thinking too deeply about the circumstances of the visit, the questions or the ever more agitated state of the police officer.

'So he'll be home, will he?'

'Probably.'

'And where's that exactly, then,' asked Tom.

'I'll get his address,' said Sorry helpfully. He disappeared into the tiny room that masqueraded as an office.

When Tom was waiting for Sorry to return with Westmain's address, he looked around. The usual sights and smells greeted his inspection.

Washbasins, towels, some debris on the floor; everything black and white; not a strict uniform for the staff but logos on the T-shirts. A lot of leather and flesh about; no wonder so many fellas enjoyed coming to these girly salons.

He noticed a sales area, not more than a few shelves really, surrounded by a few advertising posters. On the shelves were shampoos, conditioners, colouring products and there, on the bottle shelf, was a solitary bottle of Kenjaal.

He smiled inwardly. This has got to be it, I can feel it, he thought.

The radio played Boyzone as Sorry apologised to a client for keeping her waiting.

'It's on there, Officer, Number 11, The Bank, Topside Park, Bishop Auckland. Just a few minutes away… Do you know where it is?'

'No, but I'll find it. Thanks very much indeed, you've been helpful.'

Tom raced back to his car and immediately radioed the station. He quickly related his news through to Mansell, who blurted out – prematurely, thought Tom – 'Got him!'

They agreed that Tom would wait at the house and should do nothing until Mansell got there in twenty minutes or so. Tom set off and thought again, Nige is getting a bit excited; this could be absolutely nothing. An outsider might argue that this was one of the little things that would differentiate Mansell from the rest. He got excited about things, whereas the others, although interested and even a little excited at the outset of a chase, could never get quite so involved as Mansell, especially over details that could mean nothing.

It had only taken Tom a few minutes with his *A to Z* to find the house so he waited near Number 11, The Bank, and peered at the semi-detached house. It looked neat, tidy and very, very ordinary. No sign of anybody inside.

It was 6.50 and gloomy and cold. Tom sat patiently for half an hour and was just getting chilly when he saw Mansell's car turn into the street. Mansell parked next to him and Tom saw Rogers in the car. Mansell was quickly sitting in the passenger seat of Tom's car.

He didn't bother with any preamble or pleasantries but burst straight into questions.

'Tell me again, why do we think this guy uses Kenjaal? And you say he lives here, alone?'

Age, description and explanations followed. Within a few minutes Mansell felt that he had confirmed everything that he had noted half an hour earlier.

'So let's go then,' he said, in a steely tone.

Tom still thought that Mansell was overexcited, but his enthusiasm in this case was particularly infectious and he marched to the house with Mansell quite looking forward to the next few minutes.

The three of them arrived at the front door and Mansell both rang the bell and rapped the knocker. They waited in silence for a few seconds, then Mansell rapped again a little more aggressively. Nothing. Tom felt a little shiver run down his back. Westmain's absence from the house sent a frisson of excitement through him. He did not know why it was, just that it just seemed to mean something, something.

'Want me to check the back, guv?' he asked, feeling that giving respect and receiving orders could be the order of the day for the next few minutes.

'Yeah, go and have a look,' said Mansell. He went to the window next to the door as Tom disappeared around the side path.

Mansell was moving to the side of the house when Tom reappeared.

'No signs, guv... but I think there's an open window.'

Mansell looked at Rogers with a sly grin on his face. 'Let's have a look, then.'

They went around together. They looked for an open window but saw none, and just as Tom was saying they could get a warrant and come back, Mansell was pushing a brick through a patio window. He waited until the glass had stopped falling from the frame then ducked inside.

'Mind your head on the glass!' he shouted over his shoulder to his colleagues.

As Rogers and Tom entered, Mansell could be seen to be scouring the room, looking at all loose documents that were scattered on various surfaces. He moved into the next room but soon emerged to go back into the kitchen. Rogers could hear Mansell muttering, 'There's got to be something, got to be something.'

Rogers and Tom went and looked upstairs and then Mansell heard Rogers shouting, 'Sir, up here!'

Mansell raced upstairs, located Rogers and stared at the sight of twenty-eight teddy bears, all neatly lined up.

Rogers was staring in particular at the six teddy bears on the top row of the display. Each had a little ribbon around its neck, attached to which was a piece of card. On the cards were written, neatly, six names; Joyce, Helena, Donna, Laura, Wendy and Jayne. In the middle of the display was a bigger, older looking bear. It also had a name tag: it read 'Mother'.

'Fuck me,' said Mansell.

'Your profile, sir,' Rogers reminded him.

'Get the team here now!' barked Mansell.

They moved into the hall to the telephone stand and Mansell said to Rogers, 'I'll just try something.'

He took out a handkerchief and pulled a corner of it over his right index finger and hand. He picked up the receiver and punched 1471. The computerised BT lady advised that the last call to that number was yesterday at 16.41, number…

He punched 1571 and found that Westmain did have an answering service. The same BT lady said, 'You have one message, 16.41…' The phone beeped and the message was delivered.

'Hello, er, it's Sandy French at "Clean and Dry", just reminding Mr, er, Westmain that your items have been ready to be picked up for some time. We'd appreciate you calling in. We sorted that problem out. Bye.'

Mansell said to Rogers, 'Clean and Dry… it'll be a laundry. He's had some stuff done. Organise a pick-up, Will, it could be interesting.'

Mansell then pushed the redial button and waited impatiently as the phone rang. It was answered and his heart jumped when a voice said quietly, 'Hello, Dorothy Sanders here.'

He didn't speak for a second and then regained his composure. 'Sorry, Mrs Sanders, it's Len Mansell here from Stockton Police. I know that this will sound a funny question but could you tell me please where Jeff is?'

'Oh, haven't you heard, Mr Mansell? He broke his leg last week and he's in hospital for observation.'

Mansell was reeling because he already knew the next question and probably the answer. 'I'm sorry to hear that, Mrs Sanders. One other thing, did one of Jeff's friends ring recently to ask after him?'

'That is a funny question, but yes, now you mention it, somebody rang about an hour ago, I think it would be, to ask which ward he was in. Ward 44, Room C, I told him.'

'Who was the friend, Mrs Sanders, can you remember?'

Dorothy hesitated, 'You know, now you mention it I can't remember, just somebody from work I think. Silly me, I can't remember. Why do you ask, Mr Mansell?'

But Mansell was gone. He was already halfway down the garden path heading towards his car, barking instructions.

'Radio ahead! Get someone over there now. The bastard's gone to the General to finish it!'

Chapter Thirty-Two

He had sat at home that afternoon, wondering about his next move; or at least that had been his intention as he sat down in his comfy armchair. His mind had rather quickly drifted, however, and for no obvious reason, he was thinking of his girls.

His grandmother, whom he imagined he remembered but in reality didn't.

His mother – God, his deranged bitch mother! May she rot in hell. He smiled as he remembered her lying grotesquely at the bottom of those stairs.

Joyce Lindsay, who had triggered something, so he'd thanked her for that.

Helena Stockley, pretty girl, he remembered, until he'd changed all that.

Donna Mills, she had really fought, hadn't she? That's why he had to cut her so badly, before he killed her. Yeah, a really messy one, that. Bled to death, they reckoned.

Laura Bull, now she was interesting. She had tried the old, 'I really like you, I really do, don't hurt me, we can be friends' line. He had listened and then had hit back with a classic riposte he felt, saying to her, 'Be yourself. Especially do not feign affection. Neither be cynical about love; for in the face of all aridity and disenchantment, it is as perennial as the grass.'

He laughed. Yeah, that had shut the bitch up!

Wendy Fell, well, the kill was exemplary. It was just Sanders that had screwed it up.

And then lovely Jayne. He had to admit that the commendations after the event did appear to have more than the usual ring of authenticity about them. Maybe of all of them she really was a 'nice angel of virtue'.

He reminisced, almost fondly, about the long, lost years after the London trip when he dossed around in Paris, London and back at home in Leicester.

Did I learn anything from those years? He expected a revealing, insightful response. Yes, indeed: courage, faith, inner strength etc., etc. What he got was the truth. No, they were ten wasted, empty years, when you could have, *should* have, continued your plan. You did not please God in those years.

He spoke to the wall. 'I know, and I'm sorry, but be fair, God did not speak to me, not until I came back in 1988.'

He remembered how he had got the idea of the mac and the weapons inside it from one of his favourite films, *The Dead Zone*, starring Christopher Walken, whom he considered a truly great actor.

His mind flitted back to work that morning. Not the police visit; before then, when daft Jilly, a buxom, silly sixteen-year-old junior had got into an argument, amicable of course, with a client whose hair she was washing. When asked, 'What are you doing tonight, then?' the client had mentioned that she was looking forward to a television programme on fine wines presented by Malcolm Gluck.

'There's nobody called Gluck, can't be,' trilled Jilly.

At the next station Sam had been asked to deny this 'made-up name', but he said politely, 'It's true, Jilly. Malcolm Gluck, he's an expert, and when he swallows he doesn't go glug–glug, he goes gluck–gluck–gluck!' Jilly and the others within earshot laughed, and then Jilly got the giggles and couldn't stop laughing. She got worse and worse, and had to stop washing the lady's hair and wipe her tears away.

Sam had announced in a stage loud voice, 'Gluck-in-hell, Jilly, it isn't that funny.'

That had set her off again. Soon the salon was all in on the joke and they all laughed a little at Sam's remarks and a lot at Jilly's hysterics.

Sam knew that he was a popular guy, and this proved it; Sorry would not have had them laughing like that.

His thoughts switched back to his girls, not the ones that he had 'released', as he often thought of it, but those with whom he had sexual encounters. His mother had been correct on that memorable occasion when he was twelve.

Every time he got close to a woman he pictured his mother, and that rather spoiled things.

His first attempted sexual liaison had been at eighteen, when he had taken a prostitute home. He had sort of had sex, having made some penetration and ejaculated, but it was hardly a roaring success, and had cost him £50, which he rather begrudged. All he could think of as he came was his mother.

His next prostitute had taken a beating when his erection failed to materialise because his mind's eye had already been fixed on Momma.

In his wilderness years there had been no sex, and his only attempts over the last few years had been a girl picked up from a pub and taken behind the pub, merely for her to perform rapid oral sex on him, which he had reacted to and enjoyed; and two further prostitutes, with him failing to perform the act each time. One was just dismissed, but the second was severely beaten when she tried to feign affection, which he hated. Both prostitutes he met in Newcastle, and the beaten one did not even appear to have reported it, as he saw no media coverage. Strange, that, because he was sure that he had broken her cheek and jaw.

He realised that it was late afternoon and he hadn't really made a plan, but he could not resist a flick though his beloved journals. As he turned the pages, the odd phrase or line caught his eye and he would read a little further, occasionally becoming a little misty-eyed at some of the heart-rending or beautiful memories that the writing brought back.

He wiped a solitary tear from his eye as he read a passage, written at sixteen, not long after his mother's death. It dealt with memories of a time when one of the very worst punishments his mother had meted out was the light deprivation that she so favoured. It was always dark and gloomy, often totally so, when she would say, 'God has stopped our money, we can't afford light.' He knew that this memory was why he liked everything so well lit, overly so now.

He saw less serious observations scattered throughout the volumes of journals, and was a little surprised to see an early reference – at twenty-three, no less – to the first detection of his thinning hair. How come he had forgotten that?

Ha, how that has come to haunt me, he thought, with a bitter smile.

He snapped the diaries shut and for a moment, while he was reminiscing, it seemed he was feeling fey, as if some impending doom was upon him. Surely not. It was just that he was in one of those reflective moods which came upon him now and again. He was allowed that, wasn't he?

At five o'clock Sam had opened his telephone directory and run his fingers through the 'S's. He soon stopped at Sanders and as he was sure he had read in the press of Mr Gerald Sanders, he scanned the 'G's. He found the address, which he recognised as Jeff's, and dialled the number.

Mrs Sanders answered and Sam asked, 'Sorry to bother you, Mrs Sanders, could I speak to Jeff please?'

'I'm sorry, but Jeff's had an accident and is in hospital. Could I ask who is calling?'

'Good heavens! That's terrible, and after all he's been through. Is it serious?'

'No, not too serious; he's broken his knee and it'll be a while before he's right again. Who is this, please?'

'My name's Leonard Vickers, I'm a client of Jeff's and I wouldn't bother him, but it is quite urgent. I don't really want to bother him, but...'

'Well, I suppose if it's urgent, he is up to seeing people. We've just got back.'

'And how is he in himself? He's such a cheerful lad normally.'

'As well as can be expected, and I don't think he'd mind seeing you.'

'I certainly won't tire him out, Mrs Sanders. It'll just be a flying visit.'

'He's in Room C, off Ward 44. It's a bit more private, you know, we thought it'd be good for him. It's not the main building, mind you.'

'You obviously take great care of him – he's a lucky lad. Thanks for your help. Bye.'

Mrs Sanders thought the conclusion of the call a little abrupt but went back to her preparation of the tea. It would be nice for

Jeff to see a familiar face, other than his parents and friends, she thought.

Westmain had decided that afternoon that he was being hunted down. That bloody Kenjaal had brought the coppers to his door and even they would soon identify him. The choices were stark. Do nothing and just wait for the knock at the door. He could counter their arguments but Sanders would identify him. He could run, go away, anywhere, but what sort of fugitive would he make? Not a good one, if his experiences in Paris were anything to go by. Or he could go out in a blaze of satisfying glory. This appealed, and he went to his journal to write his final thoughts.

He had written for over an hour, with arguments, grievances, happy thoughts pouring on to the page. He railed at one point against God, saying that the Lord had never really played fair in all of this. He had set it up but had continually moved the goalposts; losing that job, Paris, the many missed chances, Sanders and now bloody Kenjaal. It was only his ingenuity and strength of character that had managed six murders, and that was a disappointing score. But now, well, he could sensationally kill Sanders before the police caught up with him. And who knows, if the police did foul up, then he'd go on one of those sprees that he'd once considered, and take out a bitch a night... or maybe something even more amazing, two or three a night.

Now he would prepare himself. He would pop down the shops to grab himself a super-duper, top of the range saw. After killing Sanders, he was going to cut him up into little pieces, just for the hell of it.

Chapter Thirty-Three

He pulled up into the secondary hospital car park where it was very quiet; only three other cars stood in their allotted bays. He parked near a ticket machine and strolled over to it. He already had his 50p ready and took the ticket back to his dashboard. He did not expect a car park attendant or security patrol to actually check the validity of his ticket at this time on a Saturday night, but there was no point in taking chances.

He was only a few yards from the block that he was heading for. As he crossed the auxiliary road towards his target, he noticed a building a little distance away, standing alone. He saw the sign above the front entrance which said *Dorothy Parkin Hospice*. He felt a pang of sympathy. Poor bastards, incarcerated, just waiting to die, what a horrible fate. He shook off the feeling and turned his attention back to the matter in hand.

He felt very, very sharp, very alive. All his senses were at full alert. Buzzing. This was the night to conclude the games of the last few months. The intervention of Sanders in January had certainly taken him down a different route, that was for sure, and no doubt God had some greater plan at hand; but come on, even He would have to admit that these shenanigans had got in the way of the master plan to cull women. But, heigh-ho, back to work to that effect from tomorrow, once tonight was cleared up...

He reached the automatic double doors and noticed a big sign in a neighbouring window advising the world that closed-circuit television surveillance was in operation in this hospital. He guessed that, like on the railways, there would probably be a good chance that there either would be no film in the cameras or they would not be switched on, but he was not going to be too cocky and he had prepared accordingly with this in mind. The dark bobble hat was pulled down to his eyebrows and his macintosh collar was pulled up. Not a lot of his face was exposed, and a scarf that reached up to his mouth completed the cover. It had been a chilly, breezy April day and the cold wind off the sea justified his evening attire.

The doors opened very slowly and he nearly bumped his nose, as his premature step forward was quicker than the automatic response to his approach. It crossed his mind that the doors were reluctant to let him in, guessing the outcome of his visit. He stepped inside, thinking, Typical, nothing works properly in the NHS. He moved a couple of paces further into the deserted hallway and looked at the large chart of directions displayed on the wall in front of him.

Medical Rehab Day Unit, Bone Densitometry, Laboratory Medicine, Diabetes Specialist Nurse, Rheumatology Clinic, Rehabilitation Resource Centre, and many others, were highlighted. Arrows pointed in various directions, but then he saw the numbering which made things a little clearer. *Wards 37–40 left, 41–50 right.* He knew from Dorothy Sanders that he wanted Ward 44, so he turned right and started to move slowly down the corridor. There was absolutely nobody in sight and it was very quiet. So quiet, that his shoes squeaked loudly on the polished linoleum. It was 7.50 on a Saturday night, still visiting hours, and there was nobody to be seen.

The clinical medical tang of disinfectant and cleanliness encouraged him to take a deep breath, unlike many people. Well he was different, wasn't he? He liked that antiseptic smell.

He heard the distant wail of an ambulance siren and wondered how busy it was over at Accident and Emergency in the main complex of buildings. Not as busy as later on when the pubs chuck out and the fighting and falling over starts. But here, in Rehab, it was quiet.

He read the door signs as he squeaked down the corridor: *District Health Service, Secretary, Continence Advisor*, (bet she takes the piss), *Hairdresser, Stroke Unit*. A real mishmash, he thought. Was there any logic to this layout? Crap management, or maybe no management. Now if someone as organised as himself could just go in for a while and have a good sort-out, well, the place would be so much more efficient.

He saw a sign directing down a corridor to the Chiropody Waiting Area, and he thought that there should be a supplementary sign saying, *Somewhere To Put Your Feet Up*. A lonely yucca plant, in need of love and attention, was a token gesture to decoration.

A notice warned, *No Tugs to Operate Beyond This Point*, and he joked to himself again, querying whether the corridor was really big enough to get a ship through.

Another sign instructed, *Switch off Mobile Phones*. The funny idea occurred to him of a man being connected to life-saving machinery suddenly being given extra doses of medicine or shocks or something equally humorous, just because somebody nearby was using a mobile to phone home for a football score – a bit like the mobile user inadvertently opening the neighbour's garage door, but maybe a bit more serious. He chuckled and thought, God, I feel good!

He was aware of the warren of rooms and corridors but regular updates kept him en route to Ward 44. He had only taken one turn off the original corridor so it shouldn't be difficult getting back to the entrance, he thought.

Wards 41 and 42 had been passed and he could see ahead an overhead sign announcing Ward 43, so he could not be far now from his goal.

An old man pottered past wearing a tatty dressing gown and Sam tensed in case a caring member of staff came after the wandering patient. Nobody did.

The grey and white striped linoleum suddenly gave way to carpet and he noticed that the walls had a few pictures, albeit cheap ones, hung at regular internals. Must be the posh wards, he thought, although he couldn't see what else had changed. It was still the same sort of corridor and the doors looked the same. A corridor appeared on the left and as he passed it he saw the second person since he had got there. Someone who looked like a porter was pushing a big laundry skip. Then he saw ahead of him a nurse walking slowly towards him, reading something. He pulled his scarf down and as they passed she glanced up from her charts and smiled; he offered a friendly 'Hello,' in return.

A television played nearby and he heard the lottery being drawn. A lucky night for somebody, not so lucky for others, he thought grimly.

A wall sign told him that Ward 44 was next right, and above that a large electrical panel was lit up brightly with red and green lights. For a second he thought about playing with the buttons and switches, which were conveniently labelled saying what they affected, but he dismissed the idea as being too dramatic. Create a diversion, yes; cause chaos, no. He thought it extraordinary that the panel was so exposed and scoffed at the little warning sign, *Do Not Touch.*

Sam turned right at the next corner and a sign above his head said *Ward 44, Rehabilitation.* He paused for a moment and his eyes darted left and right. He told himself to be careful, and he looked for the room that he knew was his target. He passed the communal area of Ward 44, and without turning his head, saw that the four beds were occupied by tired-looking elderly gentlemen. He moved on a little further and came to an area where four rooms were signed in big numbers and letters, 44A, 44B, 44C and 44D. For a numbing second he thought, Shit, which one of four? Then he breathed a big sigh when he noticed the much smaller slot under each number which obviously contained the name of the room's occupant. He looked around and saw nobody. He noticed a little shop, now closed, with a window containing ornaments and necessities. What a strange combination, he mused. He went to Rooms A and B and moved on, then saw on 44C, *Mr J Sanders.*

His heart thumped harder, but he praised himself for his calm manner. That wonderful old feeling of control, he thought. God, how special he was! He looked around the corridor once more and saw nobody. Just get in, he told himself. No messing, no talking, nothing, clever. Straight to him, knife, saw, away...

He opened his mac and reached inside. He snapped open the binding inside his coat and pulled out a Stanley knife. He slid the blade out to its full extent, and welcomed the feel of his old friend.

He paused with his hand on the doorknob and took a deep breath. He inclined his head to the door and could hear the television murmuring in the background. The lottery was just finishing and he thought that 'It could be you' was a rather appropriate slogan at this particular moment.

He turned the knob, pushed open the door firmly and stepped inside, pushing the door shut behind him. His hand gripped the knife and he was mentally and physically prepared to move on Jeff Sanders, slash and cut him to ribbons and make his exit. Being so prepared was probably why it was such a shock to him when he saw that the little room was empty. He looked at the bed as if he had missed something first time. It was definitely empty, as was the chair by the window. 'Shit!' he exclaimed. He wondered why it had never crossed his mind that maybe Jeff Sanders might not be there in his room. But then, why the hell should he have contemplated this? Where was he going to be on a Saturday night – down the pub?

There was a door to his left, only a foot behind his shoulder, opened, and Jeff limped out of the tiny toilet. They both got a jolting shock and stared at each other for a split second, Jeff with his mouth open in a comical pose. Then Westmain smiled and Jeff shouted, 'No!'

Sam slashed from right to left in a horizontal line that was aimed at opening Jeff's stomach. For Jeff it was too quick a motion to react to and he expected to feel a sickening pain. His faded old navy blue dressing gown was an unlikely lifesaver, but the knotted string around his middle and the baggy way that it hung off his body combined to absorb and deflect the murderous swish of the blade. Before Westmain could slash again, Jeff lunged at the nightmare that stood before him. His body weight hit his attacker hard, and as Westmain was knocked backwards his hand cracked against the bedrail at the bottom of the bed. He cried out and the knife flew on to the bed.

Before toppling completely over, Westmain managed to grab Jeff's shoulders, grasping the fabric of the dressing gown. For an absurd moment it appeared that they were about to do some ritual Cossack dancing, each placing his hands on the other's shoulders. Jeff released a hand and swung a punch at Westmain's face, landing a slap on his cheek. Westmain retaliated with a kick which caught Jeff on his bandaged knee, causing him to shout, 'Aarrgh!' loudly.

Westmain pushed Jeff away from him and turned to the bed. Seeing this, Jeff knew he had a second to act and the adrenaline sluicing through his veins assisted him in his move. He lowered his head and shoulders and ran into Westmain's midriff and chest, throwing him against the far wall. Westmain hit the wall hard, grunting 'Ugh!' as the wind was knocked out of him. Jeff spun around and opened the door. Westmain shook his head to clear the little stars that flitted in front of his eyes, and raised himself from his position slumped against the wall. He lurched forward as Jeff stepped quickly out of the door, putting his arm between the door and frame as Jeff pulled the door shut. His arm absorbed the blow without too much pain and he flung the door back.

Jeff had thought that when Westmain hit the wall that he'd bought himself a few precious seconds, enough to escape, and was horrified when his attacker recovered so quickly. As he left the room, he tried to shout 'Help!' but it only came out as a croak, the fight having taken its toll. A hand grabbed at his back and he swung around, punching wildly with both fists. Westmain was almost upon him and Jeff's left hand glanced a blow across his jaw. Still he came on, but maybe the punch had had some effect, because Westmain seemed to stumble as he snatched at his victim. Jeff backed off, back-pedalling as quickly as his bandaged leg would allow. He turned and ran, his exaggerated limp and flailing dressing gown giving him the appearance of a character from a *Carry On* film. But this was no joke, and as he hobbled in strange fashion he gasped for air. He tried to shout, but only once out of three attempts did any volume of sound leave his mouth, and that generated no response. He looked over his shoulder and saw Westmain running after him, and noticed that Westmain was looking down into the inside of his mac. Jeff guessed what this was for, but was conscious that Westmain's distraction was allowing Jeff to maintain the distance between them.

Jeff bounded along, lurching from left to right as he tried to protect his injured leg, but he could feel the pain growing rapidly down there and he knew his knee was seriously damaged by the movement. He looked ahead and from left and right, but every door seemed to lead to an administration room and there was no sign of sanctuary anywhere. Why, oh why, had he not turned from his room back towards the other wards? He was moving too fast to read every sign and he was looking over his shoulder again as he passed a sign that said, *Wards 45–50, Next Left. Theatres 1–4, Straight On.* He ignored the corridor that appeared suddenly on his left and ran on. He slipped a little and winced at the jarring pain in his knee. He lost his left slipper but gave it no thought. He panicked when the pounding of feet suddenly sounded very close and he looked back in fear and trepidation, but Westmain was still twenty yards away. The echoing corridor was playing tricks with his imagination.

Although Jeff was hot, perspiring and gasping, an enormous chill ran through him as he heard Westmain chant, 'Sammy's gonna get you!' in a sing-song voice. Then Westmain giggled, and Jeff felt his insides churn. He thought that he was going to vomit. He kept his stomach's contents down and realised, really knew it now, that despite all the titles, nicknames, epithets and so on that Westmain was totally and utterly mad – literally insane.

Jeff swung into a corridor on the right, praying for people, noise, life, but was sorely disappointed to see ahead of him a long, empty passage leading to a possible dead end. 'Dead end' was not a phrase that pleased him. He was running more freely now, crashing through the pain barrier with every step. He flicked off his remaining slipper, believing that it was slowing him down and that the floor was going to be clean enough to trust.

He was becoming increasingly anxious that there was no obvious route to safety ahead of him and he could not think clearly enough to assess what his alternatives were. He was now approaching the end of the corridor and got no encouragement from the sign on the double doors facing him that read: *Theatres 1–4*. His eyes were wide with apprehension, as he half expected the doors to be locked, but he burst through them without any resistance.

In the few second that he had, he took in that he was in a room from which led four doors marked *Theatres 1*, *2*, *3* and *4*. The room he was in was lined with cabinets and sink units, with a few tables scattered around. He did not wonder why the light was on in this ante-room, but as the squeaking, pounding feet of Westmain rapidly approached, he chose one of the doors ahead of him and jumped through it.

Westmain had been surprised at the strength and resolve of his prey, but having got his breath back he smiled at the sight of Sanders bouncing clumsily down the corridor, and the smile stayed there as he heard Sanders gasping for help. He set off after him and started to reach inside his mac for another weapon. He saw Sanders look back at him and noticed the fear on his face. As he followed his intended victim he reckoned that young Mr Sanders had made quite a mistake in going in the direction he'd chosen, and he got a huge boost when Sanders failed to turn in the direction of Wards 45–50. He can't be heading for the theatres on purpose, can he? Westmain wondered. He decided there and then that he was going to finish this, whatever the consequences.

He decided to panic Sanders so he sang, 'Sammy's going to get you!' and giggled at the sound of his voice, happy that he made such a positive decision – to end Sanders' life, whatever it took, whoever was in attendance. He was watching Sanders' movement and noticed that he was, if anything, moving more freely. That's got to be hurting, he thought.

He saw that double doors were not far away and wondered if they would be locked, thus cornering Sanders and allowing him an easy kill. He was not overly upset when Sanders burst through the doors, and he felt that they weren't going to offer Sanders much comfort.

When Westmain got to the doors he slowed down to a walk and was strolling as he entered the ante-room. He sensed that the moment he had waited for since January was now upon him as he looked carefully around the room he stood in. He looked from left to right, and then back again, kneeling down to check under the tables. He checked once more to ensure that he was not missing anything obvious and, once satisfied, turned his attention to the four theatre doors ahead of him. He felt like shouting out again, something like 'Here's Sammy!' but decided to be a little more circumspect. Sanders was not going to go without a fight, and there was no point in making it easier for him, so he stayed quiet. He stood there silently, listening intently for the slightest sound, but heard nothing. Which one to choose? he wondered. Would logic tell the way Sanders would have chosen? He decided not; it could have been left, right or the middle two.

Each door had a window in it and he walked to the door to Theatre 1 and looked in. The theatre was only illuminated by the light pouring in through the window that he peered through. He could see the operating table, with equipment of all sorts, and trolleys, some laden with utensils. It entered his head that he could soon be operating on Jeff Sanders: what an ironic setting! He moved slowly from 1 to 2, then 3 and 4. All the windows shed the same light on the same interior scene. He saw nothing and heard nothing that gave him any clues about where Sanders was cowering.

He went back to Theatre 1, alert to the possibility of Sanders rushing at him from any of the room. He was ready for any such attack, and held a sharpened screwdriver in front of him. He pushed open the door and held it open with his left hand, the screwdriver gripped in his right. He took a single step inside, barely breathing. The open door flooded the theatre with light and he quickly scanned every corner of the room. Still holding the door open, he crouched down and looked under the operating table. He was consciously keeping an ear open for any noise back in the ante-room, just in case Sanders tried to make a dash for it. He reached for a light switch and found one close to the door, which had not swung shut. He blinked as the powerful fluorescent lights blazed on. He did not see an awful lot more than he had already been aware of, maybe some extra bits of equipment, and a couple of personal items. He noticed a teddy bear with a blue ribbon around his neck and a large ghetto blaster sitting on top of a corner unit. No Sanders, though, so Westmain exited and moved to door number two.

He opened the door in similar fashion to the first, pushing it open and holding it with his left hand. Nothing stirred. He found the light switch but did not blink this time when the lights beamed brightly. He studied the walls and confirmed what he knew already, that there were no alcoves or recesses. He took a step to the left to make sure that nobody was skulking behind the operating table, but there was nothing to see. He took a step forward to double-check every angle of the room and then moved backwards to the door. He hesitated at the door, as if half expecting Sanders to magically appear from nowhere and go 'Boo!' But the silence and stillness remained as he backed out of the door.

Two down, two to go, he thought, and the acknowledgement of only two possibilities left heightened his tension further. He was enjoying this cat-and-mouse game, testing his superior skills against Jeffrey Bastard Sanders. His quarry was at his mercy but there was pleasure to be gained from these final tense moments.

Before he entered door three, he weighed up the options available to him regarding the kill. He was tempted to make a grand speech to young Jeffrey, and provide him with details of Jayne's murder, but then he stopped himself, chiding himself for unprofessional thoughts. Just do the job and get home. He allowed himself the consolation of the possibility of a little artistic licence with the body, maybe removing a souvenir or two. He grinned as he concentrated on the door, and then he saw something to raise his spirits higher than they already were. On the shiny white floor on the bottom of the door were four dark splashes, unmistakably blood. It was a remote possibility that it was some missed residue from a messy patient, but he knew three things without examining it closer. Firstly, the way that the spots glistened told him that it was fresh blood; secondly, he knew that it was the fresh blood previously owned by Jeffrey Sanders; and thirdly, he now knew that his victim was behind door three. He felt so good he wanted to boom, 'Fee fi fo fum, I smell the blood of a Sanders man!' But he stayed silent.

'Prepare to die,' he whispered, as he gently and slowly pushed the door open. The irony again struck Westmain that many bodies must have left these theatres after a slip of a knife, and now, imminently, another corpse was to be created through the work of a slicing instrument. Holding the door open, he saw nothing and slowly inched forward. Without turning his head he reached his hand to the area where the light switch was, his finger fumbling up the wall. They never reached the switch.

Jeff had burst into Theatre 3 and stopped dead in his tracks. It was dark and the light from the outer room only lit the centre of the theatre. His eyes became accustomed to the lack of light and he saw with dismay that there was no obvious hiding place. He tried to concentrate but a dozen thoughts crowded into his head. He knew that he had seconds to act and this was duly confirmed when he heard the door to the ante-room open and close.

Jesus! he thought. What to do, what to do? He decided that there was no point stumbling about in the dark, maybe making a noise so he simply, silently took a step to his left behind the door. It was hardly original, but there was literally nowhere else to go. He stood rigidly still, and tried to gather his thoughts. He carefully regulated his breathing, desperate not to pant or gasp and give his location away. The only thought that clearly entered his brain was, What the fuck was he going to do? He awaited the horrible entry of Westmain, trying to assess the wisdom of running for it.

It was then that the pain returned in a shrill, shrieking agony that made him jump. He had not given his leg any thought since Westmain had kicked him but now he wanted to scream, the pain was so intense. He glanced down and got another shock in a night of shocks when he could make out that his bandage was no longer white but had somebody become a darker colour – blood red, no doubt. He could now sense that his leg felt wet and he could not understand how he had not realised this before. He raised a hand to his mouth to stifle a yelp of pain, as it felt that a knife was being turned in his knee. The thought of the knife in the killer's hands made him grunt a sob-like sound, and he twitched in panic as he thought that his involuntary noise would bring the psychopath rushing in. He held his breath in sweating anticipation. A feeling surged in his chest that made him want to run screaming from the room, but he stood still; perhaps he was incapable of moving.

He sensed that there was movement outside in the ante-room and fought back the rising panic, but nothing happened. He heard a door open and released a long-held breath. He could see most of the contents of the theatre, and the only thing that he wanted was over at the far side of the room, a trolley housing shiny sharp implements. Could he risk moving? God, he wanted to, and the beads of perspiration on his forehead and at his temples betrayed his dilemma and fear.

He heard another door close and he realised that the maniac had tried the first two doors and now surely was about to try number three, his door.

Jeff's head screamed, Run, run, take your chances! But his body took no notice. Then a strange thing happened. Jeff, possibly seconds from another conflict with a madman intent on his destruction, thought of Jayne. This is the bastard who killed my Jayne, was all he could think. A wave of anger and repulsion rippled into his pool of fear. The fear remained in force, in command of his emotions, but his resolve stiffened a little. I'm going to hurt this maniac, whatever happens, he told himself. He clenched his fists and strained his ears to try to gain an edge when the nutter entered.

He could not understand why Westmain was not already in his theatre, and he was almost bursting in fearful anticipation. The percussion section in his chest beat and thumped louder and louder, and he imagined his heart bursting through his T-shirt and the good old dressing gown. His leg screamed and his head thumped. And then the door opened.

It moved slowly back to cover where he stood, allowing light to flood into the room. Jeff felt that the light was somehow illuminating him directly, but a sudden coolness enveloped him and for the first time in ten minutes he was able to think clearly. He looked through the window in the door and saw Westmain peering into the room. He hurled himself against the door and knocked Westmain flying. The noise of a weapon clattering on the hard floor gave Jeff enormous encouragement and he suddenly did not feel the pain in his leg. He could have run, but his instincts said, 'No point doing all that again.' Instead he attacked Westmain viciously, with all his might, pummelling blows at whatever he could make contact with – head, face, arms, chest and stomach.

Westmain had initially expected Sanders to be hiding, but as he had opened the door to number three, God had told him that Sanders would attack. As he peered into the room he was conscious of the tiniest movement to his left, through the door's window. Sanders hit him hard and the ferocity of the immediate onslaught took him by surprise.

Jeff took strength from Westmain's groans and his failure to return any blows. He felt that he was in the ascendancy, if only he could finish it. Through the flurry of blows, Jeff could see that Westmain was just covering up, trying to prevent further damaging strikes, and Jeff's emotions, released by the sight of the killer's apparent defeat, raged to the fore.

'You bastard!' he shouted, 'You fucking bastard!' The rate of punches thrown slowed. Tears coursed down Jeff's cheeks as he sobbed again, 'You dirty rotten bastard!' The strength in the punches ebbed.

'You… killed my… Jayne!' he gasped, the exertion of his attack leaving him short of breath.

Westmain was no aficionado of boxing, but he had heard of Muhammed Ali and the boxing great's method of enticing his opponents to wear themselves out by pounding away while he just covered up. Once they were exhausted he simply flicked his switch and took them apart with his devastating skill and power. This tactic was known as 'Rope-a-dope' and although Westmain could not claim to have deliberately applied it, he had just become the successful perpetrator of the methods, albeit unknowingly.

Jeff was shattered. The adrenaline, the fear, the injury and the emotion had robbed him of all strength, and he now sat astride a prone Westmain. He was almost motionless.

Jeff felt physically and mentally numb, but before he could bring himself to raise himself and make his exit, Westmain rolled violently to one side and threw Jeff off onto the hard floor.

Jeff was shocked by the impact with the floor and also by the swift recovery of his assailant. Fear swelled again in Jeff's stomach, for he knew that he was weak. As Westmain leapt across to Jeff, Jeff tried to beat him off, but the tattoo of punches that he landed on the madman carried no weight.

Jeff felt a pain, a heavy, dull pain move across his chest, and despite his preoccupation with his murderous assailant, he thought, Christ, I'm going to have a heart attack, or die of fright.

Westmain was now overpowering him, and Jeff felt that he was going to die. *Like Jayne* popped into his head and that gave him one last surge of energy. He lashed out with his good leg and caught Westmain fully in the groin. Westmain cried 'Aargh!' and slumped to the floor. Jeff scrambled towards the far side of the room and the trolley he'd seen there earlier.

Jeff was trying to ignore the new pain throbbing in the bare foot he had used to hurt Westmain. Soon he reached the trolley.

He raised himself to one knee as he looked for the instruments that he had earlier noticed. Suddenly Westmain tackled him around the waist, rugby-style, and the momentum carried them both into the trolley, knocking it over and spilling its contents, which clattered noisily over the floor. Both men knew that this was the moment, and each released the other to turn to the floor. In the half-light that barely reached the floor it would have been difficult to locate a specific instrument, even if given time by a friend. In the deadly situation that Jeff and Westmain were placed, they simply scrambled for the first thing they could find.

Each of them found an instrument and immediately turned to face his opponent. They were both kneeling, the pain from Jeff's knee now excruciating, but he had no time to think of that as they both swung their weapons at each other. Jeff struck out with a slashing motion, left to right, Westmain with a plunging thrust. A blade slashed flesh, deeply, bringing a gasp from the recipient; blood gushed from the wound.

There was a heavy silence, nothing but deep breathing, no movement. No clattering instruments, no curses or grunts. Both men knew that it was done. That single motion with the scalpel had ended it. There was no need to compound the deed.

A hand opened and an instrument fell to the floor with a soft rattle. The scalpel was still held and blood dripped from its edge. Both men were still kneeling and stayed upright as if in prayer. Then the unscathed one slowly, painfully raised himself up. In the semi-dark he was just able to make out the expression of amazement on the other man's face, his eyes large and unmoving, blood forming like a scarf around his neck. The body then slowly toppled forward, like a tree being felled, hitting the floor with a thump.

The survivor felt nothing, no victory, not even relief, as he moved slowly to the door.

Chapter Thirty-Four

'London, Darlington, Sunderland, Manchester, Stockton, Jayne Gilmour, his mother… and you never know, possibly others.'

Detective Inspector Len Mansell spoke flatly, addressing sixteen officers in the squad room at Stockton Police Station. He was conducting a debriefing of the officers involved in the Westmain case.

'We've read the diaries and books, they tell us just about everything.

'Westmain had a horrendous childhood; mother seemed completely psychotic. He did kill her, apparently.

'The first victim – in London – triggered her death by moaning about men. That was way back in seventy-eight. Nothing had been planned, but this man was a disaster waiting to happen. If it hadn't been her it would have been someone else.

'That seems to have satisfied his anger for a time, because then he went twelve years without killing, or at least the diaries don't tell us of any others, and I don't suppose we'll ever know.

'He had some rough times around 1990 and he blamed a woman from his past; that led to Helena Stockley.

'Donna Mills, Laura Bull and Wendy Fell all died because of women at his salon giving him, as he saw it, a hard time. Twice it was customers; once a colleague.

'He says in the books that these were God's signs to act on their plan.'

'Which was?' enquired Rogers.

'To rid the world of women who had breeding potential, apparently, in order to avoid further "bitch mothers" either happening or being born.'

'And Jayne Gilmour was because of that poor bastard Sanders?'

'Definitely, though Westmain again writes that it is just another version of God's green light to go and act.'

'Total nutter, then?'

'Well, he knew of the consequences of his actions and he still chose to do it, so I define him as just evil, not deranged.'

Somebody said 'Your profiling was damn close, boss.' He accepted the compliment with a grim nod. He took no satisfaction at this time for it had not directly contributed to the capture of Westmain.

When Mansell, Rogers and two colleagues had got to the hospital that night, they had raced to Ward 44. When they found Jeff Sanders was absent from his room they had charged through the wards looking for a nurse. They found one at a nurse's station between Wards 45 and 46, but she could not suggest where Jeff could be other than the communal television room. He was not there, and Mansell had ordered a full search of the hospital, requesting a lot of assistance from the station.

They started room-to-room searches and it took a long time to find anything, but then the radios cackled into life and Mansell was called to the operating theatres. When he got there, two officers were standing in an ante-room and one of them said, 'In number three, sir.'

Mansell opened the door and held it open to allow some light in. He took a handkerchief and covered a finger to flick the lights on. A huge pool of blood was spreading from under a body that lay in a neat straight line, face down. Mansell moved to the body, already sure who it was. He lifted the head a fraction as he reached across the pool of coagulating blood.

'Shit!' he said as he saw the face.

He left the theatre and radioed his colleagues. 'We've got someone loose in the hospital, possibly armed and disturbed. Find him, take care.'

Mansell had broken off for a second from his report and Rogers prompted, 'And of course there was Sanders.'

'Yes,' acknowledged Mansell, 'We can't forget Sanders.'

The funeral was held on an awful day, with heavy rain and strong wind, cold enough for jumpers and overcoats. There had been a service at the church and now the coffin was being lowered into the wet grave. Mansell stood very quietly in contemplative mood by Rogers' side. There were only a few people in attendance at the grave side.

Rogers whispered to Mansell, 'Can't believe he's dead, can you?'

Mansell said out of the corner of his mouth, 'Horrible way to go... but you can't help feel that the bastard deserved it.'

Jeff was at the opposite end of the grave to where the police officers stood, but he noticed them whispering. He presumed that they were there for the same reasons as himself. He was there primarily to actually see the burial with his own eyes, so that he could really believe it. He saw Mansell look across at him but Jeff turned his gaze away from him. He did not exactly blame them for anything, but a feeling in his gut kept gnawing away, telling him that the inescapable fact was that they had not protected Jayne... any more than he had; and he knew that he would never be able to forgive himself, so why should he absolve them?

The rain fell heavily, beating an audible pitter-patter on the coffin. Jeff looked around the grave. A vicar, two police officers, himself, somebody he did not know and that was it. He could not have been expected to know Sorry Sorensen from a hairdresser's in Bishop Auckland. No relatives, if there were any, had turned up, and the press had been prohibited by the vicar from being by the grave side. The vicar had said a few words which Jeff did not listen to and then it was over.

Mansell and Rogers glanced at Sanders before they turned and marched back to the cemetery entrance. They had met Jeff on the path to the grave earlier but both had sensed that he was in absolutely no mood for conversation. Mansell thought it was probably either because of delayed shock or the solemnity of the occasion, Rogers guessed that it was because Sanders blamed them for the death of Jayne Gilmour.

The vicar spoke to Jeff before heading back to the church, glad that it was over, because it had been a difficult service to conduct. How do you commend somebody's soul to heaven when they have led such a desperate, hellish existence?

The grave diggers waited patiently in the background as Jeff remained by the grave. His emotions swirled, conflicting and contradictory. He was unsure what he felt. It was easy to think,

Good riddance to the bastard who killed Jayne and tried to kill me, but it was somewhat unsatisfactory that Westmain had not suffered long-term hardship in prison. Just one moment of surprise and terror, as that scalpel ripped his jugular open, did not seem a huge payback for the suffering and terror that Westmain had inflicted on his victims and their families.

Just one bloody moment, thought Jeff. No lifetime of pain and guilt.

He had also taken to the grave, thought Jeff, all the answers that Jeff particularly craved. Was Westmain aware of his crimes? Why did he do it? Jeff did not know that the police had already found in Westmain's bureau the neatly written journals that told his story. In time the police would explain to Jeff the causes of the man's deranged psyche, but at that graveside on that day Jeff asked a hundred questions.

Not for the first time, Jeff wondered how it might have been a lot better for himself if things had turned out differently in that dark, eerie operating theatre. How he might have been better off had Westmain fumbled and grabbed the scalpel and it had been Jeff who snatched the plastic spatula. Jeff closed his eyes and relived that moment, that precious second when his scalpel cut through the flesh of Sam Westmain, and at the same time a plastic spatula thumped harmlessly into his chest, snapping the blade. Maybe if those two weapons had been reversed, then he would not be facing a future of grief, and maybe he could have been reunited with Jayne. The police would have caught Westmain and he would have rotted in prison for decades. Wasn't that better all round?

He bowed his head and said a prayer. 'Lord, help me though this, help my family, and look after Jayne, thank you.'

He opened his eyes, blinking away tears and raindrops, and soggily shuffled his way to the car where his parents waited. His knee hurt like hell, the doctor having said that he was lucky that he had not done long-term damage.

He arrived at the car but instead of getting in he tapped on the driver's window. The window was wound down and his father's pained expression stared out at him.

'What is it, son?'

'Can I just have two more minutes, Dad, please?'

'Of course, take as long as you like but don't get too wet.'

Jeff moved just a few yards from the car, sheltering under a huge oak.

He looked across the cemetery to Westmain's grave and through gritted teeth said, 'You bastard.'

Tears rolled down his cheeks and he felt that he had never felt as low as at that moment.

He tried to avoid self-pity but he could not suppress the thought that kept popping into his head: How can I ever get over this, what do I do to get things back on track?

He went back to the car and got into the front passenger seat, his mother having insisted that he have the one with the room.

'You can stretch your leg,' she prattled on nervously, trying to relieve the tangible tension, but Jeff barely heard her. 'It's your birthday in a few weeks, Jeffrey. What would you like?'

Her husband thought, What a stupid question, Dorothy, but he said nothing.

Jeff hadn't heard her. Nor did he know that he would receive, just a month after the funeral a wonderful birthday present in the form of Beth Middleton. She would be back in his life. For good.

As he left the cemetery gates his final thought that morning was, Please, Lord, one more thing: never again create or allow another Sam Westmain…

There had been many, many awful moments in Westmain's life, some shocking, others painful, both physically and mentally, but nothing hurt him as much as what happened in those final few moments.

As he had grappled with Jeff he had been hit by a thunderbolt. He saw the devil, a real live red devil, complete with evil snarling face, arched eyebrows, horns and tail: the real thing. And the devil was laughing, and laughing and pointing at him.

'Got you, you stupid, dumb prick, you total fool! Did you ever, really, really believe that the Lord God, the Almighty, the omnipresent asshole was on your side? Fool!' he raged, 'it was me all along! I've strung you along like a puppet and you've blindly followed. Do you think the lovely one would make it all so difficult, so painful, so impossible? Of course not! But me, well, I've had some fun, haven't I?'

Westmain was staggered and shouted, 'No, it's not true!' while he struggled with Jeff, but the devil had gone on.

'You became so easy to manipulate it had almost become boring.'

And then, to compound the insult, the devil had quoted at him from 'Desiderata'.

'Therefore be at peace with God, whatever you conceive Him to be. And whatever your labours and aspirations, in the noisy confusion of life, keep peace in your soul. With all its sham, drudgery and broken dreams, it is still a beautiful world. Be cheerful. Strive to be happy.'

The devil had finished the words and was roaring a huge, echoing, deep laugh in his face when the scalpel ripped Sam's throat open.

He died heartbroken.

Chapter Thirty-Five

In a little village in Cornwall a woman of twenty-six was taking down a leather strap from the peg on the back of the kitchen door. 'Come here you little shit!' she yelled in hysterical tones. Her cropped hair allowed the sight of red blotches that were forming high on her forehead, brought about by her absolute fury.

'Don't you dare to tell me that you didn't do that deliberately, you little shit!' she screamed.

She wrapped the strap around her fingers and it swung menacingly beneath her hand.

'Get here *now*!' she bellowed.

The boy of eleven was kneeling by the dining-room door, where he had fallen. He had been carrying a tray which held his tea of jam and bread and a glass of milk when he had slipped on the wet linoleum. It was wet because that afternoon his mother had wiped it clean with damp cloths. She was not a house-proud person but the floor had been grubby in the extreme and was becoming slippy with dirt and grime. She had not thought to dry the floor, so when the boy had entered the hallway he had not noticed the dangerous conditions. He had fallen heavily, hurting his knees and hands. The loaded tray had crashed noisily into a wall and then on to the floor, its contents shattering dramatically as shards of glass flew everywhere.

Now he was to be thrashed for his crime. The woman was seriously unstable; a potentially lethal cocktail of drugs and drink saw to that. Anything that upset her in any way and which could be attributed to her son usually led to a beating. The boy picked himself up very gingerly and said 'Ow!' loudly as a piece of thin glass pressed into his leg. As he shambled towards his mother, tears welled in his eyes.

'I–I–I didn't mean it, it was slippy.'

He did not expect sympathy, or love or a hug, just blame and beating for supposedly deliberately throwing himself to the floor.

His mother's head twitched as it often did when she had not had a fix for two or three days, and that frightened him further, for he knew that she was even more out of control on these days.

'Come here!' she shrieked, expecting the boy to walk briskly into the pain of a lashing heavy belt.

Something stirred in the boy, a strange unknown or unrecognised feeling. It was both scary and exciting, and the boy realised that for some reason, at that time on that day, he had suddenly, unexpectedly, been filled with a deep and powerful loathing, a huge hatred of what his mother was and what she represented: a painful, loveless, terror-filled life. He stopped moving towards her and looked at her directly. She immediately realised that something was different, something was wrong. Even in her partially incoherent mood, her instincts told her that something was simply not right.

She said once more, 'Come here now,' but her voice betrayed her uncertainty about the situation. She could not understand that expression that was set on the boy's face. Replacing the usual mask of fear and trepidation was now a picture of something more akin to… what would you call it – surely not? – *defiance*.

Her suspicions were confirmed when the boy uttered the most amazing words she had ever heard spoken by anybody, anywhere, in her twenty-six years.

'Fuck you!' he said, loudly and confidently. For a split second his confidence rocked and he thought that she might rush over and attack him, but that moment passed as he saw her mouth hang open and the fear swam in her eyes.

'Fuck you, bitch, never again!' he said, before turning back to the dining room. He felt wonderful, exhilarated, liberated. He went to his room and sat on the bed, shaking with excitement. He tried to recapture the sheer thrill of those few words and punched his pillow before burying his face in it and screaming a muffled, 'Yes!'

He sat up and thought that he had only just realised how much he really, really hated that bitch, how he pretty much thought all women were cows. Mother, teachers, crabby shopkeepers – name me a good one, he thought. None came to mind, so he started thinking that maybe he should do something about it, like make a statement. Make people notice. Be famous. He took out an old diary from the previous year and started to write.